Making Mountains Out of Molehills

By Earl Snort

TotalRecall Publications, Inc.
1103 Middlecreek
Friendswood, Texas 77546
281-992-3131 281-482-5390 Fax
www.totalrecallpress.com

Copyright © 2019 by Earl Snort
Not a speck of this is true. It's all a figment if my imagination.

ISBN: 978-1-59095-432-4
UPC: 6-43977-44327-4

Printed in the United States of America with simultaneous printings in Australia, Canada, and United Kingdom.

FIRST EDITION
1   2   3   4   5   6   7   8   9   10

THIS BOOK IS DEDICATED TO MY WIFE.

"TO THE ONES I LOVE."

-- MAMAS & THE PAPAS - 1967

"OH, MY LOVE, MY DARLING, I'VE HUNGERED, HUNGERED FOR

YOUR TOUCH,

A LONG, LONELY TIME."

-- UNCHAINED MELODY

- THE RIGHTEOUS BROTHERS - 1965

TABLE OF CONTENTS

ABOUT THE AUTHOR

Earl Snort is the nom de plume' of a retired law enforcement officer with more than forty years experience toting a badge and a gun.

Before that, he served in the armed forces.

He and his wife have been married nearly fifty years. They reside in the South. They have one son, also a career law enforcement officer, and two grandchildren.

This is the author's first foray into the world of writing fiction. After a lifetime of writing non-fiction to document investigations of true crime, he decided to try his hand at make believe.

He hopes you enjoy the yarn.

May 26, 2019

Prologue

He awoke to the sound of detonating claymores, shelling from incoming mortars, and automatic rifle fire. It was pitch black in his hooch, largely due to a new moon and heavy rainfall. His section mates were scrambling in the dark just like him, searching for their weapons and ammo.

He found his rifle, steel pot, which he took time to put on and fasten, and web gear, with ten loaded magazines, but only one jungle boot. Hell with it! He inserted a magazine, chambered a round, flipped the selector switch to full auto, and ran into the night, naked except for his drawers. Clothes didn't matter anyway, as hard as it was raining.

Some prudent soul fired a parachute flare over the camp, and for fifteen seconds he could see friend and foe darting about. Charlie was inside the wire! This was the second time since he had been in-country.

He started towards his fighting station on the north side of the camp where two of the six 105-millimeter howitzers were positioned. Halfway there, after another flare re-illuminated the fire base, he saw three Charlies no bigger than junior high school boys, headed his way. The surprise was mutual.

The one on the left was in the process of throwing a grenade.

He opened up with a three-round burst, hitting the grenadier center mass and taking him out of action. The grenade fell to the ground. Then he shifted right and emptied his mag into the other two before they collected their wits and shot him.

About five seconds had elapsed, and the grenade should have exploded, blasting him and anyone else within fifteen meters into smithereens. He wasn't looking a gift horse in the mouth.

Anyway it was too dark to see if the grenade was still live. He hoped no one would accidentally set it off. Still a member of the living, he proceeded 'most ricky-tick' to his 'tube,' ready to 'rain some pee' on Charlie.

Only three other Red Legs (artillerymen) were present, not enough to fire the tubes even if they had the coordinates and a fire mission. They hunkered down behind some sandbags and waited for the parachute flares to illuminate targets.

Time stood still in the absolute blackness of a moonless night, the rain coming down in torrents. More flares exploded in the sky, and for fifteen seconds at a time, Life was on fast forward. The flickering manmade light briefly illuminated small clusters of Charlie attacking in fits and spurts, and he could see they were taking more than just a few casualties. Still the enemy pressed on. Their mortar rounds pounded the base relentlessly, maiming and snuffing out the lives of hapless American soldiers. He was wide awake, pulse racing, his breathing shallow, but the nightmare didn't go away.

Rote training kicked in, shoving Fear to the back of his consciousness. Shooting from a sandbag platform, he sighted and shot as many of the enemy as he could. He was an expert marksman, able to hit a man-sized target out to 450 meters. Tonight, due to darkness and the rain, his range was reduced to a quarter of that.

The flares kept igniting. He settled down and methodically selected the easiest targets. He knew he hit eight, probably fatally, because they collapsed like the Earth opened up underneath them. There were at least that many more he shot, maybe not fatally, because they fell but did not collapse. He couldn't confirm any of these shots, visibility being what it was. Maybe that was best.

Later, without warning, Charlie broke contact one by one, and fled into the blackness of the distant wood line from whence they came. It was like the music stopped and the dancers sat down, completely winded. Just for a moment, all sound ceased. Then he heard cries of "medic, medic," and the squishing of feet transiting in the mud.

He got a case of the shakes. Fortunately, no one could see to notice and he was able to regain control over his body.

The three artillerymen and he maintained their post until Staff Sergeant Howard came around and said it was over. They collected their wits and their gear, and slogged through the mud and the rain, helping wounded soldiers who were ambulatory get back to the aid station.

He learned that three of his battery mates were wounded. More than a dozen grunts were casualties, including at least three KIA. The sector he defended was the lightest attacked, with only two casualties. He knew a carton of Purple Hearts would be awarded by nightfall, and he thanked God he wasn't one of the recipients.

When bedlam returned to order and he was released, he trudged back to his hooch. It was daybreak, but the rain kept falling. He rooted around in his ruck until he found a box of Certified Bond cigars. He sat in the doorway and smoked three. His throat was sore, but he didn't care. He couldn't relax. He would clean his weapon later and replace the spent cartridges when the adrenaline rush subsided.

He'd been in-country eleven months and seventeen days. He had thirteen days and a wake-up until the Freedom Bird would fly him back to the World.

"Please, God. Don't take me now. I've made it so far and I want to go home."

Chapter 1

Post High School Dilemma

Wednesday, June 18, 1969. Corporal Barlow K. Adams, Army of the United States, was peering out the window of the back seat of a Greyhound bus while it cruised the highway from Junction City, Kansas, en route to Arlo, Texas, and beyond. He was attired in his dress green uniform, with an array of three ribbons on his left breast.

The one nearest to his heart (red and yellow) was the National Defense Service Medal, awarded by the United States to military servicemen on active duty for at least six months during wartime.

The middle ribbon (yellow, red, and green) was the Vietnam Service Medal, bearing three small bronze stars. It was awarded by the United States to armed forces personnel who served in Vietnam from 1965 and continuing. The small bronze stars were awarded for participation in three of the nine campaigns which had taken place since the onset of the war.

The ribbon nearest his arm (green and white) was the Vietnam Campaign Medal, which was awarded by the Republic of Vietnam to military servicemen who served in the Vietnam War.

Centered below the ribbon bar was an Expert Rifleman's Badge. It consisted of a silver Maltese cross, centered with a three-ring bullseye, and bordered along the sides and bottom with a semi-circular wreath. A silver bar attached by small loops on the bottom read, 'Rifle.'

The biceps area of both sleeves bore two, inverted, gold chevrons, representing the rank of corporal, the lowest of the non-commissioned officer ranks.

On the right sleeve, near the cuff, were two, small, horizontal stripes, each stripe representing six months of overseas duty.

On the right sleeve, just below the shoulder seam was the circular red, white, and blue sprocket patch of the 9th Motorized Infantry Division, representing the unit with whom he served in combat in Vietnam.

On the left sleeve, just below the shoulder, was the olive drab, pentagonal patch bearing the red numeral one, representing the 1st Infantry Division in Fort Riley, Kansas, to whom he was currently assigned for 25 more days while he was on terminal leave before ETS (completion of his enlisted time in service.)

His circular brass lapel insignia depicted the crossed tubes of old-time cannons, representing assignment to the field artillery on one side, and 'U.S.' on the other. In fact, Corporal Adams was an assistant gunner on a 105-millimeter howitzer.

The miles passed slowly, but Barlow was in no hurry. He daydreamed about the odyssey which carried him to this point. Two years past, he graduated from Benson County High School in Baileyville, smack in the middle of the Texas panhandle, with no promising future in sight.

At age 12, his parents were killed in a fiery crash when a church bus crossed the centerline of Texas Highway 114, crashing into his parents' station wagon head-on. They were returning to Arlo from Baileyville on a Wednesday night, after competing in a bowling tournament. Both vehicles were estimated to be traveling between 50 and 60 miles per hour. The bus driver apparently suffered a heart attack and lost control. Six people, including his folks, were pronounced dead at the scene. Another fifteen were seriously injured. It was the worst traffic accident in Benson County history.

Barlow, who was in the seventh grade, and his sister, Chloe, who was seventeen and a senior in high school, went to live with his Grandma Bea, who lived four doors down. Chloe graduated and moved to Canyon, just south of Amarillo, to attend college at West Texas State University. She graduated while Barlow was in the 11th grade. She married Bert Kilgore, another West Texas State University (WTSU) graduate, as well as a member of the U.S. Air Force Reserve, who became a life insurance salesman. They moved to Bisbee, Arizona.

In the eighth grade, Barlow began working part-time at his Uncle Clive's Sinclair gas station after school, and essentially full-time during the summers. Uncle Clive made more money servicing cars than he did selling gasoline, and over the years, Barlow became a proficient auto mechanic. He didn't know what he wanted to do 'when he grew up,' but he did know he didn't want to spend the rest of his life under a car on a creeper or slumped over an engine.

On June 1, 1967, Barlow graduated from Benson County High School. The next day, his draft board classified him I-A, available for military service. He had to make an occupational decision very soon, or the decision would be made for him.

The Vietnam War was in full swing, essentially leaving him with two options. Fleeing to Canada as a draft dodger was not one of them.

Option One was, he could attend college on a II-S student deferment, valid for a maximum of four years until graduation. If he quit or flunked out, he would be reclassified as I-A. If he graduated, he would be reclassified as I-A. Either way, all he could hope to accomplish, would be to postpone the inevitable military service, unless the war ended, which did not appear to be on the horizon.

Option Two would be to join the armed forces. Actually, that sort of appealed to him. His dad was a World War II Army vet. He served in the military police in Europe with the 3rd Division. It would be nice to get paid to see the world, although today, it appeared the most likely destination for a serviceman would be Vietnam.

He checked. The Air Force, Navy, and Coast Guard all

required a four-year commitment. The Marine Corps and Army both required a three-year commitment.

The National Guard and all the reserve components required a six-year commitment. Of course, all the reserve units he knew about were full or nearly full because folks were trying to avoid Vietnam. You had to have a hook to get in. Even then, it was not a 'Get Out of Jail Free' card. He knew of a Texas Army National Guard unit deployed over there, and several guys from his high school who were in the Marine Corps Reserve had been deployed.

There was one other solution to Option Two. He could sign up for the draft, which was only a two-year commitment. Of course, he would forfeit all rights to choose a career field or a first post of duty, and he'd heard that in some instances, draftees were placed in the Marines. Barlow would rather be in the Army, but the obligation was for only two years. He decided to 'roll the bones.'

On Friday, June 9, 1967, Barlow signed up for the draft.

On Tuesday, July 13, 1967, Barlow was inducted into the Army of the United States, the organizational designation for draftees, not to be confused with the U.S. Army, or the U.S. Army Reserves, or the Army National Guard, all of whom wear the same uniform, and all of whom attend the same basic combat training (BCT.) The only distinction Barlow could discern, besides the reduced term of commitment, is that some of the drill instructors (DI's) in BCT seemed to hold draftees in contempt.

Truth is, the DI's weren't much friendlier to the national guardsmen or reservists. What they did, was to shame Regular Army (RA) trainees who were beaten in combat training competition by one of the draftees or weekend warriors. Then both victor and vanquished suffered by doing more push ups, etc. There was no way to win.

God had a guardian angel looking over Barlow and he knew it. The Army sent him to Fort Sill, Oklahoma, for BCT and advanced individual training (AIT) as a field artilleryman. The training was long - six months before he graduated from both schools. He was given a two-week leave before shipping out to the Republic of Vietnam, where, on January 29, 1968, he was assigned to C Battery, 1st Battalion, 11th Artillery, 9th Motorized Infantry Division, in III Corps Tactical Zone at Fire Support Base Danger in the Dinh Tuong province for a 12-month deployment.

The enemy's surprise Tet Offensive began on January 30, 1968. Welcome to Vietnam, Barlow! Great timing! He had a busy tour. He saw more combat than he ever wanted, but less than many others. His tour ended with him injury-free.

One of his battery mates was killed in action (KIA) and four were wounded in action (WIA) - five Purple Hearts in all, out of 52 soldiers assigned to Charley Battery simultaneously, assuming they were at full strength. With combat tours being twelve months, over the course of a year, they had at least a hundred percent turnover, since soldiers trickled in and out one or two at a time. Therefore, probably 100 soldiers served in Charley Battery while he was there. With that in mind, their casualty rate was low.

His last five months in the Army were uneventful at Fort Riley. Now he was returning to Arlo, population 1,450, honorable discharge in hand, and a little over $1,800 in his pocket.

Grandma Bea had passed away while he was in Vietnam. Uncle Clive sold her house and moved Barlow's meager belongings into his own. Chloe and he were included in her will as heirs, receiving $1,000 each. The $1,800 included his inheritance.

CHAPTER 2

RETURNING TO A HOME THAT WASN'T

On Thursday, June 19th, after two transfers, he stepped off the bus right in front of Adams' Sinclair station in Arlo. He enjoyed a warm reception from Uncle Clive and Aunt Marilyn, and both his elementary school-aged cousins. They put him up in the spare bedroom in the attic, where his few belongings were already in place. They said he could stay as long as he wanted.

Uncle Clive had expanded his business to include a used car lot with sixteen 'pre-owned' vehicles. (Why didn't he just call them used cars?) He offered Barlow a job as the salesman, paying a ten percent commission on anything he sold.

Barlow began work in the lot the following day, pondering his next move. It was swell Uncle Clive and Aunt Marilyn took him in and gave him a job. He sincerely appreciated their generosity, but knew he needed something different and more challenging. He just didn't know what.

He didn't have many lookers at the lot. In fact, he only sold one car, for which he received a $90 commission. That was about a half-month's pay in the Army. He had lots of time on his hands, which allowed him to closely inspect all the inventory.

He fell in love with a faded, mint green, 1965, Dodge 100, short bed pickup truck. It had a 225 Slant-Six, 145 horsepower engine, with a manual, three-speed transmission on the column, and an AM radio that worked as good as new. It only had 58,000 miles, with no rust or dents. The tires were well worn, and it needed brakes and a tune up. It had never been wrecked. The only drawback was it didn't have air conditioning. He decided he could live without that.

Eric Stottlemeyer had been the only owner of the truck. Barlow knew him, because he had been Barlow's 10th grade biology teacher. He also knew Mr. Stottlemeyer would never abuse a motor vehicle. Uncle Clive wanted $800 for it, but sold it to Barlow for cost at $675.

Barlow was busy all the next week. He changed the oil, gave it a lube job, changed the plugs, wires, and points, changed the transmission seals and replaced transmission fluid, put on new brake pads, flushed the radiator, installed a new fan belt, windshield wiper blades, battery, and tires, to include the spare.

Although the seat was in good shape, he purchased an Indian weave seat cover, with an open-ended pouch on both ends which ran the length of the bench seat along the bottom front, to carry his rifle out-of-sight, but easily accessible. He washed, polished, and waxed the truck twice. When he was done, it shined like a jade ashtray. Accordingly, he named his truck Jade.

Barlow settled into a routine similar to his days in school. Benson County High School was thirteen miles east of Arlo in Baileyville, the county seat. He rode the school bus to and fro. He wasn't allowed to stay after school for clubs or sports, because he worked in the service station on weekdays after school until it closed at 7. He worked on Saturdays from 8 until closing at 5.

On Sundays they attended the Arlo Methodist Church. In the spring and summer, Uncle Clive and he played in the church softball league. Uncle Clive asked Barlow if he wanted to get back on the men's team, but he declined, stating that for the time being, he had some other things he wanted to do on Sunday afternoons.

For one thing, Barlow needed some time to target practice with his Winchester, Model 1894, lever action, 30-30 caliber rifle. It was a pre-'64, one of the last manufactured, and had been a Christmas gift from Grandma Bea when he was 14. Uncle Clive liked to deer hunt, and together that became an autumn family ritual. Deer hunting was the single most thing he missed during his time in the Army.

The target practice was pleasurable, but it wasn't the only thing on his mind. Barlow was restless to hit the road and see something different while he figured out what to do with the rest of his life. Officially, that would begin on July 12th, when his ETS was final.

He could attend North Texas Junior College (NTJC) in Baileyville, in September on the G.I. Bill. He could apply elsewhere, maybe WTSU, like Chloe. Alternatively, he could find a more challenging job, in a career field other than selling or working on cars. The latter two options would disappoint Aunt Marilyn and Uncle Clive, but were he to make a break, sooner would be less painful than later.

Taking a trip to Bisbee to visit Chloe would be the easiest way out. He decided he would take all his personal belongings. This would include a few framed photographs of his parents, Grandma Bea, and Chloe, high school yearbook for 1967, diploma, and other documents, such as his birth certificate and one for perfect attendance in Sunday School his sophomore year, plus the trophy he got in the 6th grade for playing on the Benson County American Legion championship baseball team. They would know he didn't expect to return, but this way it wouldn't be necessary to come back and make a hard break even harder, if he did decide to move.

On Sunday, July 6th, he called Chloe to see if a visit would be okay. She joyfully invited him to come for as long as he pleased. That being settled, he said he would see her in a couple of weeks. He spent the following week making preparations.

Barlow had grown the two years he was in the Army. He was 5'9" tall and weighed 140 pounds when he reported for induction. Now he was 5'10" and weighed 165. His waist size had expanded from 32 to 34 inches, but he packed a lot more muscle.

He collected all of his clothes which were too small, and

donated them to the Goodwill in Baileyville. Then he stopped at J.C. Penney's and purchased three pairs of Wrangler jeans, six western cut, long-sleeve shirts, and a blue jean jacket.

Next he went to Cowboy Bob's Western Emporium and bought a pair of brown, low-heeled, round-toed, Justin cowboy boots with a matching brown belt. He took his time before selecting a beige 7X Stetson, with a medium crown and brim. It was good to be back in Texas.

After that, he went to the Army-Navy store. He bought two Army surplus footlockers - one for clothes and another for personal items. Then he picked through the secondhand Army field gear, selecting an oiled canvas tarp to cover the bed of his truck, two hanks of 500-mile-per-hour cord, a web belt, sleeping bag, two metal canteens with cups and carrying cases, a mess kit, pack, spaghetti straps, entrenching tool, and an M-14 ammo pouch (to hold small items). En route to the checkout counter, he spotted and purchased a metal Stanley thermos.

The final stop was at Johnston's Gun Shop, where he bought five boxes of 170-grain, 30-30 cartridges, cleaning patches, and a bottle each of Hoppe's Number 9 gun solvent and gun oil.

He was ready to go. His stash was down to $700. He couldn't dilly dally for too long before finding gainful employment.

CHAPTER 3

THAT FATEFUL NIGHT

On Tuesday, July 8th, after a tearful goodbye, Barlow began his journey.

The most direct route was to take US Highway 54 southwest through New Mexico to Alamogordo, pick up US Highway 70, and follow it west through Las Cruces to AZ Highway 80, and follow it south to the Mexican border at Douglas, and then west and a little north to Bisbee. According to the maps, this was about 700 miles.

Instead, he took his old sweet time on US Highway 83, all the way to its southern terminus at Carrizo Springs near the Mexican border. Then he drove west on US Highway 277 to Del Rio, sightseeing as he went.

On Thursday, July 10th, he picked up US Highway 90, and began his westward trek along the border, planning to see the Big Bend country. This stretch was sparsely populated, with stops far and few in between. He got a later start than expected from Judge Roy Bean's Saloon and Museum in Langtry. Traffic was almost non-existent, so he decided to press on, maybe as far as Marathon before seeking lodging.

It was about 11:30, along a remote stretch in Quayle County, maybe halfway to Marathon. Barlow had the vent windows angled as wide as they'd go. The side windows were rolled all the way down. The wind felt good on his face. The sky was clear. The moon was half full and there were a thousand shimmering stars to keep him company. The radio was blaring mariachi music from some all-night Mexican radio station.

After miles of emptiness, Barlow saw two vehicles with their lights on, parked along the shoulder of the westbound lane. He slowed to see if someone were stranded. As he approached, he could see that the first vehicle was a white Ford van. Just in front of it, was a Volkswagen bug jacked up on the left rear. As he passed, he glimpsed a man and a woman struggling between the vehicles. The man struck the woman in the face. She was screaming for help.

Barlow stopped about 100 yards beyond. He made a U-turn and slowly drove Jade eastbound on the westbound shoulder, facing both cars, stopping about 75 yards short. He turned his engine off, but left his lights on. He put his key in his pocket.

He stepped out of his truck. He slid the 30-30 from the front seat and chambered a round. He swung wide left onto the north side of the road, away from the cone of headlights. He stopped about 50 yards from their cars. Barlow stood in the dark, while the man and woman were in partial glare of the headlights. He saw the man wrestle the woman to the ground between the two vehicles.

The assailant shouted, "This ain't none of your affair. You need to get your ass outta here."

Barlow responded, "Let the woman go."

The assailant slammed the woman facedown to the shoulder of the road. As he stood up, he ground her face into the dirt with his foot. He pulled a handgun, Barlow wasn't sure from where, and aimed it at him. He fired three rapid shots.

Barlow could see the muzzle flashes. He heard the bullets pass wide to the right. Being in the darkness paid off. Barlow dropped to one knee, aimed for center of mass, and fired one shot. The man yelped, stumbled, and staggered north, into the dark away from the vehicles. Barlow felt sure he'd hit the guy, but was uncertain as to whether the shot was disabling.

He chambered another round and walked cautiously toward the two vehicles. The woman had scrambled from between the two cars and was squatted down by the driver's door of the van, out of sight from her attacker. The light was not good, but Barlow could see that her face was swollen and her blouse was torn. She was sobbing quietly.

She said she had been driving home to Mosby, when she had a flat. She was changing the tire, when the van pulled up. The man got out and offered to help if she would have sex with him. When she refused, he got abusive and started slapping her in the face and calling her names. She didn't know the attacker. She had never seen him before. She begged Barlow to drive her to Mosby, eight miles farther west, so she could get her husband for help.

Barlow agreed, but told her to stay put while he checked on things. He opened the engine cover on the rear of her car and removed the distributor cap. He turned off the lights, rolled up the windows, and locked the car.

Then he did the same to the van. He copied the license plate number of the van, in his shirt pocket notebook. After a careful perusal of the area and seeing nothing, they ran to Jade and got in.

Barlow checked to make sure he had both distributor caps before they left. He didn't want the assailant to escape. Then he drove 100 miles per hour all the way to Mosby. He didn't stop until they arrived at the courthouse, where the sheriff's office was located on the ground floor in the back.

The Quayle County Courthouse was a three-story, creek stone edifice, erected in 1910 according to the chiseled stone above the front door.

The deputy on duty was old and ropey, about Barlow's height, with a formidable swooping mustache. He was dressed in khaki twill trousers and a matching long-sleeve shirt with button-down shoulder straps. The departmental patch, a green circle with a yellow border and yellow letters which read, "Quayle County Sheriff's Office," was on the left sleeve near the shoulder seam. The upper right sleeve had a Texas flag patch. He had a shiny silver, five-pointed star on his chest.

He wore brown cowboy boots and a brown gun belt filled with cartridges completely around his waist. Barlow recognized his sidearm as a Colt Peacemaker with a six-inch barrel. The deputy carried himself like a man who knew how to take care of business. It appeared that he was there all alone.

The woman, Sandra Taft, ran straight to the deputy and collapsed in his arms. She sobbed hysterically, and liked to never have caught her breath long enough to report what happened.

It turned out that Deputy Sheriff Archibald Willis was her maternal uncle. Sandra told him everything.

Then he questioned Barlow, who repeated what Sandra said. He went on to say that the assailant was a white male, about six feet tall, with long dark hair like a hippie, thin, wearing jeans and a dark shirt. He was driving a 1960, white Ford Econoline van, with California license 619LNV.

Deputy Willis wanted to know how hard Barlow looked for the guy before they skedaddled.

He responded, "Not very."

He asked if Barlow actually shot the guy or if he might have missed.

Barlow said he aimed for center of mass and thought he hit him. The guy squealed and reacted like he was hit, but ran off, so he wasn't sure.

Deputy Willis opined that by now the guy had probably escaped.

Barlow responded that he took the distributor caps off both vehicles and had them in his truck.

Deputy Willis cracked a smile and said, "You're all right." Then he called Sandra's husband, Willard Taft, Sheriff Solomon Pratt, and Chief Deputy Alexander Snodgrass, the department's criminal investigator.

While they were waiting, Deputy Willis got on the teletype machine and ran registration and wanted record checks on the license plate. It was registered to a Robert Cook in Los Angeles, and had been reported stolen four days earlier.

The three men plus the sheriff's wife, Joanna Pratt, arrived about twenty minutes later. Joanna was a registered nurse. Sheriff Pratt brought her along to check the severity of Sandra's injuries, which turned out to be two black eyes, a broken nose, and multiple abrasions.

Sheriff Pratt was impressive. He was in uniform, wearing brown cowboy boots, a beige Stetson, and a brown leather gun belt with twelve filled cartridge loops, and a holstered, nickel-plated, Colt Python .357 magnum revolver with a six-inch barrel.

He was about 40 years old. He stood about 6'5" tall and probably weighed 275 pounds. He had thick black hair, combed in a pompadour. He was dark complected with black eyes. Barlow guessed (correctly) that the sheriff was part Indian and that he probably played football in high school (partially correct. He also played four years at University of Texas El Paso (UTEP) starting as center his senior year.)

Chief Snodgrass was older, maybe 50, bald, about 5'9" tall, a little overweight, maybe a 180 pounds, with light blue eyes behind tortoise shell glasses. He was not wearing a uniform. He had on black dress trousers and a crumpled white dress shirt, with brown cowboy boots and a beige Stetson. No tie or jacket. He was wearing a Browning Hi Power, 9-millimeter, semi-automatic pistol on his belt with one spare magazine. His badge was clipped on his belt, too.

Willard Taft was a big, stocky man, built like a bear, with blond hair and blue eyes. He crushed Barlow with a hug. He told Barlow over and over that he was indebted to him and promised to return the favor.

At Joanna's suggestion, Willard left to drive Sandra to the hospital in Alpine to have her checked out in the emergency room. Sandra handed Deputy Willis the keys to her auto on her way out the door. He promised to have it back in her driveway before dawn.

Sheriff Pratt, known to all as Sheriff Sol, listened to Barlow's recitation. He told Barlow to get his rifle and the distributor caps and join Chief Alex, as he was known, and him for a ride back to the crime scene. Barlow did as he was told, and climbed into the backseat of the sheriff's spanking new, unmarked, brown Plymouth Fury, four-door sedan. As soon as all were seat-belted, Sheriff Sol blasted down the highway at 130 miles per hour. Barlow should have known the car would be powered by the 383 cubic inch, 330 horsepower engine. He hung on for dear life for the four minutes it took to get there.

It was a little after 1 o'clock on Friday, July 11th, when they arrived. Somehow the sky seemed darker than before, even sinister perhaps. Sheriff Sol parked on the eastbound shoulder to avoid contaminating the crime scene.

They started at the parked vehicles, where the suspect threw Sandra to the ground. They found blood where the suspect was standing when he was shot. They spread out, guns at the ready, and began walking north where Barlow thought the suspect fled. Ten minutes of cautious searching was all it took. They found him propped against a small boulder, dead, eyes wide open, all bled out. A .38 caliber, Smith & Wesson Model 10 revolver was still in his hand. It had three expended cartridges and three live ones.

His wallet contained $80 in cash and a California driver's license identifying him as Rupert Doyle, age 28, of Bakersfield. Later that morning, Chief Alex reported that Doyle had two prior convictions, one for shoplifting and the other for aggravated assault, for which he was sentenced to five years in prison. He had been released after three years and was still on parole.

The sheriff and Barlow shined flashlights so the chief could take photographs and make measurements. They found Barlow's spent shell casing. It was 64 yards to the spot where they found Doyle's blood.

It was 4 o'clock before the chief was satisfied he had

everything he needed. Doyle's body had already been picked up by the coroner, who also happened to be the local mortician.

The sheriff and Barlow changed Sandra's flat and replaced the distributor caps. Barlow drove Sandra's car to her house, and the chief drove Doyle's van to the jail parking lot. Barlow caught a ride with the sheriff back to the jail, as the sheriff's office was commonly called. On the way back, he asked Barlow to stick around and have a chat with him in his office.

CHAPTER 4
NOT ALL GOOD DEEDS GET PUNISHED

Sheriff Sol bought them both a bottle of Coca Cola out of the machine in the hallway vending area. The sheriff sat at his desk and Barlow sat facing him in an old, wooden, courtroom chair on wheels. They sat in silence for a minute or more. The sheriff lit and smoked a cigarette for another minute before speaking.

Sheriff Sol said it would take a few days to complete the investigation. They had to send Doyle's fingerprints to the FBI and the Los Angeles Police Department where he had been arrested, to confirm his identity.

Barlow's and Sandra's formal statements would need to be reviewed and signed by each under oath. The incident would be presented to the Grand Jury to determine if the shooting by Barlow was justified, which the sheriff had already personally concluded that it was, though the decision was not his to make. Assuming the Grand Jury returned a No True Bill, Barlow would be free to go.

Barlow asked, "What if it doesn't?"

The sheriff said if the Grand Jury returned a True Bill, that meant collectively, the jurors voted there was probable cause to believe Barlow wrongfully shot Doyle. The district attorney would file whatever charge he thought appropriate. In this case, murder or manslaughter or something like that. Then Barlow would be arrested and have to go to court.

He told Barlow not to get alarmed. "Everyone in Quayle County knows and loves Sandra Taft. She said she was assaulted by Doyle and you rescued her. Both your statements marry up with the physical evidence. The Grand Jury will learn what Chief Alex and I already know."

Sheriff Sol needed Barlow to remain in Mosby until all the T's were crossed and the I's were dotted. If they could present the case on Monday morning, Barlow would be free to go Monday afternoon. The county would pay for his lodging at the Travelers Rest Motor Lodge, and for his meals at Betty's Diner, which was next door to the lodge. He asked if this posed a problem.

Barlow said it did not.

Sheriff Sol said, "Excellent" and paused again, looking Barlow directly in the eyes as he sized him up some more. He asked Barlow to tell him a little bit about himself.

Barlow told him about growing up in Arlo and joining the Army after high school. He said was on terminal leave and would ETS on July 12th, which now was in one more day! In fact, the Army had already given him his DD-214, and honorable discharge certificate when he departed on terminal leave. He was headed to Bisbee to visit his sister when this incident occurred. He had no specific plans after that. He considered going to college or he might find a job better suited to his liking, something he could make into a career.

Sheriff Sol nodded, and asked, "What was your MOS (military occupational specialty) in the Army?"

Barlow replied that he was a 13-Bravo, cannon crewman. Specifically, he was an assistant gunner on a 105-millimeter howitzer.

"Did you go to 'Nam?"

"Yes. For twelve months."

"Was tonight the first time you killed someone?"

"It was the first time I killed an American."

"How do you feel about that?"

"The guy gave me no choice. I don't have much remorse."

"You must have seen a lot of action in Vietnam."

"I saw enough. There were two times our basecamp almost

got overrun. Charley was inside the wire, so our tubes were useless. We fought like infantrymen with our rifles. I saw the faces of three Charley I shot. It was close. I shot probably a dozen more outside the wire, but I can't say for sure if they died. Then there were the artillery fire missions. I have no idea how much mayhem my tube rained down on Charlie. I know it was a bunch. We saved a lot of American lives. All the infantry boys loved us."

"Did you receive any decorations for valor or a Purple Heart?"

"No, Sir. I was never wounded and I was not a hero. I did my job and came home."

Sheriff Sol said, "Son, you're a hero to me for what you did over there, and for what you did tonight. Most folks are afraid. They do whatever they can to avoid conflict, especially if it would put them in peril. That makes you different. You're standing in front of the crowd, exposing yourself, doing the right thing. America needs more men like you. Women, too."

He went on to say that Chief Alex was a hero from World War II. He had been a coxswain in the Coast Guard and piloted Higgins boats full of troops onto the beachheads. At Anzio, he got his boat shot out from under him. He took some shrapnel in his chest and left arm and nearly drowned. They gave him a Purple Heart. Then a year later he drove another Higgins boat onto Omaha Beach. That took real guts.

Barlow said, "My hat is off to him. He is a brave man." Then he asked if the sheriff had been in the armed forces.

He said, "the Silent Service in Korea."

"Submarines?"

"Yeah. We patrolled off the coast of Korea in case the Reds decided to send a warship. We were at Inchon. We dropped off some frogmen on a secret mission and picked them up about six hours later. I was a Torpedoman 3rd Class, but I never fired a shot in anger. That's about it."

"That sounds pretty scary to me. I'd probably freak out if they put me in an iron coffin hundreds of feet below the surface."

The sheriff laughed and said, "You get used to it." Then he asked Barlow how old he was.

Barlow said he would be 21 in February.

He asked if Barlow had ever considered a job in law enforcement.

Barlow said it never crossed his mind, but it sounded like something he would enjoy.

The sheriff said the authorized strength for the sheriff's office was six full-time deputies and three part-timers. One of his full-time deputies recently resigned to take a job with the El Paso Police Department. That left him with one vacancy. "Perhaps you might be interested."

He continued, "All deputies start in the jail, which shouldn't matter to you, because you aren't old enough to buy a handgun.

"Now, because the state law's changed, new hires have two years to get POST (Police Officers Standard Training) certified by the state. It's something new and we're all sorting through it. However, our junior college in Mosby has a law enforcement program and you can get POST certified, plus earn an associate's degree in law enforcement, if you so desire. It's up to the individual, because all you have to have is the POST certification, which can be completed full-time in about twelve weeks, or part-time in less than a year. Of course, you would have to pay for that yourself, but it's not significant, especially since you qualify for the G.I. Bill. No matter how you do it, it has to be completed within two years of date of hire or you lose your job. It's as simple as that.

"The opening is on the midnight shift to assist Deputy Willis, who, by the way, is a World War I Army vet. He's the real deal. Fought in the trenches. Bayonet charges. You name it. Bonafide badass. Still tough as nails. A man's man.

"Getting back to the point, we have great benefits. The county pays for uniforms, handcuffs, flashlight, gloves, and a nightstick.

Deputies buy their own leather, handguns, ammunition, boots and hat. Starting pay is $6,000 per annum, which is paid $500 once a month, on the last day of the month.

"The benefits package includes a $20,000 term life insurance policy and major medical health insurance. Of course, employees pay half of those premiums through payroll deduction, but it isn't much.

"Deputies also pay into the state retirement system, which nets 2% a year of the average of their high three years, for each year of service, after a minimum of twenty years and age 50. If a deputy joined at age 30, and averaged $6,000 PA for his high three years, at age 50 with twenty years of service, he would be eligible to draw an annual pension of 40% of $6,000, or $2,400. That's $200 a month just for waking up. Not bad.

"Plus, it only takes ten years to get vested, which means that after ten years, an employee is guaranteed a retirement at age 65, so long as he doesn't take his money out of the retirement fund.

"Also, we pay into Social Security, so you would also collect those benefits at age 65.

"We get seven paid holidays, which are New Years, Memorial Day, Fourth of July, Labor Day, Veterans Day, Thanksgiving, and Christmas. We also get two weeks of annual leave for the first ten years on the job, and three weeks a year after that."

He went on to say, "The population of Quayle County is about 3,000 souls, 80,000 sheep, and 35,000 beeves. Mosby is the only town in Quayle County. It's unincorporated, even though it's the county seat.

"The sheriff's office provides all the law enforcement for Quayle County, although the Texas Department of Public Safety, otherwise known as DPS, does traffic enforcement on state and federal highways whenever the mood suits them, which fortunately isn't all that often in Quayle County, because then everyone would be pissed off at me, all the time, for having to pay their chickenshit tickets. Nevertheless, DPS is available to render assistance, if needed."

The sheriff finally paused and waited for Barlow to respond.

Barlow was floored. He was being offered a job as a deputy sheriff! He said, "Yes, I am very interested in applying. It sounds exactly like something I would love to do. I'm honored you would consider me, but, if I got the job, I would need about a week before starting so I could go see my sister."

Sheriff Sol laughed and said, "That's no problem, but, before you can be hired, you have to pass a background investigation. That could easily take a week."

"What all does that entail?"

"We need to see a birth certificate, Social Security card, driver's license, and high school diploma. We have to conduct state and federal criminal background checks as well as a DPS driver's license check.

"We need to verify all employment, marriages and divorces, and interview three-character references. We can do a lot of that by phone and correspondence if the applicant lives way off, like you. That can save time and money. Also, as it relates to veterans, we need to see your DD-214, which we will confirm later from DoD. That can take a couple of months, so we don't hold up hiring waiting for that."

Barlow exclaimed, "I have all those documents with me! The only employer I ever had besides the Army was Uncle Clive at his service station and used car lot. I've never been married. I can provide the names and addresses and even telephone numbers of three-character witnesses right now! I have them in my head. I don't even need to look them up!"

Sheriff Sol laughed and said, "Not so fast. You have to fill out an application first. It's 5:30 already. The sun's coming up. Let's go get you checked into the motel. You can come back this afternoon and sign your statement and fill out an application."

CHAPTER 5
WITH FAME COMES HIGH EXPECTATIONS

Barlow found the Travelers Rest to be much nicer than he had supposed. It had twelve little cabins. His had a double bed, two-seater couch, table with two chairs, telephone, TV, and large closet. He unloaded his truck before eating a huge breakfast at Betty's Diner. Afterwards, he tried to sleep, but sleep would not come. Finally, he arose at 1 o'clock and went back to the jail.

Deputy Ernest Atwater introduced him to the administrative assistant, Miss Loretta Youngblood. She was about 25 years old, single, and attractive. She was prepared for him. She handed him a two-page application for employment. She also gave him three form letters which he addressed to his character references.

Each letter informed the recipient that Barlow was an applicant for the position of deputy sheriff. It requested that the recipient list his dates of acquaintance, frequency of contact, type of contact, and relationship with the applicant. It further requested that the recipient sign and return the form in the SASE (self-addressed stamped envelope) if he believed the aforementioned applicant to be honest, trustworthy, dependable, of high moral character, brave, faithful, resourceful, responsible, neither a drunkard nor a dope nor gambling addict, and capable of successfully performing the duties of a law enforcement officer. It had space on the bottom to make comments. Finally, it provided Chief Alex's name and the sheriff's office telephone number if the recipient had any questions.

Miss Loretta advised him to call his references and give them a heads up. She said the rest of his background checks would be completed by Monday or Tuesday. She recorded all the relevant information from his birth certificate, driver's license, high school diploma, Social Security card, DD-214, and honorable discharge certificate before returning them to him.

Deputy Atwood photographed and fingerprinted him. Afterwards, Barlow went to the chief's corner in the office, where he read and signed his statement under oath.

Chief Alex said the coroner saw no reason to have an autopsy performed on Doyle at the county's expense. It was pretty obvious what killed him. The incident would be presented to the Grand Jury on Monday.

Barlow asked about Doyle and his family.

Chief said he had contacted Doyle's brother, Alonso, via the Bakersfield Police Department. Alonso said Rupert had been in trouble since the day he was born. His mother, now deceased, was the only person who ever liked him. Rupert did not have a wife or any children so far as he knew. He did know that Rupert had no money, nor a life insurance policy, and Alonzo was not paying for an autopsy or burial. He told the chief to bury Rupert in a potter's field.

Chief had also contacted the LAPD and the FBI, both of whom were waiting for receipt of Doyle's fingerprints from Quayle County to confirm his identity. Both promised expedited comparisons as soon as they received his prints.

LAPD also cleared the auto theft as a recovery by Quayle County Sheriff's office.

Chief spoke with Robert Cook and his insurance company. The insurance company had already paid Cook's claim. An agent said a representative would bring the paperwork and retrieve the van on Monday or Tuesday. He also said they would sell the van to anyone who was interested for what they paid out, which was $350, and to let him know.

Chief said one especially interesting aspect of this case, was that he cleared a burglary in El Paso. An inventory of the stolen van turned up a wallet with a driver's license in the name of Duncan Lebowski in El Paso. The El Paso Police Department took a burglary report from Lebowski Thursday morning. On Wednesday afternoon, persons unknown sneaked into his house and stole his wallet with $55 in cash, a gold Bulova watch, his Masonic ring, and revolver while he was cutting his grass. The revolver Doyle used belongs to Lebowski. The police department is scouring the pawn shops trying to locate the ring and watch.

There were also six CB radios still in the boxes in the van, but Chief had been unable to locate any theft reports so far.

Barlow asked about Sandra Taft.

Chief said she looked a sight, but Doc Boykin had reset her nose and she was going to be all right.

As Barlow was preparing to go, Chief said, "You know Kid, this is a small town and news travels fast. You're a celebrity here. Keep that in mind, because what you did is a hard act to follow. Everyone's going to have high expectations of you."

Barlow blushed and said he preferred to blend in and just be one of the guys.

The chief smiled and said, "Good luck with that. The last shootout in this town was in 1955. People will be talking about this until the next one."

CHAPTER 6

GETTING THE LAY OF THE LAND

After leaving the jail, Barlow decided to walk about the town since he had time to kill.

The main drag, four lanes wide in town with angle parking, was US Highway 90, running east and west, and called America Avenue. The primary intersection was with TX Highway 651, running mostly northeast to south, two lanes wide with angle parking. It was called Texas Street. Its southern terminus, so he had been told, was at the Rio Grande between two big spreads - the Circle Y and the Rocking T. Mexico was a wide but shallow walk across, nothing but a fence with four strands of barbed wire in between.

The town was small enough it had no traffic lights, just stop signs.

Besides the two primary arteries, there were six east-west avenues named after presidents. Four were north of US Highway 90, and two were south. From north to south, these were Washington, Monroe, Jackson, Taylor, (CSA President) Jefferson Davis, and T. Roosevelt.

There were four north-south streets, two on either side of TX Highway 651. They were named after Texas governors. From west to east, these were Sam Houston, Francis Lubbock, Edward Clark, and Sul Ross.

The avenues numbered east or west from Texas Street, beginning with 1, and the streets numbered north or south from America Avenue, also beginning with 1.

The Quayle County Courthouse sat on the northeast corner of 90 and 651. The Pecos Bank & Trust sat cater-cornered on the southwest corner. The Baptist Church was on the northwest corner and the Methodist Church was on the southeast corner. These were the four largest and most impressive buildings in town.

Other businesses throughout the downtown area included a Phillips 66 service station, which tripled as a wrecker service and the Greyhound bus stop. Then there were a mortuary, pharmacy with a soda fountain, insurance/realty office, doctor's office, saloon, farm implement business, grocery, feed/hardware store, bail bondsman/used car lot/auto mechanic business, used furniture store, two law offices, laundromat, thrift goods store, tiny Catholic Church, dry goods store, pawn/gun shop, Quayle County Works Department garage, motel, two diners, and a self-serve car wash.

Then there were the Bijou Theatre, open on Tuesday and Saturday nights (high school sports are on Fridays and church meetings are on Wednesday's), Quayle County School, grades 1-12, with a baseball diamond and basketball court in the back, a small park, combination blacksmith shop/veterinarian office, both of which make ranch calls, Masonic Lodge, library, American Legion, barber shop with adjoining beauty salon, an over-the-road trucking firm with three rigs, saddlery/shoe repair shop, package liquor store, auto parts store, lumber yard, and a vacant lot with a Mexican in a pickup truck selling watermelons and velvet Elvis hangings. Most likely there were businesses he missed, plus some of the ones he saw did not appear to be open when he passed by.

In the alleyways between the main drags, some businesses still had hitching posts and water troughs, for nostalgia he thought, until he saw two different ones with tethered horses.

Besides businesses, there were both small and large houses, and all but a few appeared to be occupied. With few exceptions, they were well-kept and homey. Wherever he walked, he saw American and Texas flags waving in the breeze. When someone passed, the stranger nodded or waved or said hello, just like in Arlo.

Walking to the eastern outskirts of town, he saw the Quayle County Rodeo Grounds. It was a little bigger than the one in Baileyville.

Likewise, on the western outskirts, he saw the new West Texas Junior College (WTJC) built in 1965. The campus was well laid out, with an administration building, two classroom buildings, gymnasium, dormitory, police training facility, and acres of parking. Besides being newer, it was nicer than NTJC in Benson County, although it was smaller.

The little town of Mosby looked prosperous, and moving in the right direction. Barlow decided this would be a good fit for him. He really hoped he would get the job.

Chapter 7
Cupid Strikes

It was 3 o'clock when he found himself standing in front of WTJC. He decided to check it out, hoping someone in the admin building was still there this late on a Friday afternoon in mid-July. He assumed most of the students and faculty would be out for the summer.

He walked into the registrar's office, where he was greeted warmly by a receptionist about his own age named Sarah Baker.

Sssssssssst! Thunk! Cupid's aim was true. His arrow struck Barlow smack dab in the center of his heart. He was so taken with Miss Baker, that he stopped short in his tracks, quit breathing, and stared like a starving child from Biafra invited to a Thanksgiving feast with all the fixings.

She was about 5'6" tall, 120 pounds, with green eyes and long brown hair parted in the middle like Michelle Phillips of the Mamas and the Papas. She had a creamy light tan on unblemished skin, with all the right parts in all the right places, without overdoing any of it. She was wearing a knee-length, short-sleeved, red cotton dress with a scoop neck and a full skirt at the waist. She was absolutely perfect.

When he recovered his wits, with a blush in full bloom, he stared into her eyes and stammered something about passing through town and thinking about attending college there and wondering if she could give him a tour if she wasn't too busy - and if she didn't mind - or if it was allowed - if that would be possible.

She returned his bold stare with one of her own and said, "You're the fellow who saved Sandra Tafts life."

He replied, "Well, I don't know about all that, but I did help her out last night."

"Sheriff Sol called Dean Kirkman and said you might show up and to do what we could to help you make up your mind about getting enrolled."

His astonished reply was, "Well I'll be doggoned."

Before he realized it, Sarah had taken him throughout the campus, introducing him to several administrators and instructors. She told him all about the school and a good portion about the town and county history while they sipped coffee in the student cafe.

She said Quayle County was over 2,000 square miles. Mosby was the only town. The primary economic engine was sheep and cattle, with the emphasis on sheep. There were also a few oil wells in the northern part of the county.

This part of far west Texas is called the Trans-Pecos. It includes part of New Mexico, and is essentially the part of the Chihuahuan Desert south of the Pecos River.

One of the most prominent families in Quayle County are the Sweeneys. In the 1880's, Clarence Sweeney, mostly known as Ripsnort Sweeney, homesteaded about 100,000 acres in the southwestern corner of the county bordering the Rio Grande River. He pioneered sheepherding in this portion of Texas, which put him at odds with the cattlemen. This wasn't an original idea. The Mexicans had been herding sheep in this area for about a hundred years.

Ripsnort was continually having problems with bandits and rustlers from both sides of the river. A man had to be cut from the right bolt of cloth if he were going to survive around here, especially then. The law was virtually non-existent, or too far away to be of any use.

Ripsnort killed so many bandits, he actually established a cemetery on his land just for rustlers and owlhoots. She's never actually seen it, but folks who have say there's thirteen graves, most of them marked with a big rock and the date the bandit was killed. Some have names and some do not.

Ripsnort died in the 1920's. He has two grandsons, Maxwell and Darnell Sweeney, who have a lot of pull. Maxwell is the county judge. Darnell is a state senator. He used to be a Texas Ranger for a number of years.

One way or another, Darnell became drinking buddies with Lyndon B. Johnson when he was a U.S. senator or maybe a representative. In 1964, he convinced President Johnson that Texas needed to upgrade their training for law enforcement officers. She thought that had something to do with the Civil Rights movement.

He got a bill passed in the state legislature to establish a standardized curriculum of training, after he convinced LBJ to give the state federal funding to build the training facilities. Then as sort of a quid pro quo, the state legislature agreed to place one of the training facilities in Quayle County, even though the Trans-Pecos is the most sparsely populated region in Texas.

Then, the state legislature decided it would be a better idea to combine the law enforcement training facility with a junior college. They built the whole complex, all of it probably funded with federal dollars, in a year-and-a-half. WTJC opened its doors in September of 1965, with 220 students, forty of whom were POST trainees only. Now it has over 400 students, mostly from the Trans-Pecos. About a hundred are enrolled in POST from agencies throughout the state.

Barlow was sold. Besides that, he was smitten with Sarah. This was a scary, unraveling, new experience for him.

He learned that working in the administration department was her part-time job. She turned 19 on July 4th. She was a full-time student who would begin her third semester in September, in pursuit of an associate's degree in animal husbandry.

She and her family are sheep ranchers. They own 3,000 acres about five miles south of town. This is a small spread by Trans-

Pecos standards. Her oldest brother, Cordell, and her dad run the ranch. Her other brother, Henry, otherwise known as Hank, is a senior at Texas A&M in the Corps of Cadets. He's working on a bachelor's degree in agriculture, but he has a two-year obligation in the Army when he graduates in May.

Barlow said he just completed a tour of duty in the Army.

She offered to introduce him to the VA coordinator so he could file for the G.I. Bill if he wanted.

He said he expected to find out if Sheriff Sol was going to hire him in the next week or so. He was also waiting to find out if the Grand Jury would rule the shooting as a justifiable homicide. Assuming they do, he needed to visit his sister for a few days in Bisbee, Arizona. If he got the job, he would definitely enroll and would be most grateful for her help.

She said the Grand Jury was a no brainer, so she'd get busy to line him up. Then she glanced at her watch and exclaimed that she had to get back to the office before they locked up for the weekend.

He said, "Don't go yet. I was wondering if you would go to the movie with me tomorrow night. I saw the Bijou is playing Butch Cassidy and the Sundance Kid. It starts at 7."

"That sounds like fun. Stop by my house about 4. My folks are having a few neighbors over for a barbecue. We can eat and talk some more before the movie."

"Are you sure? Your folks don't even know me."

"Believe me. They know who you are and they'd love to meet you. Besides, everyone's welcome at Casa de Baker. We live at the Bar B, five miles south of 90 off 651. Turn west at the old windmill. That's Apache Road. The Bar B is about a mile down the road on the south side. You can't miss it."

"What's your phone number?"

"We're in the book under Arthur Baker. That's my dad. Sorry. Gotta go. I'm late. See you tomorrow at 4."

"See you tomorrow."

Barlow floated back to the Travelers Rest on Cloud 9. The 24-hour wait was excruciatingly long. Christmas came around quicker.

CHAPTER 8

THE FIRST TASTE OF LOVE

It was Saturday, July 12th. Barlow arrived at the Bar B at 4 o'clock sharp, full of anticipation and anxiety. The gathering had already begun. There were at least a half dozen cars and trucks parked in the lot next to the barn. One of them looked just like Sheriff Sol's police cruiser.

When he got out of Jade and started walking towards the fifteen or so folks gathered under the shade trees, the first person he recognized was Sheriff Sol, standing three or four inches above all the rest.

The person he did not see was Sarah. He thought this could be awkward.

Sheriff Sol spotted him right away. He separated himself from the crowd and walked over to greet him.

"Barlow, we're glad you could make it. Let me introduce you to our hosts.

"Barlow Adams, meet Arthur and Clarice Baker. We all grew up together, although they were seniors when I was in the 7th grade. Arthur taught me how to hit a curve ball when I was still in junior high. And the beautiful young gal who invited you to this soirée is their daughter and my goddaughter."

Arthur Baker was the doppelgänger of the Marlboro Man on all the billboards. He shook Barlow's hand and said, "Nice to meet you, Barlow. Welcome. This is my wife, Clarice."

Clarice was an older, still beautiful version of Sarah. Wow! Barlow felt himself blushing. He stammered, "Nice to meet you Ma'am, and Sir. I appreciate the invitation and hope I'm not intruding."

Clarice reached over and hugged him. She smiled and said, "Sol, you didn't tell us he was such a gentleman! Welcome. Sarah's been telling us all about you. Let me introduce you to everyone else before she drags you off and we don't have time to visit. Can I offer you some refreshment? We have beer and soft drinks iced down in that wash tub over there. Pick your poison and I'll show you around."

The names and faces were a blur. He was embarrassed by all the attention. He recognized Joanna Pratt. He made it a point to remember Sarah's brother, Cordell, and his wife, Darla, when he was introduced to them. Everyone was cordial and welcoming. He made the rounds, trying to act nonchalant, all the while his insides were flopping upside down.

At last, Sarah appeared in a white, eyelet lace cotton dress and bikini sandals. She was beaming, graceful, full of energy, and bursting with confidence. She took him by the arm and gave him a tour of the house and the curtilage, bantering back and forth with all the guests.

Her confidence rubbed off on him. Before long, he was relaxed, chatty, having a great time, and enjoying his best meal in at least a year. He was a little sad to rush off to the movie, but not too sad. It was mighty nice to enjoy her company all by himself.

The movie was funny and sad and exciting and all that it should be. When it was over and he drove her home, all he could remember was that he held her hand from beginning to end. She sat as close to him as Newton's Third Law of Physics would permit, what with two bodies exerting a force on one another, the forces being equal in magnitude, but opposite in direction. Then he kissed her goodnight at the doorstep.

She said, "Meet me in the morning for church. It's the Methodist Church. Services start at 9 o'clock. It would be a lot more fun for me if you came along."

He replied, "No problem, I grew up in the Methodist Church.

I'll be there at the front door at 8:45."

He could hardly wait, especially since it meant spending more time with her. Heck, he wouldn't even mind sitting on the front row if she were there by his side.

She said, "No, Silly! Meet me at your truck in the last row of the parking lot. I'll be riding with my folks. I'll come get you. If you wait at the front door, everyone will be curious and mob you, with good intentions of course, but then I wouldn't have a chance to talk to you before the service.

"Also, maybe we could ride over to Alpine afterwards and eat lunch at the Pizza Hut, unless of course, you have something else you need to do."

"You must be a mind reader because I was just thinking how long it's been since I ate pizza and I really have a taste for one."

Then she kissed him goodnight. She smiled and said, "Go home and get some sleep. Don't be late." Then, she stepped inside and gently closed the door.

He thought, "Sleep. What sleep? How am I going to go to sleep when all I can think about is you?"

Sunday, July 13th, was the most fun Barlow had ever had that he could remember. The connection he felt with Sarah was as if they had known each other since childhood.

There was no pretense. They talked about everything that came to mind, discovering that they had the same or similar points of view and values on all the topics they had discussed. They rounded each other out, like yin and yang, both being glass-half-full people, filled with gratitude for all the gifts God had bestowed upon them. They were in love with life and probably falling in love with each other.

They both had goals, but balanced and with perspective. Neither was ossified due to single-mindedness or rigidity. Both subscribed to life as a journey and not a destination. Their relationship seemed to be blossoming, as if someone had bathed them in Ortho Grow. Maybe Cupid?

The day came to a close way too soon for them both. Sarah's folks would be full of questions they would try not to ask. They had an abiding love and respect for one another, so she would tell them a lot. She also had chores to do and work on Monday, even if was just for four hours. The clock was her friend.

Barlow on the other hand, had nothing to do. He was in limbo waiting for the Grand Jury's ruling. He wasn't much concerned about that anymore, but he was anxious for some good news about his job application. Waiting was always the hardest part of life.

Ticktock. Ticktock.

Chapter 9

A New Lease on Life

It was Monday, July 14th. Sheriff Sol was headed to lunch when he saw Barlow on the sidewalk outside the courthouse. He asked Barlow to join him at Crabtree's, the other diner in town.

During the meal, Sheriff Sol reported that the Grand Jury returned a No True Bill, ruling that "the homicide by gunshot of one Rupert Doyle of Bakersfield, California, by one Barlow K. Adams of Arlo, Texas, on the night of Thursday, July 10, 1969, near the roadside of US Highway 90, approximately 8-1/2 miles east of the Quayle County Courthouse, is hereby declared to be justified with no further investigation warranted."

The sheriff smiled and Barlow smiled wider. He asked, "What's next?"

Sheriff Sol said he had verbal confirmation of Barlow's character and suitability from all three references. Ditto regarding his employment history. All he was waiting for now was for the correspondence to arrive.

He also had approval by the Quayle County Board of Supervisors to offer Barlow the job, to begin on Friday, August 1st, if he was sure he wanted it.

Barlow let out a whoop. He thanked the sheriff enthusiastically, accidentally bumping the table and spilling their coffees. After mopping up the mess with napkins, they shook on it and resumed wolfing down their meatloaf and mashed potatoes.

Before they finished, Sheriff Sol mentioned he knew of a small house that was coming up for let at a reasonable price. He said he'd line up a look-see for Barlow after his trip to Bisbee, if he were interested.

Barlow said he was, and thanked the sheriff once again.

Before they parted, Sheriff Sol's demeanor changed from upbeat to serious and he said, "Barlow, I need to make sure you fully understand that this deputy job is completely different from one in a more populated county.

"In Quayle, we cover over 2,000 square miles. The radio doesn't have 100% coverage. We ride alone. Back-up could be an hour away. Most folks take care of their own problems, so we don't have many high-speed chases, but when we do have a problem, it's usually serious and we have to be up for the task.

"On August 1st, Judge Sweeney will swear you in, and commission you as a deputy sheriff before you're POST certified. You don't realize it, but that puts you in a state of limbo, being allowed two years to complete the course, while the law transitions from no training required like it's always been, to the way it will be in 1972, when it will be absolutely necessary before commissioning.

"POST training is not a big deal to me, because we never needed it. Ever. We pick good people, give them on-the-job training, and watch them progress. If a guy can't cut the mustard, we send him on his way; however, this is a new era. POST certification is a very big deal to the lawyers and the judges and the anti-police.

"Truth is, I can't decide if all this training is a Machiavellian invention designed to be used as a tool against the police when they make a mistake, or if it's just the Law of Unintended Consequences in that 'the road to Hell is paved with good intentions.' Ya follow me?"

"Not exactly."

"What I mean is, I can see that you have a strong moral character, you're brave, and you have a good head on your shoulders. Your intervention with Sandra Taft demonstrated that. What is it police tell citizens to do if they see a crime in progress?"

"Call the police, I guess."

"Exactly, and don't intervene. Leave it to us. We're the professionals. Be observant. Get a license plate number if you can.

"Now look at the Sandra Taft incident. Suppose you did what conventional wisdom dictates. You drive as fast as you can to the jail and report what you saw to Archie. With luck, Archie arrives at the scene in fifteen minutes. What do you think Doyle would have done to Sandra in fifteen minutes?

"Or suppose you stopped right next to their vehicles and decided to intervene physically, if necessary? Doyle had a revolver you didn't see. How would that have turned out?

"No doubt about it. You were Sandra's knight on a white charger. You handled the situation better than most lawmen. In fact, if the Army were aware of this, they'd probably award you a medal for valor not in a combat zone.

"I considered your tactics.

"You parked far enough away not to escalate the situation too rapidly. You blinded Doyle with your headlights. You armed yourself and remained in the shadows. At 64 yards, blinded with headlights, he probably would have been lucky to hit your truck with that handgun.

"He fires, allowing you to fire back. You're a deer hunter and an expert Army rifleman with recent combat experience. You aim for dead center.

"After you fired, you could have charged off into the night after him, which would have been like tracking a wounded lion in the dark. Instead, you give him time to bleed out, like a wounded deer, and you rescue the damsel in distress.

"You did everything in the safest way possible, making spur of the moment decisions. Then when questioned by police, you respond like a 10-year veteran officer.

"What you did not do, was the conventional, by-the-book solution. That's why I want you working for me, and not the Dallas or Houston or Amarillo Police Departments.

"POST will teach you the school-recommended way to perform all the necessary law enforcement tasks they can imagine - marksmanship, unarmed combat, photographing a crime scene, investigating an accident, writing a ticket, handcuffing a suspect, state law, the law of search and seizure, interrogation, mobile surveillance and so forth. I'm not saying any of that is bad. In fact, it's all good.

"What I am saying is that whatever POST teaches, the lawyers and judges and anti-police will compare everything you do by that standard. If you deviate, they will use that against you, in essence suggesting that you're a rogue or incompetent. Coloring outside the lines, using common sense, understanding that 'necessity is the mother of invention,' and not responding robotically all becomes 'failure to follow proper police procedure.' They will do all they can to keep you within that box, claiming that anything otherwise is wrong or bad or illegal.

"Believe me when I say someday you will find yourself in this trick bag, defending yourself for doing the right thing but not in the way POST mandates. Remember this. I learned it the hard way in the Navy. 'No good deed goes unpunished.' I bet you learned the same thing in the Army. You will be excoriated in court, or investigated by the FBI for a civil rights complaint sooner or later.

"I know with 100% certainty that you are up to the challenges you will be confronted with on this job. I just want to make sure you have your eyes wide open before you commit."

"Sheriff Sol, I can't tell you how much I appreciate this opportunity. I promise I won't let you down. I know I have a lot to learn. I'm willing and able. I'll make you proud."

"I know you will.

"One last thing. I got a call from my goddaughter a little while ago. She didn't know if you were leaving town today or tomorrow. She asked for you to stop by and see her this afternoon, as soon as you can. She's waiting."

"Thanks, Sheriff. I'm leaving tomorrow. I'd never leave town without seeing her first."

"Somehow I knew that. You take good care of her, Barlow. She's as good as they come. I love her like she really is my own daughter. Savvy?"

"Yes, Sir. I've never met another girl like her. I would never hurt her. I'm headed over there right now.

"Good decision."

Chapter 10
Parting is Such Sweet Sorrow

Barlow skedaddled to the college ASAP. He saw Sarah in the registrar's office helping a student, most likely. She lit up and motioned for him to take a seat. Five minutes later, she was seated next to him.

"I was afraid you might leave town and I wouldn't see you before you left."

"I could never do that. Anyway, I'm not leaving 'til tomorrow morning. Can you stay in town after work? Maybe we could eat at Crabtree's. I ate lunch there with Sheriff Sol today. It was pretty good."

"Of course I can. Must I ask if you got some good news?"

"Well, being the goddaughter of the sheriff and all, I figured you probably have the inside pipeline."

"You rat! He would never tell me something like that. Maybe my dad . . . ."

Barlow smiled. "Meet Quayle County's newest deputy beginning August 1st."

"You should have told me right away! I've been on pins and needles. I didn't want you to move away if you didn't get the job."

"We've only known each other four days. Already, I could never do that."

"Well okay then. Look it, I'll be off at four. Meet me in the parking lot. We can hang out at the library until it's time to eat. I want to know everything."

"See you then."

Barlow topped Jade off with gas, and cleaned her up at the

self-serve car wash. He called Chloe from a pay phone and told her he'd see her on Wednesday night. He got most of his belongings ready for the trip. He was waiting for Sarah in the parking lot with twenty minutes to spare.

Sarah was out the door at 4 o'clock sharp, skipping down the steps toward Jade. She climbed in the truck and gave Barlow a huge hug and a slow kiss. They spent the next two hours at the library catching up like they hadn't seen one another for at least a month. Supper at Crabtree's was country ham, lima beans, a tossed salad, with biscuits, apple pie, and lemonade.

Tomorrow would be Tuesday, July 15th. Barlow planned to arrive at Chloe's on Wednesday eve. He would stay the rest of the week through the weekend, and return to Mosby on Tuesday, July 22nd. That would give him time to find a place to live, and enroll for the fall semester, before beginning work on August 1st. He already knew he would be on midnight shift. Sheriff Sol said so.

Sarah said she would help. She also pointed out that Saturday, July 26th, was Quayle County's biggest annual rodeo, called Cowboy Days. She was a competitor in barrel racing. She wanted Barlow to attend. Everyone in Quayle County and all the counties surrounding, plus some farther Texas venues, and even some out-of-staters would be there. Of course he would come.

Saying goodnight was even harder than on Sunday. Even so, Barlow was a man on a mission.

CHAPTER 11
A LONG OVERDUE VISIT

The drive along the Rio Grande corridor was eye-opening. The wide, empty spaces, scorching sun, aridity, proximity to Mexico, coupled with the myths and legends of firefights with Indians, bandits, and all types of desperate people, both excited, and in a way, sobered him. The very nature of the desert, combined with its deadly snakes, scorpions, tarantulas, Gila monsters, and various furry and winged predators were more than enough to take the life of a tenderfoot or a careless person.

Driving along the highway at 50 miles per hour without benefit of air conditioning, in oven-like temperatures with the dry air evaporating his perspiration almost on contact, made this trip more poignant. Life is tenuous in the desert, which is what appealed to him. Knowing he planned to take this route was his primary motivation in purchasing the army surplus equipment. He brought several gallons of water and survival rations in the event he had a breakdown.

Barlow arrived in Bisbee late afternoon on Wednesday, July 16th. He had a couple of hours to catch up with Chloe and meet his 6-month-old nephew, Oliver, before Bert returned from work.

They lived in a charming old adobe, on a street lined with sycamore trees. Chloe exuded contentment and happiness. She fussed over Barlow because it had been so long since they were together. When Bert arrived, they sat down to a much appreciated roast beef dinner. Afterwards, while Chloe fed and bathed Oliver, Bert and Barlow repaired to the patio to sip shots of tequila and smoke hand rolled cigars while they compared and contrasted the Army with the Air Force. After the sweltering day, the evening breeze was bliss itself.

One day they drove over to Tombstone in Chloe's air conditioned, 1968, Rambler American station wagon. Barlow was enthralled to walk down the boardwalks of this legendary town.

At the OK corral, he studied the wooden, painted, two-dimensional, life-sized figures of the combatants placed where witnesses claim they were standing just before the gunfight erupted.

Their proximity to one another was incomprehensible. They were so close it would have been harder to miss an opponent than not. Doc Holiday began this engagement with a sawed-off, 12-gauge, double-barrel shotgun! Did the Earps or the cowboys think 'too close to miss' would encourage their opponents to stand down? Seeing this gave Barlow pause to wonder many a time later on.

Just as planned, Barlow spent five nights before heading back to Mosby. It was a great reunion. Bert and Chloe were both happy for him regarding his new job. They had long conversations about the good times before the crash which radically altered their lives. Barlow could see first-hand, just how happy Chloe and Bert were. It made him think of Sarah.

Chloe wept when he got ready to leave. It almost cut his heart out. He vowed to come around more often now that he was out of the Army.

It was a long trip back. He had lots of time to reminisce. He hadn't really thought about his folks for a long, long time before this trip. He had barely mentioned them to Sarah. He didn't know why. Maybe too hard to go there.

He regretted missing Grandma Bea's funeral while he was in Vietnam. He could have gotten a Red Cross family hardship leave to attend it, but he never applied. He had been in country eight months. He didn't apply because he couldn't imagine returning for four months to complete his combat tour. He had to gut it out because once his tour was done, he never wanted to come back. Now he was sorry he didn't. Heck, it was all he could do to visit her gravesite and that of his folks before he left on this odyssey.

He was getting maudlin. Time to put past things in the past and think about the future.

He arrived back in Mosby on Tuesday, the 22nd about 6:30 p.m. He was physically and emotionally spent. He checked in at the Travelers Rest on his own dime and got his old room back. Fortunately, it only cost $6.00 a night.

Tomorrow would be a new day. The cloudy skies from the past were dissipating. The future held out a promise of sunshiny days. Fatigued as he was, sleep eluded him. Tomorrow he would check in with Sheriff Sol before calling Sarah. Business before pleasure.

CHAPTER 12

FOLLOWING DIRECTIONS PAYS DIVIDENDS

Wednesday morning, July 23rd. He went to the jail to see Sheriff Sol. He wasn't in, but he left Barlow a message to stop at the Mosby Feed & Seed and see Willard Taft. Next, he was to go to Jake's Pawn Shop and see Jake Buchanan. Finally, he was to stop at the college and see Sarah. The note was emphatic about making these stops in that specific order.

Barlow could half-way guess why he was sent to see Willard. He probably wanted to express his gratitude again, which Barlow thought was really nice, but unnecessary.

He didn't need to be told to see Sarah, but he imagined it might have to do with getting enrolled in the POST program more than anything else.

He had no idea why he was going to a pawn shop. Nevertheless, he set out to comply with his orders exactly as prescribed, just like he did in the Army. His 'was not to ask why, but to do or die.'

Willard was excited to see him. Sandra was, too. It turned out, they were the proprietors. After a few pleasantries, not least of which was Barlow's observation that Sandra looked great and seemed to be healing well, Willard ushered him out to the parking lot and into his company, GMC cargo van. He said he had something he wanted Barlow to see.

Willard drove to 62 West Zachary Taylor Avenue, which was the very last house on the north side. It dead-ended there. To the west lay an open field. Taylor Avenue was one block north of America Avenue.

Number 62 was a small, one-story, concrete block house,

freshly painted white with forest green trim, and charcoal grey asphalt shingles on a hip roof. It had an American flag flying from an angled pole attached on the right side of the front door.

It was situated on a quarter-acre lot, with the backyard bounded by a wooden post and wire farm fence. It had a single-lane, asphalt driveway on the left side, ending at a detached, white, concrete block, one-car garage.

The yard was xeriscaped, meaning no grass, just rocks and gravel and scattered desert flora. In this case, that meant a purple sage bush, several varieties of cacti, a stunning yellow sweet broom bush, with a weathered longhorn skull in the middle of the yard for decoration. It was really cool. Barlow began to hope this was the place Sheriff Sol said might be available.

Willard unlocked the front door. They went inside and stepped into the living room. The first thing Barlow noticed, was that it was cool. An air conditioning unit was purring in a window.

The interior had also been freshly painted. The walls were a light mustard. The floors were a pale, olive green terrazzo.

The house was furnished. The living room had a couch, easy chair, ottoman, two end tables with lamps, coffee table, and magazine rack. The picture window had avocado green drapes. A black and white TV on a small wooden stand was situated in the corner.

The living room opened up to the kitchen in the rear, and to a hallway on the right.

The kitchen had a 1950's style, round, chrome-framed table with a red formica top. It had four matching chrome-framed chairs with red plastic, padded cushions and backs. The cabinets were simple, painted white. The refrigerator was small and old, and quietly humming. The stove was white enamel with four gas burners. The kitchen window over the sink had white lace curtains and overlooked the back yard.

The hallway led to the bathroom, tiny laundry room with a washer and dryer, and two bedrooms.

The street side bedroom was furnished with a double bed, chest of drawers, freestanding oval, wood-framed mirror, and two end tables with night lamps.

The backside bedroom was set up as an office with a small desk, chair, bookshelves, four-drawer filing cabinet, and a large map of the United States hanging on the wall. This map was dated 1952, predating both Alaska and Hawaii as states.

They returned to the kitchen and walked out the back door. On the west side next to the house, was a 30-foot, metal tower with a TV antenna.

The garage was empty and clean, with shelves running across the back.

Barlow's chest was thumping.

Willard asked, "What do you think?"

Barlow responded, "It's great. Who does it belong to?"

"It's Sandra's. It was her mother's. She died several months ago. We fixed it up to rent. Are you interested?"

"I am, if I can afford it. How much is it?"

Willard beamed. He said, "We planned to ask $150 a month, but we would be mighty pleased if you would take it for $125. Of course, you would be responsible to pay the utilities."

Barlow asked, "Are you sure? I don't want to take advantage."

Willard said, "We are. Shake on it, sign the lease, and I'll give you the keys. Rent's due the first of the month, but there's no charge for the rest of this month."

Barlow's face almost split in two, smiling. He said, "Thanks so very much to both of you. I'll take real good care of it."

Willard said, "Come on. I'll lock up. We'll go back to the store and you can sign the lease."

Thirty minutes later, Barlow drove out of the parking lot with keys to his own digs. Remarkable! For the past two years his home had been a single bed and a footlocker in an Army barracks, a sleeping bag in a tent, or a cot in a hooch in Vietnam. What an improvement!

CHAPTER 13

OUTFITTING FOR WORK

Next stop was at Jake's Pawn Shop. The man behind the counter said, "Welcome. You must be Barlow Adams. I'm Jake Buchanan and I own this establishment."

"Hi, Mr. Jake. Very glad to make your acquaintance. Sheriff Sol said for me to come see you."

"As well you should. I'm the local firearms dealer and police supply store, among other things. I have a contract with the county to supply uniforms and the like to the sheriff's office. Why don't you browse around while I get some things in order?"

"Yes, Sir."

Barlow looked around. Although there were a variety of pawned items for sale, the lion's share of inventory was firearms and accessories, to include at least a hundred different knives. Barlow was acutely aware that he needed to buy a handgun and his leather. He saw an entire display case of new revolvers and semi-automatic pistols, and another with used ones. He didn't know how that was going to work, because he still had seven more months before his 21st birthday. Nevertheless, he browsed around and saw several which appealed to him.

One entire aisle was dedicated to belts, holsters, slings, cleaning kits, gun cases, reloading supplies, etc. Another aisle contained boxes and boxes of just about every conceivable type of ammunition. One wall had a rack with at least four dozen long guns. This place was a cornucopia for shooters and hunters.

About ten minutes later, Jake reappeared from the back. He directed Barlow into a storage area which was curtained off. It contained shelving and clothing racks of uniforms for lawmen, firefighters, ambulance crews, gas station attendants, nurses, county works department employees, and various other occupations he couldn't identify.

Jake said that Barlow looked like a size 42. He handed Barlow a pair of khaki trousers marked 34 x 30. Barlow tried them on and they fit.

Next, he handed Barlow a long sleeve khaki shirt marked 15-1/2 x 34. Again, it fit perfectly.

He handed Barlow a short-waisted, khaki jacket, similar to a World War II Ike jacket, except it was zip up, not button up. Bingo.

Next, he had Barlow try on a khaki, canvas duck car coat. It was a little roomie, and the sleeves were about a half-inch too long, but Mr. Jake said that was what you want in a winter coat.

He had Barlow put his clothes back on, while he stuffed a cardboard box full of uniforms. He led Barlow back to the front counter.

Mr. Jake said, "Okay. The county pays for five sets of trousers and shirts, light-weight jacket, winter coat, this rubberized, ankle-length rain slicker, one pair of Peerless handcuffs with two keys, a wooden nightstick with a leather thong, a two-cell flashlight, and one pair of leather work gloves. Deputies pay for their boots and Stetsons, since they can be worn off duty. The ones you're wearing are just fine. If you tear, stain, or wear out a garment, you can exchange it for a new one, so long as the replacement isn't a result of your neglect or abuse.

"In addition, you get seven left-sleeve shoulder patches with the sheriff's office logo and seven right-sleeve shoulder patches of the Texas state flag.

"That's one pair for each shirt, the jacket, and the coat. Patches are centered and worn 1/2-inch below the shoulder seam. You can sew them on yourself or go to the laundromat and have Mrs. Martha Perkins do it for you. She charges 25 cents a patch. The county does not pay for sewing.

"I have an invoice here for you to sign affirming that I issued all these uniforms to you. The pink copy is yours.

"The county will issue the badge when you get sworn in. By the way, the badges are custom made by our very own renowned silversmith, Linus Farmer, out of sterling silver. If you lose it, besides pissing off the sheriff, you will be assessed $18.00.

"Do you own a handgun, Mr. Barlow Adams?"

"No, Sir."

"Interesting dilemma, Mr. Adams. ATF says you can possess one, but you cannot buy one. The Army or the Sheriff's Office could issue one to you, and you would be lawfully permitted to shoot it or to defend yourself with it, but you cannot buy one. Typical government bullshit, so here's the deal the sheriff and I worked out.

"You could wait until you turn 21, and buy one then. In that event, you'll be the only deputy without one, hauling around that 30-30 everywhere you go on duty, which, by the way, I hear you're deadly with, and I applaud you for it, Sir.

"You could arrange to get one elsewhere, maybe borrow one, inherit one from a family member, find one under a bush, something like that.

"Third option would be to rent-to-own one from me. The way that works, you select one you like, fill out the ATF Form 4473, and rent it from me for one dollar less than purchase price. The day you turn 21, you come in and pay me a buck and you become the owner.

"Whatever you decide, understand that you are under no obligation to purchase any unissued items from me. I do sell top notch police equipment, whatever you may need, at a very reasonable price I might add, and I won't steer you wrong, but the choice of vendor is yours alone."

"Mr. Jake, I'm prepared to rent-to-own a gun from you, especially since Sheriff Sol said it was okay. I'm pleased he worked this out for me. I figured I'd have to wait, since he said

I'm starting out in the jail. I know jailers don't carry guns."

"My dear Barlow, the sheriff's office doesn't house prisoners with such regularity as to have the luxury of paying deputies to lallygag in an empty jail like a firefighter sitting on his ass waiting for a fire! The county is hiring you to enforce the law. Enforcing the law presumes one is prepared to use force, which could escalate into the use of deadly force, most likely with a firearm, the most common genre being a handgun. Certainly you intuited this when you accepted the position."

"I did. It's just that I know the new Gun Control Act is complicated, plus the new state law regarding police certification can be tricky, too. I'm just the FNG thankful to get this job and trying not to make waves."

"FNG?"

"Army acronym for fucking new guy."

"Ah, yes. Of course. Very well. So, we cannot make a determination as to what style of leather you will need until we know what type of handgun you'll be carrying.

"Sheriff Sol is very flexible about make, model, and caliber of handgun his deputies carry. He says it's very personal, like selecting a wife. Deputies are not robots and the sheriff's office is not the Army. Do you agree?"

"Yes, Sir."

"Are you familiar with the Colt, Model 1911, .45 ACP (automatic cartridge pistol), semi-automatic pistol, with a five-and-one-half-inch barrel, otherwise known as the Government Model?"

"Yes, Sir. We familiarized with it in the Army. I've shot it, but I never qualified with it."

"Okay. You are allowed to carry a pistol such as that, even a pricey one like Chief Alex's Browning Hi Power, 9-millimeter, which comes with two magazines that hold thirteen rounds each; however, most deputies prefer revolvers. Do you have a preference?"

"A revolver, I think."

"Excellent. Now a couple of deputies, Archie Willis, for example, and Slick is another, carry a single-action Colt in .45 Long Colt caliber. The Long Colt ammo is expensive by the way, but it's an outstanding cartridge that's been around for nearly a hundred years. That being said, the trend over time, especially in the East, has shifted to double-action revolvers. Now I realize we are not in the East.

"I presume you know, that the single-actions must be cocked each time before pulling the trigger, whereas the double-actions can be shot with or without cocking. Also, the single-actions have a loading gate. You have to load and eject each cartridge one at a time, whereas the cylinders in the double-actions open outward, and you can eject all the empties at once. Loading and unloading are both a little quicker in the double-actions. Do you have a preference?"

"Yes, Sir. Double-action."

"Very good. What we have in this display case here is a variety of new double-actions by Smith & Wesson, Colt, Ruger, oh yeah, and one Dan Wesson, in .38 Special, .357 Magnum, .41 Magnum, .44 Magnum, and one in .45 Long Colt.

"Most city cops, especially in the East, are issued or carry .38's, because they are not quite as powerful and therefore are less likely to go through several walls or several people. Less collateral damage, and yet a very fine, all around cartridge.

"Most highway patrolman and rural deputies carry .357 Magnums. Same basic round as the .38, except with better penetration. It's also better for the greater distances likely to be encountered in a rural area.

"We also have the three larger calibers, a few .41's, .44's, and one .45. Generally, that means more power and more recoil, especially the .44 Magnum, if you are shooting the magnum cartridges and not the lighter load, which are the .44 Specials.

"Why don't you pick up the ones you're curious about? See if any particular one has the right feel."

Barlow handled most of the guns in the new gun display case. Most were blue steel, some high gloss, others more of a satin finish. Some were nickel-plated. Those were beautiful, easier to clean because you could see the carbon build-up after firing. They were also less apt to get rusty. The barrel lengths of the guns varied from two inches on the .38 snub-nosed revolvers, designed to be concealable, to one .44 Magnum with an eight-and-three-eighths-inch barrel, designed for hunting.

Barlow preferred the Smiths over the Colts. The Rugers were okay, but didn't offer the .41 Magnum caliber.

Jake was keen-eyed and said, "Why don't you take a really close look at this one?"

It was a Smith & Wesson, Model 58, Military & Police, .41 Magnum, six-shot, double-action revolver. It was on an N-Frame, a heavier, more durable frame designed for the punishment of a .44 Magnum cartridge. It had a blue satin finish, with a four-inch bull barrel, and fixed sights.

Mr. Jake said, "This model has a heavier barrel for less recoil and better accuracy. It has fixed sights, which take a split second longer to line up when sighting, but they don't get knocked out of alignment like the target sights are prone to do. This is the big brother M&P to the Model 10 M&P in .38 Special. In fact, both the San Antonio and the San Francisco Police Departments issue this model to their uniformed officers. How does it feel?"

"Perfect."

"That's what I thought. Take a look at this. It's a standard 158-grain .357 Magnum cartridge, with a muzzle velocity of 1,240 feet per second.

"Compare it with this 210-grain .41 Magnum cartridge, with a muzzle velocity of 1,000 feet per second. Ironically, it has less recoil but more knock-down power. The .357 is faster, with better penetration, as a rule of thumb. What do you think?"

"I like the .41."

"I thought you would. It's $119.00. If you are certain this is the gun you want, we can select your leather. You can be all rigged out today . . . or you can wait."

"I'll take the .41. What do you suggest for leather?"

"Well, the sheriff's office wears plain brown leather, as you may have noticed. Most wear products made by El Paso Saddlery, because it's the best, in my humble opinion, been around for years, but there are other, well-made competitors - Don Hume, Bianchi, Hunter, etc. I carry them all.

"Most deputies purchase the #2 Texas belt. It's a sturdy, two-inch wide belt. This one here has no cartridge loops. We also carry it with 12, 24, or 36 loops. You can even special order one with more loops, if your waist is big enough. The sheriff has the 12-loop, Archie Willis has the 36. In Quayle County, the preference seems to be 24. What would you prefer?"

"Can I see one in my size?"

"Here's a plain one. Uh oh. The only one in your size with loops in .41 has 24. Try it and see."

"They both fit, but obviously the 24-loops makes more sense than zero loops."

"Well, I also have a 12-loop cartridge slide in .41 Magnum you could use with the plain belt, or I could order one for you in either 12 or 36 loops."

"Oh, that won't be necessary. I'll take the one with 24. What about a holster?"

"Everyone here uses the Austin 1930 model, with the leather snap strap. You're right-handed, right? Here's one for a four-inch, N-Frame revolver. Slide it on the belt and see how it feels. Once you adjust it where you want it, put the gun in it and see how it rides."

"Wow. This is nice. I'll take 'em both."

"Good. Now you'll want a nightstick strap with a metal loop, a handcuffs strap, and I notice you're wearing a Buck Folding Hunter. You'll probably want this knife sheath designed for that size knife, which will slide over a two-inch belt."

"I do. How much for all the leather?"

"Altogether, $55, plus tax, of course."

"How much is ammo?"

"The .41's like I showed you are $8.40 per box of 50. You'll want factory loads for on duty, but I also sell the Lee Loader, for $12. You can reload your expended casings with the 210-grain, semi-wadcutter, lead bullets for $2.20 per box of 100. The primers cost 85 cents per hundred. An eight-ounce tin of Bullseye gunpowder costs $4.30. That much powder should last you for several years. Anyway, if you have the empty shell casings, you can load 100 cartridges for about $3.50. That's $1.75 a box."

"I'll take five boxes of cartridges, the Lee Loader, the gunpowder, two boxes of bullets and two boxes of primers. I'll also need a gun cleaning kit and patches. I already have the solvent and oil."

"The gun cleaning kit is 75 cents. Patches are 50 cents."

"What's the damage?"

"That's $118 for the gun rental, $55 for the leather, $42 for the cartridges, $12 for the Lee Loader, $4.30 for the Bullseye, $4.40 for the bullets, $1.70 for the primers, and $1.25 for the cleaning kit and patches. That comes to $238.65 plus sales tax. Can you handle this today or would you like for me to open up an account for you?"

"No, Sir. I got it, but I appreciate the offer."

"Okay. Before we wrap up, you need to complete this ATF Form 4473. I'll hold it in abeyance. When is your birthday?"

"February 28th."

Barlow filled out the form and signed a lease agreement.

"Okay. If I don't see you before then, come back on February 28th, and pay me that buck you owe me. I'll tear up the lease and you will own the gun. Also, don't forget your receipt."

"Thanks, Mr. Jake."

"Thank you, Barlow. Don't be a stranger. We can chew the fat if you don't need to buy anything and I'm not busy."

"Will do.

"By the way. Is there much of a chance for an accidental discharge loading bullets with the Lee Loader?"

"Not any chance, if you ask me, unless you are a complete imbecile. I've never heard of, nor read about anyone having an accidental discharge while reloading ammunition.

"You could have a reloaded shell blow up when you shoot, if you put too much powder in it. However, the kit comes with a pre-measured scoop. Even if you rounded the scoop, you won't have a shell blow up. If you put in two scoops, assuming they would fit, you might have a shell blow up. I've never heard of anyone being that stupid. This ease your mind?"

"Yes, Sir. Thanks for the clarification. I don't know anyone who reloads."

"You will. Most cops shoot a lot to stay proficient. Ammo is expensive. Most departments only qualify once a year. That's why you reload."

"Understood. Thanks."

CHAPTER 14

ATTENDING TO THE MUNDANE

Barlow collected his haul and filled up the cab of his truck. His excitement meter was nearly pegged out, and he still had two stops to make, the laundromat being added.

His money was rapidly diminishing. He was down to about $250. His first paycheck wouldn't be due 'til August 31st. That was more than five weeks away. He would have to watch his spending a little more carefully.

The laundromat was on the way to WTJC. Miss Martha greeted him by saying, "You must be the new guy Sheriff Sol hired."

"Yes, Ma'am. The name's Barlow Adams. Nice to meet you."

"What have you got here?"

"Five shirts and two jackets that need these patches sewed on."

"I know the drill. That will be $3.50. You can come back in an hour if you like. We're open 'til 6 o'clock. Otherwise, they'll be ready tomorrow."

"Great."

"Also, just so you know, we wash, dry, and fold clothes for folks who don't have time to do it themselves. It's 25 cents a load, 35 cents to dry, and a $1.00 drop-off fee. We also launder and press trousers for 40 cents each and shirts for 35 cents each."

"That's good to know. I very well may have something in a few days. See you later. Nice meeting you."

CHAPTER 15

SWEET TALKING MAN

MIXES BUSINESS WITH PLEASURE

Last stop was the college. Sarah lit up like the desert sun when she saw him walk in.

"Well, Mr. Adams, I was beginning to think I was the last thing on your mind since you got back into town."

"Au contraire. You were the very first thing on my mind once I left Bisbee, but it was two very long days driving back. Anyway, I smelled like a water buffalo, plus I needed to find lodging. I thought about coming over Tuesday night, but didn't want to wear out my welcome with your folks. You can understand.

"Besides that, I went to see Sheriff Sol first thing this morning. He gave me a list of things to do in a specific order, and he told me not to come here until I got everything else done first, so here I am."

"So here you are, on an errand, planning to enroll I presume, and voila! Mission accomplished."

"Well . . . that's one way of looking at it. Another way is that I was in this very office less than two weeks ago. I had a chance encounter with a bewitching angel in human form. She enchanted me. I can't get her out of my mind. I think she likes me. I want to spend as much time as I can with her.

"The thing is, I need to be gainfully employed with a roof over my head, rather than rambling about like the itinerate ex-soldier that I am.

"This stunning member of the fairer sex hails from a prominent family with friends in high places, no less than the high sheriff, as an example, who, without a doubt, and rightfully so, would run off any potential suitors who couldn't provide for her and, perhaps even more importantly, make her happy. And that, my dear lady, is why I'm here.

"I want to, no, I need to enroll in college so I can keep my new job, and through permanent, gainful employment, do right by this angel, thereby continuing to afford myself the opportunity to visit with her, just like I'm doing right this very moment."

"Why, Rhett Butler! You sweep me off my feet. How about a little less talk and a lot more action?"

"I was hoping you would say that. Can you stay after work and eat supper with me tonight? I was thinking about cooking some hamburgers at my place. I'd have to go to the store first to get the fixings, and we'd probably have to eat off paper plates . . ."

"What place? What haven't you told me?"

"Well, today I leased Sandra Tafts mother's house at 62 West Zachary Taylor Avenue. She died a few months ago. You probably already knew that. Tonight's my first night there. I don't know if the house came with dishes. I need to get some things. Not sure yet what. Would you be my very first guest?"

"You rat! You let me prattle on, pretending to be neglected while you had exciting news to tell me? Yes! I will eat with you in your new home tonight! I'll bring the food. Can you get some beer or bourbon or something like that to help celebrate?"

"Well, I haven't been to this one yet, but the American Legion sells drinks to vets regardless of age. I've never heard them ask for your driver's license - just a membership card, which I happen to have. They might sell me a six-pack. Or, I do have a nearly full bottle of Old Crow bourbon I'm rather fond of. And, my brother-in-law gave me an unopened bottle of Jose Cuervo. We could do tequila shots."

"That's it! We'll do shots! I'll get some limes and salt, too.

"What about school? Did you come to enroll? We can also sign you up for G.I. Bill benefits."

"Yes. In fact, I've already completed the application and signed the release for a copy of my high school transcript to be mailed to the registrar. Here's $10 for the application fee. I want to enroll in the law enforcement associate's degree program. I studied the catalogue and I know what classes I'd like to take first semester. I need morning classes because I work the midnight shift. How do I do this?"

"Come with me."

She took him to see Mrs. Leona Dalrymple, the assistant admissions officer. Thirty minutes later Barlow was enrolled with his first semester schedule in hand. He signed up for six classes.

On Mondays, Wednesdays, and Fridays, he had English 101, College Math 101, and Spanish 101 at 8 o'clock, 9 o'clock, and 10 o'clock, respectively.

On Tuesdays and Thursdays, he had Patrol Procedures 101, Texas Law 101, and LEO (Law Enforcement Officer) Physical Education 105 at 8 o'clock, 9:30 o'clock, and 11 o'clock, respectively.

This was a sixteen-semester-hour caseload, with all classes except physical education being three hours. It allowed him to get out the door by noon on most days.

Tuition was $100 per semester, plus a $25 lab fee for PE (due to firearms training.) Payment was due by first period, the first day of school, which was Tuesday, September 2nd, Monday being Labor Day. Barlow deferred payment, trying not to cut himself short. With payday falling on August 31st, a Sunday, he hoped the county would pony up on Friday, August 29th.

Enrollment completed, Sarah walked him over to Mr. Conrad Dawkins, the Veterans Administration coordinator. He assisted Barlow in signing up for the G.I. Bill benefits, which were $288 per month for up to 36 months for a full-time student. This was enough time to complete a bachelor's degree at nine months per year for four years.

Mr. Dawkins said it normally took four to six weeks for the checks to begin. The checks would cease during summer vacation, unless he enrolled full-time for the summer term. Furthermore, the maximum was eighteen months of benefits for an associate's degree; however, benefits were available up to ten years after ETS, if he decided to pursue a bachelor's degree.

During the process, Mr. Dawkins mentioned that he was a captain and the commanding officer of Battery A, 491st Field Artillery, Texas Army National Guard in Alpine, which is a 155-millimeter, self-propelled, howitzer unit. He has a vacancy for a fellow artilleryman. Barlow could keep his stripes if he signed up within 90 days of his ETS.

This caught Barlow completely off guard. On one hand, he wanted to say, "I'm proud to have served, but my obligation is over and I'm done."

On the other hand, he knew the money would be helpful. Also, he enjoyed being an artilleryman. Besides that, if he served eighteen years in the National Guard, coupled with his two years of active duty, he would receive a small pension at age sixty. This was tempting.

What he said was, "Gee, Sir, I appreciate the offer, but I'll have to think about it. I'm not sure how I'll handle a full-time job while being a full-time student. Let me see how it works out and I'll let you know."

Captain Dawkins said he understood, but if Barlow waited too long, he'd have to come in as a private first class.

CHAPTER 16

SPENDING TIME WITH THE ONE YOU LOVE

It was 4:30 when he finally finished. Sarah had been off since 4:00 o'clock. She was waiting for him in the lobby. After a short tete-a-tete, she left for the grocery. Barlow gave her his second key in case she finished first.

He checked out of the Travelers Rest. The owner, Mrs. Patricia Norris, a sweet old widow woman, didn't charge him for the late check-out. Miss Pat was a little sweet on him, and she asked him to come by and visit once in a while if he had some free time. He said he would. They chatted a bit before he left. This delayed him somewhat, so he was in a hurry when he picked up his garments at the laundromat before heading home.

Sarah did finish first. She found some old dishes and pots and pans and silverware in the cabinets. The Tafts were taking really good care of Barlow. She washed and put away the things they didn't need for supper before he arrived.

Barlow had a veritable truckload of stuff to put away. With two of them working together, it didn't take long.

Sarah cooked hamburgers, new potatoes, and corn on the cob for supper. They had orange sherbet for dessert. Then they took kitchen chairs out under the lone shade tree in the backyard.

Barlow smoked his pipe. They toasted each other with tequila shooters. They held hands and laughed and fell into a peaceful rhythm that ofttimes manifests itself with lovers in sync.

At 10 o'clock, Sarah left for home, more sober than not. Today had been a great day.

On Thursday, Barlow went through the house carefully. He found some towels, sheets, blankets, tablecloths, broom, mop, bucket, even four folding lawn chairs, plus other everyday household items he never had the need to purchase in the past, and thus, never considered. He realized and came to appreciate even more, what the Tafts had done for him.

He went to the grocery and stocked up on grub as well as non-food items, such as paper towels, dish soap, etc. Sarah was coming over for supper again. She had decided to make spaghetti with a tossed salad.

That afternoon, he did a little target practice with his new revolver. He shot one box of shells. Sweet! He was pleased with his choice. It shot true and the recoil was not significant. At 25 yards, he could drill a tin can five out of six shots. He knew with practice he would be six for six and then could begin to extend his range.

That evening with Sarah was every bit as special as the one the night before. He knew he was hopelessly in love. He could no longer bottle up his feelings for her. This was quickly becoming an all or nothing proposition.

How quickly life changes! Two months ago he was still in the Army, pondering what his future would hold. He thought it was looking mighty bright today. Brighter than he ever could have imagined.

By Friday, he was bored. He went for a three-mile run, just to burn off excess energy. He ran four. He was ready to begin his new job. He couldn't wait for it to begin.

He reloaded the one box of empty shell casings with the Lee Loader. Worked like a champ. Still restless. Too much time on his hands. Fortunately, the Bakers had invited him for supper. They said to come over whenever he was ready, so he did - at 2 o'clock!

For the Bakers, the entire day had been set aside in preparation for the big rodeo on Saturday. Their enthusiasm was catching. Barlow pitched in, helping to wax and shine Sarah's saddle, muck out stalls, groom two horses, and even fix a flat on their two-horse trailer. The work morphed into cold beers and a mutton stew with frijoles, tortillas, a tossed salad and sopaipillas. Their way of life enamored him. He couldn't explain why, exactly, but now he was excited about the rodeo, too.

On Saturday, he understood why.

Sarah picked him up before 8. She was driving an old, black, 1956 Studebaker pickup truck that clearly showed its wear and tear. She was pulling the two-horse trailer.

The rodeo grounds were already a beehive of activity. The periphery was jammed with trucks and trailers and makeshift campsites. Vendors selling food, drinks, and all types of western attire and cowboy paraphernalia were already in full swing. Sarah parked where she could find an open space. They led both of her horses to one of the open stables and put them in adjacent stalls.

At 10 o'clock, the festivities began, initially with events for children, shifting to teens, and finally to amateur adult and professional rodeo cowboys and cowgirls.

There were six different heats in barrel racing for amateur women. Sarah astonished Barlow with her skill. She placed second behind a young woman from El Paso. Barlow watched from the stands with her parents and Cordell and Darla, when they weren't taking turns attending to her or the horses. It was thrilling to watch her race. She had a lot of local fan support, too. Now he was one of them.

He saw Sheriff Sol and all the deputies, including Chief Alex, in uniform, providing security, while enjoying the festivities. Barlow was envious.

Sheriff Sol said, "Don't worry. This is the last time you'll be here as a civilian. Next year you'll have to earn your keep. Better enjoy it while you can." He also told Barlow to report for duty at 8 a.m. on his first day at work.

The rodeo itself, ended at 6; however, that didn't stop the festivities. People were mixing and milling around, drinking and eating, selling and buying horses and saddlery, and in no hurry to leave. Little by little, the crowd thinned out as folks packed up, and by 10 o'clock, only those who'd driven from far away and were camping out were still there. There had been no fights, no arrests, no law enforcement issues whatsoever.

Sunday was church and a fried chicken dinner at the Bakers'. Barlow and Sarah took a long horseback ride, covering nearly every square inch of the Bar B. He rode a twelve-year-old bay mare named Ruthie, who was even-tempered and patient with tenderfeet.

By the end of the day, Barlow felt reasonably proficient, and began imagining himself as a real vaquero. 'Pride goeth before a fall,' and fall he nearly did, after four hours in the saddle when he disembarked. His legs ached, and he stumbled around like a bowlegged infant learning to walk.

It's always nice when one is a guest and able to provide amusement to his hosts, and Barlow did. It was all good-natured, and he handled the ribbing well. He also vowed to spend as much time as God would allow, learning to ride the way a Texan was born to ride. Sarah enthusiastically promised to make that happen.

CHAPTER 17
DAY ONE

Finally, it was Friday, August 1st. Barlow didn't need an alarm clock to wake up with the early bird. He was ready to go at 6:15. The gun belt was a little stiff, but he knew it would conform with wear. He could see no reason to burn daylight, so he arrived for work way early.

While locking Jade, he debated whether to put the nightstick in its belt holder. He'd never seen a deputy carrying one, but he also didn't know protocol. Finally, he decided to leave it in the truck.

The courthouse entrance to the Quayle County Sheriff's Office was unlocked, like always. Deputy Willis was seated at the front desk, all alone. He waved Barlow in, and pointed to a percolator on a credenza behind him.

"Welcome, Rookie. Grab a cup of joe and have a seat. Currently, we have the establishment all to ourselves. By the way, you're about a light-year early."

"I know. Guess I couldn't wait to get started. I left my billy club in the truck. Should I go get it?"

"I 'spect that will be all right for today."

"Okay."

"Since you're so early, let me save the sheriff some time by explaining our operation here. He won't be in for awhile. Maybe that way you can get done early, so you can go home early, and get some sleep, so you can be back tonight at 11:45 to begin your shift."

"Yes, Sir."

"Barlow, my given name is Archibald. Most people call me

Archie. I prefer you call me Archie, or Arch, unless we're dealing with a member of the public who doesn't know me, and nearly everyone roundabout here does, but if it's a stranger, you refer to me as a Deputy Willis and I will refer to you as Deputy Adams. Do that with all the deputies. Understand?"

"I do."

"Good. Call Sheriff Sol, Sheriff Sol, unless it's in public. Then call him Sheriff Pratt. Call our investigator, Alexander Snodgrass, who is also our chief deputy, Chief. He likes Chief, or Chief Alex. Understood?"

"Yes."

"Call our clerk, Loretta Youngblood, Miss Loretta."

"Okay."

"In seniority or rank, we have the sheriff, the chief, then me. Next we have Deputy Ernest Atwater, also known as Ernie, Deputy Noble Bustamante, otherwise known as Chunk, followed by Deputy Kirk Shoemaker, who's just Kirk, and, in a couple of hours, in theory, followed by you. Do you have a nickname?"

"No."

"Middle name?"

"Knotts."

"Knotts?"

"It's my mother's maiden name."

"Okay. Might want to keep that to yourself. Guys are always breaking balls around here, and if that gets out, someone's bound to call you Knothead. Anyone ever call you that?"

"Well, I've been called a knothead and a knucklehead, but not because of my middle name."

"How about Barlow from Arlo?"

"Nope."

"Fair enough, so the guys will call you Barlow or Rookie or Rook, if they're ragging you a little bit. Don't take it the wrong way. Kirk was the rook for the past four years. He's the one most likely to bestow that title onto you. Understand?"

"I do. I just spent two years in the Army and being called a rookie or a rook is mild compared with some of the things we called each other. By the way, Sheriff Sol said there were nine deputies. What about the rest?"

"I was getting to that. Look around. See the radio on the desk on the far corner over there?"

"I do."

"That's our commo system. The office is Quayle Base. All cars are Quayle, followed by a number. The sheriff is Quayle 1. All the sheriffs in Texas are the name of their county, followed by 1. Pecos 1. Brewster 1. El Paso 1. Got it?"

"Yes."

"So the Chief is Quayle 2, I'm Quayle 3, Atwater is 4, Bustamante is 5, Shoemaker is 6, and you'll be 7. That's our full-time staff. Follow?"

"Yes."

"Okay, we have three part-time deputies. Dewey Carruthers is Quayle 8, Randall Meacham is 9, and Clarence Oldman is 10. You'll work with all those guys.

"All the deputies, full or part-time, are POST certified, since they were already on board before the law changed, and were grandfathered in. They're all experienced. You're the rook, so even though you're Quayle 7 and in theory, outrank the part-timers, they, in fact, all outrank you until you get certified. Do what they tell you and learn from them."

"Yes, Sir."

"Also, all the radios have channels F1 and F2. 'F' stands for frequency. Stay on F1. F2 is a statewide band which allows us to talk to other jurisdictions. The base station pulls more watts than the car radios, so if a unit from one of the adjacent counties or the state patrol is in hot pursuit, they'll radio their base and have it call our base, who in turn, will call our mobile unit and tell it to switch to F2. Base will stay on F2 and relay, until such time as our unit can talk to the other unit. Our base will remain on F2 monitoring until such time as the visiting unit leaves Quayle County. Got it?"

"Yes, Sir."

"One last thing regarding radios. This county is so big, we don't have enough repeaters to be heard by Base in the farthest reaches. The guys will show you the dead spots. Memorize them because your life may depend on it someday."

"That's good to know. Thank you."

"Okay, Sheriff Sol's personal office is this room here. He usually leaves his door open, but we stay out of it when he's not here, unless he tells us otherwise or it's an emergency. You'll have to define emergency for yourself and pay the price if you screw up either way.

"We have a gun rack over there. We have two Remington Model 870, 12-gauge, pump shotguns, one Winchester lever-action 30-30, and one Remington, Model 700 bolt-action, in 30-06, with a Redfield 3x9 variable scope. That's our sniper rifle, which we've never used except at the range. Atwater practices with it quite a bit on his own time, and he's our designated sniper. Next time he takes it out to practice, you can tag along and try it out if you want."

"Yes, Sir. I'd really like to do that."

"We have a key to the gun rack on the key ring for each vehicle, and speaking of which, we have five.

"The sheriff and chief have unmarked units, but everyone in the county knows them on sight. You've ridden in the sheriff's new Fury. It's brown. The chief has a blue, 1967, Jeep Wagoneer in four-wheel drive. They take their units home, and are available to respond 24 hours a day.

"Then we have three marked units. I'm sure you've seen them parked right outside. They're all painted white with the sheriff's office decal on the front doors. They have the big red, 'bubblegum machine' flashing light on the roof, a Federal siren under the hood, and a spotlight mounted into the left front doorpost. They also have a wire mesh cage behind the front seat. Also, the door handles and the lock posts have all been removed from the back seat for our safety.

"The newest is a '68 Ford. Then we have a '66 Chevy. The oldest unit is a '65 Dodge. We try to alternate. If the county has money to purchase a new car, we try to rack up mileage on the oldest one. If it doesn't, we use the other two a little more often to keep the oldest one running for as long as possible.

"The keys are kept on the key hooks over here. There's two sets of keys for each unit. Each set of keys has a brass disk with a number on it. That's the county property number. We don't pick the number. The county assigns them in numerical order each time they purchase a new vehicle. The marked units are 78, 81, and 87, with 87 being the Ford since it's the latest acquisition of the three.

"We have a vehicle sign-out book on the table below the keys. Each time, before you grab a set of keys, you sign the unit out by date, unit number, time out, time in, ending mileage, and operator's name.

"In the remarks section, you write in things like, needs an oil change, left rear tire was replaced, windshield is cracked, things like that so we can make sure the units are all properly serviced and repaired. The county takes this seriously, so the sheriff takes this seriously, so you better take it seriously. Got it?"

"Yes, Sir."

"We get all our fuel and servicing at Buck Boyd's Phillips 66. When you buy gas, or get a car serviced, and so forth, he'll do it and no money changes hands between him and you. He will give you a receipt with the date, county property number, and mileage, which you will sign and give to Miss Loretta. If something major needs to be done, check with her or the chief or the sheriff first. Got it?"

"I do."

"Good. Also, you never return a unit unless it has at least

three-fourths of a tank of fuel. Also, take time to fully check out a unit before you drive away, absent an emergency. We already covered the definition of an emergency. Check the tire pressure, fluid levels, lights, wipers, brakes, etc. Especially check the brakes on the Dodge. It seems to chew up brakes like cotton candy.

Don't forget to check the spotlight. Those things are always stripping a gear and won't rotate properly. If it's busted, Buck Boyd can replace it for you. Annotate all that type of thing in the log book. Remember, we all know you're a mechanic, so we expect rigorous vehicle checks by you."

"Yes, Sir."

"Also, this is desolate country. You don't want to get stranded, so in the trunk, we keep a footlocker with emergency items, blankets, flares, jumper cables, tool kit, rope, 35-millimeter camera with film and flash attachment, shotgun shells, fire extinguisher, first aid kit, etc. There's also a shovel, a two-gallon jug of potable water, and a 5-gallon jerry can full of gas secured with a metal strap. Replace the water often. Make sure everything's in there for you or the next guy."

"You bet."

"Good. Come with me back here. Even though we usually refer to the sheriff's office as the jail, the jail itself, is behind this locked door. The key is kept in this desk drawer, here. The sheriff and Miss Loretta and I have our own, but don't lose this one or forget to put it back where it belongs when you lock up."

"Yes, Sir."

"Okay. This key unlocks this regular wooden office door, which leads to this little foyer, where we get to the big iron door. The same key also unlocks this small cabinet on the wall here, which contains these three big brass keys. This one unlocks the big iron bars door. This one marked 1 unlocks the first cell, on the left, and the key marked 2 unlocks the second cell on the right. These brass keys are as old as the building itself. If there's a back-up set, I don't know about it. A jail break with deputies locked inside would be a serious catastrophe, especially if the prisoners took the keys with them. Savvy?"

"Yes."

"Good, because anything to do regarding the jail itself is serious business.

"You can see each cell has a pair of stacking metal bunks with a commode and sink. That means our maximum capacity is four prisoners, unless it's just for a few hours. Then, if you have a female prisoner it gets even more complicated. Thank goodness we haven't had a female in at least ten years.

"Straight back past the cells we have the jailer's room, unlocked by the same office door key. This window in front of the iron bars can be opened for ventilation. That's the only source of ventilation in the jail. That's why it's so darn hot in here most of the time. No a/c for the prisoners.

"We got a desk, telephone, pair of chairs, oscillating pole fan, coat rack, trash can, a sink and a commode for us, an open shower for the inmates, under supervision, when it's absolutely necessary, a large, locked closet where we store black-and-white, striped, inmate uniforms, shower thongs, towels, blankets, sheets, pillows, first aid kit, soap, cleaning supplies, paper towels, and toilet paper. In the corner here, we have a smaller locked closet, where we store a bucket, mop, broom, etc.

"We don't put the inmates in stripes unless they'll be spending more than one night.

"If we have an inmate, we must have a deputy on site, around the clock, and he has to make hourly checks, at a minimum, which he documents in this logbook here. We don't want any jailbreaks, nor do we want any suicides.

"We feed inmates from carry out food prepared by Betty's Diner, on paper plates, with plastic utensils.

"We usually don't have many prisoners because it takes a lot of manpower and money to make sure nothing bad happens to them. Usually, Judge Sweeney fines people convicted of misdemeanors, or gives them a suspended sentence. If someone's arrested on a felony, he generally convenes a trial within a week.

"If a person is convicted of a felony, he pronounces sentence as soon as the verdict is rendered. If the sentence involves incarceration, he signs a commitment order at the same time. If the Department of Corrections, otherwise known as DOC, can't pick up the convict within a day or two, we transport the prisoner ourselves, just to get him out of here. That's only happened once that I can recall in the last dozen years, because the judge's brother is a state senator and he can move mountains in this state.

"The main thing to understand is we make arrests when they need to be made. At the same time, we try like hell to avoid transitioning from lawman to jailer, especially with this dungeon, but it really wouldn't matter if we had a brand-new jail. Housing prisoners is an expensive proposition without an upside unless you can turn a profit by putting them to work."

"Got it."

"Okay. Lock up and we'll go back in front.

"See this map on the wall here? It's a plat map of Quayle County, which is exactly 2,198 square miles. This is the only map you'll ever see that has all the roads, goat paths, buildings, and landmarks on it. You can't buy a copy and take it with you, so you either memorize this one, or you draw your own map from this one, in sections, so you can put it in a binder.

"Much of the county appears vacant, but believe me, every square inch of it is owned by somebody, of which more than 90% is owned by private individuals. The federal, state, and county governments own less than 10%. Surprising, ain't it?

"The sheriff's office is responsible for protecting all of it. We don't want the Mafia burying bodies out there, or children getting lost, or idiot motorists running out of gas or breaking down and dying out there. Neither do we want coyotes smuggling illegal aliens or outlaw motorcycle gangs setting up shop on us. If a citizen calls and needs assistance, and he lives in East Roosterfart sixty miles from here, you need to know the quickest way to get to him. Savvy?"

"Savvy."

"I know this is overwhelming, but you will get a complete tour of our kingdom before the month is out. In your short time with us, you've met more than a few citizens. You need to put names with faces and faces with vehicles and ranches or businesses plus houses they own. This is going to be much harder for you than a local, but within a few months to a year, I guarantee you will know all of this. To be any good at this job, you have to."

CHAPTER 18

THE SHERIFF'S WELCOME

It was almost 8 o'clock. Sheriff Sol, Chief Alex, and Deputy Noble Bustamante, also known as Chunk, all walked in together.

"Sheriff Sol exclaimed, "Well, look what the cat dragged in! How are you, young man?"

"Fine, Sheriff."

"Good. Archie, you been showing Barlow the ropes?"

"You bet, Sheriff. He showed up early, so I been giving him the ten-cent tour. He knows radio procedure, vehicle protocol, a little bit about these long guns here, and he's familiarized regarding the jail."

"Very good."

"Barlow, you get a chance to meet Chunk yet?"

"No, Sir."

Chunk was maybe 35 years old, 5'8" tall, about 220 pounds, and built like a whiskey barrel. He had no discernible fat. He was just thick with large bones. He was dark-complected with short black hair and brown eyes. It was obvious that he was of Mexican descent. He carried a six-inch, nickel-plated, .45 Long Colt, Smith and Wesson, Model 25 revolver in a rig with 36 loops.

"Glad to meet you, Sir."

"Ho! Ho! Sir. I like this kid already, Sheriff. Call me Chunk, Kid."

Sheriff Sol told Barlow to grab another cup of java and have a seat in his office. In the interim, Chief showed up for work and took his seat at his desk in the rear of the squad room. Chunk and Archie were making the shift change.

Barlow topped off, and took the same seat in front of the sheriff's desk that he sat in on that first night. The sheriff hung his hat on the coat rack and settled behind his desk. He lit up a smoke.

"You smoke, Kid?"

"When I do, it's cigars if I'm flush, or my pipe when I'm not and I have time to fiddle around keeping it lit. Mostly though, I just dip Copenhagen."

"Yeah, I used to dip when I was on subs. No smoking under water. I went back to Lucky Strikes when I got out.

"Well, well. We are glad to have you on board. I have a few things for you here, badge and identification card, once the judge swears you in. In the meantime, sign the card so everything will be according to Hoyle for the judge.

"Also, I have this diary for you. Our method of keeping track of things here, is by our diaries. Everyone has one. We get a new one each year.

"What you do each day is record the weather, shift worked, times clocked in and out, and what you did. If it's a day off, just write in 'day off' or 'holiday' or 'annual leave.' You don't have to record anything else on those days, unless for some reason, you're called into work or you wind up taking action, like maybe helping a stranded motorist, even if you're in your own vehicle.

"On duty days, you might not have anything more than 'Temperature in the 90's. Clear sky. Worked in the jail 8-4 shift. Arrived 7:45. No prisoners. No calls. Cleaned long guns. Took Unit 78 to Boyd's for new tires. Departed 4:10.'

"If you make a run, document the time you were notified, where you departed from, who called, what the problem was, where you went, what you did, what time it was when you finished up. It doesn't have to be "War and Peace".

The narrative might say, 'At 8:45 a.m., Horace McGillicuddy, Circle M Ranch, called the jail and said his favorite donkey was stolen last night between 10 p.m. and midnight. I responded and obtained a description. Searched unsuccessfully from 9:30 until 10:30 before discontinuing. Complete report is on file, Item # 69-699.' That kind of thing. Understand?"

"Yes, Sir."

"Always record license plate, wanted, or criminal history checks, informants contacted, assistance to other agencies, really anything you think might be significant, like a BOLO, (that means 'be on the lookout') from another agency, or something which might come up at a later time, like 'Joe Lunchbox saw a strange red Ford pickup truck in the middle of the Slash Q ranch on Sunday morning during church services.' That might be important later if the Slash Q started having sheep disappear."

"Yes, Sir."

"Okay. Periodically, Chief or I will review your diary. We do these spot-checks on everyone. We'll sign off on the last entry, and pick up where it left off when we do it the next time. This diary is designed for you to keep notes to assist in writing incident reports, or witness statements, or even in preparation for courtroom testimony.

"I understand."

"Good. For the first few months, we'll review your diary more frequently than usual to make sure you're catching on to what's important and what isn't. If you have a question, ask any of the other deputies. They'll help you out."

"Yes, Sir."

"Today you're working an 8 to 4 shift. Put that down after you annotate the weather, but also put the actual times worked. Like today. What time did you arrive?"

"6:20."

"Okay. Put that down. I'm going to try to get you out of here early because you're pulling a short change tonight. Don't worry if you don't get exactly 8 hours. We're not clock watchers. You will end up donating plenty of unpaid overtime in this job anyway. Got it?"

"I do."

"Did Archie show you the vault?"

"No, Sir."

"Okay. Follow me."

The sheriff led him into another room where a vault, not dissimilar to a bank vault, only smaller, was located. He dialed the code and opened up. They walked in.

Each side had shelves, but the left side was bare except for the six CB radios recovered from Rupert Doyle and Duncan Lebowski's stolen wallet and revolver. This was the evidence side. They also had a box full of labels and evidence forms, and an evidence log, which the sheriff explained.

The right side had several cardboard boxes. This side was for departmental equipment. He saw extra handcuffs, belly chains, ammunition, firearms cleaning equipment, targets, a camera, two tape recorders, blank tapes, bolt cutters, first aid kits, fire extinguishers, and the like.

The very back had a large wooden cabinet. He opened the door. It was a gun cabinet with a rack containing four Thompson, .45 ACP submachine guns, and dozens of twenty-round magazines. He picked one up, jacked the charging handle to make sure it was unloaded, and handed it to Barlow.

"Ever fired one of these?"

"Heck, I've never even seen one."

"Didn't think so. Old Sheriff Oscar Delaney bought these back in 1931, when they only had three deputies. Bonnie and Clyde, among some others, had everyone worried. I still issue these on occasion if the situation warrants. The first chance we get, I'll have someone take you to the range and get you qualified."

Before he locked up, he picked up an old, canvas and leather-bound docket book, and signed them both in and out. It was only one-fourth used. The first entry on page 1 was dated October 7, 1910.

They went back to his office.

He said, "I see Jake got you all rigged up. What model revolver is that?"

"It's a Smith Model 58 in .41 Magnum."

"Good choice. Shot it yet?"

"Yes, Sir, but just one box. I'm passable up to 25 yards. I need more practice, though."

"Define passable."

"I can consistently hit a tin can five out of six times."

"I'd call that more than passable. If you can do that consistently under some pressure, you'll be our best shot. That's why Chief Alex carries that thirteen-shot Browning Hi Power. He figures he'll finally get lucky before he needs to reload. I'll get Chunk or Atwater to take you to the range very soon to get you qualified.

"Did you get signed up for the POST course?"

"Yes, Sir. I decided to sign up for the whole enchilada and go for the associate's. School starts Tuesday after Labor Day, so I still have a month."

"Good deal. Just don't get behind in those POST classes. You only have two years from today. It can sneak up on you if you get busy."

"No, Sir. I won't."

"Well, go see if Chief or Chunk have anything for you. I'll call upstairs to the judge's office and see if he's ready for us."

"Yes, Sir. Thank you."

CHAPTER 19
NOW IT'S OFFICIAL

The judge was free, so at 9:30, Sheriff Pratt, Chief Snodgrass, and Barlow walked up the stairs to his courtroom. The judge was already in his robes, seated behind the bench. Mrs. Eloise Goodman, his clerk and sometimes court reporter, was seated at her desk. Otherwise, the courtroom was empty.

They approached the bench. The judge appeared to be preoccupied, intensely studying the grain of his desk, or the shine, or perhaps the dust motes.

Mrs. Goodman softly whispered, "Judge Sweeney, the sheriff is here to see you."

He looked up and said, "Good morning, Gentlemen. What business do you have before the court today, Sheriff Pratt?"

"Your Honor, I've brought Barlow K. Adams before the court today to be sworn in as a Quayle County deputy sheriff."

"Yes, of course. Good morning, Mr. Adams."

"Good morning, Your Honor."

"Sir, are you the young man who dispatched that villain, Rupert Doyle?"

"I am, your Honor."

"Well done, young man! I've read the report. I must say I was impressed with your civic-mindedness, your situational awareness, and your demeanor under fire.

"I also understand that you are a veteran of the War in Vietnam."

"Thank you, Sir. I am. I was just trying to be of assistance when I saw Mr. Doyle strike Mrs. Taft."

"Your derring-do speaks well of your character, Sir.

"Do you understand the solemn responsibilities conferred upon a deputy, and the august esteem this court holds for lawmen, Mr. Adams? My very own brother was a Texas Ranger for a dozen years. I hold him in great reverence."

"Yes, Your Honor."

"Very well. Mrs. Goodman, please place the Holy Bible under Mr. Adams' left hand. Mr. Adams, please raise your right hand."

They both complied. Chief Snodgrass took an angle so he could photograph the ceremony.

"Repeat after me."

Barlow repeated: "I, Barlow K. Adams, do solemnly swear, to protect and to serve, the United States of America, the State of Texas, and the County of Quayle, to defend them against all enemies, foreign and domestic, to impartially, honestly, and bravely enforce the laws of this state with all fidelity, to the best of my ability, until such time as I am relieved of this responsibility, so help me God."

Judge Sweeney said, "By the power vested in me by the County of Quayle, in the State of Texas, I hereby appoint Mr. Barlow K. Adams to the office of Quayle County Deputy Sheriff, on August 1st, in the Year of Our Lord, 1969."

"Sheriff Pratt, please pin the badge of office on Deputy Sheriff Adams."

He did. The chief took photographs. Congratulations were conferred. Hands were shaken all around. They departed the courtroom in single file. Barlow was all smiles and full of nervous energy.

CHAPTER 20
FIRST GRADED EXERCISE

When they returned to the jail, the sheriff corralled Deputy Bustamante, and said, "Chunk, show Deputy Adams, here, how to check out a unit. I'm pretty sure he knows where things are in Mosby. Have him drive to the northwest corridor. Point out the landmarks, ranch boundaries, sheep trails, abandoned buildings, attractive nuisances, things to watch out for. You know the drill. Try to get back by 2 o'clock, if you can. I want him to get off a little early today since he's making a short change.

"One more thing. Pick up a lunch to go for both of you at Betty's Diner. It's on the county today, in honor of the investiture of Deputy Adams."

"You bet. Thanks, Sheriff."

Barlow was excited, but cautious. He knew this was a training exercise, but it was also a pop quiz from Archie's early morning instruction. Chunk told him to grab the keys to 78. Barlow remembered that this was the oldest car in the fleet. He signed the log book.

Chunk signed out a shotgun. Barlow noticed that it had a sling with fifteen cartridge loops. The top ten held 00 buckshot. The bottom five held one-ounce, rifled slugs.

Chunk filled the magazine with four buckshot. Then he chambered a round, put the safety on, and added one more round. Now the gun was filled to capacity.

When they went to the lot, Barlow unlocked a 1965, Dodge Polara, four-door sedan. He rolled down the front windows, pushed the vent windows open all the way, and cracked the back windows about an inch. It was already 92 degrees and this unit did not have air conditioning. Barlow wondered if the other marked units did.

Barlow popped the hood. The 383 cubic inch, 270 horsepower engine was clean and well maintained. He checked the belts, and all the fluid levels, to include the windshield washer reservoir. All was in order.

He checked the glovebox and found a tire gauge. He checked all four tires on the ground plus the spare. All were within the recommended 30-35 PSI.

While he was in the trunk, he checked the emergency equipment in the footlocker. Everything Arch said was there. He checked the water thermos. It looked fine. He checked the fuel in the jerry can. It was full. Everything was in order.

Before closing the trunk, he turned on the ignition. The unit had 116,235 miles. The gas gauge reflected that it was three-fourth's full. He went back to the trunk and emptied the jerry can into the gas tank.

Chunk smiled and said, "I heard you were a mechanic. Worried about how long that can of gas has been there?"

"Well, I had no idea, plus I thought this might be a graded exercise, so I decided to err on the side of caution. Besides, I want to go through the drill of buying gas."

"Well, now you get to do it twice - going out of town and coming back in. I'm glad you checked the can. It's often overlooked. I happen to know that this one was recently filled, because this is my favorite unit, and I did it last week."

"Okay. Not trying to be a smart ass. I just want to do things right."

"You are. Let's mount up."

They got in. Chunk secured the shotgun in a vertical rack between the driver and passenger.

Chunk pointed out the on-off/volume dial for the radio, as well as the F1-F2 toggle switch. He told Barlow to make sure the radio was turned off at end-of-shift because otherwise, it would drain the battery.

He had Barlow flip the emergency light switch and step outside to insure the light, difficult to see close up in brilliant daylight, was oscillating and flashing properly. It was. He turned it off.

He had already seen the toggle switch for the siren. He knew it needed to be checked, so he flipped it on. Nothing happened. Before Chunk could open his mouth, for some unknown reason, Barlow pushed the horn button in the middle of the steering wheel. Instead of a honk, the siren began to wail, almost deafening both of them. He let up immediately, sheepish look on his face, ears ringing profoundly.

Chunk said, "Sorry about that. No matter how hot it is, before you use the siren, it's a good idea to roll up the windows. Also, don't forget to switch it back to horn. Guys do a lot of times and it's embarrassing."

Barlow asked, "Do any of the marked units have air conditioning?"

"No. The county says horses aren't air conditioned and to consider the vehicles our horses. Both the sheriff and the chief paid the extra cost for air conditioning in their units, but the difference is, they're allowed to use them just like they were their privately-owned vehicles."

"What if the car already came with air conditioning as standard equipment?"

"Well, you haven't met the Quayle County Board of Supervisors yet. They're all good guys, but some of them are tighter than two coats of paint. They'd probably say the county couldn't afford to pay for the extra gas it costs to run an air conditioner, and tell the sheriff to take it out."

"Well, I've never had air conditioning in a car before. My truck doesn't have it and none of the Army vehicles I was in had it either. I was just wondering."

"My car doesn't have a/c either, but my old lady says the next time we buy one, it better have it. I told her that would be a few years down the road.

"We got a '61 Plymouth Fury, four-door sedan, red with a white roof, tricked out just the way I want it, with rolled and tucked red leather interior, and mag wheels, and it's paid for. It's got a 383 cubic inch V-8 with 330 horsepower.

"Why would I want to buy some weenie Valiant station wagon with a Slant-6, 115 horsepower engine? Just because it has a/c?

"Anyway, before you pull out, call Quayle Base and let them know we're leaving Mosby, headed for the northwest part of the county. But before you do that, there's something else you need to know.

"I'm Quayle 5 and you're Quayle 7. When two deputies ride together, the unit becomes the two numbers, with the lower number first. In other words, you and I are unit 57. Savvy?"

"I do.

"Quayle Base, this is Quayle 57, departing Mosby for the northwest corridor."

Miss Loretta responded, "Quayle 57, this is Quayle Base. 10-4. We hear you loud and clear. How me?"

Barlow, responding in Army vernacular, replied, "Quayle Base, we copy Lima Charlie," (phonetic for L and C, and understood as loud and clear.)

Chunk smiled and said, "Well, listen to you! A rookie who's an old hand on his first day."

Barlow blushed, but he knew it was just good-natured ribbing.

When they arrived at Betty's, Chunk told Barlow to sit tight, while he got their grub. He said he was going to get two bologna and mustard sandwiches, some chips, and a slice of apple pie. He asked what Barlow wanted. Barlow said he'd take an order of ham biscuits and the apple pie, plus a Pepsi.

Chuck said, "Roger that. DX the Pepsi. I always bring a cooler with a six-pack of RC Cola. It's in the trunk. I'll share that with you. You might want to get a cooler for yourself. They sell them at Goode's Dry Goods for $1.99."

They stopped by Boyd's and topped off the car and the jerry can. The procedure for charging the county was easier than he thought. It was 10:45 when they actually began the trek north out of town on TX 651. Unit 78 ran like a scalded dog. The Pecos Bank sign said the temperature was 93 degrees. The wind felt good on Barlow's face as he accelerated.

Chunk directed Barlow along county roads, some of which were unpaved.

The county roads were not marked on the official state map. They kicked up a plume of dust. Chunk pointed out a number of ranches, commented on what he knew of the owners, mentioning past issues, if any, as well as potential problems or concerns.

They stopped at the intersection of CO 10 and CO 19. An abandoned adobe gas station/cafe with a large metal awning, where the two gas pumps had been, provided shade for their lunch.

While they ate, Chunk told Barlow a little bit about himself.

He said his dad and two brothers own and operate Quayle Trucking Firm. Chunk has a CDL and drives part-time for them. Mostly they haul livestock, but they also have one reefer for loads requiring refrigeration, which pays better.

He graduated from Quayle County High School in 1957. He spent six years in the national guard artillery unit in Alpine. His wife is named Rosa, and they have two daughters, ages ten and eight, and a son, age seven.

He's been a deputy six years, and it's the best job he's ever had. He can't imagine doing anything else. Sheriff Sol is the absolute best.

He and his old lady got a small place, twenty acres, on CO Road 12, two miles north of town off Highway 651, where they raise chickens, a seventeen-year-old mule named Hector, and a pair of chihuahuas named Pancho and Sancho. They call it the Crooked H. Named it after his mule, Hector, who has a crooked face. Strange birth defect but it doesn't affect his smarts or ability to work. He's really good at pulling a plow.

His old lady likes to garden and cook. She's a really good cook. You can tell just how good by looking at him. Ha!

He invited Barlow to come visit on his day off.

Barlow thanked him. He said he would take him up on that one day soon and he would bring his appetite. Also, some iced cerveza.

Chunk replied that was the general idea and that they wouldn't have it any other way.

CHAPTER 21

THE ROCKING A

They were wrapping up lunch. Quayle 57 received a transmission from Quayle Base. Miss Loretta said the office got a call from Alberto Gomez up at the Rocking A, about an abandoned vehicle. Quayle 57 was told to respond.

Chunk responded "Wilco," meaning 'will comply.' Before they left, Chunk told Barlow to enter this into his diary and get caught up since reporting for duty.

"Put down getting sworn in, being assigned with me to patrol the northwest sector, and getting this call at 12:22, departing from this location."

That done, Chunk directed Barlow to proceed east. He said the Rocking A was about forty miles away. Since this was not broadcast as an emergency, they would go Code 1, meaning 'proceed with the flow of traffic,' even if there wasn't any. In other words, obey the fifty miles-per-hour speed limit.

Code 2 was lights and siren optional, usually just lights, for something like an accident or runaway horse. Code 3 was balls-to-the-wall with lights and siren for bonafide emergencies.

Barlow responded that being a Code 1 call didn't matter to him because he was happy just to respond on his first run.

En route, Chunk said that Alberto Gomez was a good guy, in his fifties, who mostly earned a living in highway construction. He had a passel of kids, mostly grown, who had moved all around, and a battalion of grandkids. Alberto used to be big into cockfights, mostly in Mexico, but not so much anymore. Also, he'd never given anybody any trouble.

When they arrived, Alberto was waiting for them at his gate

by the road, in his twenty-year-old, battered and faded, red GMC pickup truck. He was alone.

Chunk made the introductions. Barlow and Alberto shook. Chunk and Alberto updated one another on old friends and family members. It had been several months since they had seen one another. Ten minutes later, pleasantries completed, they were both up to speed and ready for business.

Alberto got back in his truck, and led them up his driveway and then down a dirt road, which evolved into a goat path along, and into, a dry gulch.

A faded yellow, 1959 DeSoto Adventurer was parked in the gulch, out of sight from anyone who wasn't almost on top of it. It looked quite serviceable despite it's age.

Alberto said he didn't know how long it had been there, but perhaps a week. He saw it when he was searching for one of his ornery cows that's bad to wander off. He thought maybe the coyotes had killed her. He was probably going to have to go ahead and take her to the auction. She wasn't ready yet and wouldn't bring much, but whatever he got would be more than if the coyotes got to her first.

Chunk, leading the way, told Barlow to be careful where he stepped.

Barlow asked, "Rattlesnakes?"

Chunk laughed and said, "Could be. I was thinking more on the lines of not disturbing evidence. Look for footprints or tire tracks or anything that doesn't belong and could have been left by whoever parked the car here."

Barlow was more than a little embarrassed. What a moron! What was he thinking?

He looked carefully, proceeded with due caution, but didn't see anything that resembled a clue, or a snake. He did see dozens of shallow and partial footprints on top of each other, which were probably made by Alberto, making it impossible to segregate any useful tracks.

The front windows of the car were rolled down. The ignition had been hot-wired. Nothing was in the car besides the spare and jack in the trunk, an ashtray full of Camel cigarette butts, and the owner's manual in the glove box.

Chunk called Base with the Texas license plate number and the VIN, which he copied from a small aluminum plate attached to the inside of the driver's side door post.

A short while later, Base responded that the license plate and the VIN matched. The vehicle was registered to Euliss and Olive Trent, of 402 Main Street, Pecos, Texas. It was reported stolen a week ago.

Chief Snodgrass wanted to know if the car needed to be towed or if they could drive it back to the jail.

Chunk said, "Stand by." Then he asked Barlow to see if he could get the car running.

In the interim, Chief told Chunk to take photographs and to collect any evidence. He also told Chunk to take a written statement from Alberto and anyone else there who might have seen anything. He said he would call the Reeves County SO to see if they had any further information.

Barlow fiddled with the hot-wire, but the ignition wouldn't turn over. He checked the gas gauge, which indicated the car was below empty. He fetched the jerry can and emptied it into the gas tank. After a little prodding with the carburetor, the engine fired, and it was up and running.

Chunk told Barlow to see if he could get it turned around and out of the gulch.

He did, driving it past both of the other vehicles. He told Chunk he thought it would make it to the jail.

Alberto's statement was brief. He said he couldn't understand how the vehicle got ditched on his property. He had no suspects. No one else had been around.

Chunk and Barlow wondered if any of Alberto's two dozen sons, sons-in-law, nephews, or grandsons might have been involved, simply due to the drop site. Someone could hunt for months and never find the car in this location; however, neither one mentioned this until after they were back at the jail.

At 4:15, they departed en route the jail. Chunk drove the DeSoto, allowing Barlow to notify Base. Barlow, thinking ahead, had already recorded all the pertinent information into his diary before they left.

It was after 5 o'clock by the time Barlow gassed up and pulled into the jail parking lot. Chunk was already inside. Chief Snodgrass had been waiting for them.

He said Olive Trent is an 82-year-old woman whose husband is in a wheelchair. They don't get out much. The car was stolen on Thursday night, July 24th, from their driveway. Reeves SO had no suspects and no leads. Mrs. Trent is a smoker and the cigarette butts were probably hers.

They considered that the car might have been stolen by someone planning to commit an armed robbery. Of course, it could have been stolen by adolescents joyriding. That was more likely the case, because none of the adjacent counties had had a robbery in the past week.

He asked Chunk about Alberto's boys. Chunk said one or more of them were probably the culprits, because who else would have ever come up with the dump site? Also, maybe the thieves had planned to sell the car in Mexico where no questions are ever asked. Alberto's boys would certainly know how to pull that off.

Chief told Chunk to show Barlow how to write an incident report. Then he told Barlow to go home as soon as he was done. Sheriff Sol had wanted him out of there by 3, so he'd be rested for his midnight shift. He also told Barlow he would check his diary tomorrow to see if he was on the right track.

Barlow's first incident report passed Chunk's muster and was duly filed on the monthly incident clipboard for August. It was first in sequence for the month. That's because it was the only one.

CHAPTER 22

MRS. PEABODY IS PEEKING

Barlow didn't arrive home until 6 o'clock. Sarah had just locked up, getting ready to leave. As soon as she saw him, she stopped and waited.

"I thought you were getting off early."

"Me, too. Chunk and I caught a run up in the northeast corner. We wound up recovering a car stolen from Pecos."

"Well, well. Not only do you look the part, very impressive in your uniform, you know, but you're the real McCoy."

"Thanks. I would've called if I could."

"I know. I have to get home, plus you need to get some sleep. I made some tuna fish salad and put it in the fridge. Also, I got some fresh peaches. They're really good."

"Are you sure you can't stay, even for a little while?"

"No. I told Mom I'd be home at 6:30. She's planning supper around me, but tomorrow's Saturday, and I could stop by about 5 and we could go to the Bijou for the 7 o'clock.

"Paint Your Wagon is showing. Lee Marvin and Clint Eastwood are in it. If you want, I could make you a chicken fried steak and mashed potatoes for supper before we go."

"That would be outstanding. Come before 5, if you can. I'll probably already be up. Also tell your folks 'Gomer says hey'."

"Aren't you going to reimburse me for the tunafish salad and the peaches?"

"Oh sure. How much?"

"Just for you, Mr. Adams, I have a special. One kiss, if it is done to my satisfaction. Otherwise, it might take two."

Barlow stepped up close and hugged her tight. Then he gave

her a long, lingering kiss. He let her go, smiling. Not to be outdone, she stepped up and gave him a short French kiss in return. Then she broke off and hurried to her car, laughing as she went. They both looked up and saw the neighbor lady, Mrs. Peabody, watching from her picture window. Sarah waved and the old lady waved back.

"Better be careful, Deputy. Mrs. Peabody may call the sheriff and tell him you're smooching in uniform. I bet there's some kind of regulation against that. My parents would probably wonder about your intentions."

"My intentions are to make myself irresistible to you, so you will want to spend more time with me."

"You already did that. I'm beginning to think you're trying to seduce me."

"Perish the thought, but if you don't escape soon, before Mrs. Peabody looks out again, I may just sweep you up into my arms and carry you into the inner sanctum and dot, dot, dot."

"What's dot, dot, dot?"

"I understand that's how romance novels tease the chicks who read them. Then they're not X-rated and the drug stores can sell them in the open."

"How would you know? Do you read chick books in your spare time?"

"No, but I have an older sister, or did you forget? By the way, Mrs. Peabody is peeking again. She's probably heard every word. You better get home or your dad will be getting a call from the sheriff, no doubt."

"Good day, Deputy Adams."

"Good day, Miss Baker."

Barlow had a real hard time falling asleep. The alarm woke him at 10:30. Getting out of bed was a chore. He put on a pot of coffee before stepping into a cold shower. He ate two tunafish salad sandwiches and made two for later on. The peaches were really sweet. He packed one of them, too.

CHAPTER 23

LEARNING THE FINE POINTS OF ADMINISTRATION

Barlow walked in the jail at 11:45 Friday night. It was a six-hour turnaround, otherwise known as a short change. On one hand, he was eager to work the Saturday midnight shift. On the other hand, he wondered what he would do for eight hours. They had no prisoners and town was as quiet as a mausoleum.

He was surprised that Archie was not there. A deputy he hadn't met was holding down the fort, leaning against the bannister which separated the foyer from the office, arms folded across his chest.

This deputy was older, 55 probably, whipsaw thin, about 5'6" tall, 135 pounds, with silver hair, and skin like oiled leather. His most impressive features were his piercing, light blue eyes, punctuated with his distinctive Wyatt Earp mustache. He was wearing a Stetson, with a taller crown than most, creased vertically in the front. The brim was quite a bit wider, too.

Just like Arch, this guy was wearing a Colt .45 Peacemaker with a belt full of cartridges, with two obvious differences. Archie's cartridge loops didn't go underneath his holster. This deputy's did. He had enough spare ammo to save General Custer from massacre by Sitting Bull at the Little Big Horn. In addition, he was wearing a Marine Corps Ka-Bar sheath knife, with a seven-inch blade, on the left side of his belt. Wonder how many scalps he had taken with that?

The deputy was the prototype Texas lawman, except for his diminutive size. Even so, Barlow recognized that his stature was probably not a valid indicator of his lethality. Clyde Barrow was only 5'4" and his lethality was legendary. What about Attila the

Hun? He was a dwarf!

That decided it for Barlow. He was going to grow a mustache like Archie's or better yet, like this guy's, beginning right now. Sarah better like mustaches!

"Well, my word. Deputies sure are getting younger these days. You must be that gunfighter feller I heard tell about."

Barlow's face turned bright crimson. He replied, "No, Sir. No gunfighter. Just a guy passing through who saw a woman in trouble. Lots of folks would have done the same. Name is Barlow Adams. I'm the FNG. Very nice to make your acquaintance." He extended his hand.

The deputy had a good grip and a solid shake. He never once broke eye contact. He said, "There's lots who think they would, but they're ain't many what do. Glad to shake your hand. Gladder still that the sheriff brought you on board. What's an FNG?"

Barlow blushed again. "It's an Army acronym. Means fucking new guy."

The deputy erupted with laughter, bent over double at the waist. He said, "That's a new one on me. I was in the Marines during WWII, fought in Guadalcanal and Iwo Jima, but I'm behind the times. The name is Clarence Oldman. Most guys call me Slick, on account of my fancy haircut," at which point he whipped off his Stetson and took a sweeping bow, showing off a military bootcamp buzz cut.

Barlow smiled and said, "Slick, what you lack in tonsorial styling, you more than make up for it with that fabulous mustache. You and Archie have both inspired me, and I can only hope that the mustache I just decided to grow, will be as splendid as yours."

Archie walked in and said, "Slick, are you trying to run off our rookie before we get any work out of him?"

Slick smiled and said, "I think he's here to stay, Arch. Excuse me girls, but I have important business to attend to."

Archie asked, "Planning to pleasure Emma Dean two nights in a row? Ain't that tempting Fate, with that wore out ticker of yours?"

Slick replied as he was walking through the door. "My ticker may have high mileage, but it ain't wore out. You're just jealous because your off-duty gun is broke, and there ain't no remedy in the world what would raise up your flagpole again, Old Man. It's up to me to pleasure all the lonely old women around here, because you're over the hill. With that, I bid you both adieu."

"Daggone you, Slick! Go on and get your bony carcass outa here!"

No sooner than Slick made his exit, Archie resumed Barlow's schooling, as if there had been no break since he reported to duty at 0620 this morning. He started with the precise amount of coffee needed to brew a pot.

It morphed into the records system. All official police actions were logged into a huge leather-bound book, just like the one in the vault. This particular book was entitled 'Sheriff's Office - Book 2.'

He learned that not all police actions were official. There were many unofficial actions a deputy might make.

For example, he might scoop up a kid who was cutting school and take him to his parents or the principal.

Another example was he might be driving by the tavern and see an otherwise solid citizen, who had never been in trouble, stagger out of the tavern pie-eyed. He might decide to drive him home instead of arresting him for public drunkenness.

Things like that. Those actions did not require an incident report. This was called officer's discretion. He would live or die by that. Good discretion was good law enforcement. Bad discretion usually resulted in the officer getting jammed up. He would learn to distinguish between the two, but until then, he should rely on the judgment of a senior deputy.

Each official action, whether self-initiated, or the result of a request for assistance, required an incident report, which required an item number. Item numbers began with the last two digits of the year, followed by a hyphen, followed by sequential numbering.

The call Chunk and Barlow made was the most recent entry in Book 2, numbered 69-426. After the item number, were the date, victim/caller, location of event, responding officer(s), and brief description. Barlow's first call read, "69-426, Aug. 1, 1969, Alberto Gomez, Rocking A Ranch, DY Bustamante & DY Adams, Recovery of vehicle stolen from Pecos County."

Barlow flipped back to page 1. It was dated November 14, 1955.

Archie said Book 1 was in the archives at the Clerk of Court's office, along with numbered boxes of incident reports in chronological order, from 1910 through 1967. 1968's incident reports were in the filing cabinet by Chief's desk. 1969's incident reports were hanging on the back wall.

He said item number 10-1 was reported on October 7, 1910, which coincided with the day Quayle became a county. It recorded the arrest of a pickpocket who stole a bystander's wallet during the swearing in ceremony for the county officials. The wallet was recovered intact.

Archie said the thief, Amos Goddert, was fined $25 and sentenced to thirty days at hard labor. They made him shovel and dispose of all the horse droppings along America Avenue, which, at the time, was all there was to Mosby. They also made him dig outhouses. He said it was a real shit job.

Archie explained the twelve clipboards lined up on hooks across the back wall. Each clipboard had a pair of six-inch long, metal binder rings, where the incident reports were hole-punched and filed in reverse, chronological order. January through July's clipboards were full. August's clipboard had one item number: 69-426. The other months' clipboards were empty.

At the end of the year, these incident reports would be filed in the chief's cabinet for one year, before being boxed and stored in the archives.

To find a documented incident, first search Book 2, approximating the date of the incident, in chronological order until the item number was located. Use the item number to check the clipboards for an incident reported in the present year, the chief's file cabinet for the preceding year, or the archives, for anything older.

Archie stressed that a wise and prudent deputy would take pen and paper with him when pulling an item number or a file. He would make notes and return the original immediately afterwards, in its proper place. A lost file or missing document was a serious transgression and offenders were severely punished.

He said all incidents requiring investigation were assigned to the chief. In some instances, the chief delegated the investigation, usually to the deputy who caught the squeal.

Miss Loretta creates a file folder for all investigations. The investigative file folders are annotated with the item number on the outside. They're filed in chronological order in the chief's cabinet. An investigation is considered open, if they are ongoing or the case has not been adjudicated in court. The top drawer contains all open cases, regardless of the year they were opened. The second drawer contains closed cases for the current year or the previous year. Closed cases older than that are in the archives.

Arch said to talk to the chief or the sheriff before touching any open investigative file folder, unless the investigation was assigned to him by the chief.

He recommended reviewing all the item numbers hanging on the wall and any closed investigations for 1969, to get a feel of what had recently transpired. Time permitting, he suggested Barlow read 1968's reports before they got boxed and placed in archives.

Barlow reviewed files until 4 o'clock, when Archie told him

to stop. They ate their meals and took a break. Then they cleaned firearms.

First, they cleaned their own sidearms.

Next, they cleaned all four Thompson's. Archie was thorough and patient like the Army DI's had been during basic, insuring that Barlow understood the procedure and followed it exactly. They disassembled, cleaned, and reassembled. Again and again and again. Barlow became an extremely proficient disassembler and assembler of the Thompson submachine gun. The question was, would he become a proficient marksman with it?

Lastly, they cleaned the 870's and the two rifles. This was chump change. They were done by 6:30.

Barlow cleaned out the waste baskets, carried out the trash, dusted the furniture with Pledge, and swept the floors. It was like getting ready for S.A.M.I. (Saturday Morning Inspection) in the Army.

At 7:30, everything was shipshape. A little before 8:00, the chief and Chunk showed up for work. Chief forgot to inspect Barlow's diary.

8:00 o'clock. End of shift. Barlow was in the rack by 8:20, zonked by 8:25.

CHAPTER 24
ALL IS REVEALED

Barlow awoke at 4:30 to the sound of Sarah unlocking the door. He usually slept nude, so he scrambled to throw on a pair of jeans, and was somewhat successful when she stepped into the bedroom holding a sackful of groceries.

She smiled and said, "My, my! Did I just see what I think I did? Were you in your nudies, Deputy Adams?"

"Sorry. I was out cold."

"Do all your girlfriends get to see what I just saw?"

"You're the only girl friend I have, so the answer would be 'not usually.'"

"Well, I would imagine since you've been here, you've become friends with Miss Loretta, and some other females you've met, like Alice at the drugstore and Betty at the diner."

"True. I'm friends with all of them. Let's just say you are my special girlfriend. I don't go out on dates with them."

"And what makes me so special?"

"I know things about people. I know you were born special. Plus, I can't get you out of my mind. I want to be with you whenever I can. So besides being special to your family, you're extra special to me."

"What if I said the same thing about you?"

"I was hoping you would."

"Then in that case, I think I shall kiss you."

"You're burnin' daylight, Darlin'!"

He took the sack of groceries out of her arms and placed it on the bed. Then he reached over and wrapped her in his arms like she was freezing to death. He smelled the faint scent of her hair and body lotion. Instant stimuli. The pheromones were in full play. There was no way she didn't notice.

Her body melded perfectly into his own. He kissed her longingly with a passion that even surprised him. The kiss lingered. His manhood was throbbing violently. He did not want to break off.

They were locked into each other's eyes. It was like he could see deep into her soul, and vice versa. His innermost self was completely naked, no cover for safety, fully exposed.

Sarah hugged him tighter. She whispered, "Don't let me go."

"I won't."

"Promise?"

"I promise."

"Then I am your girlfriend and not just a female friend?"

"Yes."

"Then I can tell people you are my boyfriend?"

"Yes."

"I like that."

"Me, too."

They lingered. After a while, she said, "Are you hungry?"

He replied, "I was until a few minutes ago. Now I'm interested in what we're doing right now."

"Me, too, but I haven't eaten since breakfast. I need food first. Why don't you take a shower while I start cooking? If you have any of that bourbon you mentioned the other night, you can pour us a drink when you're done."

"You got it. Just because I'm feeling a little randy doesn't mean I'm not hungry."

"Don't be a tease! Go take your shower!"

He returned and poured them both a taste of Old Dr. Crow while Sarah finished cooking.

Over the meal, they discussed things only partially explored at this point in their brief, but magnetically charged relationship.

They delved into family history, political views, religious

beliefs, wins and losses, and regrets, in more depth than before on their trip to Alpine. The admiration they felt for each other continued to intensify.

Sarah said that in Mosby, everybody knew everything about everybody; that there really were no secrets; that out of politeness, folks seldom spoke out loud, the things other people thought were secrets about themselves.

He said Arlo was the same way. It wasn't mentioned, but each understood they were talking about sex, and who was discreetly doing it with whom, imagining that nobody else had a clue.

Time got away from them. Suddenly it was 6:45. They hustled to make it to the movie on time.

On the way, Sarah said that Cordell and Darla mentioned they were going too, and that they would save seats for them. Barlow figured the Baker jury was probably still out on him.

He understood. If he ever had a daughter as beautiful and charming as Sarah, he'd probably want to ride in the back seat whenever she went out on a date. It was an absolute impossibility for a red-blooded male not to have some of the thoughts about her that he was having. You'd have to be queer not to.

They had a great time. Cordell and Darla were fabulous company. They finished the evening at the soda fountain in the drugstore with ice cream sundaes.

Sarah returned home with him for ten minutes of making out in the cab of his truck, spooning, as Grandma Bea would have said.

Then she got in her car and left. As she drove off, she said, "I better see you in church bright and early, Mr. Adams. God knows you're having way too many impure thoughts."

Chapter 25

Ancient History, Lusty Talk,

and Disappointment

At 11:50 p.m., Sunday, August 3rd. Barlow reported for work on the midnight shift again with Archie.

He was a whipped dog. He didn't get enough sleep on Saturday after work, plus he stayed up too late because of his date. Then he was up too early for church. Afterwards, they packed a picnic lunch and rode horses all afternoon until 6 o'clock. Riding was still a new activity for him and his muscles ached all over. He fell into bed completely wiped out at 7. He was running on fumes.

Thankfully, Archie had mercy on him. They didn't do much besides clean house, smoke, drink coffee, and chew the fat. Who knows? Maybe Archie had a full weekend, too. Whatever the reason, Barlow was thankful for the respite.

The night was dragging. Barlow was having a hard time staying awake. He said, Arch, there's something I've been wondering about."

"What's that?"

"Well, the day I applied for this job, Chief Alex mentioned that there hadn't been a gunfight in Mosby since 1955."

"Hmmm. Well, I s'pose he's right. We've had the occasional shooting, and one murder as I recall, but only one gunfight since 1955, that is, until you rolled into Quayle County."

"What happened in 1955?"

"Well, we went through a lean spell here for awhile. Going back to the '30's, Quayle 'bout always had three deputies, but in the early '50's, we was down to one, and that was me.

"The sheriff back then was Lattimer Goulds, but he was up in his late sixties, and in poor health, so in November of '52, he decided not to run for reelection. I thought about running, but to tell the truth, the Board of Supervisors was a trio of bitter old skinflints, and they didn't cotton to me, and I liked them even less. I knew I couldn't get elected, even if I was the only one runnin'.

"For one thing, they wanted the sheriff to work twelve hours a day, six days a week, and the pay 'tweren't for shit. When you work that many hours, you don't have time to make a living on the side, raising a few cows or even a henhouse full of chickens.

"Old Lattimer didn't mind 'cause there wasn't much to do so far as sheriffing was concerned. You might say he was retired on active duty. If you don't know, the standard abbreviation for that is R-O-A-D. All he did was sit on his ass and read the paper and listen to the radio. Then he got to where he couldn't even do that, which is why he up and decided not to run.

"Poor old soul. His body really was wore out. In his early years he was a cowboy, then a rodeo man, then a rodeo clown. He'd also been a professional boxer for awhile. He even worked for the railroad as a superintendent of the track-laying coolies. He couldn't help it. He died right after that on Christmas Eve. Left behind a sweet little wife.

"Well, we had an old widow woman in town, Miz Baldwin, who had a nephew named Dudley Donaldson, who was fixin' to retire from the El Paso Police Department after thirty years. Miz Baldwin was chummy with one of the county supervisors. Real chummy if you get my drift. Long story short, the Board of Supervisors contacted Dudley and offered him the job if he would move to Mosby. Of course, he'd have to get elected, but the fix was in so it was a done deal.

"Dudley agreed. He sold his house in El Paso, or maybe it was rented, almost overnight as I recall, and he and his wife up and moved next door to his Aunt Nellie on Jeff Davis Avenue. He won the election and that was that.

"Well, Dudley was the real deal, a bonafide big city lawman who wasn't afraid of nobody or anything, and I really enjoyed working for him. We still had a hiatus on hiring, so he decided that he'd work day shift, and I'd work afternoons. We didn't work on Saturday or Sunday or mids unless something special needed to be done.

"So it was on a Wednesday, I remember that, in February of 1955. It was unusually hot and sunshiny that day. Anyway, Dudley was here in the office and I was off duty at home, shoeing a horse, I think.

"Right about lunchtime, two mutts drove up in a black '48 Merc with a monster V-8 engine, and parked on the street almost in front of the courthouse, headed west.

"What were their names? Let's see. Oh yeah, the driver was Everett Beauchamps, and the other guy was . . . Ted something or other, I can't recollect right now. You can go to the archives and pull up the file. Interesting read.

"Anyway, they left the windows rolled down in the car, and walked across the street to the bank, but they was both wearing calf-length rain slickers and there weren't a cloud in sight. I think it was the Baptist preacher, who was locking up and headed for lunch, who saw it. He thought it was suspicious, so he walked straight to the jail and told old Dudley.

"Well Dudley carried a Long Colt .45 like me, but he decided to lock and load one of the Thompsons and take a couple extra mags, just in case these jaspers was bank robbers, which they was. Even up the odds a little bit if they broke bad.

"These tools was walking out the front door of the bank, headed back to their car, just as Dudley was crossing the street in their direction. They locked eyes on each other right away. Beauchamps had a Colt Government Model .45 in each hand, and the little fella, Ted, had a sawed-off shotgun in his right and a big, heavy cloth sack of money in his left. Hell, they even stole all the change! Lucky for Dudley his left hand wasn't free. Took him a second or two to drop the poke so he could commence shooting.

"Well, Dudley never even hesitated. He opened up with that chopper and emptied the clip into both of 'em. He shot Beauchamps' head clean off above the chin. Brains and eyeballs and teeth was scattered everywhere. Ted's chest looked like it had been stitched by a Singer sewing machine. Bloodiest mess you ever seen outside of a battlefield.

"That ended their crime spree. Turns out these two jaspers was wanted by the FBI for robbing a bank up in Bastrop, I believe, and Amarillo. They'd killed a bank guard in one of 'em. They was headed for the hangman's noose if they was caught, but they wasn't. Dudley done the FBI's job for 'em."

"Whatever happened to Dudley?"

"Now that's a real sad story. He got cancer and died a couple of years after that. He was too sick to run for reelection, and that's when Roger Elliott got elected."

Archie glanced up at the clock and saw it was 4:30. He got a sly look on his face and suggested that Barlow check the amended work schedule.

Barlow went to the bulletin board to take a peek. Wow! Good news! Good news!

Sheriff Sol scheduled him to work the afternoon shift with Deputy Kirk Shoemaker Tuesday through Friday. Afternoons meant patrol work, not jailhouse work.

It also meant at 8:00 o'clock, end-of-watch this morning, he was free until 4:00 o'clock Tuesday afternoon. This was known as a long change.

There was a downside, however. He would have no time with Sarah except for phone calls. He hated that, but it was just for a few days. He needed some sleep, but he was eager to do some real police work.

The other good news was that Sheriff Sol gave him Saturday

and Sunday as days off.

News flash! He could stay up all night tonight and sleep until noon on Tuesday. He hoped Sarah wasn't tied up tonight. His mind was racing. Suddenly, his fatigue vanished. A long sleep could wait for another day!

It was agony, but he managed to wait until 7:30 to call.

She was finishing breakfast. She said, "What's up?"

"Hey, I just learned that I'll be working the afternoon shift Tuesday through Friday. I'm off on Saturday and Sunday. I was wondering if you wanted to get together this afternoon after work."

"What did you have in mind, Mr. Adams? After my shock on Friday afternoon, seeing what I saw and not being able to unsee it, I just don't know if it's prudent for me to stop by your house anymore. I had to pray extra hard in church Sunday morning, in case you didn't notice, asking Jesus to restore the innocence that I lost so unexpectedly.

"Was it an ethereal experience, an amalgamated vision of science and art coupled with beauty, or was it simply carnal? You are a very seductive man, Mr. Adams. I am so confused."

"My word. I do apologize. It sounds like I ruint you, even if it was purely by happenstance.

"Perhaps we should forsake one another forevermore and pretend this never occurred. Go on about our lives like we live in separate universes.

"Another possibility, I suppose I could talk to your father. Try to make amends in some fashion. Whatever he thinks might be reasonable. Buy him a horse or something to compensate for sullying your reputation. Wonder if that would be enough or if I'd have to throw in a saddle.

"Or maybe we could simply designate my house as off limits to you.

"Better yet, maybe we don't, but I buy some heavy duty sweat pants and an athletic supporter with a stainless steel cup, and I wear that to bed, like pajamas, to forestall any future unforeseen incidents, that is, if you still want to come over, although I confess that I always sleep better au naturel."

"Oh, no, no, no, no, no. Please, Mr. Adams. I must bear my abashment alone, lest I transcend into a state of shamelessness. It would never do for even a scintilla of this scandal to come to light. My father would be devastated. My poor mother would fret herself to death. My friends would shake their fingers at me and say, "Tut. Tut. You floozy!

"And now that I'm ruint, I would never be perceived as a paragon of virtue by any other suitor, were one to happen along. I think it's best that we maintain the status quo, if just for appearances sake.

"Besides that, your house is so charming. I do so love to visit. And you certainly deserve your beauty sleep in the manner to which you are accustomed. You must never do anything which would interfere with peaceful slumber. A growing boy needs his strength. It's important to me that you continue to grow and reach your fullest potential.

"Maybe I could just avert my eyes if something like this should ever rise up again. In fact, I believe that's the best solution. That way, if I did happen upon your bewitching body sleeping in its natural state, I could always avert my eyes, and feel my way around the problem by use of my tender hands. That way, if I accidentally did feel something with which I am unfamiliar, I shan't be irrevocably shocked.

"That's what we'll do. I shall stop by about 4:30 with fixings for supper. I don't know what yet. Please recharge your batteries in your customary fashion. I'll see you then. Ta ta."

Jimminy Cricket! She was killing him! He wanted her so bad. He throbbed so violently, it ached like an abscessed tooth! He knew he couldn't go on like this much longer.

8:00 o'clock. End of watch. Archie and he passed the baton to Chief Snodgrass and Deputy Shoemaker.

He went home, stripped off, and fell into bed. It didn't take long to dream the dreams of the not so innocent.

Ring! Ring! Ring! Ring! Ring. Ad infinitum.

Barlow opened one eye and looked at his alarm clock. It was 5:15. Oh Jeez! Sarah would be here any minute!

He stumbled out of bed and scrambled to the kitchen in his birthday suit. He caught the phone on its 20th ring.

"Hello?"

"Barlow. Good. I'm sorry I woke you."

He had been fast asleep just moments ago. Now his heart was pinging. "Sarah, where are you? I though you would be here by now. Anything wrong?"

"Oh, Barlow. I'm so sorry. Mom called me at work just before I clocked out. My Granny Parker is in the hospital. They think she had a heart attack. Mom and I packed a bag and we're headed out the door to go see her. We probably won't be back for a couple of days. I wanted to let you know before we left."

"Oh my gosh! Do you think she'll be all right?"

"I think so, but we'll know more when we get there."

"Are you going to Alpine?"

"No. She lives in Del Rio with my Aunt Lacy. That's where we're going. We'll stay with her until Granny is out of the woods, at the very least."

"Is there anything I can do?"

"No. Well, there is one thing."

"What's that?"

"You could have some patience with me. I was really looking forward to getting together tonight."

"Me, too. Of course, I will. You know me. I'm a reservoir of patience."

"Sure, you are. I think I experienced some of that patience when I woke you up Saturday night. If I recall correctly, it was pulsating with every beat of your heart."

"Oh, Jeez, Sarah. Don't tease me. You're exercising my

patience real hard right now."

"Good. Hard is good."

"Oh, Lordy. Have some mercy. How long do you think you'll be gone?"

"Did you say long? Long is also good."

"How would you know? Are you speaking from personal experience?"

"Shame on you! I'm as pure as the driven snow. I'm saving myself for my husband, whenever I get married. However, I may have read something on this subject in one of those romance novels you told me about."

"Romance novels say dot, dot, dot."

"That's how little you know about romance novels, Mr. Adams. There's romance novels, and then there are risqué Victorian romance novels, such as "The Pearl," for those knowledgeable in English literature. I may have stumbled upon such a book unwittingly. I blush now recalling the incident."

In the background, Barlow heard Clarice saying, "Come on, Sarah. We need to go. Aunt Lacy is waiting for us."

"Oh, okay. Coming.

"Barlow, I gotta go. Mom's waiting. I'll call you first chance I get. See you when I get back. And Barlow, one of these days I'll make it up to you. The wait will be worth it. I promise. Bye now."

"I know it will. Bye. Be safe."

Barlow hung up. He had to shake it off. Sarah had his number and she knew it. She loved to torture him. She was beginning to consume all his thoughts.

So this was love . . . . 'Unchained Melody' by the Righteous Brothers came to mind. 'Oh, my love, My darling, I've hungered for your touch a long, lonely time, and time goes by so slowly . . .'

Chapter 26
An Education in Traffic

Tuesday, August 5th, 1530 hours. Barlow was both excited and nervous. He didn't know Deputy Shoemaker. They'd been introduced briefly, and had seen each other in passing once or twice. That was it.

Kirk Shoemaker was about 35 years of age, 6'1" tall, 175 pounds, muscular, with close-cut black hair and brown eyes. He was clean shaven. His uniform was tailored and heavily starched. He wore the twelve-loop gun belt, and carried a nickel-plated Smith and Wesson Model 15, .38 Special caliber revolver with a four-inch barrel. He was the only deputy Barlow had seen so far who carried a .38. He was their poster boy.

He was quiet, reserved, and extremely 'strack' (meaning squared away in Army parlance.) One might even describe him as aloof. This made him somewhat of a conundrum for Barlow. He didn't know what to expect, so Tuesday afternoon he arrived a half hour early. Deputy Shoemaker was already at work, visiting with the sheriff in his office.

Deputy Shoemaker said, "Barlow, you're driving today," so he went about the business of checking out their unit with the same degree of anal retentiveness as he did on his first day with Chunk. When they were ready, Barlow called Base, reporting Quayle 67 in service.

Once they cleared downtown, Deputy Shoemaker said, "Barlow, my name is Kirk. I was the rookie until last week when you came on. I'm probably the most 'by-the-book,' aggressive deputy here, although I'm pretty mellow by big city or DPS standards. Sheriff Sol paired us together this week so I can teach you traffic enforcement. Are you ready?"

"Yes, Sir."

"Don't call me Sir. I'm only 34 years old. I was an enlisted man in the Air Force. I work for a living. For the next few days I'm your partner. We rely upon each other not to get hurt. We do our job, but we both go home at end of shift without knife or bullet hole perforations or broken ribs or skinned knuckles. Got that?"

"Savvy."

"Good. Stay on 90 westbound until we get to the county line. Keep your eyes open for anyone who's driving erratically, recklessly, or more than 15 miles over the posted speed limit."

"Gotcha."

"Okay. Traffic enforcement is not a big part of the job for most sheriffs' departments, but you need to know how to do it, and what the sheriff expects from you, and all the rest of us when it does come up.

"Traffic is mostly the responsibility of the state troopers, but they only work the federal and state highways in most jurisdictions, unless there's a fatality. If we have a fatality, we secure the scene and call them to take lead. It's not that we can't work fatalities, but they're specifically trained to do that and we are not. Fortunately, we don't have many fatalities here. When we do, it's usually on 90, and the cause is usually speed and/or alcohol.

"If you haven't noticed, you will someday, that big city police departments have traffic divisions made up of marked and unmarked units and motorcycles. Traffic is all they do except for backing up the beat cars. They write a lot of tickets, mostly for speeding. DPS does the same thing.

"Beat cops write tickets too, but usually only for flagrant violations or to remind the punks and assholes who's in charge. Most beat cops with more than a year on the job consider traffic cops douchebags because they think a good day at work is writing 25 or 30 tickets. They rely on radar guns to clock speed, and once the violator crosses the magic number, that's it. They write a ticket. They don't care who it is, or if he had a reasonable excuse. They're automatons. It's kind of hypocritical. Who hasn't violated the traffic laws sometime or other without a good reason?"

"I get that. I've never had a ticket, but all my friends who've been stopped by DPS got written up. No one ever got a break."

"There you go. Now you understand what the sheriff does not want us to do. Consider yourself a beat cop.

"I'm sure that when you take the traffic enforcement class in WTJC, you'll learn all about the three holy 'E's' of traffic - engineering, education, and enforcement. It sounds corny, but actually it makes a lot of sense.

"Engineering is when you, as a quote, dedicated and responsible lawman, end quote, see something dangerous on or along the roadway and you either rectify the situation yourself, or report it to the public works department for correction.

"In theory, if the roadway isn't banked to the inside along a curve, you should contact the works department and have them come out and pave it properly. Good luck with that. However, if a tree or bush is obstructing vision at a crossroad or covering up a road sign and you don't want to cut it down yourself, write up a work order and get Chief Alex or Sheriff Sol to sign off on it and the road crew will come out and fix it. Understood?"

"Understood."

"The next 'E' is education. Simply stated, if you stop a motorist for a broken taillight or speeding or running a stop sign, but it's not too serious, if he's polite, and even the least bit repentant, or 'deserving' as we like to say, you give him a polite verbal warning and send him on his way. Tell him if you catch him again, you'll issue a citation. Be nice. Make a friend if you can. Got it?"

"Yes."

"Good. The third 'E' is enforcement. Enforcement is what we

get paid to do, if it's warranted. A guy is running wide open down the highway, 20 or 25 miles over the limit, or he never even braked at a stop sign, or maybe he nearly caused an accident, or he did cause an accident and you saw it. By all means, 'issue a citation,' (using the proper police parlance for ticket writing.)"

"What if he's been drinking or he's drunk?"

"What do you smell? Is it alcohol? How strong is it?

"What do you see? Are there any empty or opened beer cans or whiskey bottles in sight?

"Is his speech slurred? Are his eyes bloodshot? Are his clothes disheveled?

"If he's drunk, or you think he's drunk, get him out of the car. Frisk him first. Then see if he can hold his arms out wide and touch the end of his nose with the tip of his index finger on each hand, one at a time. Make him do that two or three times. This is hard to do if you're drunk.

"Ask him to stand first on one leg for fifteen seconds, and then switch to the next. If he's drunk, he won't be able to do it. However, some people with a disability can't do it either, so this isn't the end all, be all.

"Ask him to walk a straight-line toe-to-heel along the highway about twenty yards, preferably on the striping, if it's safe, and to do an about face and come back to where he began. To a drunk, this is like walking on a balance beam in gym class.

"If he can't do all of these fairly easily, he's probably drunk.

"Hell, ask him how much he's had to drink. Half the time they'll tell you. If he can't perform these simple tests, or even if he can, but he still appears drunk to you, hook him up. You might want to call ahead first, and see if either Chief or DPS can perform a breathalyzer on him at the jail. None of the rest of us are certified. If for some reason, no one is available, he'll probably get off scot-free.

"Understand this. You'll be making an arrest for probable cause based upon your observations and whatever training you get. You don't want to get in the habit of arresting folks for DWI and them not blow at least a .10 on the breathalyzer. On the other hand, better to arrest someone you think is drunk and lose the case, than to let him go and ten minutes later he runs over a pedestrian and kills him.

"Also, breathalyzers don't measure drug usage. He could be stoned on pot or speed or whatever. Only a blood sample can establish that and even then, you have to know what to tell the lab to look for. So, if you think you might have a DWI and you're patrolling by yourself, best bet would be for you to call for back up until you know what you're doing. Even after that, it's never a bad idea to have some back up."

"Got it."

"Okay. We're looking for a violator. So far we haven't seen a blessed thing. That's pretty much the norm in Quayle County.

"Bottom line. Traffic enforcement is pretty basic. Writing a ticket is not brain surgery. The violations with their statutes are listed on the inside cover of the ticket book. Make sure you take your time and fill out the citation correctly and completely. Write the court date for three weeks down the road, Monday through Thursday, at 10 o'clock. No Fridays or weekends, or holidays. Sometimes, that means the violator will get more than three weeks. Point out the mailing address and the amount of the fine, in the event he chooses to accept responsibility and mail it in to avoid going to court. Most folks will, if you treat them nice.

"And one last thing. The violator gets the original. The court gets the second copy. Miss Loretta gets the third copy. You get the bottom copy. A wise and prudent officer will make notes on the back of his copy, for things such as who all was in the car, what everyone was wearing, anything relevant the offender said, or something unusual like the car had three Dobermans in the back seat, things like that.

"You wanna know why? Sometimes the guy will be a 'no show' and we'll have to hunt him down and arrest him on a failure-to-appear (FTA) bench warrant. It could take months to find him. Then when we do, if the guy doesn't plead guilty right then, Judge Sweeney will set a new court date. By then, you might have forgotten what happened. The guy may have a mouthpiece or a lying witness who wasn't even there, but you're not sure. You can't remember. If that happens, the judge has no choice but to dismiss the case."

"We're at the county line. Want me to turn around?"

"Do it. It's starting to look like we might have a slow day. That's fine with me, but I'm sure you'd like a little excitement, and I don't blame you."

CHAPTER 27

MALE BONDING

They patrolled up and down Highway 90 and Texas 651, all the way to the county line in each direction without seeing a viable moving violation. They did clock one dude speeding ten over, but Kirk told Barlow that would be considered a chickenshit violation absent extenuating circumstances, such as recognizing the driver as an habitual traffic offender, or seeing equipment violations, such as a broken taillight or smoking exhaust, or for 'contempt of cop', as in passing a marked unit which is already driving the speed limit, indicating disrespect for law enforcement.

At 6:30, they pulled in at Betty's Diner for coffee and hamburgers.

Kirk already knew Barlow's bona fides, but Barlow knew next to nothing about Kirk. While they were eating, Barlow threw Kirk a slow pitch to see if he were willing to open up.

"Is that a Model 15 you're carrying?"

"It is. You've obviously spent a little time studying handguns."

"I have. Besides that, you're the first deputy I've seen here carrying a .38. Most of them seem to prefer the .357."

"You are correct again. They do. I like the Model 15 because that's what the Air Force issued me. I carried one for four years, except it was blued. I bought the nickel because it's easier to clean and less susceptible to rust. I understand why guys carry the .357, but I don't expect to shoot at anything more than fifty yards away, so why put up with the extra wallop?"

"Mr. Jake told me that most police officers carry a .38 Special, especially in the East. Assuming he's right, it validates your position. I wanted something with a little more oomph, so I bought the .41. I don't have any experience in law enforcement, so what I think doesn't carry much weight. Not only that, but from what I've observed here, everyone pretty much has a different idea about which type of gun is best for police work."

"To each his own. I've never fired a shot in anger. Maybe if I ever do, I'll feel differently about it. Whatever works for you is right for you."

"How did you like the Air Force?"

"How did you like the Army?"

"It wasn't bad. The training was excellent. I had good NCO's and officers overall, especially when I was assigned to the 9th ID. I enjoyed being assigned to the field artillery. Vietnam wasn't exactly a picnic, but it could have been worse. I survived, as did most of my friends. No complaints."

"That's what I heard."

"What about you? What did you do in the Air Force?

"Short story or long?"

"Long."

"Well, I'm from Alpine. My dad's a barber. My mom's a checker at the Piggly Wiggly. I have a brother and a sister who are both married and still live there.

"I finished high school in '57. Thought I wanted to be a high school history or geography teacher, so I enrolled at Sul Ross State Teachers College right there in Alpine. Lived at home the first couple of years.

"For fun, starting in high school, I did some small time rodeoing as a bull rider. I chose bulls because I didn't grow up on a ranch and we didn't have any horses. It was a no brainer. I won a few buckles and enjoyed a small amount of notoriety.

"I met my wife at a rodeo. In 1959, she was crowned the Pecos Rodeo Queen. That's when we met. She lit up my life. Her name is Penelope, but everyone calls her Penny.

"Turns out she was also a student at Sul Ross. We started

dating. It was serious for both of us, right from the start. Two years later, she got a degree in elementary ed and I got mine in social studies. We decided to get married.

"I knew I wasn't destined for the Professional Rodeo Cowboys Association (PRCA) Hall of Fame. Besides that, rodeoing didn't pay much more than cover costs, plus the risk of injury was high. I lost my interest in teaching by the time I graduated. I didn't know what I wanted to do other than get married. The draft was still in effect, and it had a substantial influence on my thinking.

"It really wasn't a hard decision once I examined all the facts. I joined the Air Force in July of '61, two months after graduation. Before I left for basic training, Penny and I got married. She's from Mosby, so she came home and moved back in with her folks. I went off 'into the wild, blue yonder.' While I was gone, she worked at the drugstore and did a little subbing at the school whenever they needed someone, which wasn't often.

"Basic was at Lackland Air Force Base in San Antone. Then I went to tech school at the Army Military Police School in Fort Gordon, Georgia. That was a pleasant surprise. I was offered OTS (Officer Training School) since I had a degree, but wasn't sure that was my forte, so I turned it down. I figured that might seal my fate and I'd be conscripted into something boring like being a medical orderly, but it didn't work that way. They assigned me to air police. Anyway, after tech school, I got two weeks leave before reporting to Offutt Air Force Base in Omaha. I scooped up my bride in November, and off we went to a land of hot muggy summers and frozen tundra in winter.

"I was still an Airman 3rd Class when I reported for assignment at the Air Police Squadron. I spent two years guarding nuclear weapons facilities. That was my life, day after day. It really sucked. I got to thinking maybe the Air Force did decide to punish me for not volunteering for OTS. I couldn't wait to ETS. I made 2nd Class and then 1st Class, but the job was the same. Then I got lucky as hell.

"In December of '63, they PCS'ed (permanent change of station) me to Ramstein Air Force Base in Kaiserslautern near Frankfort. I was assigned to garrison police duty.

"I found my niche. We were the base police force. We also had liaison duty with the local authorities whenever an airman got busted off base. That's where and how I learned to police. Besides that, Germany was a nice place to live. Neither one of us had ever been out of Texas until I joined the Air Force. This was our adventure.

"My ETS was up in July of '65. Vietnam was in full swing, so I didn't re-up. My wife was pregnant with our son, Roscoe, and she wanted to go back home, so we did. I was lucky again, because Sheriff Sol had a vacancy. I never had a day of unemployment. Besides that, my wife got on as the 3rd grade teacher at Quayle School.

"Then in September of '65, I joined the Air Force Reserve. I do weekends once a month and two weeks each summer at Lackland with the security police, which is what they call the AP's now. I made sergeant two years ago. I'm on the list to make staff sergeant. I really like it. It's extra money, plus I get to attend a lot of law enforcement schools.

"Roscoe is four now. We have a nice little house we like. I love my job. Our folks are nearby. We see our families frequently. Penny is happy. Roscoe's happy. I'm happy. Life is good."

"Wow. That's where I'd like to be in a couple of years. You are a very lucky dog, indeed, although I suspect hard work and merit had no small amount of influence on the outcome for both of you."

"Shut the fuck up. Time to get back to work."

They finished eating and went back on patrol. However, they never saw a moving violation of sufficient consequence to even pull over the violator. No one called in a motor vehicle accident. Not a surprise to Kirk, but a disappointment to Barlow.

Thus endeth Day One in Barlow's OJT in traffic enforcement.

CHAPTER 28

ACCIDENTS AND TICKETS

Day Two started with a bang, or rather a crash, in front of the pharmacy on America Avenue.

Old Mr. Willoughby was backing out of the angle parking. Apparently, he wasn't paying close enough attention, because he backed into a farm truck belonging to the K-Bar-V Ranch, which was driven by a ranch hand named Kirby Oswald.

The farm truck was a 1953 Chevrolet bucket of rust, so the damage to the right rear fender hardly showed, and it certainly didn't matter. Mr. Willoughby's left rear taillight assembly on his 1959 Cadillac was busted, and since his automobile was in pristine shape, it was destined for the auto body shop to make it like new again. Unfortunately for Mr. Willoughby, the accident would be charged to him.

Normally, since this was on a federal highway, DPS would have been dispatched to write the report. However, since Barlow was in training and the accident was a simple one to resolve, Kirk volunteered Quayle 67 to handle the run.

Barlow acted like he knew what he was doing.

He spoke to both drivers and listened to what each had to say. There was no conflict. Mr. Willoughby acknowledged his carelessness and Kirby Oswald was both polite and humble. Easy-peasy.

Barlow asked each for their driver's licenses, vehicle registrations, and proof of insurance. Both complied.

This is when Barlow encountered a fly in the ointment.

He noticed that Kirby's driver's license was expired by seven months.

Kirby said he hadn't realized that. He said he hadn't had a ticket in five or six years, and that was in New Mexico for driving a K-Bar-V truck with bald tires and a worn-out exhaust system. The New Mexico State Police impounded the truck. Mr. Vandergriff had to bring his new truck to Las Cruces to tow the old truck back to the ranch. Then on top of that, the cops made Mr. V. pay for a tow and the two tickets. Cost him $90! He was spitting mad. Everyone knows they're all a bunch of mongoloids in New Mexico.

Then it hit home. "You ain't gonna tow the truck are you Deputy?"

Kirk asked, "What do you think, Deputy Adams?"

"Well, the way I see it, I have to write old Kirby here a ticket for driving on an expired license. No choice about that.

"I was wondering though, if we don't get an urgent call right away, after I finish filling in the accident report, maybe you or I could drive the truck back to the K-Bar-V while the other one of us drove Kirby back in our cruiser."

Kirk asked, "How's that sound to you, Kirby? There's a good chance if you get your license renewed before court date, Judge Sweeney will dismiss the case."

"I'd be mighty obliged to both of you. I appreciate your understanding. I'm real sorry."

There you have it. Two birds with one stone. Maybe three. Maybe four.

First, Barlow wrote up his first accident report.

Second, he wrote his first ticket.

Third, he made allies out of Kirby Oswald and Mr. Vandergriff.

And fourth, he learned where the K-Bar-V sheep ranch was located and all about it and the family who owned it.

Barlow wrote one more citation while working with Kirk.

The next day, some yahoo named Dwight Fortenberry from Ozona passed CO 16, headed northbound on TX 651 at a high rate of speed. Quayle 67 was on CO 16 almost to the intersection, but apparently Mr. Fortenberry didn't notice them, in that he had a tremendous rooster tail of dust in his wake.

Barlow turned to follow in pursuit. Kirk told him to hold back and gradually increase his speed until he could pace the earthbound rocket ship. They followed for four or five minutes, watching their certified speedometer rise up to 73 miles per hour. Then the driver eased it back to 68 and maintained speed.

Kirk told Barlow to goose it, and when he caught up with the violator, to turn on his emergency light and siren, but not before. Barlow didn't ask why. He just did what he was told.

When he caught up, they rolled up their windows and he switched on the emergency equipment. The violator slammed on his breaks and pulled over to the side of the road.

Kirk told Barlow to put his billy club in its ring on his belt when he exited the vehicle.

After the dust settled and they could see clearly, Kirk called Quayle Base requesting a license plate check on TX BA5-311. He said it should come back to a white, late model Plymouth. He also reported the traffic stop on TX 651 about ten miles south of the Crockett County line.

Miss Lorretta said the system was slow today and that it might take a few minutes. Kirk responded that they would be out of the unit and they would check back in a few.

They got out of the cruiser and approached the Plymouth from both sides.

Barlow could see that the car was empty except for the driver, who was a fortyish white male, balding, overweight, and a little fidgety. He asked the driver to show him his license, vehicle registration, and proof of insurance.

The driver was already prepared. He handed the documents to Barlow.

The driver was the aforementioned Dwight Fortenberry, age 45, of Box 136, RR2, Ozona, TX. The vehicle was registered to

Dwight and Gladys Fortenberry at the same address, on a 1967 Plymouth Fury sedan, white in color.

Barlow asked, "Sir, where are you going?"

"Back home, officer. I'm running late to an appointment with my wife."

"What type of appointment?"

"Well, if you must know, we have a meeting scheduled with our bank. We're contemplating selling our house and buying another one."

"I see. Where were you coming from?"

"Well, not that it's any of your business, but I was checking on a fellow from Langtry who was interested in buying my house. I wanted to make sure he was, in fact, owner of a ranch he claimed was his."

"Mr. Fortenberry, Langtry is way off the beaten path from here. There's a much more direct route to Ozona from Langtry than coming through this way."

"I didn't say I was coming directly from Langtry. Anyway, this is none of your affair! What is it that you want?"

"Mr. Fortenberry, I was just trying to learn a little bit about you. Whether you had a true emergency to justify your speed. What you've said doesn't really add up. Do you know the speed limit on this highway?"

"Yes. It's fifty MPH, like all unmarked Texas highways."

"Right you are. How fast were you driving?"

"Oh, I don't know! Maybe sixty. I didn't check. What's the big deal? You and I are the only two motorists on the road right now. It's not I like a robbed a bank or anything!"

"Funny choice of activities that you mentioned. You were, in fact, driving like you just robbed a bank. I clocked you at 73 miles per hour. Another two, and we'd be calling for a wrecker and taking you to jail."

"This is outrageous! I will protest your conduct when I see the judge."

"Patience, Mr. Fortenberry. That's all I need from you right now. It will just be another few minutes."

Barlow and Kirk went back to the cruiser. Kirk called base, who confirmed that the Plymouth was registered to Fortenberry. Kirk called in his DOB and asked for a wanted check. Shortly thereafter, Miss Loretta replied that he did not have any outstanding warrants.

Kirk told Barlow to issue the citation for speeding 73 in a 50 miles per hour zone. He said if Fortenberry had been a little humble, he would have suggested cutting him some slack and writing it for 65 in a 50. That way, the fine would be less, plus he'd only lose three points on his license instead of six. However, Fortenberry didn't deserve a break. He also reminded Barlow to write some notes on the back of his own copy.

"Make sure you write enough detail to remember everything.

"If Fortenberry does come to court, and he doesn't lose his self-righteous attitude, Maximum Max will probably goose him for the maximum fine of $100. That's why you annotate everything that's relevant or noteworthy, to provide the judge with a clear picture of what you witnessed, if you are called to testify. Yes, indeed. Mr. Fortenberry would be better served to mail in the minimum $20 fine and the $15 in court costs."

Barlow tore off Mr. Fortenberry's copy of the ticket. He walked up to the Plymouth and handed it to the livid motorist. He pointed out the address of the courthouse, the date and time of his scheduled court appearance, and the amount of the fine if he decided to mail it in.

Fortenberry stared at Barlow with a look on his face that would freeze a glass of water on an August afternoon in Quayle County, Texas. His face was contorted. His temples were pulsating; however, he kept his mouth shut and drove off as sedately as a preacher's wife in a funeral motorcade.

Barlow returned to the cruiser.

Kirk said, "Come on. Let's head back to Mosby. It's time to

eat."

"You got it. But first, why did you tell me to catch up slowly without lights and siren?"

"Think about it. We needed to pace him long enough to determine his exact top speed. Besides, who knows what he had under the hood of that Plymouth? His car is newer than ours, and maybe he could have outrun us. Those are our official reasons.

"But the underlying reason was to give him enough slack that he thinks maybe he could outrun us. Then, he just might decide to go for it. If he does, we have a full-blown chase with the hounds after the fox. When we catch him, and we inevitably do, he goes 'directly to jail. Do not pass Go.' We tow his car; he loses his license; he pays a huge fine; and, his auto insurance skyrockets. Basically, he completely screws himself. Savvy?"

"Savvy."

"Good, because you saw for yourself, he's a deserving asshole, even if we didn't know it at the time.

"And there's another thing you need to consider. Fortenberry was up to something he didn't want us to know about. Could be that documentation of his being where he was at the time we stopped him, might be problematic for him if it came to light by whomever he's hiding it from. Paying a fine might be the least of his worries."

Food for thought.

Friday was a wash, and so was the weekend. Sarah didn't return home until Sunday evening. He needed rest. He got rest. Just not peace of mind.

CHAPTER 29

LEARNING HOW TO SMOOTH TALK AN ARREST

Sheriff Sol assigned Barlow to work with Deputy Ernie Atwater for the first two days on second shift during the week of August 11th. After that, he would return to first shift to work with Arch. This was a real treat, since it was the first time he worked day shift since his first day on the job.

Deputy Atwater was a big guy, like Sheriff Sol. He was 37 years old. He stood 6'4" tall and weighed a good 250. He had brown eyes, bushy eyebrows, and thick, black, curly hair. In fact, he was hairy all over. He had more hair on his arms than Chief Alex had on his head. And even though he was clean shaven, he had a 5 o'clock shadow, no matter what time of day or night it was.

Another thing, he always looked like an unmade bed, no matter what, even though his uniform was always clean and pressed, although far from being heavily starched. He wore a cartridge belt like Slick's with cartridges all around his waist. Probably had 100 loops. Ha! He carried a Smith and Wesson, Model 28, .357 Highway Patrolman, with a six-inch barrel and target grips. It looked small on him. He could have carried a sawed-off bazooka. It would have looked appropriate.

He was jolly and treated everybody like he was thrilled to see them. So far as Barlow knew, he didn't have an enemy in the world. He had sixteen years on the job, and was fourth in seniority behind Sheriff Sol, Chief Alex, and Arch. He was also the SO's designated sniper.

That first morning, Ernie told Barlow to check out a shotgun and join him in the parking lot. By the time Barlow did, Ernie already had unit 81, the '66 Chevy Impala, fired up and ready to go. It was 8:05 when Quayle 47 pulled out of the lot.

Ernie said, "Sheriff assigned you to work with me today and tomorrow because we have two bench warrants to serve. He wants you to learn how to find folks who don't want to be found, and how to arrest and process prisoners."

"Gosh, this is great! What do we have?"

"Well, right now we have a warrant on Jasper Elrod, a real piece of work. He's bad-tempered and usually ready to fight at the drop of a hat. He failed to appear on a disorderly conduct charge. He lives up off CO Road 15 in a shack with his wife and three delinquent, teenaged boys. The entire clan is rowdy, overgrown, stupid, lazy, worthless, and eager to fight."

"What did he do?"

"Well, Arch was on mids. About two months ago, in the wee, wee hours, he got a call from Mrs. Elrod. She's a slob, mouthy, and a bad drunk just like Jasper. She said he was knocking her around and she was afraid he was going to kill her.

"The sad truth is, even if he did do her in, it wouldn't be no big loss to Quayle County or the rest of the world. She's real trouble. She's a nasty brawler, an incorrigible thief, specializes in shoplifting, and someone you'd really prefer to avoid. Not only that, she's probably been arrested as many times as Jasper. So, whatever she says, you have to take it with a grain of salt. The situation could easily be just the opposite of what she claims.

"So Arch woke up the sheriff to see how he wanted to handle it. Sheriff Sol told him to wake up Slick, and for the two of them to make a house call.

"When they arrived, the hullabaloo had shifted from the house out into the front yard. They saw Jasper bitch slap Rose a couple of licks. She was motherfucking him at the top of her lungs, and trying to brain him with a baseball bat, but 'tweren't no use. She was blind drunk and her glasses were missing and she couldn't see a thing. She slipped and fell on her ass.

"Archie and Slick bailed out of the car to stop the fight. Jasper looked up and decided to go after Slick, who was riding shotgun, which he left in the car when he sized up the situation. I'm guessing Jasper went after Slick instead of Arch because Slick's considerably smaller.

"Who knows for sure? The headlights were in his eyes, probably causing him to have night blindness, plus he was shit-faced, too.

"Anyway, he took a swing at Slick and missed. Slick reared up and kicked Jasper in the balls as hard as he could and down he went like a sack of horseshoes. They hooked him up and stuffed him in the back seat."

"What happened next?"

"Well, they checked out Rose and the boys and the house. For a change, the boys were subdued. Slick said the house was about what you'd expect - a total mess. He also said there had to be at least a hundred empty beer cans scattered everywhere. Some of the furniture was knocked over. That was about it."

"Was the wife hurt?"

"No, not really. She had a black eye and a few minor abrasions, but nothing serious. Arch tried to get her to sign a complaint on Jasper, but nothing doing, so order was restored and Jasper was removed from the scene of the crime, as it were. All's well that ends well."

"They were drunk, right?"

"Oh, hell yes. They were both rip-roaring drunk."

"Why didn't they take Rose in too, and charge them both with being drunk? And, how come they didn't charge Jasper with resisting arrest or assault on an officer?"

"Well, there's no crime being drunk on your own property. The statute is for being drunk in a public place. And as for charging Jasper for resisting arrest or assault on an officer, that was Slick's call. I'm pretty sure he felt like charging Jasper with DC was sufficient. Hell, you can get fined up to $500 and/or serve up to six months in the county jail upon conviction.

"Not only that, I heard Jasper's balls swole up like grapefruits. They said he couldn't walk straight for more'n a week. Slick might've thought he broke his stones for good and figured that was punishment enough.

"You got to understand. Jasper's a ne'er-do-well. He scavenges old derelict cars and scrap metal, which he sells to a junkyard in Alpine. He ain't had a job in probably twenty years. No telling how much he steals off folks when they ain't looking. He used to be a Trailways bus driver, but he couldn't stay sober and lost his Class A license. By then, nobody was willing to take a chance on him, and rightfully so.

"They ain't got any money. They draw commodities from the county because they're poor, because neither one can hold down a job, and because they spend every last cent on beer. Whatever amount Jasper gets fined, in theory anyway, is like taking food off their table. And, if he serves time, the result is still the same.

"Not only that, you can't go off and leave three minors in the house alone.

"Besides, you've seen the jail, but you haven't had to pull jail duty yet. It's like serving time yourself when you're guarding one of those jailbirds."

"So what do you think Judge Sweeney will do?"

"That's a good question. You got to be wiser than King Solomon to resolve a situation like this. If I had to guess, he'll probably draw some time.

"Maybe we'll get lucky and Judge Sweeney will put him on the county road crew. Make him pick up trash and things like that. Then we wouldn't get stuck babysitting him around the clock, plus he'll have to work his ass off. But he'd probably rather do hard time and just lay about in the cell."

"So what's our plan?"

"Well, we'll drive right up to the front door and see if he's there. If he is, we'll hook him up. If he wants to fight, we'll beat the stuffing out of him and take him to jail anyway. If the old lady or kids get froggy, we'll do the same to them."

"What if he won't answer the door or his wife won't let us in?"

"Barlow, we have a warrant signed by the judge. We can bust the door down if we have to. Any damages will be on him, so long as he's there. If he's not there, we'll try to figure out where he is or when he's likely to come back. I hope you're prepared to stay all day and all night if we have to. I don't aim to go back until he's in cuffs."

"Good thing I brought a lunch."

"Good thing you did, but I don't think you need to worry. If his junky, faded blue, '50 Ford, stake-bed truck is there, he's there. If it isn't, he's probably picking up junk. He ain't a hard worker. He'll be back before long."

Barlow's excitement was brimming over. He couldn't wait to make his first arrest. He just hoped he didn't have to beat the stuffing out of Rose or the kids.

When they turned off on County Road 15, Ernie slowed down to a crawl so as not to kick up a dust storm and announce their arrival any sooner than necessary.

Ernie pointed out a "Grapes of Wrath" backwoods, white trash shanty on the left side of the road. He identified Jasper, who appeared to be loading old washing machines and rusty car bumpers onto the back of a raggedy old truck that looked as if it were long overdue for the junkyard, itself.

Ernie said, "Take it easy when we drive up. He knows nothing good for him is gonna come out of our little visit. Take your stick, but hold it down alongside your leg.

"I'll do the talking. If he rears up and wants to fight, and you can get a clear lick without hitting me, clock him good. If he runs, tackle him. Cuff him first chance you get. And if you see me whaling on him, stay out of the way. I don't want to hurt you by accident. Any questions?"

"No, I think you covered it."

"Good. Here we go."

Jasper threw a rusty radiator in the back of his truck. Then he started walking over toward the cruiser. At the same time, Rose and the three boys stepped out of the shack and stood near the front door taking it all in. A grubby female sumo wrestler with Larry and Curly and Moe in the cheap seats waiting for the American Wrestling Association match to begin between the favorite, Jasper the Jaybird and the Polecat Police tag team.

"Is that you, Ern?"

"Yep. It's me."

"What're y'all doing way out here?"

"You remember that time Slick and Arch had to come out and bust up the fight betwixt you and Rose?"

"Yeah."

"Well, you never showed up for court. You pissed off Judge Sweeney. He issued a warrant for your arrest. We gotta take you in."

"Aw come on, Neighbor. I thought me and Slick was through all that. You know my balls swole up like melons and turned all black and blue? I wasn't able to fuck for nigh on a month."

"Well, I figured it was bad, but not that bad. But this ain't betwixt you and Slick. You all are square. This is between you and Judge Sweeney. How's come you failed to appear in court?"

"Well, Hell's bells, Ern! I ain't had no money to pay a fine. I can't do no hard time in jail. You know, I gotta feed my kids."

"I know that, Jasper. It ain't up to me. You gotta appear in court and talk to Judge Sweeney about that. Maybe he'll cut you a break if he ain't too mad on account of you blowing him off like he ain't a judge."

"Could I turn myself in next week?"

"You know better than that. Sheriff Sol told me not to come back 'til you was in cuffs. Why don't you just turn around and put your hands behind your back and come in peaceable this time? I can tell Sheriff Sol and the judge you cooperated. That ought to count for something. I don't think you really want to fight, do you?"

"Come on, Neighbor. I'm beggin' you."

"You know I ain't gotta choice, Jasper, but you do. What's it gonna be?"

"Who's this scrawny little feller with you? I ain't never seen him afore? Ain't he a little puny and underage to be a deputy?"

"This here is Deputy Adams, Jasper. He might not look like much to you, but he's the guy what shot and killed the turd that was trying to rape Sandra Taft. You heard about that didn't you? You really don't want to mess with him. Sheriff Sol sent him here with me, just in case you decided to break bad. You ain't gonna do that are you now?"

"Sheriff sent him here to shoot me?"

"Only if he has to, Jasper. He's here to settle things if you and I can't get 'er done. Understand? You can't win today. What do you say? Surrender peacefully?"

Jasper started shaking. Then he said, "Oh, all right. Don't clamp 'em down too tight. You know you're fucking me up real bad, don't you?"

"I do, but it ain't my call."

Jasper turned around and put his hands behind his back. Ernie cuffed him before frisking him. He pulled out a rusty Barlow knife, a snotty bandana, a moldy wallet with $28, and a set of keys. Jasper said it was okay to give his property for the wife to hold.

Before they put him in the back seat of the car, Jasper told his family he'd call as soon as he found out what the judge was going to do. The four of them just stood there like deaf mutes, never saying a word. Barlow wondered if they even understood.

Ern backed out of the driveway and headed towards the jail.

Barlow's mind was spinning. Ern just demonstrated why everyone seemed to like him so much. However, he sort of made Barlow the Boogerman. He wondered if this was a one-time deal or if other folks in Quayle County would see him this way.

CHAPTER 30

WATCHING THE ADMINISTRATION

OF JUSTICE UP CLOSE

It was 11:15 when they returned to the courthouse. They escorted Jasper down to the dungeon.

Miss Loretta called the judge's chambers to let them know the warrant on Jasper Elrod had been served. Miss Eloise Goodman, Judge Sweeney's clerk, said for them to bring him to the courtroom at 2 o'clock.

In the interim, Barlow completed the booking slip, defendant personal history sheet, took two mugshots, and made a bonafide effort to fingerprint Jasper.

They really didn't need another set of his prints on file, but this was a training exercise. Barlow had to learn how to make legible prints. Ernie was patient, demonstrating the way to do it without making smudges or smearing the loops, arches, and whorls. Barlow printed Jasper eight times before Ernie decided that one set was passable.

Barlow looked up the next item number in Sheriff's Office - Book 2. He annotated this arrest and incident, taking the next item number. He wrote the incident report. He referenced this item number with the old one when Jasper was arrested on Wednesday, June 4th. He would have done the property report, except that Jasper didn't have any personal property.

Ernie called Betty's Diner and ordered a hamburger with fries and a small Coke for Jasper. Thankfully, Betty's delivered.

By 1:25, Barlow had completed his prisoner processing. He washed and wolfed down his lunch.

At 1:45, Ernie and Barlow fitted Jasper with ankle and belly chains and walked him up the stairs to the courtroom. At Ernie's direction, Barlow escorted Jasper to the nearest seat in the jury box. Then he took a seat nearby.

Ernie sat at the table reserved for the prosecutor.

At 1:47, Mr. Samuel Davis, Esquire, the public defender, arrived. He walked over and began whispering to Jasper. A minute later, he escorted him to a seat at the defense table.

At 1:55, DA Able DeWitt arrived. He took his seat.

At 1:59, Miss Goodman and Bailiff August Bellweather arrived. They each took their seats.

At 2:00 o'clock sharp, Mr. Bellweather stood and said, "All rise. Hear ye, hear ye. Order in the court. The District Court for the County of Quayle, in the State of Texas, the Honorable Maxwell Sweeney presiding, is now in session. All ye who have matters before this court come forward and ye shall be heard. God bless this honorable court."

Judge Sweeney swooped in like an angry bird in his black robes and took his throne behind the bench. He said, "Be seated." Then he studied a sheaf of papers placed on his desk by Miss Goodman for several minutes.

Finally, he asked, "Mr. District Attorney, what have we before the court this afternoon?"

DA DeWitt rose and stated, "Your Honor, today we have Mr. Jasper Elrod in custody, who was arrested this morning on a bench warrant for contempt of court for failure to appear, and for disorderly conduct."

"I see. What's the docket number?"

"Docket number 69-08-0015."

"Mr. Davis, do you represent Mr. Elrod?"

"I do, Your Honor."

"Mr. Davis, how does your client plead to these charges?"

"Your Honor, Mr. Elrod would like to plead guilty to both counts."

"Mr. Davis, please present your client before the court."

Jasper stood up beside Mr. Davis.

"Mr. Elrod, is it true you wish to plead guilty to the charge of disorderly conduct, and to my charge of contempt of court for failure to appear?"

"Yes, Your Honor."

"You are aware, aren't you, that you have the right to plead not guilty and to face the accusers against you?"

"Yes, Your Honor."

"Do you know if you plead guilty, I can and will impose sentence at this time. You may be incarcerated for up to six months and fined up to $500 on each count. Are you quite certain that you still wish to plead guilty?"

"Yes, Your Honor."

"Did anyone threaten you if you didn't plead guilty or promise you a lenient sentence if you did?"

"No, Your Honor."

"Do you affirm that you are, in fact, guilty of disorderly conduct and contempt of court for failure to appear as scheduled, after you were released on your own recognizance?"

Jasper whispered to his lawyer, "What's recognizance?"

Mr. Davis whispered back, "The judge let you go without making you post a bond, because, on your word, you promised to return voluntarily on your next scheduled court date. Remember that?"

"Oh, yeah. I'm guilty, Judge."

"On both counts?"

"Yes, Sir."

"Mr. Elrod, why did you disregard your promise to return to court?"

"I don't know. Stupid, I guess. I didn't have the money to pay a fine and I didn't want to go to jail."

"A man is only as good as his word. You understand that don't you?"

"Yes, Your Honor."

"You know if you ever appear before me again on other charges, I will require you to post a cash or bail bond pending trial, right?"

"Yes, Your Honor."

"Very well. I accept your plea.

"Mr. DeWitt, do we have an officer here for the allocution, with respect to the charge of disorderly conduct?"

"Your Honor, we don't have either of the two initial arresting officers here, but we do have today's arresting officers, and Deputy Atwater is prepared to testify based upon his knowledge of the original incident, if that's agreeable to Defense."

Sam Davis rose. "That's agreeable to Defense, Your Honor."

"Very well. Deputy Atwater, please take a seat in the witness box and be sworn in."

Ernie took his seat and Mr. Bellweather administered the oath.

Then Mr. DeWitt said, "Deputy Atwater, please tell the court what happened in the early morning hours on June 4th at the Elrod residence in Quayle County, to the best of your knowledge."

"Your Honor, Deputy Archibald Willis received a call at the sheriff's office from Mrs. Rose Elrod, Jasper Elrod's wife. She said Jasper was beating on her, and she was afraid he would kill her.

"Deputy Willis and Deputy Clarence Oldman responded to the scene, where they observed both parties attempting to strike one another; however, I don't think either deputy actually observed either participant strike a blow.

"When Jasper saw Deputy Oldman approach, he took a swing at him, but missed. Deputy Oldman subdued Mr. Elrod and placed him under arrest."

Jasper jumped like he'd been bitten by a horse. "Judge, Slick kicked me in the balls! He liked to have kilt me! I didn't mean him no harm. I was drunk. That's all."

Bang! Bang! Bang! Judge Maxwell hammered his gavel.

"Order in the court! Mr. Elrod, you are out of order! Did you take a swing at Deputy Oldman or did you not?"

"Well, yes, Your Honor. I done that. I just wanted you to know he kicked me in the balls. He didn't have to do that. He coulda just thumped me one time with his stick. That woulda sobered me up and I'da stopped doin' wrong. My balls swole up and turned blue. I was dern near crippled for 'bout a month. Me 'n the old lady couldn't do it for at least that long. I'm sorry for what I done. I apologize to Slick, but he owes me one, too."

"Deputy Atwater, you may step down.

"Mr. Davis, do you wish to add anything?"

"No, Your Honor. I think that sums it up very well."

"I agree. Mr. Elrod, on the count of disorderly conduct, I sentence you to serve sixty days at hard labor in the county jail. I suspend the sentence for sixty days, under the following conditions.

"I spoke with Mr. George Cramer, Superintendent of the Quayle County Public Works Department. Are you familiar with Mr. Cramer and where his office is located at the county garage?"

"Yes, Sir."

"Good. Right now he happens to be shorthanded for entry level road crew workers. He agreed to employ you on a two-month temporary basis at my request. You will be paid the standard minimum wage of $1.10 per hour, to work forty hours per week, Monday through Friday, beginning tomorrow morning at 8 o'clock. Payday is each Friday at close of business.

"If you fail to appear at work sober, or if you are late even one day, he will call me. I will rescind this order, and you will serve the full sentence in the county jail where you will not be paid; however, you will work hard labor and you will do it for free. Very likely, you will do the same work, maybe even harder work, except you will be under the supervision of a deputy sheriff and not a public works department foreman. Do you understand?"

"Yes, Your Honor."

"Good, because I mean every word.

"In addition, I fine you $20 for contempt of court. You will pay that fine, plus $30 in court costs, by the completion of your sixty-day sentence. That's a total of $50 payable in cash to the Clerk of Court not later than October 9, 1969. If you fail to pay even one red cent by that date, you will be incarcerated at the rate of $2.00 per day until the debt is fulfilled. Is that clear?"

"Yes, Your Honor."

"Very well. Forty hours times $1.10 per hour is $44.00, before taxes. You will have eight weeks to earn $352.00 before taxes. You can continue to sell scrap metal to the junkyard on your own time. I expect you to work hard and to pay your debt to society. I mean it! If you botch this opportunity, you will rue the day you pleaded guilty to these charges. Understood?"

"Understood."

"Very well. Deputy Atwater, you may release this man from custody.

"Mr. Bellweather, not having any other matters before this court, it is hereby adjourned.

"Mr. Elton, I better never ever see you again in my court. I mean it!"

The ferocious bird of prey lifted off his perch and flew back into his inner sanctum.

CHAPTER 31

A HAPPY REUNION

It was 3 o'clock when they returned to the jail.

Jasper called his wife. He left to sit on one of the park benches in front of the courthouse while he waited for her to pick him up in his rusty chariot. It would be at least an hour in the hot sun. Barlow hoped it was a happy reunion.

Ernie showed Barlow how to close out a case, now that it was adjudicated.

3:45. Barlow finally had the opportunity to call Sarah at work. She answered on the first ring.

"Registrar's Office. Sarah speaking."

Barlow pinched his nose and began to speak softly in an effeminate, high-pitched, nasally lisp, doing his best to eliminate his North Texas drawl.

"Hewwo. Hewwo. Ith thith the pwathe where thumwone can thine up for cowwege cwatheth?"

"Yes it is. How may I be of assistance?"

"Do you have any cwatheth in athwowogy?"

"I'm sorry. Did you say anthropology?"

"No. Athwowogy. You know. Weading the athwowogical thine. Wike Wibwa or Pitheth."

"No. I'm sorry."

"Would you wike me to wead your thine?"

"Oh, no. Look, I really must go now."

"Wait. Your name is Tharah. You are bee-you-ti-vul. Would you wike to go out with me tonight? I been mithing you all week."

"Wait a minute. . . . Barlow, is that you?"

"Yeth. I'm tongue-tied. Thum angew named Tharah catht a thpell on me. I won't wetuwn to nomaw untiw you kith me."

Sarah smiled. She made a smooching sound and blew into the mouthpiece. "There I just blew you a kiss. That's more than you deserve. What are you, some kind of a nut?"

"I'm nuts about you. Did you miss me as much as I missed you?"

"You know I did. I was wondering all day if you would call."

Barlow sang, "'Buffalo Gal, can you come out tonight? Can you come out tonight? Can you come out tonight? Buffalo Gal, can you come out tonight and dance by the light of the moon?'"

"You think I have anything in common with a buffalo besides being a mammal? The way I recall it, buffalo gals were the fat homely chicks who worked in the brothels of the wild west towns.

"You want to go dancing in the pasture with a buffalo gal, dodging all the buffalo chips, Cowboy? Who's going to provide the music, coyotes?

"What exactly are you trying to say? I've been gone an entire week and I missed you terribly, but you aren't scoring any points, Mister."

"Touche! Not at all what I meant to convey.

"My interpretation of a buffalo gal is that she's a young, single woman who lives on the frontier. I'd say we live in a semi-frontier community. It is the frontier to someone who lives in Dallas or Houston. That's all. I never considered that a buffalo gal has the connotation of being a coyote ugly member of the world's oldest profession. Besides, I already said you were an angel. You ever seen any ugly angels?

"Let me start over. How would you like to break bread with me at Betty's or Crabtree's and then watch TV over at my house?"

"Well stated, Mr. Adams, on your second try. Nooooo. I don't think so. Too much time wasted in public. I told you how much I missed you. What if you pick up whatever you want for supper at the grocery and I'll cook it for you, and then we can cuddle up on the couch and watch TV?"

"You have a deal! Is there anything which sounds particularly good to you, Miss Baker?"

"Fried chicken and mashed potatoes, but that would take too much time. Pick up some minute steaks and whatever you want to go with it. Corn on the cob or baked beans or new potatoes. I don't care. If they have any pies in the bakery section that look good, get one of them, too."

"I'm on my way. See you soon."

"Don't dawdle. I missed you for way too long, Mr. Adams. Time is precious."

"Missed you more. Bye."

Barlow got a head start. He bolted out of the office at 4 o'clock and flew to the grocery. He got minute steaks, new potatoes, applesauce, and a peach pie.

He beat her home just long enough to use the bathroom and wash up.

When she stepped into the living room, it was like two electromagnets of opposite poles were sharing the same force field. She jumped into his arms. He lifted her off her feet and held her like he was afraid she would evaporate.

She had tears of joy in her eyes. She kissed his lips and neck and whispered that it wasn't any fun in Del Rio without him.

He sang softly, "'Ain't no sunshine when she's gone. It's not warm when she's away. Ain't no sunshine when she's gone. And she's always gone too long. Anytime she goes away.' I think they wrote that song for you."

"Don't, Silly. You're making me cry. Sit on the couch and hold me tight. Then I'll make supper."

"All I got was peanut butter and jelly."

"That's fine, as long as you bought some pie. What type did you get?"

"Peach."

"Good, I love peach. Now sit down and shush up and hold me tight. My hug-o-meter is sitting on empty. Just be still and let me luxuriate in your arms."

He held her for several passion-filled minutes. She smelled so uniquely pleasant and tantalizing. Sarahscent, he thought to himself. Nothing in the world like it.

Eventually, she collected herself and went poking around in the kitchen, looking for food. She found his recent purchases.

"You rat! I knew you were lying. I'm hungry, too. I didn't eat lunch. This looks really good. Do you still have any of that bourbon left, or the tequila?"

"I have some of both. What's your pleasure?"

"Bourbon."

"My favorite. Looks like I need to replenish soon. I really need to find a reliable source. It wouldn't do for the underage, puny, scrawny deputy to get caught trying to procure the demon alcohol."

"Ask, Slick. He's simpatico and he'll keep his mouth shut. I don't think Sheriff Sol cares that you drink, but he would care if it were reported to him that you were caught buying underage."

"How do you know Slick's simpatico?"

"Come on, Barlow. This is a small town. Slick services all the single women over 40 who are in need of male companionship. Everyone knows that. I heard he's a master at it, too.

"I bet he thinks you're just like him. Single, and servicing all the young chicks who are . . . horny, shall we say? Of course, he would lend you a hand."

"One of those secrets no one says out loud?"

"Now you got it."

"And I'm the new Lothario for the young gals?"

"Probably so. You're young, single, good-looking, and I know from personal experience that you're randy. Why wouldn't he think it?"

"Heck, Sarah, I don't even see any girls socially, except for you. Do you think that he thinks that we're . . . . .?"

"Probably. It wouldn't matter to him. He wouldn't think less of me, although many others would.

"He sees you as a younger version of himself. You're a lot like him, you know. Good looking, brave, combat veteran, lawman, passionate about life, and women, I might add, who does everything with zest or gusto. You should be flattered. Next time you see him, slip him a $5 and ask if he could get you a bottle."

"Well, I hope he does think that well of me, although we've never spoken about women. Maybe I'll give it a shot. We do need some more adult libations."

"Trust me on that."

"Well I have another question. Do you think Sheriff Sol cares if you drink?"

"He knows Mom and Dad let me drink beer at their soirees. But he might think you were trying to take advantage of me. I think it best he doesn't know until we're both 21."

"So do you think I'm plying you with alcohol to take advantage of you?"

"Oh my! You naughty boy! I would certainly hope so!"

"Huh?"

"What would be the corollary? That you don't need to ply me with alcohol because I'm such an easy target? Worse yet, we both need to get wasted because I'm so grisly you couldn't perform otherwise?

"Did you forget? I'm the one who asked you for an adult beverage."

"You slay me! You're the most beautiful woman I've ever seen. I'm aching inside because I want you so bad. I'm about to explode. I've never felt this way before."

"I know. Me too. I like to tease you. It arouses me to arouse you.

"I'm so bad! Wicked! Unladylike. The preacher would be mortified if he knew the thoughts I've been having. Not kidding.

"I don't know what I'm doing. I'm a complete mess. I never ever wanted to be with a man before I met you. Now I think about it all the time. I'm afraid I'll lose complete control if I allow Mother Nature to take her course. I might become insatiable, a nymphomaniac.

"What if you get tired of me and leave? I couldn't stand it.

"I keep reminding myself that we've only known each other for a month. Are we in love or are we in lust?

"Oh, Barlow! I hate doubting you, or myself."

"So you do want me as much as I want you?"

"Yes, Silly. Of course. I do, but I need some time to sort it out. This isn't like me. I'm all over the place. I don't want you to get frustrated with me and go find someone else who isn't so conflicted."

"Hey. Hey. Hey. Cupid shot me in the heart the exact moment I laid eyes on you. I haven't been the same since. I'm smitten. I could never leave you."

"You think Cupid did this to us?"

"Well, he did to me. You haven't said anything about yourself."

"Cupid's not real, Silly. He's just a chubby little nudie boy with a bow and arrow on Valentine cards."

"How do you know he isn't real? Maybe he's one of God's angels. Who's to say he isn't? Not all God's angels are listed by name in the Bible. All I know is what I felt as soon as I saw you. That's as real as it gets to me."

"Barlow, you do make a compelling argument. I'm not about to naysay it. I hope you are 100% correct. Perhaps I felt the same thing at the very same time, but didn't know what it was."

"There you go."

"So it's okay, then? You don't mind if I take some time to work through this? You won't seek solace elsewhere?"

"Sarah, Sarah, Sarah. I'm in this for the long haul. Like infinity. I don't want any other woman. It's fine. Take your time.

I can wait. But here's the deal. I can resist anything but temptation. If you tempt me too much, I may not be able to hold myself in check."

"Fair enough and thank you. I'll try not to tease you so wickedly, but I still need your hugs and kisses. And I promise, I'll figure this out before long."

"I know."

They ate. They snuggled. She went home at 9 o'clock.

CHAPTER 32

A MISCOMPREHENSION IS EXPLAINED

Tuesday, August 12th. Barlow rolled in for work early, at 6:30. Archie was still on duty, all alone. Just what he was hoping for.

"Well, look out! It's Barlow from Arlo! Get yourself a cuppa joe. How you been doing, Deputy?"

"Great, Arch. How about yourself?"

"Well, this job gets funner and funner each day. I'll never retire. They'll have to kill me to get rid of me."

"How's that?"

"I heard Old Jasper Elrod told Judge Sweeney and the whole wide world that his balls swole up after our little misunderstanding and he couldn't service Old Rose for at least a month."

"True. All true."

"Hell, he'll never live that one down! What was he thinking? Some jaybird will throw it in his face and he'll fly off the handle and beat the shit out of that fool, and then we'll have to babysit him for at least two months!"

"Oh, I hope not."

"Me neither.

"I also hear you and Ernie got another scofflaw to go hogtie today."

"We do, but I don't know who it is."

"Well, I do. Right here's the file with his picture.

"His name is Duncan Fish. He's a white male, 37 years of age, 5'11" tall, 175 pounds, slight beer belly, reddish hair, blue eyes, born in Eagle Pass over in Maverick County, but last known to still be living in McCamey in Upton County. He's your basic shithead."

"That's what we got him on, being a shithead?"

"We ort to 'ave. Too bad it ain't in the statute book. You don't know this guy, Barlow.

"Let me start from the beginning. Sheriff Sol, Ernie, and Duncan Fish all turned eighteen in 1950.

"Know what was going on? I'll tell you what was going on. Korea, full bore. Sheriff Sol enlisted in the Navy. Ernie enlisted in the Army, and this piece of shit gets hisself classified IV-F.

"You wanna know why? Because he already had a felony conviction for armed robbery at age sixteen. That's why! He robbed some ma and pa grocery in Eagle Pass, shot the place up, luckily no one got hurt, tried to outrun the police, crashed his car, and got caught.

"The judge let him off easy. Give him five years instead of life, because he was still a juvie. Somehow or other, he got hisself paroled in two.

"Then he gets on the rodeo circuit, something he learned to do in Huntsville. Ain't that sweet? He's riding for pussy and belt buckles, while Sheriff Sol and Ern are fighting the Reds in Korea.

"Apparently he couldn't handle prosperity. There was this calf roping cowboy named Eugene Potts. He and Duncan were neck and neck in competition. I read about them in the papers all the time. Eugene began pulling ahead and Old Duncan got jealous. He planted a burr under Eugene's saddle in one of the big competitions, and Eugene took a spill. Fortunately, he wasn't hurt too bad, but he lost the competition.

"The good news is, Duncan got caught and the PRCA barred him for life.

"After that, he went to work in the oil fields. I lost track of him and all his wrongdoing.

"Then several months ago, May 2nd, to be exact, this stellar citizen began stealing chickens over at the Slash 6, close to where Alberto Gomez's Rocking A is at.

"Miz Kitty Loveless is a widow woman. Owns the ranch and lives by herself. Doesn't even own a dog, but I believe she does have a cat. Her husband, Hugh, died a few years ago. She's one of the widow women Slick services ever so often. He's kinda sweet on her, too. When you see her, you'll understand what I mean.

"Anyway, she noticed that her chickens started disappearing. No signs of coyotes or foxes. She started staying up at night with the lights off to see if she could figure out what was going on.

"Well, about 2 a.m. on May 2nd, she hears a car quietly coming up her drive. It has the lights off. It stopped about halfway up. Fortunately, it was nearly a full moon, plus the farm yard light, and she could make it out clearly. It was a turquoise, 1965, Studebaker Daytona sedan! Turquoise! She didn't know the make or year or model, but she recognized it because of the color.

"She sees a man get out and creep up into her chicken house. She recognized him, too! He scooped up five or six chickens, put 'em in a gunny sack and ran back to his car.

"About the time he goes to get back in his car, she unloaded with two barrels of 00 buck. Blasted the heck out of the car, but he got away. Didn't matter none. She knew who it was and so did we.

"Yessir! You guessed correctly! It was Duncan Fish. He took that car off of an old, drunk, retired railroad engineer, named Jesse Whitcomb, in a poker game at the Horned Toad Saloon in Dryden. He probably cheated to win, too. The car was white, but Old Dunc, our self-proclaimed stud duck of McCamey, Texas, painted it turquoise to impress all the cougars in all the low rent honky-tonks, something like an advertisement. Wanted them to know when he was in their neighborhood, in case any of 'em were in need of a tune up.

"She says it ain't so, but I suspect maybe Dunc the Hunk plied his peckerwood charm on Miz Kitty once upon a time, afore Slick started stopping by.

"Later that morning, our very own Deputy Randy Meacham drove up to Upton County and joined forces with one of their deputies. They went out to Duncan's most recent girlfriend's place, a woman named Aline Tucker, him not having a place of his own, at least back then. His car was there in the yard, riddled with buckshot holes in the left rear fender and quarter panel.

"They also found the gunny sack, splattered with feathers and chickenshit all over it, and later, they recovered four of what turned out to be six stolen chickens according to Miz Kitty.

"Later on, besides her say so, Duncan admitted two of 'em got away and fussed that they shouldn't be held against him. It's probably the truth, as they really didn't have time to pluck and fry and eat two chickens, with as much fornicating as they was doing in such a short period of time.

"You see, Duncan and Aline was busy playing bury the bone, and they never knew the police was there until it was too late. Randy snatched him up right out of the saddle and put the bracelets on him without so much as a fight. Brought him straight back to Mosby.

"Said he had to fumigate the car when he was done 'cause Duncan smelled like b.o., stale whiskey, cigarette smoke, cheap perfume, raw sex and who knows what all. Said he liked to never got the smell out of the car. After that, I changed Dunc the Hunk's name to Dunc the Skunk.

"Anyway, Dunc the Skunk posted a $5,000 bond and that was it. Never came back.

"Truth is, I'm surprised Big Buddha (Ralphie) Krebbs, or Stubby Markwell, the bail bondsmen, ain't picked him up yet. They stand to lose all five grand if he don't appear in court. In fact, I'll check on that later on before I wrap up. If they have any new information on him, I'll call you all on the radio. If that don't work, I'll leave a message for you all at the Upton SO.

"So, the rest of the story is, we ran Duncan's rap sheet in May, and he has at least five additional arrests prior to the one for impersonating the Chicken Man.

"They was all misdemeanors except for the armed robbery and a grand larceny from a saddle and tack business in El Paso. Hell! I believe it's the one where Jake buys our gun belts, where Old Dunc absconded with a saddle and bridle, plus the saddlebags, all of which was decorated with silver conchos. Very distinctive. EPPD recovered the goods, but Duncan drew a lenient judge again, so he only got a year to serve on that one.

"But you wanna know what the best part of this sad sack story is?

"Stealing a fowl worth more than $2.00 is a felony! They passed that law back during the Depression when the farmers and ranchers was getting robbed blind by all the hobos. It's still on the books.

"That bastard is up for his third felony! I bet Maximum Max lowers the boom and sends him up the river for five years!"

"I hope we find him today."

"There's no doubt you will. Ern's a bloodhound. It might take all day, but I'll bet a dollar to a doughnut hole right now, you'll find him."

"Not betting against Ern or myself.

"Say, before he gets here, there's something I need to ask. It's real personal and private."

"Whatever can I do for ya, young laddie?"

"Well, it's like this. When we were arresting Jasper yesterday, before he surrendered, he asked Ernie who the scrawny, puny, underaged deputy was, which I will tell you right now, I took offense to.

"Ern said I was the dude who shot and killed Sandra Tafts attacker. He said Sheriff Sol sent me up there with him in case things broke bad.

"Then Jasper asked if the sheriff sent me up there to shoot him.

"Ern said, 'Not unless he has to.' That seemed to

discombobulate Jasper, and he just up and surrendered.

"Do you think folks around here look at me like some kind of a dangerous killer?"

"There's some what probably do. Mostly the ones who wouldn't fight for theirselves or anyone else, no matter how bad things got. The ones what thinks violence is never the answer. You know the type. I wouldn't worry none about them.

"Ern said that, 'cause Jasper's a known police fighter, and he's truly dangerous. He really is. He's the sort who'd go into a blind rage and kill you or another deputy to avoid arrest, and then feel real bad about it later on, for a little while at least, until something else crossed his mind. He ain't a deep thinker.

"Jasper was sizing you up, thinking he could devour you in two bites 'cause he's so much bigger and stronger, but mostly meaner.

"That's why he took on Slick, 'cause he's littler than me. Besides, Jasper knows I'm too old to put up with his shit. He probably figures, correctly too, that I'd just blow a hole in him the size of a baseball and be done with him. Call the hearse to haul his carcass off.

"But he fucked up. He underestimated Slick. Thought he'd be a cupcake. Gobble him up in one bite. He ain't the first asshole who's made that mistake and paid for it dearly. Slick's as lethal as a pygmy rattler.

"Yep, he really fucked up! Cost him a whole month of pleasuring Rose, plus now he's proclaimed it to the whole wide world. Ha! What a dumbass!

"Ern wanted Jasper to fear you, so you will never have to fight him, and now I bet you never will.

"You know, we wouldn't have to fight any of these badasses, if they thought we took a hiatus on giving them a chance to kick our asses, and instead, went straight for the six-shooter to settle all issues of resisting arrest, quickly and permanently. All that by-the-book, Marquis of Queensbury rules and Dudley Do-Right nonsense be damned! You know, like Ripsnort Sweeney did around here when he tamed this land, or the Texas Rangers when I was coming up. Not like, in fact, just the opposite of the TV cops you see on Dragnet, who never get shot or hurt, or if they do, have a full recovery in thirty minutes.

"What you gotta remember is, you ain't getting paid to fight or get killed. You get paid to enforce the law fairly and objectively, without favor to no one. The idea is, you come home in one piece at the end of shift, and if anyone does go to the hospital or the morgue, it's the violator. Savvy?"

"Savvy. I was hoping that's what Ern was doing. I just wasn't sure. I hope I don't sound like a wimp."

"Put your mind at ease, Laddie. Seriously. Ern was doing you a solid regarding that jackass. Jasper'll never look at you again, without thinking you'd blow him away if he got out of line. And, you need to consider that a serious option each time you have contact with him. If he ever got you on the ground, he'd kill you for sure."

"Thanks, Arch."

It was 7:45. Ern came in. He told Barlow to check out a shotgun and the Chevy while he got the file together and made a call.

Issue resolved. Barlow was loving life, once again.

CHAPTER 33

ANOTHER LESSON IN POLICING

"You know how to get to McCamey?"

"Roger that. I looked it up."

"Good. Did you pack a lunch?"

"I did. It's in the trunk in the cooler next to yours."

"Very good."

"Quayle Base, this is Quayle 47 en route to McCamey."

"Quayle Base 10-4. Good hunting."

"Arch fill you in?"

"He did. I looked at Fish's photos. I think I'd know him anywhere. Are we going to the girlfriend's house?"

"Maybe. I called Deputy Marvin Early from Upton SO. He's going to meet us at the Sinclair station in town. By the way, they call him Deputy Dawg 'cause he has a long hound dog face and big ears. He's a good guy. Takes the joshing pretty well. He's bringing another deputy with him. They're not sure Duncan's still with that gal."

"How come?"

"They said she was humiliated having three cops bust in on her when Dunc the Hunk was knocking the bottom out of it. Said she was squealing so loud, they heard her outside and thought Dunc mighta been whaling on her. That's hows come they rushed in. Instead, she was in the throes of ecstasy."

"Well, I reckon she would be embarrassed."

"No. I don't think you really do. Can you truly imagine it? Think of your grandma catching you in the backseat with your girlfriend, or better yet, the high school principal. Everyone in town would know. The story would be told over and over again, and exaggerated until it came out you was begging her to spank you so you could get it up."

"Oh, my gosh! That's dreadful! Are you serious?"

"Serious as a cocked .45 pointed right between your eyes."

"That would be pretty awful. Probably be the end of everything that's near and dear to me."

Barlow was silent for a few minutes, contemplating the ramifications if it were Sarah and him. Finally, he asked, "Life gets kinda gritty, doesn't it?"

"It does, Barlow. Look, I know you probably saw and did lots of things in Vietnam you probably wished you hadn't. Same thing for me in Korea. We bury those things in the deepest corners of our mind, because they happened thousands of miles away and bear no semblance to reality as we know it here in the States.

"Law enforcement is similar. Just like soldiers, we see and do things that a lot of people never get confronted with. An accountant in a nice office is unlikely to get the shit scared out of him very often, or be forced to make split-second, life and death decisions like a lawman. Sometimes we get cornered into making a bad decision versus a worse one. Your life, your partner's life, maybe a citizen's life, plus your job, and maybe even your freedom are always on the line. You're still playing for all the marbles, just like a soldier in a combat zone.

"The difference is, it never stops. Your combat zone is right here, in America, where you live and the bad guys don't wear uniforms. You can't rationalize that what happened was 'a long time ago in a land far, far, away.' It's here, now. Today. Every time you suit up.

"But that's also the thrill of it. That's why you do this instead of fixing cars. You like the challenge, seeing and doing something different most of the time, catching bad guys, saving maidens, being the hero.

"The key is to not get dragged down into the mire and

depravity that you will encounter, oftentimes when you least expect it. Women will offer you sex, and crooks will offer you money just to look the other way. If you fall short, just one time, even for something minor, you'll be a target for blackmail the rest of your life. Eventually it will all come out and you'll go from hero to pariah in a split second."

Barlow was quiet again. All he said was, "Sobering thoughts. Thanks for putting this all in perspective for me."

Later, he asked, "What's Aline Tucker look like?"

"Not bad for a steamer. Nice body. About 40. Red hair. Definitely a game jersey with sort of a practice helmet, but not quite. Like the song says, she's a 10 at closing time."

"Well, did she kick him out?"

"Marvin's not sure. They was separated for awhile. He heard they got back together, but he hasn't seen 'em together. Also, they don't know what he done with his car. They ain't seen it in about a month. They think he stashed it on account of him not showing up for court. They're pretty sure he's laying low."

"How long since they've seen him?"

"Well, about a week for Marvin, but someone he knows seen him at the Pink Pussycat Roadhouse night before last. Said Marvin was alone, hitting on this fat chick named Queenie."

"Are you kidding? What on Earth for? Is he that desperate now?"

"Believe he is for money. Queenie's a divorcee with a big house in Rankin. Ex-husband had lots of oil wells. Now he has a gorgeous 21-year-old stripper girlfriend and a few less oil wells. Queenie drives a Cadillac Sedan de Ville. Bright red. Supposedly she pays generously and gives nice jewelry to stud muffins who can ring her bell. If he ain't with Aline, we'll check her next."

"He'll be tough to find if he isn't driving that Studebaker."

"As long as he's still in Upton County, Marvin and us will find him. If he's moved to another county, well, we probably won't round him up today."

"Man, oh man, I hope we find him. I go on mids tonight, and I probably won't get another chance to catch this guy."

"Well, don't give up yet. We ain't even started. I'm pretty sure we'll catch him."

"This guy a fighter?"

"Oh, hell no. A guy who won't fight when he's interrupted fucking ain't no fighter. But he is fast and might be a runner, so be prepared."

"You mean to run him down?"

"Barlow, you're a good kid. You're in great shape. Now look at me. Do you really think God made this body for running? The deal betwixt you and me is this. You chase 'em and catch 'em, and hold 'em for me. I'll beat the tar out of 'em for making you run. Savvy?"

"Savvy. You coulda told me this yesterday."

"Yesterday we was after Jasper. Jasper don't run. He fights, and he fights dirty. He gouges eyes, bites ears, head butts, anything to win. That's why it's so funny Slick ended their little set to by kicking him in the nuts. That's something Jasper would do. Got a big dose of his own medicine. Serves him right."

They continued the banter the whole way to McCamey, something over a hundred miles. Deputy Dawg and his partner were waiting at the Sinclair when they arrived.

"Well hello there, Dawg! How's it hanging?"

"Loose as a goose, you old buzzard. Hey, you figure you don't hafta shave and you can wear wrinkly clothes on account of you ain't working in Quayle County today? Sheriff Sol see that stubbly face of yourn?"

"You said it! Sheriff Sol don't mind. He knows I have more hair on my ass than the likes of you. What's it matter? Besides that, old Dunc the Hunk won't pay it no never mind. He sees your butt ugly face, he'll just keel on over an' die from fright."

"Sheeeit. You figure on plucking him up outa the saddle like Randy done? Could be a mite tough if he's plowing Queenie.

She's a big old gal, used to getting her own way. Won't like it one bit if you cause a coitus interruptus like what happened to Aline. She might take a squat on you and rub your little pecker down to a nub."

"Jeez, Dawg, you're making me squeamish in front of my new pard. This here is Barlow Adams. He's a newbie, but he's a scrapper."

Dawg extended his paw. "Glad to meetcha. Any friend of Ern's is a friend of mine. This here is my partner, Enos 'Copperhead' Bowling. Call him that on account of his bright red hair that he wears all slicked back. With those squinty eyes, makes him look like a snake."

They shook hands all around.

"Well, you boys need to make a pit stop, or are you ready to visit Aline Tucker?"

They opted for the former. Ern said, "Barlow, let's top off before we hit the road. We don't wanna get stranded."

Barlow asked, "How do we pay for it?"

"Ern said, "Got five bucks you can spare until we get back to the jail? Turn in a receipt and Miss Loretta will make you whole. If you don't, I'll get it; but normal procedure is for the driver to pay. I just never thought about it when I told you to drive."

"No, I got it."

Barlow topped off. It took 8.3 gallons at 33.9 cents per gallon, or $2.82.

Just before they departed, Dawg said, "Ern, there's something you orta know before we put the habeas grabbus on Fish."

"What's that?"

"Sheriff told me this morning that Dunc broke into his sister's house last night and stole some cash, a little jewelry, and his brother-in-law's Luger that he brought back home from World War II. If we catch him, we're locking him up here. We'll hold him on your warrants, and wait for you all to file a detainer, but you won't get to drag his ass back to Mosby. We got first dibs. I hope that don't sour our relationship. I didn't know this when you called."

"Hell, Dawg! That suits us to a 'T!' Now we don't have to take turns babysitting him in our calaboose.

"Does that suit you, Barlow?"

"Suits me. All I care about is being in on the arrest."

Dawg responded, "Oh, you'll be in on the arrest. Things has changed, though. Now he's armed. We're not sure if he'll try to shoot his way out of capture."

Ern asked, "Well, does he have any ammo for that gun? It fires a necked-down 7.65 by 21-millimeter cartridge. They ain't as common around here as they are in Germany."

"Oh, he's got ammo, all right. Casper Downs loved that gun. He had a couple of cases of ammo, plus a spare magazine. He kept it in a Nazi gun belt with a holster that had a spare magazine pouch. Dunc didn't steal the leather, just the gun, spare magazine, and a case of ammo. He's got 1000 rounds."

"How's the sheriff know it's Dunc?"

"They was coming back home when they saw Dunc driving off like Mario Andretti in that turquoise Studebaker. They didn't know why he was in such a hurry until they got home and saw their front door was busted open and their stuff was missing."

"What time was this?"

"Not sure, but I know it was after midnight."

"You all still think he's at Aline's?"

"Not for sure, but that's the best place to look first."

"Well let's go then. If he pulls that pistol, don't expect us to hold back. We'll drill him like an oil well."

"You'll have to shoot fast to beat us. Come on. Follow me."

CHAPTER 34

SEARCHING FOR AN ARMED FUGITIVE

When they saw the house, they slowed down to a crawl to check it out. Dunc's car was not in sight, but Aline's blue, '67 Mustang convertible was.

Ern told Barlow to take the rear. Dawg said the same to Copperhead. Ern said he and Dawg would take the front. Further instructions were to wait unless Dunc burst out the back door, or they heard shooting or hollering to come help.

Before they could get completely situated, Aline answered the door. "What is it, Dawg?"

"Miss Aline, is Duncan Fish here?"

"Why, what'd he do?"

"Well, this deputy here has paper on him for failure to appear in court in Mosby. You remember when we arrested him here back in May?"

"How could I forget? I'll never live down the embarrassment! He shamed me, Dawg. I'm not that kind of woman. He sweet talked me into letting him have his way. I thought he loved me, but he was just using me. I'll never live this down as long as I live."

"Miss Aline, we don't think no worse of you at the sheriff's office. We know what kind of low-down varmint he is. We can just imagine what he must've said to get you to let down your guard. We know you're a good church woman, who was momentarily deceived by Satan, hisself. You don't have to hold your head down around us, Darlin'."

"Well, that makes me feel a whole lot better. I been too ashamed to go to church until recently. Some of those old biddies still give me awful looks and turn their backs on me whenever they see me."

"Miss, Aline, I bet more'n one of them has been deceived by the Devil, theirselves. You just ain't heard about it."

"You're probably right, Marvin. Would you fellas like to come in? I could make some coffee."

"No, Ma'am, we just need to talk to Duncan iff'n he's here."

"No, he ain't! I never want to see that awful man again!"

"Would you have any idea where he might be staying?"

"Well, I don't keep tabs on him, but I heard he taken up with Peggy Higginbottom, but I think they parted ways. Something about she needed him to fix the toilet that was leaking and he told her to go pee in the yard."

"How long ago was that?"

"Oh, I don't know. Last week sometime when I was at the IGA. Nancy Weeks told me. She would know because she and Peggy spend a lot of time together at Amos' Bar and Grill trying to get picked up by the likes of men like Duncan Fish."

"Well if he ain't with Peggy, where might he be?"

"I really couldn't tell you. He likes to go to the Pink Pussycat. I know he's broke. Queenie Melton is always there looking for male companionship. I heard she pays for it, too. Usually goes after the real young boys, teenagers if possible, because they have more stamina, or so she says. I wouldn't know myself.

"He might be staying with her until he's got a bankroll, but I hafta say, Marvin, pleasuring that woman, fat and mean as she is, would be far more work than a shiftless bum like Duncan Fish is used to doing."

"Well, thanks for your time, Miss Aline. Look forward to seeing you again."

"You, too. Bye, now. You stop by anytime. Ya hear? Bye."

Ern called off Barlow and Copperhead. They loaded back up, Dawg leading the way.

Before they left, Dawg said, "Queenie will be a delicate

situation. She's mean, rich, has a nasty lawyer named Oscar Krauss on retainer, usually has a few boy toys hanging about which she likes to sic on people like they was junkyard dogs, and she files complaints on everyone about everything. However, Sheriff Harned is real pissed off about his sister's house being burglarized, and he don't care whose toes get stepped on to catch Duncan Fish. If Queenie's harboring a fugitive, Sheriff Harned will stick it up her ass, fancy lawyer or not."

Ern said, "Why would she have boy toys hanging around if she goes to the Pink Pussycat every night to pick up a new guy to get laid?"

"Because they say she's a nymphomaniac and can't get enough. Word is, she'll take on six or eight guys at one time and wear 'em all out. And since she pays 'em well to do it, they all just suck it up. I hear tell she pays guys as much as $100 a night! If you could do it with your eyes screwed shut, it just might be worth it."

It didn't take long to get to Rankin. Queenie had a big sprawling ranch house with stables in the back. The whole thing was surrounded by a white rail fence. A half dozen well-kept Arabians were grazing in the side pasture.

Barlow watched a couple of boy toy cowboys start heading their way from the nearest stable. He could see they were well muscled and would probably be a handful if they were in a position to dictate how a fight was going to go down. Forewarned is forearmed. He'd definitely get out with his stick on this occasion.

Before they got out, Ern said, "You and Copperhead take a look in the outbuildings. They're all wide open. See if you can find Duncan's car. Let Copperhead take the lead. He may know these guys. Be nice if they let you. If not, if they threaten or impede you in any way, take 'em down and put 'em in cuffs. Dawg and I will deal with Queenie. But, if Duncan ain't here, we'd prefer to leave without having to haul assholes to the Upton

County Jail. Saavy?"

"You got it."

Copperhead knew the two guys. He said, "God dang, Butch, you're crawling kinda low on your belly, ain't cha, working for Mrs. Melton! Shit, Clint, don't tell me your doing a little work between the sheets, too?"

Butch said, "Hell, Copperhead, this is easy money for a man who can go more than a couple two-minute rounds a night. And, if you ever had a mind to do something kinky, this woman will definitely oblige you. We make more money in a few days than you make all month. Plus, we don't pay no taxes and she buys all the beer and groceries. If I only last here a month, I'll have at least $2,000 in my pocket, plus I got this new, gold, Ball railroad watch, and this here gold onyx ring with my initial on it. The sheriff's office gonna do all that for you?"

"No, I reckon not. You boys are rolling in clover. Ha! No pun intended. Say, the reason we're here is, we're looking for Duncan Fish. You all seen him?"

"Oh, yeah, that asshole was here for a couple of nights. She run him off last night. He was some kind of pissed off. Thought we might have to kick his ass, but it didn't come to that."

"Gosh, what brought all this about?"

"Well, Queenie can be a difficult person. She has meltdowns, temper tantrums. I 'spect she got a hair up her ass and just up and told him to shove off."

"What time was that?"

"Oh, about 10 o'clock. Then me'n Clint spent the next couple of hours riding her like she was some deranged elephant. Truth is, Dunc is a real hombre when he's in the saddle. We was wishing he coulda been here to spell us. She liked to have broke both our backs."

"Any idea, where Dunc would go?"

"Well, I'm not sure. Let me think. You got any ideas, Clint?"

"Not really. I heard when he's out of options, like every time he gets his ass run off, he stays with that old Apache woman who lives in a 20-year-old house trailer about five miles down Highway 349. You turn off at the old Marathon station on a skinny little goat path. Go another mile or two. It's in the middle of nowhere. You'd never find it, if someone didn't tell you how to get there."

"What's her name? Know what she drives?"

"Yeah, they call her Thundercloud. She's usually on horseback, an appaloosa or a paint, but I have seen her a time or two in a wore out old Ford pickup truck."

"What color?"

"It was probably green at one time. It's so faded it's hard to say."

"Is she friendly?"

"Most of the time. She wears a long hunting knife, real sharp because she skins with it, and she carries a hundred-year-old 30-30, but I never heard of her threatening anybody.

"You know, she's an Indian. She can hunt out of season whenever she wants. Nobody's going to say anything. Plus, you know, she eats ever bit of what she kills. She probably even boils the horns and eats them, too."

"Well, thanks guys. We appreciate it. You all take care."

"You, too. By the way, what's he done?"

"Oh, right now Quayle County's got paper on him on account of he failed to appear in court."

"What did he do in Quayle?"

Barlow said, "If you can believe this, he broke into some widow woman's henhouse and stole six chickens."

"That stupid bastard. That's just like him to do something as dumb as that."

"Well thanks again, Guys."

"Da nada."

The senior deputies were already waiting for them when Barlow and Copperhead returned to the cars.

Barlow asked, "She tell you anything helpful?"

Dawg said, "Not really. She said she ran him off last night about 10 or 11 o'clock. She doesn't know where he went and she doesn't care. Did you all learn anything?"

Copperhead said, "Yes, in fact, we did. Butch didn't know, but Clint said whenever Dunc is homeless, he stays with an old Apache woman named Thundercloud at her house trailer down off 349 where the old Marathon station is."

"Dawg said, "I know her! I've been to her house. She's a pretty good shit. Come on. Follow me."

CHAPTER 35

DUNC THE HUNK TAKES A DIVE

The trip to RR 4, Box 64, Rankin, Texas, residence of Thundercloud Hopewell, took less than a half-hour. Duncan's car was parked out front. The bullet holes had been fixed. You could never tell it had been shot up.

As per their plan, the four deputies drew their firearms, took cover, and spread out. The front and rear doors to the trailer were on the same side about twelve feet apart. The windows, front and back, were too small for a man to crawl through. If Duncan were inside, the only avenue of escape would be through the front doors where the deputies were waiting.

Besides the trailer, the yard contained an open, three-sided shed with a paint mare in a stall. Miz Thundercloud had a clothesline with sturdy posts and cross beams made of twelve-inch diameter tree trunks, with a pulley, which also doubled as a place to hoist and skin animals. She also had a 55-gallon drum where she burned trash, a small chicken coop with a dozen chickens, a hand water pump, a small garden, wooden frames of various sizes to dry skins, assorted buckets, tools, and a hose all coiled up. It was obvious that she lived off the land.

The old, faded Ford was parked in the rear. The left front tire was flat. That was the whole shebang, besides an outhouse in the very back. Barlow checked it, just to be sure. It was smelly and had a nest with wasps buzzing all around, but otherwise unoccupied.

Dawg said, "They know we're here. I'll knock on the door. Hopefully, we can handle this peacefully."

He knocked on the door and then stepped down off the steps

back into the yard.

"Miz Thundercloud, this is Dawg. Would you answer the door please?"

The door opened a crack. "What is it Dawg? Why do you come with armed men to bother me? I have wronged no one."

"Miz Thundercloud, we've come for Duncan Fish. Will you ask him to come out?"

"Why should I do that? He's my guest."

"We have a warrant for his arrest. He needs to come with us. We don't want any trouble from anybody, but we're prepared to do what it takes."

She shut the door. They could hear some muffled talking and shuffling of feet.

A minute passed. Then two. They were about to make a forced entry when the door opened a crack, such that those standing on the right could see Duncan Fish. He said, "Dawg, why are you fucking with me? I'm sick and tired of being hounded by the law."

"Duncan, come on out. Hands in the air. I mean it. We don't want to shoot you but we will. Is that what you want?"

"Fuck you, Dawg. I ain't scared of you or none of your asshole deputies. Maybe you're the one what'll get shot."

"Suit yourself. Tell Miz Thundercloud if she doesn't want to get hit by a stray bullet, she ort to come out now."

Duncan started to say something, but his words erupted into a grunt and a squeal and a thud as he came flying out the door, landing on his face next to a fire ant hill. He had Casper Downs' pistol in his hand, but he dropped it when he landed.

Ern was the first one to get to him. He kicked Dunc hard in the gut, rolled him over on his stomach, and snapped the cuffs on his wrists. He jerked him up and pushed him face down over the hood of the cruiser. He took everything out of his pockets before turning him over to Copperhead, who put him in the UCSO cruiser.

Barlow picked up the gun. It was loaded with a round in the chamber.

Dawg shouted to Miz Thundercloud. "Did you throw him out?"

"Dern right, I did! I don't want my place all shot up. I didn't know he was wanted by the law. Get him outa here. Duncan Fish, don't ever harken my door again! You hear? If you do, I'll skin you alive, carve you up like a rattlesnake, and make a pair of moccasins outa your hide for my daughter-in-law. She's partial to snake."

"Miz Thundercloud, can I come in and get his belongings?"

"You can look, but he don't have nothing in here. Check his car. What all are you looking for?"

"He broke into Sheriff Harned's sister's house last night. Stole that pistol and some jewelry and cash and a watch, I think."

"Well Dawg, come and see. Satisfy your curiosity. That stuff ain't in here, or it better not be. If you find it, take it. Take his car, too. Get it outa my sight. Then you all go and leave me alone. I never have a problem at all until I truck with the white man."

Dawg searched the trailer, but like the old woman said, nothing there belonged to Duncan or the Downs'.

Copperhead popped the trunk and found the opened case of ammo, a spare Luger magazine, a Hamilton watch, a silver charm bracelet, a set of silver cufflinks, and a man's Upton County High School ring.

Dawg searched Duncan's wallet and found $154 in cash. No doubt that most, if not all of it, came from the Downs' house, but it might be hard to prove.

Copperhead drove Dunc's car to the sheriff's office. Dawg transported the prisoner. Barlow and Ern brought up the rear. Sheriff Harned was waiting for them when they arrived.

"Well, boys, looks like you all been doing the Lord's work. Congratulations! You all toss that piece of shit real good?"

"Dawg said, "You bet, Sheriff. We got everything out of his

pockets. He ain't holding so much as a gum wrapper."

"Good. Put his ass in holding. I need to talk to Ernie and his sidekick. Boys, come on into my office."

Ernie and Barlow followed him. He motioned for them to take seats in front of his desk.

"Monica, bring us a Coca Cola!"

"Coming, Sheriff."

"Well, Ernie, introduce me to your partner."

"Sheriff Harned, this is Deputy Barlow Adams. He's our new hire. A good man."

"I can see that he is."

Sheriff Harned extended his hand and offered it to Barlow. Barlow grabbed it and held on for a vigorous shake.

"Boys, did Dawg tell you all what Mr. Fish did in Upton County last night?"

Ern answered, "Yes, Sir. I think we recovered all the loot."

"That's what Copperhead said. Glad to hear it. You all understand that all the felony charges we're fixing to stack on him take precedence to us, over chicken thieving and jumping bail."

"We do, Sheriff. It's okay by us. We'll need to give Sheriff Pratt a call first, before we go, but I'm sure he won't mind."

"Feel free to use my phone. Rest assured, though, I already talked to Sheriff Sol and he's fine with it, too. We'll be glad to serve your warrants on him, and as soon as Chief Alex gets a detainer, he can serve it or we will. Don't make no never mind to me. One thing's for sure. Old Dunc the Hunk won't be released from this jail until DOC comes to take him back to the Texas State Penitentiary in Huntsville, or the judge tells us to release him to you all to face charges in Quayle. Are we square?"

"We're square."

"Good. Go ahead and call Sol. When you're done, I'd be glad to treat you all to the finest beef brisket barbecue in all of Texas."

"Where's that?"

"Polecat Ollie's right down the street."

"Thanks, Sheriff. We won't be but a minute."

Ern called Sheriff Sol, who was solidly on board. He told Ern that they did a great job, and he really appreciated the way he took Barlow under his wing and gave him a little seasoning.

After they ate an ample and tasty meal topped off with pecan pie, they took a leisurely ride home, arriving at 4 o'clock on the dot.

Barlow turned in his receipt and got reimbursed. Sheriff Sol congratulated him on his good work over the past few weeks. Then he shooed him out the door to get some sleep.

Barlow was euphoric. What a job! He couldn't believe they paid him good money to do this.

CHAPTER 36

FIRST TROUBLE CALL

The rest of August passed quickly. One nice aspect of the way Sheriff Sol ran the SO, was that nobody worked on Sunday, unless they had a prisoner, which was uncommon. The deputies rotated as the Sunday duty deputy, meaning they were available for emergency calls, which seldom occurred. This meant Barlow and Sarah had been able to spend Sundays together so far, and should be able to continue to do so.

Barlow's other day off varied according to the needs of the office. He was fine with that, just like he was fine predominately working the midnight shift. It was a fair trade off for the opportunity to go to WTJC.

The sheriff had thoughtfully rotated Barlow to give him an opportunity to work with the other four full-time deputies. They were an excellent group of guys. Each one had been helpful in teaching him the ropes.

His first paycheck was disbursed on Friday, August 29th. This was a relief and a much needed shot in the arm. He opened a passbook savings account at the Pecos Bank & Trust.

On September 2nd, he paid his tuition. Classes began. They were interesting, and his instructors were knowledgeable as well as helpful.

On September 10th, his first G.I. Bill benefits check arrived. It went straight to savings.

Life was good, better than he deserved. He was so busy, juggling work, school, and sleep, that time spent with Sarah was reduced to just two or three days a week. That time together was the icing on his cake.

Life had settled into a rhythm. He was marching along. Progress was visible, but sometimes tedious. Halloween was around the corner. Then on a waning Wednesday eve, October 29th, life got real serious again in a matter of seconds.

It was 11:30 p.m. Archie and Barlow had just made the shift change and taken over from Dewey Carruthers. The weather was delightfully crisp in the evenings and early morns. All was well.

Arch was putzing around in the office. Barlow began reading an English assignment.

The telephone rang, interrupting Barlow's concentration and Archie's sudden quest to tidy up the office. Arch took the call.

After a brief conversation, in which his demeanor stiffened visibly, he hung up and told Barlow to "saddle up."

Barlow asked if he should grab a shotgun.

Arch said, "No. Just your stick."

Barlow retrieved it from the coat tree, where he'd hung it earlier. He had to scramble to catch up with Arch, who was already out the door.

"What's up?"

Arch said the call was from Old Man Spellman, owner of the Dry Gulch Saloon, an establishment Barlow had yet to acquaint himself with. A couple of outlaw bikers were pretty rowdy, and they were picking on a sad sack customer named Clifford Biggs. Spellman said he thought they were going to mop up the floor with him.

Archie briefed Barlow regarding tactics along the way, as he raced the half-mile to the saloon, sans emergency lights or siren.

He said, "We'll go in quietly. I'll go through the rear door. Give me a minute before you go in the front. I hope to slip in so they won't see me. I want to see how you handle this situation. Be calm, but firm. I won't step in so long as you have things under control. Got it?"

"Yes, Sir."

Arch was true to his word. He pulled into the gravel lot with no sound, except for the crunching of tires. They eased their doors shut.

Barlow noticed there were only three cars, a pickup, and two choppers parked in the lot.

Archie walked around to the back. Barlow's heart was pounding. This was his first trouble call. He took a couple of deep breaths as he counted to 60.

1 - 100. 2 - 100. 3 - 100. At 60 - 100, he opened the door and stepped in quietly.

Old Man Spellman was standing behind the bar. Archie was behind him, barely noticeable in the shadows.

A waitress was standing, arms crossed, at a table occupied by an elderly couple who were nursing their drinks, off to his right. They acted as though they were oblivious to their surroundings. Fat chance!

A pudgy, shoe salesman type of guy, was sitting at a table to his left. This would be Clifford Biggs. Two scary looking bikers were hovering over him. Both were covered with tattoos, wearing filthy jeans, tee shirts, and blue jean jackets with patches that read, 'El Diablos M/C', and '1%-er.' They also had a twelve-inch red, black, and yellow circular patch with the face of the devil surrounded by flames centered in the middle of the back.

The bigger of the two, a bearded, 6-foot, 275-pound, beer-bellied, loudmouth was shoving Biggs in the chest, calling him foul names, daring him to stand up and fight, and threatening to filet him like a fish.

The other biker was about 5'10" and 185 pounds. His muscles were ripped. He had shoulder-length scraggly hair. He was wearing a long, decorative knife in a bright metal sheath. He was egging on Fatso, shouting, "Do it, Screech! Do it! Look at that pile of shit, bawling like a little girl. What a turd!"

Biggs was looking down, hanging onto the table for dear life, tears flowing down his cheeks in torrents. Neither Biggs, nor the bikers, seemed to notice Barlow, or if they did, they didn't care.

Barlow approached within six feet of the table, and still the bikers ignored him. Fatso shoved Biggs hard, sending him and his chair crashing to the floor.

Barlow spoke in a normal tone of voice, "Knock it off."

Fatso backed up a step, and said, "Lookie here, Joe, a baby cop! Don't he look like he's about to shit hisself?"

Joe laughed, and stepped closer to Fatso. He said, "Get outta here, Boy! Yore momma's lookin' for ya. She needs ya to tuck her into bed, since Screech and me done fucked the shit outta her. She's all wore out."

Barlow spoke louder. "That's enough! You're both under arrest! Get on your knees with your hands locked behind your head!"

Fatso snorted like a pig, and Joe hooted as if this were the funniest command he had ever heard. Fatso's eyes narrowed and he took two quick steps toward Barlow, fast as a runaway freight train, arms wide open like he wanted to hug and squeeze the everlasting life out of Barlow.

It happened before anyone could blink. Barlow put both hands on his nightstick about ten inches apart, as if he were planning to break a plate glass window, only he wasn't. He put all his strength into it, and jammed the stick as deep into Fatso's belly as it would go.

Fatso gasped for breath and dropped to his knees. He heaved and puked big gobs of vile, undigested food and beer all over the floor and Biggs.

Joe got a wild look in his eyes and an even nastier-looking scowl on his face. He stepped around Fatso, all the while pulling the eight-inch dagger out of its sheath, as he closed the distance to Barlow.

Barlow backhanded his swing of the nightstick with everything he had, striking Joe on the outside of his elbow. The crack of bone could be heard from across the street. Joe dropped the dagger, grabbed the fractured arm across his chest, and howled like a gut-shot coyote.

By then Arch was behind Joe. He shoved Joe viciously to the floor onto his stomach in all the vomit, wrenched both his arms behind his back, and snapped the bracelets as tight as they would go. Joe continued to howl, and writhe about, begging for mercy.

Fatso was docile, but only because he was still sucking wind. Barlow shoved him facedown into his own barf, and cuffed him behind the back, too.

Barlow straightened up, feeling a little woozy and weak in the knees. He looked over at Arch, who said, "My, my, Deputy Adams! Aren't you the gnarly one? I'm glad you're on my side."

He pulled up a chair, and told Barlow to sit down and keep an eye on both maggots. Then he bent down and retrieved Joe's dagger. It was an ornate Nazi war trophy, replete with scrollwork and a silver Swastika on the hilt.

"Well, lookie here! I ain't seen one of these in more'n twenty years. I'll bet this will knock the sheriff's socks off."

After a pause, he said, "Everybody sit tight. I gotta call the chief. He'll want to come down and talk to everyone. Barkeep, get my pard an RC Cola. I 'spect he's a mite thirsty about now."

Barlow sipped the drink and replayed the chronology of events in his head, over and over. He truly had no plan of attack for either assailant. He reacted without conscious thought. It was pure reflex. He pondered that. He got off lucky. He'd have to do better if he wanted to remain in law enforcement and live to a ripe old age.

In the meantime, the waitress cleaned and mopped up the mess. Also, Doc Boykin arrived and examined both bikers.

CHAPTER 37
MORE LESSONS ABOUT THE LAW

Fatso, otherwise known as Maynard Creech, a/k/a Screech, had a substantial, purple bruise on his torso above his navel, but was otherwise okay. No medical attention needed.

Joe, otherwise known as Joseph P. Schitt, a/k/a Joe Shit the Ragman, was in pretty bad shape. His elbow was busted to smithereens. Doc stabilized it, so he could be transported to the hospital in Alpine.

Sheriff Sol rolled in with Deputy Ernest Atwater and Deputy Dewey Carruthers. They were instructed to take Joseph Schitt to the hospital in Alpine, and stay with him until otherwise relieved.

Chief Alex called ahead to Chief Deputy Arnold Buckman in Brewster County, who said he would detail a deputy to assist.

The chief took sworn statements from Old Man Spellman, the waitress, Eloise Huff, Clifford Biggs, and Mr. and Mrs. Shelby and Maurine Winters.

Sheriff Sol called Buck Boyd and told him to get a wrecker and put both motorcycles in the secure impound lot. Then he told Arch and Barlow to take Maynard Creech to jail. Maynard was a lucky dog, though he would hardly think so. The weather was cool. Otherwise the jail cells were stifling.

Sheriff Sol spoke with both deputies, individually and then together, before they wrote their official statements. Barlow wrote the incident report while Archie fingerprinted and photographed Creech.

Sheriff Sol told Barlow to charge both men with disorderly conduct, resisting arrest, and misdemeanor assault and battery of

Biggs (threatening and shoving him.) Creech was also to be charged with misdemeanor assault on Barlow (charging, but not touching him.) Schitt was to be charged with felony aggravated assault on Barlow for pulling the dagger. He said if DOC confirmed that either of the mutts were on parole or probation, Chief would tack on those charges, too.

Barlow asked about charging them with being drunk in a public place.

The sheriff asked, "Did they look drunk to you? Were they staggering or did they have slurred speech?"

Barlow replied, "Not when you put it that way. I just thought since they were drinking beer . . ."

Sheriff Sol interrupted, "Listen. We don't want to charge them with anything indicating impairment, because we don't want to open the door to diminished capacity as a mitigating factor. The defense will say, 'Mr. Schitt was too intoxicated to realize he was taking his knife out of the sheath. The deputy says he was staggering drunk. It was just a big misunderstanding.'

"These mutts were definitely imbibing, but by Jove, they weren't drunk! Understand?"

"Yes, Sir."

"Good. You're learning. Everyone will back you up on that."

Sheriff Sol reviewed and approved all the paperwork after it was completed. He personally supervised Barlow through the booking paperwork, to include the personal history, personal property, and evidence forms (for Schitt's dagger.) He told Barlow that before long, he wouldn't need anyone looking over his shoulder while he completed booking, with the exception, perhaps, of fingerprinting. Barlow smiled to himself, but he concurred wholeheartedly.

Archie ran criminal history, wanted, and DMV record checks on both prisoners.

Creech had been arrested six times, all misdemeanors, except for a grand theft (auto), for which he served two years in prison.

Schitt had a four-page rap sheet. Besides a myriad of misdemeanors, his felony arrests included armed robbery, possession of a controlled substance, felon in possession of a firearm, manslaughter, burglary (twice), aggravated assault, and parole violation. Neither man was on parole or probation now.

For certain, Schitt had three felony convictions, because his rap sheet reflected three separate incarcerations at the Texas State Penitentiary in Huntsville. This made him a 'three-time-loser.'

Sheriff Sol said, "As a three-time-loser, the district attorney, Able DeWitt, could charge Schitt with being an habitual offender, otherwise known as the 'high bitch.' Conviction of the high bitch is a mandatory 25-year sentence without parole, running consecutively with any other sentence he gets. Basically, that's a true-life sentence.

"Likewise, DeWitt could use the high bitch as leverage to entice Schitt to plead guilty to agg assault, thus avoiding trial. He would receive a lengthy sentence, but not forty or fifty years.

"And just so you know, charging Schitt with the high bitch would require a whole lot of legwork for us. DeWitt would need certified records from each venue which convicted him, plus proof he was the person in prison who actually served those sentences. This is normally done by fingerprint comparisons and mugshots, or eyewitness testimony.

"Also, the severity of the sentence absolutely guarantees a court fight. We'd be looking at a delay in trial, which could mean housing him in jail for weeks. Nobody here, and I mean nobody, wants that."

Then Sheriff Sol said Barlow was in for a long day, and for him to call someone at the college to let them know he would be absent due to his required presence in court. Most likely DA DeWitt would expect him to testify at Creech's initial appearance.

This brought up a more detailed explanation of the justice system so Barlow would understand the nuances involved with arresting someone.

Sheriff Sol said, "Creech has neither asked for an attorney, nor a telephone call, and he's entitled to both. Therefore, unless one of the club's gang attorneys on retainer has ESP and just happens to appear in court, Creech will be represented by Sam Davis as court-appointed counsel. Schitt hasn't made a request either, but he isn't going to court today."

He continued, "Creech has two options when he appears in court this morning.

"One is, he can plead not guilty and receive a trial date. Of course, he would have to post bond if he wanted to be released from jail pending trial.

"The problem for Creech, is that it's unlikely Judge 'Maximum Max' Sweeney will set a bond for less than $10,000, what with Creech being a felon outlaw biker from out of town, and all. He's a serious flight risk.

"So, if Creech doesn't have the money to post bond, which is refundable after the case is adjudicated, he would have to hire a bail bondsman to post it. A bondsman charges a non-refundable fee of 10% to 15% to post a bond, taking into consideration the risk that the defendant might fail to appear in court, commonly referred to as jumping bond or skipping bail. The bondsman forfeits the full bond amount on all skips.

"Bottom line is, if Creech doesn't come up with the jack to post bail, he'll cool his heels in jail pending trial. That would suck for all parties concerned, but Creech doesn't know that. He's only concerned about himself. Now that he's experienced Quayle County's spartan accommodations, I'm sure he wants out in the worst possible way.

"Creech's other option would be to plead guilty and get sentenced today, but he won't do that unless he thinks it's in his best interest.

"Before court, DeWitt will offer a plea bargain to Sam Davis. If Creech agrees to plead guilty, the DA will agree to recommend a sentence which would be lighter than if he went to trial and lost.

Judges don't have to accept plea bargain agreements, but they usually do. I think Creech would plead out if it gets him out of jail sooner, rather than later.

"Everything's up in the air for the time being. All will be revealed, as it relates to Creech, at 10 o'clock court. Go home, shower, change uniforms, eat, and be back before then.

"Oh, yeah. Be prepared to testify this afternoon before the Grand Jury, regarding the proposed indictment against Joseph Schitt. Afterwards, you can split and grab some shuteye before reporting for mids. By then, I hope to know if Schitt will remain in custody at the hospital, or in jail. Of course, there's always the possibility we'll have a prisoner at both locations."

As Barlow was walking out the door, Sheriff Sol said, "Barlow, you handled yourself like an experienced hand tonight. Everybody's real proud of you. Keep up the good work."

CHAPTER 38

TESTIFYING IN COURT

It was 10 o'clock, Thursday, October 30th. Barlow, Chief Alex, and Sheriff Sol were in the courtroom with their prisoner.

DA DeWitt had presented defense counsel Sam Davis a plea bargain offer, which he was now discussing with Creech. He had very little time left to take it or leave it. There was a good chance of a trial forthwith, if Creech declined the offer. Barlow was sitting on pins and needles.

Bailiff August Bellweather rose and banged his mallet on the block.

"All rise. Hear ye. Hear ye. The District Court for the County of Quayle, in the State of Texas, the Honorable Maxwell B. Sweeney presiding, is now in session. All ye who have matters before this court come forward and ye shall be heard. God bless this honorable court."

Judge Sweeney swept into the room, robes flapping like he was riding a cyclone. He took his seat behind the bench. "Mr. Clerk, what matters do we have before the court, today?"

"Just one, Your Honor. The State versus Maynard Creech, docket number 69-10-0021."

"Are all parties present, Mr. Clerk?"

"Yes, Your Honor."

"Counsels, please state your names before the court."

"District Attorney Able DeWitt, representing the State, Your Honor."

"Mr. Samuel Davis, Esquire, Your Honor, court-appointed counsel for Maynard Creech, who is here beside me."

"Very good. And what is the matter before the court today, Mr. DeWitt?"

"Your Honor, this is the initial appearance for Mr. Creech. The Sheriff's Office has filed a complaint against Mr. Creech, alleging the following misdemeanor violations: one count each of disorderly conduct, resisting arrest, simple assault and battery of a private citizen, and simple assault on a law enforcement officer."

"I see. And how does Mr. Creech plead to these counts, Mr. Davis?"

"Your Honor, if it please the court, the defendant and the District Attorney have reached an agreement, in which Mr. Creech will plead guilty to all counts. The State is recommending maximum fines of $100 each on disorderly conduct and resisting arrest; a $250 fine for simple assault and battery of a citizen, and a one-year sentence in the county jail to be suspended for five years, for simple assault of a law enforcement officer. In addition, Mr. Creech agrees to pay $15 court costs for each count.

"Furthermore, the defendant is prepared to sign the title of his motorcycle over to the Clerk of Court, in lieu of paying cash for the fines and court costs. I have the title with me. The Blue Book suggests that the value of the motorcycle is between $500 and $550. Also, Mr. Buck Boyd, the county's temporary custodian of the vehicle, who is also a licensed dealer of motor vehicles, has examined the motorcycle and will attest that the Blue Book value is an accurate assessment."

"Is this true, Mr. DeWitt?"

"Yes, Your Honor."

"Mr. DeWitt, does the State have a witness for the allocution, regarding the facts of this case, were it to go to trial?"

"Yes, Your Honor. The State calls Deputy Sheriff Barlow Adams to the stand."

Barlow walked up to the stand, faced the clerk, placed his left hand on the Bible, and raised his right hand.

"Do you solemnly swear to tell the truth, the whole truth, and nothing but the truth, so help you God?"

"I do."

"Please be seated."

Barlow sat.

DA DeWitt said, "Deputy Adams, in your own words, tell the court what happened late last night and early this morning, October 29th into the 30th, 1969, which lead to the arrest of one Maynard Creech."

"Yes, Sir. Around half past 11 or a quarter to 12, Deputy Archibald Willis received a telephone call at the Sheriff's Office. Mr. Elmer Spellman, proprietor of the Dry Gulch Saloon in Mosby, called to report an assault taking place on one of his customers by two individuals.

"Deputy Willis and I responded to the scene. Deputy Willis entered the saloon from the back door and I entered from the front.

"Upon my arrival, I saw the defendant, Mr. Creech, badgering a man later identified to me as Clifford Biggs, who was seated at a table.

"Mr. Creech was cursing Mr. Biggs, pushing him in the chest, and ordering him to stand up and fight like a man. He said he would filet Mr. Biggs like a fish if he didn't. Then he pushed Mr. Biggs so hard that he fell out of his chair onto the floor.

"At that time, I identified myself as an officer of the law, and told Mr. Creech to desist. Mr. Creech ridiculed and taunted me. His associate made salacious comments about my mother.

"I told Mr. Creech and his associate they were both under arrest. Then Mr. Creech ran towards me with his arms wide open, like he was going to tackle me. I took a step towards him and thrust the end of my billy club into his stomach before he could reach me. He fell down and I handcuffed him."

"Is that everything relating to Mr. Creech?"

"Yes, Sir."

"After subduing Mr. Creech, was it necessary to subdue another person?"

"Yes, Sir."

"Was that other person working in concert with Mr. Creech?"

"Yes, Sir."

"Was he arrested?"

"Yes, Sir."

"Your Honor, unless you or Mr. Davis have any further questions for Deputy Adams, this concludes the allocution."

"Do you have any questions, Mr. Davis?"

"No, Your Honor."

"Deputy, you may step down.

"Mr. Creech, you've heard the testimony of Deputy Adams. Is this the truth?"

"Yes, Sir."

"You did everything Deputy Adams said about you?"

"Yes, Sir."

"Do you have anything you'd like to say on your own behalf, Mr. Creech?"

"Just that I'm sorry, Your Honor, and I apologize to the deputy and the man I was picking on."

"Indeed. Mr. Creech, do you belong to the El Diablos Motorcycle Club out of El Paso?"

"Yes, Your Honor."

"How do you make a living?"

"I'm a mechanic."

"Not a drug dealer, nor pimp, nor extortionist, nor shylock, nor thief, nor chop shop mechanic?"

"No Sir."

"Do you have a family?"

"I'm divorced."

"Any offspring?"

"What's an offspring?"

"A child. Children. Sons or daughters."

"A daughter."

"How old?"

"Six."

"Are you paying support?"

"I do when I can. I'm a couple of months behind right now. Business has been slow."

"How much do you owe?"

"$350."

"And yet here you are, prepared to forfeit a $500 motorcycle to pay your fines, in hopes that you will avoid going to jail?"

"Ain't no way I could ever get caught up in jail, Your Honor, and the support keeps stacking up, even if I am in jail."

"Do you know that I don't have to follow the District Attorney's recommendation, and that I can sentence you to jail right here in Mosby for up to a year on both assault charges, and I can stipulate that the sentences run consecutively, thereby incarcerating you for two years, and that there's no such thing as 'good time' in jail like there is in prison?"

"Yes, Your Honor."

"Did anyone threaten you if you didn't plead guilty, or promise that I wouldn't sentence you to jail?"

"No, Your Honor."

"Did you plead guilty because you are, in fact, guilty of all these charges?"

"Yes, Your Honor."

"All righty then. I hereby find you guilty on all four counts. I fine you $100 on count one for disorderly conduct; $100 on count two for resisting arrest; $250 on count three for simple assault and battery on a citizen. In addition, I sentence you to serve one year in jail on count four for simple assault of a law enforcement officer. Furthermore, I hereby suspend the sentence for five years.

"If you are brought before me for any reason within the next five years, I will incarcerate you in the Quayle County Jail for 365 days. Trust me when I tell you that is very, very hard time. We have no air conditioning, no radio, no television, no telephone calls, no library, no dessert, and you will do hard manual labor, without pay, Monday through Friday, for 52 weeks.

"Do I make myself clear?"

"Yes, Your Honor."

"You better be. In addition, I impose a $15 court fee on all four counts. Furthermore, I accept title to the motorcycle in lieu of all fines and court costs.

"One last thing. Mr. Creech. It is nigh onto 11 o'clock. I'm giving you until 3 o'clock to get out of Quayle County, or I will rescind the suspended sentence. I never want to see you in Quayle County again. Is that clear?"

"Yes, Your Honor."

"Sheriff Pratt, I order you to take this man to your office, and allow him to make calls until he makes contact with someone who will pick him up.

"Then I want a unit to transport him to the rest area three miles west of Mosby on Highway 90, and drop him off there for pick up. At 3 o'clock, I want a unit to patrol west on 90 all the way to the county line. If Mr. Creech is found after 3 o'clock, anywhere in Quayle County, I want him arrested and brought back to this court forthwith. I don't care what time it is. Am I clear?"

"Yes, Your Honor."

"Mr. Clerk, is there anymore business before the court?"

"No, Your Honor."

"Court dismissed."

"All rise."

Chapter 39

Going Before the Grand Jury

Chunk was at the office when they returned. Sheriff Sol put Chunk in charge of babysitting Creech while he made calls, and hauling him to the rest area on Highway 90.

Miss Loretta said Deputy Atwater had called to report that Schitt was undergoing surgery. The doctor said he would probably release him in the morning.

Sheriff told Chunk to rouse Deputies Shoemaker and Oldman, and send them to Alpine to relieve Deputies Atwater and Carruthers. He said Archie and Barlow would relieve Kirk and Slick if Schitt remained in the hospital overnight.

Sheriff said he had something to do, but he would be back in time for Barlow's 1 o'clock Grand Jury appearance.

He said Barlow could crash on the couch in his office if he wanted, but to make sure he was ready to testify. He reminded Barlow that Grand Jury testimony is recorded, just like courtroom testimony. He didn't want Barlow to deviate whatsoever from his affidavit, or this morning's testimony, since the Schitt case would most likely go to trial.

On his way out the door, he told Chief Alex to call the El Paso SO and their PD, to learn all he could about the El Diablos. In particular, he wanted to know if they should expect retaliation from the gang.

Chief said he was on it.

Barlow was worn out, but too wired to sleep. He poured a cup of coffee and began rehearsing his testimony in his mind.

At 12:45, the sheriff and Barlow walked up the stairs to the Grand Jury witness waiting room. DA DeWitt was already there.

He looked at Barlow and said, "This will be similar to court, except there will be no judge, no defendant, and no defense counsel - only eighteen jurors, a court reporter, you, and me.

"I will go in first and tell the jurors the essence of the case. Then you will be called. The foreman of the jury will swear you in. Then I will ask questions and you will answer.

"There's one huge difference here from court. The jurors are allowed to ask questions once I'm done. Sometimes they get carried away, go down rabbit holes, ask off-the-wall questions. I will try to keep them on track.

"For Christ's sake, Barlow do not speculate. Stay on script. Keep it short and sweet. The defense gets a copy of the transcript of the entire proceeding. When everyone runs out of questions, you will be excused.

"Then the jury will deliberate on the proposed indictment. In this case, whether they think there is probable cause to charge Schitt with the felony count of aggravated assault. It isn't necessary for the misdemeanor charges to be presented to the Grand Jury - just felonies. Assuming they think there is, they will return a True Bill.

"When Schitt gets released from the hospital, he will have an initial appearance, arraignment regarding the indictment, and bond hearing before Judge Sweeney at his earliest convenience. The judge will determine bond amount and set a trial date. We'll worry about that later. No questions?"

Barlow shook his head.

"Good."

DA DeWitt went into the Grand Jury room.

The sheriff and Barlow cooled their heels for twenty minutes, not saying a word. Barlow was nervous, but confident. He was as prepared as he ever would be. He reminded himself that he was the good guy and Schitt was the villain.

When Barlow was called and entered the room, he saw twenty pairs of eyes watching. He recognized several of the jurors from around town. The foreman swore him in and he took his seat.

DA DeWitt began with the preamble regarding the date, matter at hand, and the identity of Barlow as a witness.

He asked Barlow to state and spell his name. Then he asked Barlow about his background, to include education, military service, length of time employed at the Sheriff's Office, and POST qualification. Then he asked Barlow to tell the jury what had happened the night before, which resulted in his appearance before the Grand Jury.

Barlow recited the same testimony he provided for Creech's allocution.

"Once Creech was down on his knees, Schitt maneuvered past him and headed in my direction with a knife he was pulling from a sheath on his belt. I struck Schitt on the right elbow with my nightstick, which resulted in him dropping the knife. By then, Deputy Willis had come around the bar, and he tackled Schitt, dropping him to the floor. Then Deputy Willis handcuffed Schitt while I handcuffed Creech. Deputy Willis recovered the knife, which turned out to be a Nazi dagger with an eight-inch blade.

Barlow stopped his recitation, expecting DA DeWitt to ask for clarification. He didn't, but a juror did. He asked if Barlow thought Schitt planned to stab him with the knife.

Barlow responded, "Well, I didn't think he just wanted to show it to me."

The jurors erupted in laughter.

Then DA DeWitt asked, "Just for the record, did you fear for your life?"

"I did."

The jurors had no further questions and Barlow was excused.

Five minutes later, DeWitt returned to the waiting room. He said the Grand jury returned a True Bill. He told Barlow to sit tight and wait for the jurors to vacate the courthouse.

They waited in silence for about five minutes. DeWitt poked

his head out the door and gave an 'all clear.'

Sheriff Sol said, "Son, you're a fast learner. Be back at the jail at 11:45 to go with Archie to babysit Schitt. Be alert. I'm not kidding. These Diablos are some bad hombres. No telling what they're apt to do. Try to get some sleep."

CHAPTER 40

FROM LAWMAN TO JAILER

Barlow went home and fell into bed. He was too tired to sleep, but he did. His alarm was set for 11. He was in a coma when it went off. He stood under a steaming shower until he ran out of hot water. He made coffee, dressed, and scarfed down two peanut butter sandwiches and demolished a pint of milk. He gobbled down a Snickers Bar for dessert.

He filled his thermos full of black coffee. He packed a lunch of two bologna and mustard sandwiches, Hostess snowballs, and an apple.

He arrived at the jail at 11:35. Arch was already there. So was Deputy Randall Meacham, who had been called in to man the desk.

Arch said, "Barlow, you ready to go?"

"Yes, Sir. Want me to grab a shotgun?"

"I'd be upset if ya didn't."

They were rolling at 11:40. Archie drove. With no traffic, they covered the 90 miles in an hour. Archie knew where to park, and the location of the ward for psychotics and prisoners.

The hand-off was brief. Slick and Kirk said the doctor would return at 5 o'clock to check Schitt's arm, plastered in an L-shaped cast from shoulder to wrist, with a brace fastened to his chest to relieve the strain.

Schitt was asleep under heavy sedation. The idea was to get him on his way before the hospital and the world woke up, in an effort to be back at the jail before any of the Diablos attempted to visit, or perhaps stage an escape.

Archie said the El Paso Diablos had about thirty members and a dozen wannabes. Their primary source of income was trafficking in methamphetamine and prostitution out of a biker bar north of the El Paso city limits. They were not brazen enough to declare war on cops, but they were willing to take on cops they outnumbered. They were reported to 'disappear' their enemies.

He said it wouldn't be beyond them to try to rescue Schitt in the parking lot or at a remote service station, if the circumstances favored them. Chief even said they might come after the two of them individually once they knew who they were. He told Barlow to keep his gun handy at all times, and to maintain situational awareness everywhere he went, to include at home and at school.

It seemed like they had barely settled in for the night, at 4 o'clock, when the surgeon showed up. They hadn't even eaten their meal.

The surgeon awakened Schitt, who was dopey but still in pain. After a brief but thorough examination, he declared Schitt well enough for transport. It was obvious the hospital preferred not to be in a free fire zone. By 4:30, they had Schitt belted and wedged in the backseat behind the screen, and were cruising back to Mosby just as fast as they came.

Before shift change, Schitt was wearing stripes and uncomfortably ensconced on a two-inch thick mattress on a metal bunk. The weather unexpectedly had turned warm. The jail was stuffy and smelled like disinfectant. He whined incessantly about needing more pain meds. He got one every four hours, just like doctor's orders. Life is tough for those who choose the Owlhoot Trail.

Schitt was arraigned at 10 o'clock. Fortunately, Barlow's presence was not required. His days and nights were running together. Was this Thursday or Friday? Had he missed one day of classes or two? It was Thursday. No, Friday. He'd missed just one. Hell, it was Halloween! He tried to get himself together before joining his 8 o'clock class ten minutes late.

CHAPTER 41

SARAH'S SURPRISE

Barlow had a hard time concentrating. He wondered if the Diablos were going to seek revenge, or otherwise cause trouble for him or Mosby at large.

At noon, he was intercepted by Sarah after he left his PE class. He was dragging ass. She said, "Long time, no see, Stranger. You look like you could use some rest."

"Roger that. It's been a long week, and it's gonna get longer until we're through with our outlaw biker. We're all working extra hours."

"Don't I know it? What say we go back to your house and I fix you something better than a peanut butter and jelly sandwich for lunch?"

"What about your 1 o'clock?"

"Oh, that's American History. I have an A so far, and we aren't having a test today, so I think it'll be okay. Besides, I have to be back at 3 to work in the office."

"Okay. Let's do it."

Sarah followed Barlow home. They rummaged around and found some cheese and Campbell's tomato soup, so she made soup and grilled cheese sandwiches served with potato chips.

She could see he was fading fast, so she pushed him into the bedroom and onto the bed. She lay down beside him and began running her fingers through his hair. She pressed her body closer to his. She kissed him lightly and ran her tongue over his lips. She had crossed the Rubicon.

She had his undivided attention. His arousal sparked hers into high gear, as in 'Damn the torpedoes. Full speed ahead.' It wasn't even awkward. They both shucked their clothes and intertwined under the sheets.

She rolled him over onto his back and straddled him like a horse. This was her first time ever. She felt only the slightest pain as she placed him inside. She was wet and relaxed, and he was harder than Chinese arithmetic. She began slowly, savoring the sensation, but lost all control as he began his own thrusts. Sarah was riding a runaway stallion intent on winning the Kentucky Derby.

She clinched him inside and out, and on and on he ran. She sensed the finish line but couldn't see it. Her body was overwhelmed by sensations she never imagined.

She was out of breath. The ride got rougher. One violent push and Mount Vesuvius erupted. She was gushing and so was he. It was over.

She collapsed on his chest. They were gasping for air. She had never been so content. She didn't want to move, ever. She thought it was over. Time for her to clean up. She wondered what this would mean for them. He rubbed her back softly. She savored his touch. Without warning, his manhood woke up just as hard as before.

He rolled her over. His joystick found its way into her tingling honeypot without effort. She was instantly aroused.

It was so different. He was in control. It was slow and lasted longer. He found her special erogenous spots. When it ended, he whispered that he loved her.

He rolled to his side. She nestled against him. In ten minutes he was in Never Never Land. She eased out of bed and pulled the covers over him.

She showered, cleaned up the kitchen, and set his alarm for 11. She needed to compose herself before reporting for work. She looked in the mirror. She glowed. A blind man could see that she'd just made love. She was euphoric.

How was she going to conceal this from work, let alone her

mother? No wonder her mom was so perky on some mornings! Now she understood.

It was 2:45 when she floated into work. She got busy filing reports until she could wipe the smile off her face.

At 9:30 Barlow awoke with a start. He tumbled out of bed and into the shower. He dressed and went to the kitchen in search of food. It was tidy and clean. No dishes in the sink. No mess on the table. There was a note. It read, "Love you, too. Call me."

He called the Baker residence. Clarice answered.

"Hello, Mrs. Baker. This is Barlow. Is Sarah there."

"Hi, Barlow. When are you going to come out and see us again? We've missed you."

"I've missed you all, too. Things have been topsy-turvy at work, but I'm hoping to be off on Sunday. Probably won't be, though. It's because of me we're all tied up."

"Nonsense. What would those thugs have done to poor old Clifford if you hadn't stepped in? Wait a minute. Here's Sarah. Come see us soon, okay?"

"I will, Mrs. Baker. Tell Arthur hello for me."

"I will. Bye."

Sarah picked up the phone. "Hey, Barlow. I'm surprised you're up so early."

"Well I just woke up feeling better than I ever have my entire life. Thanks for everything . . . like cleaning up, you know. Are you alone?"

"Pretty much, if I don't talk too loud."

"Do you feel okay?"

"I feel great, and before you ask, I've been on the pill for a month now. I'm safe."

"Does your mom know?"

"What do you think?"

"I don't know."

"Well Doc Boykin wouldn't tell her, but she's not blind. I think she might have suspected something tonight, but if she did, she didn't say anything. Just gave me that all-knowing mother look."

"Geez, I hope not. I don't want your ma and pa all mad at me."

"They both love you. Don't worry."

"Maybe we shouldn't do it again."

"Fat chance, Mr. Adams. I'm already waiting for the next encounter. Besides that, you're the one who opened Pandora's box."

"Me? I distinctly recall that you started it."

"Well if I did, you inserted the key. Now that the mystery is out, I want you to unlock it again."

"Better be careful what you ask for, Miss Baker. This old hoss might wear out your brand-new saddle."

"You have to break it in first, Mr. Smartypants. Did you call to let me know when we can see each other again?"

"No. Just responding to a note I found on my kitchen table. Feelings are mutual, times two. I won't know if I have to work on Sunday until I go to work tonight. Hope not, but we'll all be working extra until we get rid of Joe Shit the Ragman."

"You think that gang will cause trouble?"

"Don't know, but we're all keeping a weather eye out."

"Tomorrow morning, I'm going to help Daddy round up some sheep in the outback, but we won't start before 8. We should be done by early afternoon. If you don't have to work, maybe you could stop by and visit with Mom and Dad. They both would love to see you. We could eat here.

"Of course, you might want to eat fast if you expect to get lucky. That is, the Wild Bunch is playing at the Bijou and you would have to be lucky to get there by 7 once my folks start talking to you."

"Seeing a movie? That's your idea of getting lucky?"

"It's supposed to be a really good one. A cowboy show. You'll like it."

"That's not my idea of getting lucky, even if I do get to see the show."

"Who knows? Maybe you'll get lucky after the show. I don't need to be home until midnight. Getting to church on time might be a little tough, but it might be worth it if you don't fall asleep on me."

"You have no mercy."

"Mercy is exactly what I have that felled you like a sequoia."

"I suppose it was all work and no play, what with you chopping all that wood."

"I have an affinity for wood, especially ironwood."

"I seem to recall something about that."

"Then show me again. Saturday night. Gotta go. Love you."

"I love you, too, Paula Bunyan."

"Who?"

"You know, Paul Bunyan, the legendary lumberjack . . . his sister, if he had one?"

"Chop, chop, Mr. Adams. Bye now."

CHAPTER 42

FEAR OF RETALIATION

Barlow arrived for work early. He was working with Slick because Archie was off, except Slick wasn't there yet. Kirk Shoemaker was completing the 4-12 shift, and he had all the skinny.

"No news this, but Joe Schitt is a monumental pain in the ass. Always complaining. Good thing you broke his arm because he's dangerous and the pain takes some of the spunk out of him. Check him a quarter after each hour and don't forget to log it in. If he's asleep and you don't hear him breathing, wake him up to make sure he's still alive. He gets pain pills at 12:15, 4:15, 8:15, and so forth. Log that in.

"Somebody has to walk the perimeter once an hour to check for signs of trouble. Log that in, too, and also anything unusual or suspicious.

"Maximum Max set Joe Schitt's bond at $50,000 cash - no surety. Joe Schitt said he'll get his own attorney. Max Max said the attorney has to file with the clerk of court by Monday, November 3rd, at 10 o'clock, because trial is scheduled for Friday, November 7th. Otherwise, Sam will remain as court-appointed counsel.

"That ain't likely to happen. DeWitt received a call from a big bucks dope lawyer named Elton Stonebreaker, who said he represents Joe Schitt. He's filing for a bond reduction hearing and a postponement of the trial.

"DeWitt said he would oppose both, but not to be surprised if the trial gets set back a week or two. DeWitt thinks Stonebreaker will stall until he can bleed his entire fee up front from the Diablos.

"Chief said Joe Schitt was pretty high up in the Diablos chain of command. He also said a joint BNDD-DPS-EPSO-EPPD Task Force is working the Diablos, and Joe Schitt is second on their target list. BNDD is the Bureau of Narcotics & Dangerous Drugs if you haven't heard of them. They're federal.

"Chief suspects they've got a snitch inside because EPSO said they'll give us a heads up if the Diablos plan to swarm Mosby on trial day. Also, they said it wasn't out of their comfort zone to send a crew over to bump off the arresting officers.

"Also, Sheriff Sol said you're off Sunday, but you will work mids the next six nights in a row."

Barlow said, "Thanks for the update."

He didn't mind the OT. It was all straight time, but he worked more hours per day for longer stretches than that in the Army, and the Army didn't pay OT, and for that matter, neither did Uncle Clyde. Anyway, he was trying to build up his savings account. This would add nicely to the G.I. Bill checks, both of which had been deposited into savings and were drawing 2% interest.

Barlow's major concern was about getting ambushed. His house was a cracker box with nothing more secure than the locks in the doorknobs. A six-year-old could defeat that. Also, much of the time he left the windows cracked to let a breeze in. None of this was unusual. Most folks in Mosby didn't lock their houses or their cars.

To even the odds a little against a burglar, he left the curtains open when he was out. Also, he started leaving an eighteen-inch branch which fell off a tree in his front yard, on the porch by the door, making it necessary to remove before entering, and an RC Cola bottle on the back porch by the rear door, as tells.

He turned off all indoor lights, and left porch lights off when he departed at night, to be a more difficult target in darkness. Hell, if he had some Claymore mines, he'd put them around the perimeter. He didn't, so he had to rely more on his wits and instinct.

Beginning now, he checked his truck for bombs before he opened the door. In the past, he would have thought this paranoia, especially in backwater Mosby. Today, he thought it prudent. Even so, he was careful not to let the other deputies or Sarah catch onto his extra vigilance. He didn't want the ribbing or concern.

Friday's shift was anticlimactic. Slick and he checked on Joe Schitt like ordered. He was sullen, but not nearly as insufferable as he had been the night before. All quiet around the courthouse, 'not a creature was stirring, not even a mouse.'

Barlow wrote a three-page essay on one of Walt Whitman's boring poems. He completed all the problems for his math class.

School was pretty good for the most part. He would have tried out for the WTJC Javelinas basketball team, except if he made it, that would have left no time for sleep. He contented himself by wearing a yellow and green Javelinas sweatshirt when he had an opportunity to attend their games.

By 4 o'clock, Barlow had completed all his homework and then some. He ate. Then he got out his Lee Loader and reloaded 150 cartridges before end of shift. He decided to ask Sarah if she would mind going shooting instead of to the movie. He needed the practice, but he didn't want her to know why. If he sensed disappointment, he would stick with the movie.

He was late calling. Sarah and Arthur and Cordell were already rounding up sheep. He told Clarice to let Sarah know he'd stop by about 3. No need to confuse her. He decided to pack extra ammo and call an audible if it seemed feasible. Otherwise, they would stick with Plan A.

CHAPTER 43

TARGET PRACTICE AND MORE LUSTY TALK

When Barlow arrived at Casa de Baker, the family was sitting under a copse of live oak trees, drinking longneck Shiner Bocks from an old metal cooler filled with ice. The sky was crystal blue. It was hot in the sun.

Sarah, Arthur, and Cordell were all dusty and sweat-soaked. Clarice and Darla were wearing sun dresses and looked like they were headed to church or the movies. When Sarah saw Barlow pulling into the driveway, she exclaimed, "Oh my God! He's early!" and ran into the house to get changed.

Arthur told Barlow to grab a beer and have a seat.

Barlow said, "I was hoping Sarah might consider having a little target practice instead of going to the movies, but maybe that's something we could save for another day."

Darla said she'd go inside and ask, and then she was gone.

Arthur said to tell Sarah the movie would still be showing next weekend.

Cordell said, "I bet I know why you changed your mind. From what I hear, you need to be prepared."

Arthur said, "Amen."

So much for subtlety or secrets in a small community. Sarah was right.

Barlow replied, "Well, I try to be prepared all the time, but practice makes perfect, and anyway I just enjoy shooting."

Cordell responded, "From what I hear, you shoot like a Kentuckian. I heard you drill whatever you aim at."

Barlow said, "Well, I take that as a high compliment. My daddy was from Kentucky and so was his whole clan. I don't believe he ever missed anything he shot at. He said his daddy was the finest marksman he ever saw, and that was saying something because the whole darn clan was good."

Arthur laughed and said, "Sounds like the Hatfields and McCoys. I'm especially glad to know that. If you decide you want to practice with your rifle, let me know. We'll bait the south end and you can help us get rid of some of the coyotes that're killing our lambs and raiding the henhouse. They're a little too skittish for Cordell or me to get a good shot at."

Barlow responded, "The Hatfields are from West Virginia. The McCoys are from Kentucky. My dad, and therefore yours truly, are related to the McCoys by marriage, although I never met any of them.

"I'd love to thin out the coyote population for you. Probably have to wait, though, until we're shed of the Diablos."

Then Arthur said, "Not a problem. By the way. Don't run off when you all get done. We're planning to barbecue some fresh mutton after while. We could use your help making sure we don't have any leftovers."

Barlow said that sounded great. They bantered another fifteen minutes until Sarah showed up in jeans with her .22 revolver belted around her waist, wearing a Stetson, and looking every bit a poster child for cowgirls. She was also toting a large sack of tin cans.

They saddled up Bonnie and Clyde, a pair of horses which had not been ridden earlier in the day. Barlow strapped on his gun belt, and grabbed his 30-30, a bandoleer of rifle cartridges, a sackful of .41 caliber reloads, and a canteen of water.

They rode down to the south end and tethered the horses under a tall, ancient, gnarly cedar tree.

For the next hour and a half, they blasted the tin cans into shards of metal. They took turns, betting a nickel on each shot. Sarah was mighty good with her H&R revolver. Barlow shot it a few times, himself, and learned just how much a six-inch barrel enhanced accuracy. However, he was deadly with his .41, and bested her often enough that when they finished, she owed him $1.35.

He said, "You don't have to fork over my winnings in cash. I'll take it out in trade."

She said, "You'll be the loser because I planned to give it to you anyway, free of charge, Mr. Smartypants."

"In that case, you keep my winnings and I'll double them, no triple them, because I plan to accept your generosity with vim and vigor. Lots of vim and vigor. Probably way too much for the likes of you."

She laughed and said, "You better save your energy, because that's mighty bold talk for a young man suffering from narcolepsy."

He replied, "That's a very unfair assessment. You caught me on a day in which I hadn't slept but four hours in the previous 24. If I'm fully rested, I'll have you begging for mercy, and you will have a smile on your face that you can't wipe off."

She responded, "That's the general idea, you slick talkin' man. Hurry up! I'm getting hungry. Help me get the last of these cans so we can get back to the house and refresh ourselves. In fact, you better get real refreshed, Mister, because you'll need every bit of your strength to keep up with me after church tomorrow."

"I'll hold you to that."

It was a great evening. Clarice and Darla prepared a feast with baked sweet potatoes, fresh corn on the cob, tossed salad, homemade biscuits, and cherry pie.

Arthur barbecued the mutton. It was moist and tangy, with a honey, tomato, and onion sauce. They washed it down with frosty longnecks of beer.

Barlow helped clean up and departed at 9 o'clock, so everyone could get some rest before church.

As Sarah and he were walking to his truck, holding hands,

Sarah said for him not to confuse tonight's cherry pie, of which he ate two pieces, with dessert, because she planned to stay in town after church and provide dessert for him after they ate at Betty's.

Barlow asked wouldn't they go to Hell if they did it on the Sabbath.

"Hell? Did you say Hell? Mr. Adams, I plan to take you to Heaven tomorrow afternoon! Don't get the two confused!"

"Of course not, Miss Baker, but if it were Hell, I'd follow you all the way there and back with a bucket of gasoline in each hand."

"Mr. Adams, you are most certainly a smooth-talking man. My mother warned me about boys like you."

"Well, you must not have listened."

"I listened just fine. It's just that I know a good thing when I see it. Even so, I can recognize a snake charmer when I see one."

"Miss Baker! Did you mean to say you are a snake which needs charming?"

"I meant to say snake oil salesman, but you got me all flustered. Please leave now before I catch the vapors. All your talk about taming my inner lioness has left me breathless. You have breached the walls of my defenses. I beg you to go. I shall expect complete satisfaction from you tomorrow afternoon."

"And satisfaction you shall have. Good evening, Miss Baker. Please convey my appreciation to your family for a fine meal and exquisite company."

The church service was good. Barlow needed it. Nevertheless, he did feel ashamed for having the thoughts which were racing through his mind. He knew a wedding ring would square his actions with his faith. He also knew they both needed to finish school before tying the knot. Besides that, her folks needed more time to know that he would always be there for her.

They ate a turkey dinner with all the fixings at Betty's. They topped it off with dessert at his house afterwards. He was a real glutton. He had three servings. She left at 6 o'clock with a smile on her face from ear to ear. It was true. She couldn't wipe it off.

He managed to catch a catnap before work. It wasn't enough.

CHAPTER 44

THE CIRCUS COMES TO TOWN

Sunday night to Monday morning was a very slow shift. Snails move faster than the minute hand on the clock.

The unexpected Las Vegas style arrival, dramatic court hearing, and fireworks in the District Attorney's office later that morning would be riveting, but Barlow would miss it all because he would be in class.

Sheriff Sol took a few precautions for the big day, to include sending Deputy Dewey Carruthers to the western county line as an early warning device, in the event an entourage of Diablos decided to ride into town.

Deputies Noble Bustamante and Randall Meacham were both assigned in town on the day shift, with Chunk in the courthouse and Randall in a unit nearby. Deputies Ernest Atwater and Clarence Oldman were working the afternoon shift, with Ernie inside and Slick relieving Dewey at the county line.

Chief Alex had been dispatched to Waco, Dallas, San Antonio, and Huntsville by DA DeWitt to get certified copies of Joe Schitt's three felony convictions and his prison records, to include photographs and fingerprint cards. He'd be gone several days, driving from one end of the state to the other and back. DeWitt had decided to be prepared to indict Schitt for being an habitual offender, if he so much as got a hint that Stonebreaker was taking the case to trial.

Too bad Barlow wasn't there to see it, because it was quite a spectacle.

A little after 9 o'clock, Elton Stonebreaker sailed into Mosby on his magic carpet, otherwise described as a gleaming, onyx and chrome, 1969 Cadillac Sedan de Ville, driven by a duded up, musclebound chauffeur in a black driving uniform replete with a billed cap, and a Playboy-bunny-gorgeous secretary. He was escorted by three Diablos in colors riding hogs, which no one except Deputy Meacham seemed to notice.

Mr. Stonebreaker was wearing a brilliant, cobalt blue, western cut, sharkskin suit, pleated white shirt with a ruby red tie, alabaster white Stetson with a four-inch brim, and shiny blue, pointy-toed, high-heeled, snakeskin cowboy boots. His belt and hat band matched his boots. He stood all of 5'6" tall and weighed slightly less than 250 pounds. Like 249.

His skin was pinkish. His eyes were pale blue. His fingernails were manicured. His hair was the color of straw. He was wearing a gaudy gold watch with diamonds, a Rolex perhaps, and a gold pinky ring with a gigantic diamond on his right hand. He carried a slimline, emerald green, lizard skin valise, with his initials in gold script letters below the gold locking latch.

Any other time, the citizens of Mosby who happened to witness the arrival of a big shot, would have been gawking at the stunning, blonde secretary in the short, red, form-fitting, décolleté dress, and the four-inch spike heels.

She was an apparition of the Goddess Aphrodite in the flesh. So beautiful, in fact, someone suggested that she could bring tears to a glass eye. A woman of her pulchritude is seldom ever seen anywhere, except on the big silver screen in Hollywood. But, on the other hand, absolutely no one had ever seen a man dressed as resplendently as Mr. Stonebreaker, not even at the movies.

Then the worm turned.

Stonebreaker strutted and the blonde sashayed into the courthouse. She was poetry in motion. The lecherous thoughts of the otherwise benign male onlookers clashed with each other in the Realm of the Netherworld, fighting for conquest and supremacy, with each step she took up to the courthouse doors. No doubt a dozen wives and girlfriends were the satisfied beneficiaries of this vision after the lights went out that night, and many more nights thereafter.

The bikers and chauffeur remained outside with the gleaming chariot under Randall's watchful eye. Finally, the passersby moved on, now that the meteor shower had passed, but you can bet the image, etched indelibly in the minds of many, still lingered for months afterwards.

A little while later, the bikers rode down the street to the Dry Gulch Saloon. They drank one beer each. Randall was watching, waiting for any sign of trouble, but they were model citizens.

Sheriff Sol was in the DA's office with DeWitt when Elton Stonebreaker and Miss Goodbody arrived. Stonebreaker said he was present to sign on as Mr. Schitt's counsel, and that he was going to request that the judge hold a bond reduction hearing forthwith.

DeWitt called the judge's secretary and passed along the message. Judge Sweeney made Stonebreaker cool his heels until noon before appearing in court. With time to kill, and billable hours, otherwise known as his earnings meter running full tilt, Stonebreaker told Sheriff Sol he wanted to speak with his client.

Sheriff Sol walked him down to the jail. He had Chunk search him for weapons. Then Chunk escorted him into the cell block, locking him in with his client. Chunk stationed himself in the jailer's room where he could partially observe, but not hear, the meeting.

Thirty minutes later, Stonebreaker left, sweating like a sumo wrestler in a Turkish steam bath, his skin a marbled red in the face, muttering about the inhumane treatment his client was receiving.

At noon, Judge Sweeney convened court. He accepted Elton Stonebreaker as Joseph Schitt's attorney of record. He held pat on the $50,000 cash bond, but postponed the trial until Friday, November 14th. DA DeWitt objected, but was overruled.

Then DeWitt informed the court and defense counsel that he planned to supersede the indictment on Thursday, November 6th, adding a count against Mr. Schitt for being an habitual offender.

Stonebreaker jumped to his feet. He was outraged. He shouted, "This is an ambush! You're all in cahoots trying to railroad my client! This is villainy at its very worst! It has all the earmarks of a kangaroo court! I demand additional time to prepare for this unwarranted and absurd additional count! This smacks of prosecutorial abuse!"

This outburst mightily offended Judge Sweeney. His face turned beet red. He was apoplectic. He pounded his gavel like he was smashing Brazil nuts. He exploded, "Counsel is precariously close to being charged with contempt of court! You temper your tongue, Sir!"

He shook his finger at Stonebreaker and added, "I'll lock you in a jail cell next to your client for the next ten days so you can devise your strategy together. One more incendiary remark will clench your fate!"

Stonebreaker, who was sweating profusely, and who now realized the ice under his feet was cracking and that he was about to take an icy plunge for which he had no stomach, humbly apologized. He changed tactics and pleaded, "I beseech you, Your Honor. Going to trial on such short notice is unprecedented, and will, of course, be a basis for an appeal if you proceed."

Judge Sweeney cooly responded, "Request denied. You can appeal all you want, all the way to the highest court of this land. You'll lose."

Then he ordered, "Mr. District Attorney, turn over all discovery material to defense not later than Friday morning, November 7th, at 10 o'clock."

As a postscript, he added, "This is a simple case, no more than a half-dozen witnesses, all of whom live in town except for one, and none of whom are to be harassed or intimidated. Thus, I can't fathom why defense needs more than ten days to prepare."

Then he pounded diamonds into dust with his gavel, and said. "Court is out of session." He swept out the door behind his bench like a fading phoenix.

Immediately afterwards, DeWitt and Stonebreaker returned to the DA's office. The effulgent Bufo toad caught his reflection in the glass. It pleased him greatly. He smiled smugly and said, "We'll plead the case for a maximum five-year sentence."

Now on his own turf, it was DeWitt's turn to flex and to demonstrate that he, too, had a case of the red ass. He said, "Initially I had planned to offer ten years, but deep down inside, I knew it would be a waste of my time. That's why I sent my investigator to collect the evidence needed to secure a conviction on the Habitual Offender Act.

"The aggravated assault case is already 'money in the bank.' My final offer is twenty years in prison, at hard labor, in lieu of trial, which, as we speak, I can just about guarantee will be less than half the prison sentence envisioned by Judge 'Maximum Max' Sweeney."

Stonebreaker appeared to be thunderstruck. He bellowed, "Twenty years is preposterous for no bigger of a dust up than this was!"

Then, the more he thought about it, the madder he got. His face turned purple. His beady, little blue eyes bulged. Spittle was coming out of his mouth. He got tongue-tied, unable to formulate his words. Finally, he roared, "I'll eat you in court!"

DeWitt roared back, "The only one who's going to get eaten is you, Stonebreaker, most likely by the judge, who doesn't cotton to high-priced, fancy pants lawyers! I suggest you tone it down a notch if you want to stay out of jail!

"Furthermore, for your information, both vics are well-liked in this community, whereas Joe Shit the Ragman is an anathema to the citizenry of Mosby and Quayle County. It won't take fifteen minutes for them to return a guilty verdict on all counts. Twenty years is so much better than life!"

Stonebreaker sputtered, "Your key witness, the baby cop, is a stone-cold killer, wet behind the ears, suffering flashbacks from

Vietnam. I'll make mincemeat of him."

"Give it your best shot, Counselor. Your stone-cold killer is a bonafide hero in this town. You're hallucinating. You must be ingesting some of that poison your client peddles."

Stonebreaker became sanctimonious. He pontificated, "Thank you, Mr. DeWitt. You just made the case for me, that my client could never, ever receive a fair trial in this backwater county. This will oblige Judge Sweeney to grant a change in venue. I'll get the case transferred to El Paso or Amarillo, where he can get a fair trial."

DeWitt snapped back, "That will never happen! All the witnesses except Creech live in this county, although Creech probably won't return even if he is subpoenaed. Nobody besides the witnesses and the deputies have ever seen Mr. Schitt, let alone talk to him. The newspaper here is a six-page weekly with negligible influence to sway the as-yet-to-be determined jury. No appellate court in the state would overturn Judge Sweeney's ruling to hold the trial here.

"Unless you're pleading your client to twenty years, we're done here. See you in court a week from Friday. One more thing. I suggest you get paid in full before trial; otherwise you'll be doing this case pro bono. Good day, Counselor!"

Stonebreaker stormed out of DeWitt's office. He and his secretary piled into his big fancy machine and left town - very slowly. All three bikers followed. Not one traffic law was violated. By 3 o'clock, everyone in the community knew what had transpired.

When Barlow reported for work that night, he asked if Meacham copped the license plate numbers on the choppers. The answer was 'yes.' All the bikes were properly registered, nothing out of order, and the riders did not have any outstanding warrants. Furthermore, EPSO had been contacted, and were mailing photos and rap sheets on all the Diablos they have on file.

CHAPTER 45

EYE OF THE STORM

The following ten days were uneventful. It was like being in the eye of a hurricane. Everyone followed the new protocol like his life depended on it. Maybe it did. Chitchat was held to a minimum.

Barlow had a hard time concentrating at school. Sarah was sensitive to his somber mood. She didn't push, but somehow managed to be present when he needed her. The whole town acted like the gunfight at the OK Corral could erupt in Mosby at a moment's notice.

On Thursday the 6th, Chief returned with the evidence needed for the high bitch. He testified at the Grand Jury. A superseding True Bill was returned against Joseph Schitt.

On Friday, November 7th, the Chief Alex and Deputy Atwater drove to Elton Stonebreaker's office, surrendering all discovery material, and a copy of the superseding indictment. It went as slick as snot on a doorknob. They were in and out in ten minutes.

Chapter 46

Preparation for the Big Ball

On Thursday, November 13th, Elton Stonebreaker and his party checked in at the Travelers Rest. He met with Joseph Schitt for three hours that afternoon. No one had seen nor heard from a Diablo. Everyone was on edge.

That day, Sheriff Chester Fentress, EPSO, called and spoke with Sheriff Sol. He said to expect the entire El Diablos Motorcycle Club at trial.

Arch and Barlow worked their standard midnight shift Thursday night through Friday morning, November 13/14. They both were scheduled to testify later that day. Barlow obtained another excused absence from school.

It was 3 a.m. Barlow was surprised to see Sheriff Sol and others show up for work, but Archie wasn't. Archie already knew. The sheriff had activated the Sheriff's Posse. Heck, Barlow didn't even know such a thing existed!

By 4 o'clock, over sixty members of the mounted posse were assembling in the Rodeo Grounds. There were almost as many horse trailers parked there as on rodeo days. Slick was in charge of posting the posse, most of whom were mounted. A few had been detailed on foot posts around the courthouse, but they brought horses, nevertheless. All were armed with handguns. Most had long guns in their saddle scabbards.

Betty's Diner and the American Legion were open to accommodate the needs of the posse. It was curious that the public works department did not put out any port-a-potties. Sheriff Sol said the Diablos could stand in line at the courthouse if they needed to go. He also instructed his deputies to arrest anyone caught pissing in the bushes. Zero tolerance today.

Except for the unpaid posse, all full-time and part-time deputies were on the clock. Sheriff Sol said Judge Sweeney and the Board of Supervisors approved overtime for the regulars until Joe Schitt was out of the county, plus expenses for all the posse, until the Diablos were out. Expenses meant food and drink plus fodder for the animals.

At 6 o'clock, Deputy Meacham radioed that 32 Diablos motorcycles and two biker vans had just crossed the Quayle County line, headed for Mosby. Trial wasn't scheduled until 10. Moments later, he radioed that two El Paso news trucks from different stations were also headed to town.

Barlow couldn't imagine all this hullabaloo for an aggravated assault trial. Just imagine what it must be like in L.A., whenever anyone from the Charles Manson cult appeared in court! Helter Skelter wouldn't begin to describe it.

Around 6:45, Barlow heard the motorcycles. They arrived, crawling down the street to the Dry Gulch Saloon. Old Man Spellman was already open. It was reported that the price of a draft beer had increased from 50 cents to $1.00. Apparently, neither greed, nor shame, has any bounds.

Both sides of America Avenue were flanked with mounted members of the posse spread out about fifty yards apart.

Chief was roaming around in his Jeep Wagoneer, taking photographs.

Chunk and Kirk were sitting in a unit watching the tavern. In addition, Slick had detailed a half-dozen of the mounted posse all around it, off premises, to watch for violations of public urination.

The regular townsfolk began showing up for work, but most businesses remained closed. Everyone was curious. This was better than the circus.

Dewey Carruthers and a member of the posse had been detailed to the lockup itself, to process prisoners.

Sheriff Sol assigned Ernie Atwater and himself as Joseph Schitt's custodians.

At 7:30, Randall Meacham returned from the county line and set up a checkpoint at the foot of the courthouse steps to search visitors for weapons before they could enter. He had four of the largest, toughest members of the posse to assist.

Doors of the courthouse opened at 8 o'clock, like always. Folks were already lined up to get in. This would prove to be interesting, in that the courtroom itself only accommodated eighty persons. It looked like all the courtroom benches would be filled to capacity before any of the Diablos arrived.

Everyone even remotely involved with the sheriff's office had an assignment, except for Arch and Barlow. That's because they were the star witnesses. So this is what it felt like to be a celebrity. Barlow decided he'd rather be invisible. He felt like a bug under a microscope.

At 8 o'clock, Mr. Elton Stonebreaker, Esquire, and his party of five, rolled up to the front of the courthouse like Hollywood celebrities.

The five included the chauffeur, who remained with the blinding, black, behemoth, luxury land cruiser; the voluptuous secretary; a scrawny, bald, little, weaselly-looking assistant of some sort who was carrying three, bulging, leather valises; and, two Diablos outlaws wearing their colors. The older biker's jacket bore a patch identifying him as the club president.

The crowd made way for Stonebreaker and his entourage to jump the line. The deputies searched them thoroughly, but found no weapons. Once inside, Stonebreaker went to the jail to confer with his client. The others made a beeline for the courtroom. They took seats on the left, in the front, behind the railing separating the public from the attorneys' tables. Left is reserved for defense. It was clear they knew their way around a courtroom. Lots of experience, no doubt.

Barlow and the other witnesses gathered as instructed, at the office of District Attorney Able DeWitt.

DA DeWitt told them to wait there until such time as they were called to testify. They were sequestered, meaning that they were not allowed to hear the testimony of the other witnesses until after they had testified, themselves. This rule was designed to cut down on perjury.

After they testified, they could remain in the courtroom to watch, or they could return to the DA's office, whichever they preferred.

He reminded them to answer all questions truthfully. They were to say they didn't know the answer to a question if they didn't know. Ask for clarification if they didn't hear or understand a question. Don't exaggerate. Don't be scared. Don't get mad. The jury would be evaluating the truthfulness of their testimony, looking for signs of deception as well as believability, so look at the jury when you are answering a question.

Looking around the room at one another, it was apparent that all except Archie would have preferred running down the street naked during the Fourth of July parade, rather than to testify against a coldblooded killer. Oh, yeah. They all knew Joe Shit the Ragman had been arrested for aggravated assault. They all had friends and family on the posse. It was different today. This was not a festival. Everyone had to cowboy up.

CHAPTER 47

OPENING VOLLEY

Trial was called to order promptly at 10 o'clock. The courtroom was packed. This was high drama for sleepy, little Mosby.

Many of the observers were there to see what Deputy Adams would say. Although everyone knew who he was, most had never spoken to him. This was a good opportunity to size him up.

Gossip around town was that his good looks were deceiving. He was so young, so quiet, unimposing in stature, not the type of person one would expect to shoot dead Sandra Tafts attacker, or to stand up to a dangerous outlaw biker like the scary looking Joe Shit the Ragman.

The observers were both mesmerized and aghast at Elton Stonebreaker's appearance and commanding presence. He was attired exactly as he had been ten days ago, except this time his outfit was fire engine red. Only his tie was cobalt blue. His voice was stentorian. He commanded attention, like a ringmaster at the circus. He was the unequivocal center of attention.

Judge Sweeney called the courtroom to order in his typical, no nonsense fashion. In spite of Stonebreaker's flamboyance, everyone could see that Judge Sweeney was still in control. They all knew he would brook no deviation from proper courtroom etiquette and decorum.

The voir dire was quick and efficient. Even though Judge Sweeney and DA DeWitt knew all 24 prospective jurors personally, this was not Old Home Week. In thirty minutes, twelve jurors and two alternates were selected, with only four strikes.

The District Attorney's opening remarks were brief.

He outlined his case as a straightforward assault on a respected citizen, with threats of bodily harm, pushing and shoving, compounded by the uttermost intimidation by the two outlaw motorcycle gang members.

It escalated into life or death violence by both outlaws when a sheriff's deputy attempted to defuse the situation. The criminal case against one of the bikers had already been adjudicated, and was not in dispute today.

Today's case was about the unlawful actions of the other biker, the defendant present before the court, who attempted to slash the deputy with an eight-inch dagger before being subdued and arrested.

In addition to securing a guilty verdict on each count related to the assaults, the county would prove beyond a reasonable doubt, that this defendant, with his extensive criminal record, was guilty of being an habitual felony criminal offender, and should be convicted of such.

Mr. Stonebreaker didn't wait for the DA to conclude his opening remarks. He jumped to his feet and objected that his client had just been defamed by the District Attorney, who called him an outlaw biker. Now that the DA prejudiced the jury against him, the judge had no other choice but to rule this a mistrial and to censure the DA for this scurrilous debasement of his client.

The jury didn't know what to think. Some didn't understand what Stonebreaker said, but it certainly didn't sound good for Mr. DeWitt.

Judge Sweeney coughed lightly into his hand and cleared his throat. He looked first at defense counsel and then at the jury. Then he said, "By definition, an outlaw is someone who lives outside the law, someone convicted of violating the law. The defendant's past criminal conduct is well documented, not even in dispute, in fact. The district attorney's accurate description of the defendant as an outlaw is no more inflammatory than it would be to call a cardinal a red bird. He is what he is.

"In fact, the court believes the defendant is proud of being an outlaw. It gives him stature in his community. If he feels defamed, he did it to himself. Motion denied. Defense counsel needs to sit down and wait his turn."

Mr. Stonebreaker sat down. The judge was still in charge.

When his turn did come, Mr. Stonebreaker stood up abruptly, tugging at the lapels of his $500.00, custom made suit, and marched directly in front of the jury. He stared into the eyes of each juror, discomfiting them no small amount, before speaking.

He boldly declared, "The district attorney is making a mountain out of a molehill. Did you hear me? A mountain out of a molehill! In fact, this is a case of prosecutorial abuse due to overcharging my client over a minor disagreement between barroom patrons, further compounded by gross overreaction by a wet-behind-the-ears, unqualified, adolescent, rookie deputy, and a vicious, over-the-hill, senile deputy, both of whom used excessive force, and in so doing, violated my client's civil rights. Very soon, both of them will be facing an investigation for criminal and civil violations by the FBI for their unwarranted abuse.

"Look at my client! Notice the cast from shoulder to wrist! Look at that awful contraption cobbled together, holding his arm in place away from his body! Does that look like it's comfortable to you, or does it look like he is in excruciating pain? That's what your deputies did to my client! Remember that when you hear their rendition of events on that godforsaken, regrettable night."

With the exception of Judge Sweeney and DA DeWitt, the entire courtroom was riveted by Mr. Stonebreaker's theatrical performance.

Observers already forgot this was about poor, passive Clifford Biggs who nearly got stomped into hamburger at the hands of Mr. Stonebreaker's outlaw client. They disremembered that Clifford would never challenge a fourth grader, let alone a murderer. What about Deputy Adams? Did he go berserk? They were confused and doubtful, and the first word of sworn testimony had yet to be uttered.

Score: Stonebreaker one; the State zero.

CHAPTER 48

OLD MAN SPELLMAN SETS THE STAGE

Testimony commenced with DA DeWitt calling Dry Gulch proprietor, Elmer "Old Man" Spellman to the stand.

He testified, "That night was nothin' special. It was a typical, quiet, weeknight. I only had three customers, when the two strangers come in. They was all about theirselves, talking loud, swearing, being obnoxious. They bellied up to the bar, and ordered a couple of drafts. After awhile, they tried to get my other customers to cozy up to them.

"The problem was, they was scary and my other customers wouldn't look at 'em. They tried to ignore 'em.

"This guy, the defendant, and his pal was on their third beer, when they began picking on Clifford Biggs, calling him dirty names, daring him to fight, stand up like a man, and things such as that. Cliffy comes in near ever' night. He don't bother nobody. His wife up and died a couple of years ago, and Old Cliff, he ain't been the same since. Then they started poking him, slapping his face, not too hard, just enough to agitate him and make him fight.

"They said they'd cut him into pieces like a fish, and this guy here, I seen he had a big old, fancy knife on his belt. It had a real long blade, and I thought they might be serious, so I called the sheriff's office and asked Deputy Willis to come as fast as he could.

"A little bit later, Deputy Adams walked in the front door. I didn't see Deputy Willis at first, because he didn't make no noise and sneaked in the back. I don't know why he done that. He usually comes in the front.

"Deputy Adams told the two strangers to leave Cliffy alone. Then they started making fun of the deputy, calling him names.

One of 'em made a really nasty comment about his mother, so the deputy said both the guys was under arrest. Then the other stranger charged straight on, right at Deputy Adams, like he meant to body slam him. The deputy stepped back real quick like a cat, and jabbed the guy in the gut with his billy club. The guy started throwing up all over the floor and fell down on his knees. He was groaning and heaving real bad. Then this guy, Mr. Schitt…"

The courtroom erupted in laughter. Judge Sweeney pounded his gavel like he was killing cockroaches, yelling, "Order in the court. Order in the court. I will fine the next person who violates the sanctity of the court, so help me God! One more peep from anybody! The more the merrier. Twenty dollars for anyone who has an outburst like this again!"

The courtroom hushed up real fast.

DA DeWitt instructed Mr. Spellman to refer to the defendant as the defendant.

Mr. Spellman finished up stating, "The other guy fell down and started puking. Then the defendant, scrambling quick as a lizard, come around the table and grabbed his sticker, but before he got it out, Deputy Adams hit him on his knife arm with his billy club.

"Then Deputy Willis was there. I saw the knife scooting across the floor. Deputy Willis grabbed the defendant from behind and handcuffed him in the back. This guy was howling like he got gutted hisself. Looked like his arm might've got broke. Then Deputy Adams handcuffed the other guy. That was it."

DA DeWitt showed the Nazi dagger to Mr. Spellman and asked if he could identify it.

He said, "That's the knife the defendant had."

"Your Honor, I request that the Clerk of Court enter this dagger with the scabbard as prosecution Exhibit 1."

"So be it."

Stonebreaker jumped from his seat and objected that

Spellman never had custody of the knife and therefore could not introduce it as evidence.

Judge Sweeney asked Spellman how he could be sure this was the knife in question.

Spellman said, "Deputy Willis showed it to me after the fight and I held it. I never seen such a fancy knife, with the Nazi cross and all the silver and onyx trim."

Judge Sweeney said the objection was overruled.

DA DeWitt took the knife and walked over to the jury so they could all get a good look. Then it was Stonebreaker's turn for cross examination.

He asked, "How long have you owned the tavern?"

"Eleven years."

"How many days a week is it open?"

"Six."

"What hours?"

"Normally noon 'til 2 a.m."

"Do you own a motorcycle?"

"No."

DeWitt objected, saying this was irrelevant.

Stonebreaker said it was extremely relevant because it would show that Spellman has a bias against motorcyclists.

Judge Sweeney overruled the objection.

Stonebreaker asked the question again.

Spellman said, "No."

"Have you ever ridden a motorcycle?"

"Once as a passenger."

"Did you like it?"

"No."

"Do you get many motorcyclists as customers?"

"Not too many."

"When you do, do you call the Sheriff?"

"Not unless it's necessary."

"Has it been necessary before this incident?"

"Once or twice."

"Was it once or twice?"

"Twice."

"Why did you call the Sheriff?"

"Because the first time they was grabbing my waitress in her private parts and the second time they was busting up my bar."

"What did the Sheriff do?"

"Locked them up."

"Both times?"

"Both times."

"So you don't like motorcyclists."

"Not the ones what cause trouble."

"So by your own admission, you are biased against my client."

"I didn't say that."

"Oh, but you certainly did! I'm through with this witness, Your Honor."

DA DeWitt got up and asked permission to re-direct. The judge granted it.

He asked, "Mr. Spellman, did you have anything against the defendant or his partner, Mr. Creech, when they entered your establishment."

"No, Sir."

"Did you treat them any differently than your other patrons?"

"No, Sir."

"Do you hate the defendant?"

"No, Sir."

"Is your establishment, in fact, open right now and servicing the needs of other members of the El Diablos Motorcycle Club?"

"It is."

"Did you tell the truth in your testimony this morning?"

"Yes, Sir."

"No further questions. You may step down. The county calls Mr. Clifford Biggs to the stand."

Score: Stonebreaker one; the State one.

CHAPTER 49

CLIFFORD BIGGS COWBOYS UP

Whereas Elmer Spellman appeared as if he wanted to be somewhere else, such as selling overpriced beer to outlaw bikers, Clifford Biggs, when he shuffled in, head down, taking small steps like he was walking to the gallows, looked like he would burst out bawling if someone gave him a hard look. He didn't make eye contact with anyone. He didn't want to be somewhere else. He wanted to be anywhere else.

"Mr. Biggs, can you tell us where you were on Wednesday night, October 29th, into the wee hours of Thursday morning, October 30th?"

"I was sipping a gin and tonic at the Dry Gulch like I usually do."

"What, if anything, was different about that night?"

"Late that evening, two guys, a Mr. Creech, I believe, and a Mr. Schitt barged in, talking loud, and ordered beer at the bar."

"Can you describe Mr. Creech?"

"He was mean-looking and great big, like a bull."

"Is he in the courtroom today?"

"No."

"Can you describe the other man?"

"He's sitting next to the man in the fancy red suit."

"Are you referring to the man whose arm is in a cast?"

"Yes."

"I would like the court and the jury to note that Mr. Biggs has identified the defendant."

"So noted."

"What happened then?"

"After a while, I seen them staring at me. I looked away, but Mr. Creech said, 'What are you looking at, you little worm?'"

"He called you a worm?"

"Yes, Sir."

"Then what?"

"Then Mr. Schitt started laughing and said I didn't have enough backbone to qualify as a worm. Then he come over and shoved me and said for me to stand up and pull up my shirt, so he could see if I had a backbone."

"What did you do?"

"I looked away down at the floor. He shoved me again, so I clung to the table so I wouldn't fall off my chair. He kept pushing and shoving me."

"What happened next?"

"Mr. Creech come over and picked up my drink and swallowed some of it. Then he spit it out all over me and said it tasted like . . . a bad word."

"What bad word? You need to tell us."

"He said my drink tasted like spider piss and only a woman or a queer would drink something like that. Then he asked me if I was a worm or a queer. Then he poured the rest of my drink over my head."

"What happened next?"

"Then Miss Eloise ran over with a towel and she mopped the drink off of me and the floor."

"When you say Miss Eloise, do you mean Miss Eloise Huff, the barmaid?"

"Yes."

"Okay. What happened next?"

"Then Mr. Creech handed her a dollar bill and told her to go fetch me a beer. He said I needed to learn how to drink like a man. I said, 'No thanks. I don't like beer.' Then I said I wasn't thirsty no more and I was going home."

"What happened next?"

"Then Mr. Creech shoved me back in my chair and said I was insulting them and acting like I was too good to drink with them. Then Mr. Schitt called me a name and asked if that was so."

"Was what so?"

"If I was too good to drink with them, I guess."

"What name did he call you?"

"He called me a rank, tunafish-smelling pussy."

"What happened next?"

"I said I wasn't too good. I just wasn't thirsty no more. Then they both started in on me, pulling my ears and my nose, poking me in the chest, pouring beer on me, telling me to stand up and fight."

"What did you do?"

"I bent over the table and clung to it and prayed to God this would all stop."

"Did it stop?"

"My prayer was answered. They kept on until Deputy Adams come in and told them to knock it off."

"What happened then?"

"They both laughed real loud and started in on him."

"What did they say?"

"Well, Mr. Creech had just said he was going to filet me like a fish. Then Deputy Adams come in and Mr. Creech said he looked like a baby cop. Then Mr. Schitt told Deputy Adams to go home because his mother was calling him. Then he said something really bad."

"What did the defendant say?"

"I'd rather not say."

"It's all right. The jury needs to know."

"He said Deputy Adams needed to tuck his mother in bed because they both just finished . . . ."

"Finished what?"

"Fucking the shit out of her."

"Those were his exact words?"

"Yes, Sir."

"Then what happened?"

"Then Deputy Adams said they was both under arrest.

"That must've made Mr. Creech awful mad, 'cause he come running at Deputy Adams, yelling 'ahhhhh' real loud like a wild animal.

"Then Deputy Adams poked him in the stomach with his nightstick. Mr. Creech stopped like he'd been shot, and started wheezing, like his lungs had collapsed, and he started throwing up all over hisself, and all over me, and then he fell to his knees and kept on vomiting.

"Then Mr. Schitt grabbed this big knife that was in a metal sheath hanging off his belt, and he come runnin' at Deputy Adams. Deputy Adams was turned away from him, more towards Mr. Creech, but he musta heard something, 'cause he looked up in the last second, and swung his nightstick backhanded, and hit Mr. Schitt on his arm. Then Mr. Schitt dropped the knife and started screaming bloody murder, and Archie, the other deputy who was back by the bar, ran and tackled Mr. Schitt and wrassled him to the floor.

"Mr. Schitt was hollering all sorts of things, like he was real mad and his arm was paining him. Archie didn't pay him no never mind. He grabbed both of his arms and handcuffed him behind the back. Then Deputy Adams went over and handcuffed Mr. Creech behind his back. Then as quick as he could, Archie picked up the knife so no one would get hurt."

"Did you go home then?"

"No. After a while. First, I had to tell Sheriff Sol and Chief Snodgrass what happened. Then I went home."

"Mr. Biggs, did you ever do anything or say anything to Mr. Creech or Mr. Schitt to provoke them into assaulting you?"

"No, Sir. I just wanted to be left alone."

"No further questions. Your witness, Counselor."

Mr. Stonebreaker stood up slowly, adjusted his jacket, flicked his wrists such that his shirtsleeves poked out far enough so everyone could see his diamond cufflinks. He strolled over to the witness stand. He stood as close as he could directly in front of Clifford Biggs. Then he smiled magnanimously at the jury like he was running for office, before turning an icy stare at Mr. Biggs who was looking down, and who appeared as if he were trying to squirm his way into Judge Sweeney's lap.

"My, my, Mr. Biggs, your story sounds like you were saved from a fate worse than death by Deputy Do Right, er Adams, excuse me, Your Honor, just in the nick of time."

DA DeWitt stood up. "Your Honor. That sounded like Counsel was testifying. I didn't hear a question. Furthermore, it sounded like he was denigrating Deputy Adams."

"Very careful, Mr. Stonebreaker. You're skating on paper thin ice. Ask a question or sit down."

"Pardon me. Let me rephrase, Your Honor. Isn't it true, Mr. Biggs, that you embellished your story, akin to a mother telling a fairy tale to a child?"

"Weren't no story. It's the gospel truth!"

"Is that so?"

"Yes, Sir."

"Harrumph! Isn't it true you were eyeballing Mr. Creech and my client like they were scum of the earth, while they were peaceably having a cold beverage?"

"No, Sir!"

"Come on. Do you really expect us to believe that my client and his colleague verbally assaulted you for no good reason?"

"That's what happened!"

"So you say. Even if it were true, that they misunderstood the insolent glare you directed their way, didn't Mr. Creech offer to buy you a drink to make amends?"

"He drank my gin and tonic! Then he spit it all over me. Then he poured the rest of it on my head. Then he told Miss Eloise to fetch me a beer. I didn't do nothing to either of them."

"Didn't you insult them by refusing Mr. Creech's generous offer?"

"Generous offer? My drink cost 75 cents! Their draft beer cost 50! I didn't ask for it. I just wanted to go home and let bygones be bygones. They wouldn't let me!"

"If you say so. Did you see the unprovoked altercations between the boy deputy and Mr. Creech and my client?"

Bang! Bang! Bang! Bang! Bang! Bang! Bang!

"Mr. Sweeney. You've been warned! You're in contempt of court. I fine you $100. Another remark like that and I will put you in a jail cell right next your client!"

"Very sorry, Your Honor. The deputy's name escaped me for the moment. I was merely trying to distinguish him from the older deputy."

"Fiddlesticks! Pay the Clerk of Court before day's end, or so help me God, I'll issue a warrant for your arrest and make sure it's executed by the Texas Rangers! Do I make myself clear?"

"Most assuredly, Your Honor. I'm sending my assistant forthwith to pay the fine. May I continue, Your Honor?"

"Watch yourself, Mr. Stonebreaker. Proceed with an abundance of caution."

"Yes, Your Honor. Mr. Biggs, did you see either altercation?"

"I saw them both."

"What exactly did you see?"

"I saw Mr. Creech take off towards Deputy Adams like a raging bull. Then Deputy Adams poked him in the gut and he fell down."

"Come on, Mr. Biggs. Like a raging bull? Are you sure he wasn't just headed over to the deputy to apologize?"

"No, Sir. That's not what happened."

"Didn't the deputy use excessive force under the circumstances? Jabbing him so hard he expelled all the contents of his stomach?"

"I don't believe he did."

"Don't believe? That sounds like you're hedging your bet. Didn't he use way more force than was necessary to subdue Mr. Creech, all because he was enraged regarding the untoward remarks regarding his mother?"

"I don't think he did."

"Isn't it true the deputy had no cause to arrest Mr. Creech or my client, and the only reason he did was because of those remarks?"

"They was shoving me and threatenin' to cut me up! Ain't that reason enough to arrest them?"

"But he didn't arrest them when he first came in. He waited until they insulted him. That's how we know it wasn't about you. Isn't that true?"

"He told them to back off me as soon as he come in. Then they turned on him. I don't know what more he could 'ave done. Anyway, Sheriff Sol and Mr. DeWitt believe he done right. Both of them jay birds was arrested."

"What about the savage beating Deputy Adams gave my client? He broke my client's arm in eighteen places! He may never regain full use of it again. Don't you call that excessive force?"

"No, Sir. Mr. Schitt was gonna stab him. I call what Deputy Adams done self-defense."

"How about the way Deputy Willis wrenched my client's arms behind his back, squeezing the handcuffs down as tight as they would go, cutting off all circulation, especially after everyone could see how badly Deputy Adams broke his arm in eighteen different places? Wouldn't you call that excessive use of force and a violation of my client's civil rights?"

"First off, nobody knew his arm was broke. At least I didn't. Besides that, he tried to stab Deputy Adams! I didn't see nothing like what you just said!"

"My, my. And you claim to have seen all this with your own two eyes?"

"Yes, Sir!"

"How on Earth could that be? By your own admission you clung to the table and prayed to God this would stop. Didn't you have your eyes screwed shut the whole time you were praying?"

"Not all the time. I did at first. Then I opened them. I saw it all."

"Even with your head bowed face down into the table or rolling around on the floor?"

"Not after the deputy told them to knock it off. I looked up to see who was coming to help."

"And you saw everything clearly with tears and gin and tonic and beer running down your face and into your eyes?"

"Yes, Sir. I saw it all!"

"Mr. Biggs, I find your entire story unbelievable and preposterous.

"Your Honor, I have no further questions for Mr. DeWitt's star witness."

"The ice is starting to crack, Mr. Stonebreaker. Do I need to remind you where you'll be sleeping tonight if I have to call you out again?"

"My apologies to Mr. Biggs and to the Court, Your Honor. No affront intended. I suppose my skepticism got the better of me."

"Better keep your skepticism to yourself, Mr. Stonebreaker. The next time I'm coming down on you like a ton of bricks."

"Yes, Your Honor."

"Mr. DeWitt?"

"No re-direct, Your Honor."

Then he paused while he considered whether it was necessary to call his other eyewitnesses - the barmaid, Eloise Huff, or the elderly Mr. and Mrs. Winters. He decided that their testimonies would be repetitious and that they wouldn't make his case any stronger, so he changed direction and said, "Next, I'd like to call Deputy Adams to the stand."

"You may step down, Mr. Biggs. You are free to go. You may

take a seat in the courtroom, or in the District Attorney's office."

"If it's all the same to you, I'd prefer to wait in Mr. DeWitt's office."

"So be it. Please tell Deputy Adams that his presence is needed."

Score: Stonebreaker one; the State two.

CHAPTER 50

BARLOW'S TURN IN THE RING

Barlow entered the courtroom and stood before the clerk. After being sworn in, he took his seat.

DA DeWitt said, "State your full name."

"Barlow Knotts Adams."

"How old are you?"

"Twenty."

"When will you be 21?"

"In February."

"How long have you been a deputy?"

"About three-and-a-half months."

"What did you do before that?"

"I was in the Army."

"How long?"

"Two years."

"Were you deployed overseas?"

"Yes, Sir."

"For how long?"

"Twelve months."

"Where to?"

"Vietnam."

"Did you participate in combat action?"

"Yes."

"Were you shot at, or mortared, or otherwise in mortal peril?"

"Yes, Sir."

"Did you engage the enemy by cannon, machine gun, grenade, rifle, or pistol fire, or by bayonet, or hand-to-hand?"

"Yes."

"Which?"

"By howitzer fire and rifle fire."

"Did you receive any decorations for valor?"

"No."

"Did you receive an Honorable Discharge?"

"Yes."

"What did you do before serving in the Army?"

"I was in high school. I also worked part time as a mechanic in my uncle's service station."

"Did you graduate from high school?"

"Yes."

"Have you completed the Texas Police Officers Standard Training certification?"

"No."

"Are you currently enrolled?"

"Yes."

"When do you expect to complete the course?"

"In May of 1971."

"Please tell the court what happened on Wednesday night, October 29th, which resulted in your court appearance here today."

"I was working the midnight shift with Deputy Willis. It was a little before midnight, before Thursday the 30th, when we received a telephone call at the jail. Deputy Willis answered and spoke with someone . . ."

"Do you know who that someone was?"

"I didn't at the time, but I later learned it was Mr. Elmer Spellman, proprietor of the Dry Gulch Saloon."

"What happened next?"

"Deputy Willis spoke for a minute and hung up. He said there was a disturbance at the Dry Gulch, and for me to get my nightstick and go with him to the tavern."

"Did he say anything else?"

"He said a couple of outlaw bikers were roughing up a

customer . . ."

"Objection, Your Honor, to the deputy calling my client an outlaw biker."

"We've covered this ground, before, Counselor. Overruled."

"Did Deputy Willis tell you anything else?"

"Yes. He said he would take the rear door and for me to take the front."

"Why did he say that?"

"Because this was my first time as a deputy responding to a trouble call and he wanted to see how I would handle it."

"What happened next?"

"Once we arrived, I waited for Deputy Willis to slip in the back. Then I went in through the front."

"Was Deputy Willis already inside when you entered?"

"Yes. He was standing in the shadows near the back door."

"What did you see?"

"I saw the tavern owner behind the bar. The waitress was standing next to a table with an older couple. All of them were watching two men wearing El Diablos Motorcycle Club jackets, who were picking on another man, subsequently identified as Mr. Clifford Biggs."

"What do you mean 'picking on?'"

"Well, the first biker was really big, about six feet tall and maybe 300 pounds. He was calling Mr. Biggs foul names, daring him to fight. He was shoving Mr. Biggs, saying he was going to filet him like a fish."

"Did that biker have a knife?"

"Not that I could see."

"Then what happened?"

"The defendant here, was egging it on, telling the first biker to do it."

"What did you do?"

"I approached the table and told both men to 'knock it off.'"

"Did they?"

"Well, yes, but then they started in on me, verbally, but they didn't lay hands on me."

"What did they do?"

"Both called me names. They told me I better leave. Then the defendant made a false, vile statement about my mother."

"How did you know it was false?"

"Well, for one thing, my mother has been dead for eight years."

"What did you do?"

"Well, I'd already seen the first biker shoving and threatening Mr. Biggs, and the defendant was disorderly, inciting further assaultive behavior, and it was obvious they weren't going to heed my order, so I said they were both under arrest, and to get on their knees and put their hands behind their heads."

"What happened next?"

"The first biker ran at me with his arms wide-stretched, like he wanted to wrestle. I jabbed him in the stomach with my stick and he stopped short. He fell to his knees and started vomiting. Then the defendant here, rushed me from the other side of the table. I saw he was pulling a sheath knife, so I whacked him on the elbow one time, and he dropped the knife. By then, Deputy Willis was on him. He tackled the defendant and recovered the knife. I turned my attention back to the first biker, and handcuffed him."

"Is this the knife?"

"Yes."

"Did you fear for your life when the defendant pulled this knife?"

"Yes."

"Your witness, Counselor."

Mr. Stonebreaker remained seated, studying his notes. Finally, he arose and approached the witness stand. He brushed away an imaginary piece of lint from the sleeve of his jacket. He stared sat Deputy Adams a full thirty seconds without speaking.

Barlow stared back.

Neither man blinked.

Finally, Stonebreaker said, "You're awfully young for a law enforcement officer, aren't you?"

Barlow wanted to say, "You're mighty short and fat for a high-priced drug lawyer," but he responded, "I already said that I'm twenty years old."

"Answer the question!"

"What do you mean? You know my age. Are you asking if I'm the youngest deputy in Quayle County? If so, the answer is 'yes.'"

"By at least ten years, I'd say."

"Is that a question?"

"No. You haven't answered my original question. Would the clerk please read my original question to Deputy Adams?"

"You're awfully young for a law enforcement officer, aren't you?"

DA DeWitt stood up. "Your Honor, Counsel is badgering the witness. Twice the witness has stated for the record that he is twenty years of age."

"Overruled. I'll allow it."

"Your Honor, I'm not sure how to answer the question. Is he asking my opinion?"

"Your Honor, it's a simple question that requires a yes or no answer."

"Mr. Stonebreaker, we're not going to parse the definition of young in this court. I will allow the witness some leeway."

"Sir, I was in combat while I was still eighteen. Then I grew up real fast. Since I returned, I don't feel all that young. I might have, had I gone straight to college where nobody was trying to kill me. No. I don't think it's young. Not anymore."

"I'm glad you mentioned your combat experience. Tell me, how did you get appointed as a deputy sheriff with no law enforcement experience, not even as a military policeman, in a community so far from your home where no one even knew you?"

"Sheriff Pratt asked me to apply. I did and he hired me."

"How did you come to make Sheriff Pratt's acquaintance?"

"I was passing through town and I assisted a motorist. It came to the sheriff's attention and I met him as a result."

"What type of motorist assist draws the attention of the county sheriff?"

"A citizen was being assaulted along the side of the highway, late at night, and I intervened."

"How was the citizen being assaulted, Deputy?"

"She had a flat tire. A stranger stopped and asked if she wanted help. She said yes. Then he said he wanted sex in return. She said no. He must have figured since no one was around, he'd take it anyway. He started beating her and ripping her clothes off of her.

"I happened to be passing by when I saw him strike her. I stopped and got my gun. I told him to stop. He shot at me three times and missed. I shot him and he died. I met the sheriff. He had a vacancy. I applied. He hired me. That's how this twenty-year-old became a deputy sheriff in Quayle County. Does that answer your question?"

"Hardly. Did you kill men in combat?"

"Yes."

"And then you killed this alleged would-be rapist?"

"Yes.

"And then you became a deputy?"

"Yes."

"And you subsequently responded to a call of an altercation at the Dry Gulch Saloon?"

"Yes."

"And you are a student, not a graduate of the Texas Police Officers Standard Training Course?"

"Yes."

"Have you completed a course in threat assessment or unarmed combat?"

"Not in POST."

"Where?"

"In Army Basic Combat Training."

"But the Dry Gulch Saloon is not in Vietnam, is it Deputy?"

"No."

"Indeed not! So you were untrained and unqualified to respond to this call, weren't you, Deputy?"

"Not true. I was and I am qualified. Besides that, I am not required by state law to be POST certified for twenty-and-a-half more months. Your client tried to stab me with a knife! I could have shot him. He has a broken arm. I'd call that a blessing if the shoe were on the other foot."

"It's hardly a blessing, Deputy! Don't you think it was premature, even irresponsible, for Deputy Willis to order you to take the lead in this, your very first, trouble call?"

"Not at all."

"Really?"

"Really."

"By what reasoning, for God's sake?"

"Mr. Stonebreaker, you better not use the Lord's name in vain in this court!"

"No, Your Honor. It's just that I am astonished by the lack of professionalism exhibited by the sheriff's department in this incident, and I'm trying to understand why."

"That's not your assignment, Mr. Stonebreaker. Confine yourself to the facts surrounding the incident which landed your client before my court. My patience is wearing thin with you. This isn't some big city courtroom which condones or allows lawyers to showboat. Is that understood?"

"Yes, Your Honor."

"Deputy, answer the question. Mr. Stonebreaker, you better be ready to make your point or move on."

"Sir, I'm a new, unproven deputy. The sheriff's office needs to know if I can resolve issues like this without making things worse. It was an opportunity for me to get some OJT."

"OJT?"

"On-the-job training. This was an opportunity for a seasoned deputy to watch and evaluate my performance. If Deputy Willis saw that I needed assistance, he was right there to help, which he did when both bikers decided to jump me."

"Good grief, Deputy! And you pat yourself on the back and say you did a great job and even call the outcome a blessing? How could you possibly have performed any worse? You may have maimed my client for life!"

"It could have turned out worse a lot of ways. I could have run away. I could have let your client or Mr. Creech filet Mr. Biggs like a fish. I could have overreacted and beaten your client senseless for trying to kill me. I could have let both defendants escape. I could have died at the hands of your client. Instead, both were arrested and brought to justice. Deputy Willis' decision to let me be lead in this situation definitely resulted in a positive outcome for this community in my opinion."

"Oh, good grief! And what about Deputy Willis' manhandling of my client after you viciously broke his arm? Wouldn't you agree it was unnecessary, cruel and unusual punishment, in fact, a violation of my client's civil rights, the way Deputy Willis jerked poor Joseph's broken arm and yanked it behind his back, and then the way he crushed the manacles down on his wrists as tight as they would go? Was my client not weeping and screaming to high heaven for all the world to see because of the excruciating pain he was in?"

"Deputy Willis saw poor Joseph try to stab me with his dagger. It fell to the floor, momentarily out of sight, at least to me. Deputy Willis followed proper police procedure in cuffing your client before he or Mr. Creech, for that matter, could have picked it up and used it against us. How is that a violation of civil rights?"

"So your testimony is that both you and Deputy Willis performed your jobs flawlessly?"

"Few things are ever flawless, but I say we came as close to it as we could under the circumstances."

"Thank you, Deputy Adams! You've just established my argument regarding your youth, lack of training, inexperience, and proclivity towards violence. You are either the world's greatest prevaricator, acting like you actually believe what you say, that you performed your job well by current police standards, or you are too inexperienced to know a proper police performance from a poor one.

"You missed the essence of Wednesday night's drama completely, I believe, because of your youth and inexperience. I actually think you believe you did a good job.

"Simply put, this was a minor disagreement among three drunks at a dive, late at night, some minor joshing around, which I admit, my client and his buddy carried a touch too far, pouring a drink on Mr. Biggs, but they did try to make amends by purchasing him a beer.

"The cops get called because the inbred, sorry, Your Honor, I meant to say incompetent, barkeeper was too afraid to cut them all off and shoo them out the door, so Andy and Barney barge in, and Barney misreads the scenario. He's trying to impress Andy, but he overreacts because of an injudicious remark by one of the drunks who was from out of town and dressed funny, and voila! Barney gives it all he has and jabs a police baton with all his might into the stomach of one drunk so hard, he vomited for five full minutes!

"Then my client, also completely inebriated, runs to see how bad his friend is hurt, but his sheath knife is cockeyed and interfering with the movement of his legs, so he tries to readjust it, and Barney freaks out, misreads the situation again, thinks he's about to be emasculated, and delivers a grand slam blow right on my client's elbow.

"The damage to my client's elbow was exacerbated by the complicit and reckless assistance of a senior citizen deputy, who used the exact opposite of tender, loving care on an injured citizen.

"What we wind up with, is both out-of-towners under arrest, one maimed for life, and now maybe going to prison for the rest of his life. Isn't that true, and all because you were and still are, too young and untrained to handle a minor incident of this sort? Isn't it true?"

Bang! Bang! Bang! Bang! Bang!

"Mr. Stonebreaker, I heard at least three extremely injudicious remarks in this tirade masked as a question. This is absolutely your very last warning. I'm exercising every bit of restraint that I possess, not to find you in contempt for the second time.

"Mr. Spellman is not an inbred, and neither Andy nor Barney work for the Quayle County Sheriff's Office. It is against my better judgment that I am letting those inflammatory remarks go unpunished, but you are playing with fire. A wise and prudent man would proceed with the utmost caution."

"Yes, Your Honor. My sincere apologies to the court and the deputies."

"You may answer the question, Deputy Adams."

"Yes, Your Honor.

"My answer to Mr. Stonebreaker is an emphatic 'No!' I must be testifying to an entirely different matter than the situation you just described!

"First off, I didn't see any drunks on the call I responded to.

"Next, what I saw was Clifford Biggs being tormented by two bikers. I told them to stop. When I realized they were going to ignore my commands, I arrested them both.

"Furthermore, Maynard Creech was very light on his feet for a big man, and without provocation, he charged me. I used the minimum force necessary to subdue him. Then before I could cuff him, your client decided to intervene. He scrambled around the table, drawing his knife, for what possible reason other than to stab me?

"Fortunately for all of us, one blow subdued him, too.

"Then Deputy Willis came to my aid. How many times do I need to tell you the same thing before you stop badgering me?"

"Tut. Tut. What a textbook example of gilding the lily in an effort to embellish your so called, nearly flawless, police procedure!

"You testified that you were in fear of your life. Why didn't you just shoot my client dead like you did the alleged wannabe rapist?"

"I probably should have, but my back was partially turned to him. He jumped me while I was still dealing with his partner. I was busy trying not to get stabbed. It was all I could do to give him a backhand to slow him down. It was a close call. I most certainly was afraid of being stabbed, if not stabbed to death."

"We'll see what the FBI has to say about that. No further questions.

"Deputy Adams, you may step down. Please tell Deputy Willis it's his turn."

Score: Stonebreaker one; the State three.

Chapter 51

Archie TKO's Stonebreaker

Barlow told Archie. Then he grabbed an open seat at the prosecutor's table.

"Deputy Willis, state your full name for the record."

"Archibald Xavier Willis."

"How long have you been employed as a deputy sheriff for Quayle County?"

"Oh, it's been 27 years this stretch."

"What do you mean, 'this stretch?'"

"Well, I was a deputy after I returned from World War I, from 1919 to 1936. Then politics changed and I was let go. Then in 1942, they changed again and I was rehired."

"So altogether, you've been a Quayle County deputy sheriff for 44 years?"

"I reckon so."

"Are you POST certified?"

"Oh, I'm like everyone else who has unbroken service since 1967. I was grandfathered in."

"So you never graduated from a police academy?"

"That's right."

"Do you think that has hindered you in the performance of your duties, especially in the modern era?"

"Shucks, no. What are they going to teach an old dog like me? I seen darn near everything that can happen in a place like this."

"You mean Quayle County?"

"Yes."

"Far West Texas, the Trans-Pecos, southeastern New Mexico?"

"Sure."

"Have you trained deputies in your career?"

"You bet."

"How many would you say?"

"Oh, fifteen, maybe twenty. It sort of depends on your definition of training. Some men come by it naturally, have a good head on their shoulders. They don't need much supervision or babysitting. Others take more time to learn the ropes. Some never get it, and eventually get run off or quit on their own."

"What about Deputy Adams?"

"Oh, he's a natural. Good disposition, fast learner, takes correction well, a good hombre to partner with."

"Looking back to October 29th, is that why you let him take the lead in the Dry Gulch incident?"

"You bet."

"Were you afraid he was too inexperienced?"

"Not at all, but he had to prove it to hisself and to me."

"And did he?"

"Well let me ask you this. How many green deputies could subdue two criminals, one armed with a knife, with only two blows without getting injured or killed hisself, or breaking up all the furniture in the saloon?"

"Your point is well taken, Deputy.

"Did you see Mr. Schitt and his partner, Mr. Creech, curse, shove, poke, pull the ears, tweak the nose, threaten, pour an alcoholic beverage on, or otherwise harass, assault, or batter Mr. Clifford Biggs?"

"I did. All but the pulling of ears, tweaking of the nose, and pouring of beer on his head."

"Did you see Mr. Biggs do anything to bring this kind of behavior upon himself?"

"No. Just the opposite."

"Did he insult or engage in fighting words with Mr. Creech or Mr. Schitt?"

"No. He was crying and trying to get away from them."

"Did you see Deputy Adams enter the tavern?"

"I did."

"What did you observe?"

"Well, I saw him attempt to cool off the situation by telling the two bikers to lay off Mr. Biggs. They both mocked him, and Mr. Creech said the most disgusting, disrespectful thing you could imagine about his mother. Finally, Barlow had no other choice. He placed both men under arrest.

"Soon as he told 'em, Creech charged him, and Barlow put him down with one jab to his gut. Creech goes at least 280 pounds, and it ain't all fat.

"Then his pard, Joseph Schitt here, he charged Barlow from the other side of the table. Schitt was pulling this eight-inch, fancy dagger out of the sheath, and I thought for sure he'd slice Barlow afore I could get there. Barlow pivoted and swung his club backhand, and connected right on Schitt's crazy bone. He dropped the knife, and I tackled him from behind, and cuffed him afore he could snatch it back up.

"Barlow cuffed Creech, and I secured the knife. It was all over but the wailing and gnashing of teeth in about ten seconds."

"Did Deputy Adams overreact, use excessive force, or otherwise violate the civil rights of either defendant?"

"Absolutely not! Many a lawman would have shot Schitt dead. I would have. Others would have given Creech a blow to the head after he fell down, just to make sure all the fight was out of him and to keep him out of commission. They would've been completely justified, too. These owlhoots got off lucky."

"Did you use excessive force handcuffing Mr. Schitt?"

"No doubt he says I did. Heck, he darn near stabbed my partner. He's a bad hombre. I got to him as quick as I could, and grabbed him tight until I could get the cuffs on him. If he said it hurt, he's no doubt telling the truth.

"All I was thinking at the time, is that I got to cuff him afore he gets to the knife and sticks me or someone else. He can holler all he wants, but I did not use excessive force! Neither did Barlow!

Like I said, Barlow or I would have been justified shooting him."

"One last question. Were either Mr. Creech or Mr. Schitt, or for that matter, Mr. Biggs intoxicated when you arrived at the scene?"

"Nope. They all appeared sober to me."

"Thank you, Deputy Willis. Your witness, Counselor."

This time Stonebreaker did not walk over to the witness stand. He stood and addressed Archie from the defense table.

He opened with, "My, my, Deputy Willis, you're a salty dog, aren't you?"

"Mr. Stonebreaker, I may be a salty dog, but I'm not a fancy pants, loudmouth shyster like you!"

The courtroom erupted in laughter.

Bang! Bang! Bang! Bang! Bang!

"Order in the court!"

Bang! Bang! Bang!

The courtroom returned to a mausoleum-like silence. Judge Sweeney let the silence linger for a minute or more.

"Mr. Sweeney, you fired the first volley.

"Deputy Willis, you've appeared in my courtroom a hundred times or more. You know better than that! Another repartee like that and Mr. Stonebreaker, you will be spending the night in jail. And Deputy Willis, you'll be paying a healthy fine, if you're not staring across the cell block at each other. Am I clear, ladies?"

"Yes, Your Honor."

"You bet, Your Honor."

"Very well. Carry on, Mr. Stonebreaker, but make no mistake. I've exhausted my patience with you. Next slip and you're a gone pecan."

"Yes, Your Honor. What I meant to convey, Deputy Willis, is that you have a plethora of experience in the deputy business. Correct?"

"Well, I don't know about that, but I been around enforcing the law long before your pappy decided to have kids."

"To put a fine point on that, my father wasn't born yet in 1919, when you first began. So in your vast experience, I'm sure you've seen scores of barroom incidents, been called to put out the fire, as it were, many, many times."

"It's been a lot."

"I have no doubt. Have you broken up a lot of fights?"

"Of course, but this here was no fight. Clarence Biggs wasn't fighting. He was being provoked to give those yahoos an excuse to stomp a mud hole in him."

"And you know this how? You read minds because you're clairvoyant?"

"Mr. Stonebreaker, I'm no mind reader. Like you said, I'm a salty dog. I seen flare-ups like this all my life. You could ask anyone in the saloon that night what was fixing to happen. They'll all tell you the same thing. Why do you think Old Man Spellman called the sheriff's office?"

"So you watched the interplay between your trainee and Mr. Creech?"

"He ain't a trainee. He's a deputy sheriff, and yes, I saw the whole thing."

"Then you saw the rookie deputy sheriff inflict a vicious thrust with his truncheon into the solar plexus of Mr. Creech."

"It was a jab to his gut, simple as that, period."

"So you watched that take place. You saw it?"

"How many times do I have to repeat myself? Yes! I saw it."

"So then you personally observed Deputy Adams' overreaction with that mighty jab that was way too excessive, using far more force than needed, so hard, in fact, that it caused Mr. Creech to regurgitate violently for several minutes."

"It was not an overreaction. It was self-defense. If Barlow wouldn't have poked Creech hard enough to put him down, he would have taken Barlow to the ground. With his momentum and two-to-one weight advantage, it's no telling how bad he would've hurt Barlow, maybe even kilt him. I say Barlow was more than justified in his use of force which was not excessive."

"No doubt you would say that, if for no other reason than to justify your even greater use of excessive force on my client, when you violently wrenched his shattered arm behind his back, and savagely clamped your manacles on his wrists so hard it cut off all circulation on each one! You are likely more responsible for injuring his arm than Deputy Adams!"

"Is that a question or an accusation?"

"You senile old reprobate, masquerading as a pathetic, washed up version of Wyatt Earp or TV's Marshal Matt Dillon! Look at you! The FBI will make you rue the day you abused my client! You went too far, this time, you old geezer!"

"You're worse than your client! You know that, you lyin' little weasel?"

Bang! Bang! Bang! Bang! Bang! Bang! Bang! Bang! Bang!

"Sheriff Pratt approach the bench!"

"Here, Your Honor."

"Sidebar, please."

"Yes, Your Honor."

Judge Sweeney bent down and whispered to the sheriff, who leaned up to hear. "Sheriff, are you fully staffed today?"

"Yes," he whispered back.

"Can you accommodate another overnight prisoner?"

"Yes, Sir. With pleasure."

"Very well. You may resume your position at the rear of the courtroom."

"Mr. Stonebreaker approach the bench."

Stonebreaker had a panicked expression on his face as he mustered all his bluster and dignity while waddling to the bench.

"Mr. Stonebreaker, you weary me with your insolence. I've warned you repeatedly. I find you in contempt of court for the second time today. I sentence you to jail, to serve from the completion of these proceedings today, until the stroke of midnight. If I find you in contempt one more time, you will serve seven 24-hour days to the minute. I mean it! Your conduct today has been reprehensible! I'm still debating whether to file a bar complaint against you. Do I make myself clear?"

"Yes, Your Honor. I apologize to the Court and to Deputy Willis."

"That's a good thing, Mr. Stonebreaker, because Deputy Willis will be your jailer tonight. Understood?"

"Yes, Your Honor."

"Mr. Stonebreaker, do you have any more questions for Deputy Willis?"

"No, Your Honor."

"Good, you may return to your seat. Deputy Willis, you may step down and approach the bench."

Stonebreaker's face was ashen. He looked stunned. In fact, some would report that his knees were wobbly on the way back to his table.

"Deputy Willis. You were on firm footing until you referred to Mr. Stonebreaker as a 'lying little weasel.' No matter what the provocation, you do not address anyone in my courtroom in that fashion, even if the person is a lying little weasel. You will adhere to the proper decorum a civilized society demands from its law enforcement officers.

"Therefore, it is with a deep sense of regret, I find it necessary to hold you in contempt of court. I fine you $10, to be paid forthwith to the Clerk of Court. Furthermore, I order you, through Sheriff Pratt, to be on assignment as the jailer until midnight tonight. Of course, you will be paid for these additional overtime hours. Are we clear?"

"Yes, Your Honor."

"Very well. You will remain in the courtroom to escort Mr. Stonebreaker to his cell after today's court session is over."

"Mr. DeWitt, call your next witness."

"Yes, Sir. The county calls Chief Deputy Alexander Snodgrass."

Score: Stonebreaker one - the State four.

CHAPTER 52
THE COUP DE GRACE

Stonebreaker stood up and said, "Judge, may I address the court?"

"Mr. Stonebreaker, I'm pretty sure I already know what this is about. You will have an opportunity to address your concerns during cross or closing arguments. I am allowing into evidence, the testimony of this witness and the records he brings with, so long as they comport properly with the rules of evidence and procedure. Please take your seat."

Chief Snodgrass had a file full of documents. He stood before the clerk and was sworn in. He took his seat in the witness stand.

"Chief, there is a single count on the superseding indictment against Mr. Schitt, which is unrelated to the Dry Gulch incident. Would you inform the jury about the nature of that count?"

"Yes, Sir. Mr. Schitt was already a three-time convicted felon in the State of Texas before he entered the saloon. Texas jurisprudence has a provision for charging, convicting, and sentencing three-time-losers, as they are commonly called, simply because they are habitual offenders, which is irrespective of any new or additional convictions."

"How can you be certain Mr. Schitt already had three felony convictions to his discredit?"

"Well, first I conducted a computerized criminal records check with the FBI and the Texas Department of Public Safety. Both computerized records reflect that he was convicted of armed robbery in Waco, Texas, on February 21, 1955. He was sentenced to serve 10 years in the Texas State Penitentiary in Huntsville. He was released on parole on March 26,1960.

"Then he was convicted of possession of a controlled substance, specifically methamphetamine, on July 7, 1960, in Dallas, Texas. He was sentenced to serve 2 years at Huntsville. He also received two years for his parole violation, to run concurrently with the controlled substance conviction. He was released on May 23, 1962.

"Then he was convicted of aggravated assault and felon in possession of a firearm on November 3, 1964, in San Antonio, Texas. He was sentenced to serve three years on each count at Huntsville, both sentences to run concurrently. He was released on October 31, 1967.

"I have certified, exemplified copies of each conviction with me today, each of which I obtained in person."

"What does certified, exemplified mean?"

"It means the conviction documents are signed and sealed by both the sentencing judges and the clerks of court who maintain the records, attesting that the documents are true and correct."

"And how can you be sure that the defendant is the same person who was sentenced and imprisoned all three times?"

"I went to all three local jurisdictions . . . "

"Do you mean the police departments in Waco, Dallas, and San Antonio?"

'Yes, Sir, plus the sheriff's offices in each one. I obtained mugshots and copies of original fingerprint cards at all six. Then I went to Huntsville and obtained inmate records, to include mugshots and copies of fingerprint cards for each incarceration.

"Next, I had a DPS fingerprint expert examine each set of fingerprints. I have his report in which he confirms that each set of fingerprints match and that they all belong to Mr. Schitt.

"Furthermore, I brought all the mugshot photographs with me for the jury to compare with the defendant sitting in the courtroom today."

"Thank you."

"Your Honor, I tender all these records to the Clerk of Court, requesting that they be entered as prosecution Exhibits 2 through 21."

"So be it."

Stonebreaker reviewed all the evidence as the Clerk of Court logged it in. Then DA DeWitt passed each item one by one down the jury box. When each juror had satisfied his curiosity, DA DeWitt collected the evidence and returned it to the Clerk. Then he said, "Your witness, Counselor."

"No questions, Your Honor."

"The witness may step down. Call your next witness, Mr. DeWitt."

"The prosecution rests, Your Honor."

"Very well. Call your first witness, Mr. Stonebreaker."

"May we have a recess for lunch, Your Honor?"

"It's only 11:45, Mr. Stonebreaker. How many witnesses do you have?"

"A moment if you please, Your Honor."

"Very well."

Stonebreaker had a short tête-à-tête with his client. Then he addressed the Court and announced, "The defense rests."

Judge Sweeney said, "Very well. You may commence your closing arguments, Mr. Stonebreaker.

Stonebreaker stood and walked over to the jury box. He looked each juror in the eye. He said, "My client has a checkered past. He's made some serious mistakes, and it's cost him dearly - about ten years in prison to be exact. He served his time like a man, no whining, no complaints.

"It was wrong for him to make sport of Mr. Biggs, but the truth is, all he took was a little of Mr. Biggs' dignity. He did him no physical harm. You heard no evidence that Mr. Biggs suffered any physical hurt or that he needed medical attention. Nevertheless, my client is remorseful and wishes he could take everything back, every insult, each poke, every mean thing he did to him.

"As it relates to Deputy Adams, my client's actions were misinterpreted. For an instant, he saw red and felt rage when he saw how viciously Deputy Adams brutalized his friend. He lurched to avenge the wrong perpetrated by Deputy Adams, but in the next instant, a blink of the eye, he realized his purported actions were suicidal, so he tried to cease his forward momentum, but the World War II family heirloom brought home by his father, a decorated combat soldier, the Nazi ceremonial dagger, got tangled with his legs, and the knife began to fall out of its metal sheath.

"You all saw the knife and the sheath. You saw how loosely the knife fits, and how easily it can get dislodged. So he tried to grab it by the handle, to keep it sheathed, but it was too late. By then Deputy Adams had seen my client take the knife by the handle, and he mistakenly perceived a threat to his safety. He did a pivot and backhanded my client on the elbow with his police truncheon, breaking a number of bones. No one knows exactly how many, because Deputy Willis wrenched my client's hands behind his back and did even more damage. Suffice it to say, my client has eighteen breaks in his arm, and it may never function properly again.

"This maiming of my client was the result of an overzealous, inexperienced deputy with little or no formal training in enforcing the law. It was compounded by the incompetence of Deputy Willis, who assigned Deputy Adams to sort out this truly, insignificant horseplay, and then who has steadfastly tried to cover up Deputy Adam's rookie mistakes.

"We hold both deputies responsible for the egregious and excessive use of force. That's why we referred this civil rights violation for investigation by the FBI. Had it not been for the District Attorney's rush to exact frontier justice in such short order, no doubt the FBI would have concluded their investigation, and my client would have paid a substantial fine, but he would now be free, and all the while these rogue deputies would be the ones sitting behind bars, not him.

"Also, you must remember that this was a most insignificant incident. The only injuries occurred to my client and to his pal. No one else was assaulted! No one else was hurt! Now my client is facing charges that could literally put him behind bars for the rest of his life. For what? Pardon my French, but for being a horse's ass to Mr. Biggs? That's ludicrous! It's making a mountain out of a molehill!

"I know you all are devout Christians. You study the Good Book. When you deliberate guilt or innocence, remember the passage in the Lord's Prayer. 'Forgive us our trespasses, as we forgive those who trespass against us.' I implore you to render a not guilty verdict on each count. Thank you and God Bless."

"Your turn, Mr. DeWitt."

"Thank you, Your Honor.

"Fellow citizens and neighbors, members of the jury, that was an eloquent plea by my esteemed colleague. His rendition of the events in question could fell Mother Theresa to her knees in prayer, could it not? I know how hard he tugged on your heartstrings, because he tugged on mine.

"He sized you all up as the faithful Christians you are, and made it sound like returning guilty verdicts on each count would be turning your back on Jesus.

"You must stay focused on the testimony that we presented to you today. Each witness placed his hand on the Holy Bible and swore to tell the truth and nothing but the truth.

"I wonder . . . . Did any of you see Mr. Stonebreaker, or me for that matter, raise our hands and swear on the Bible that we would tell the truth? No? That's because we didn't.

"We are both officers of the court, but we cannot testify. We present evidence and witnesses before you, but we don't testify! Keep your eye on the ball! Don't be swayed by smoke and mirrors.

"You all know Clifford Biggs. You heard what he said. Do you believe he provoked either Mr. Creech or Mr. Schitt, or that he was responsible for the reprehensible verbal and physical attacks they both inflicted on him?

"What about Mr. Spellman? Did he have a reason to lie about what he saw?

"What about Deputy Adams? Would any of you have wanted to face those two bikers on your own, all by yourself, at least initially? Do you believe he overstepped? Could any of you have done what he did? Do you think his life was in peril when he intervened? Was this all one big joke, or was it a matter of life or death?

"Then there's Archie. You all have known him since your youth. Do you really think he embellished the truth to make himself or Deputy Adams look better than they actually are? Do you trust his word? Is he the evil man as portrayed by opposing counsel? Is he a sadist bent on inflicting pain and injury on folks because he's a deputy and can get away with it? Think about it.

"What about all the records Chief Alex brought back? Do these records reflect the misadventures of a choirboy, or do they tell the story of a hardened, career criminal?

"If each of you believes beyond a reasonable doubt, that Mr. Schitt did everything these witnesses told you, and you can marry up these misdeeds with the individual statutes the judge will explain and put before you, then it is your solemn duty to return guilty verdicts on each count, so help you God. Remember. Even Jesus had to overturn the tables of the money changers in the Temple. The wages of sin is death, even today.

"It is not your responsibility to worry about any sentence which may be imposed. That's Judge Sweeney's job. I know each of you will discharge your duties as jurors faithfully, and in accordance with the law. God speed."

Judge Sweeney took his time, and methodically charged the jury with the elements of each crime. He patiently answered all questions. Then he sequestered them in the jury room, with instructions to the clerk to have the jury meals delivered forthwith.

He recessed the court, but admonished all affected parties to remain nearby. He said he would reconvene at 2 o'clock unless the jury was still out. He said everyone should be back in the courthouse by then.

Score: Stonebreaker one; the State five plus one equals six.

CHAPTER 53

THE VERDICT

When Barlow got up to leave, he saw Sarah and Clarice waiting for him in the hallway.

Clarice said, "Barlow, I just never imagined that the outlaw bikers were as evil as they are. They scare me to death! Now I understand why Sheriff Sol activated the posse, including Arthur and Cordell."

Sarah said, "You were great. All of you were. I feel so bad for poor Mr. Biggs."

Barlow said, "Thanks. These guys are all bad news. If you think about it, they're organized crime just like the Mafia. I hope the jury convicts. Either way, we still may have a problem. You can see they're not scared of us. If they were, we wouldn't have been treated to a parade of motorcycle outlaws this morning. I hope they all leave Quayle County and never come back. From what we're hearing though, this won't be the end of it."

Clarice said, "Come on. We brought some drinks and sandwiches. Let's eat in the car away from all this hubbub."

Barlow was relieved at this invitation. He wasn't ready to return to the jail, and he especially didn't want to stand in line at the diner or American Legion. Mostly, he was drained and he didn't feel like discussing the case, even with his closest friends.

Clarice's car, a pale metallic green, 1960, Imperial Crown sedan, was parked in the back of the courthouse lot, and it was plenty roomy for a three-person picnic. Not only that, it afforded as much privacy as anyone would find downtown today in this circus-like atmosphere.

When they finished at 1:30, he led them through the sheriff's office and thence to the courtroom, avoiding the mob at the front of the building. He bumped into Sheriff Sol, who whispered that the jury had a verdict, and suggested they find seats in the courtroom before they were all taken. He also told Barlow to stay behind after the verdict, no matter which way it went, because his assistance would be needed.

They found aisle seats halfway back on the prosecution side.

At 2 o'clock sharp, Judge Sweeney entered the courtroom and took his perch on the bench. The jury was already seated. So were Stonebreaker and his client, both of whom appeared to be staring into outer space. The silence was palpable, even unnerving.

Judge Sweeney surveyed the courtroom. A hundred or more pairs of eyes were intently fixed on him. Finally, he looked over at the jury box and said, "Mr. Foreman, has the jury reached a unanimous verdict on each count?"

The foreman, Conrad Hightower, rose. He said, "We have, Your Honor."

Judge Sweeney directed his gaze at the defense table, and asked, "Will the defendant please rise?"

Both Stonebreaker, who was intently trying to read Conrad Hightower's body language, and Schitt, who appeared disinterested and lackadaisical, stood.

"On the first count charging disorderly conduct, how does the jury find?"

"Guilty, Your Honor."

"On the second count charging assault and battery of a citizen, how does the jury find?"

"Guilty, Your Honor."

"On the third count charging resisting arrest, how does the jury find?"

"Guilty, Your Honor."

"On the fourth count, charging aggravated assault on a police officer, how does the jury find?"

"Guilty, Your Honor."

"On the fifth and final count, charging the defendant of being an habitual offender, how does the jury find?"

"Guilty, Your Honor."

"Thank you, Mr. Foreman. Please be seated.

"Mr. Stonebreaker, do either you or your client have anything you'd like to say before I pronounce sentence?"

"Your Honor, I will speak on behalf of my client.

"As you might imagine, this verdict comes as an unpleasant surprise. My client simply stopped in Mosby to 'whet his whistle,' as it were, before resuming his ride to El Paso. Nothing that transpired here was planned or even contemplated. He regrets his boisterous and unwarranted ribbing of Mr. Biggs, and he seeks forgiveness from all aggrieved parties.

"We beg for leniency, Your Honor. The sum of the potential sentences is staggering. It's conceivable that Mr. Schitt may never draw a breath of free air ever again, all over a minor misunderstanding, in which no one except for my client and his running buddy, Maynard Creech, were even injured.

"A harsh sentence would reflect poorly upon this county, and perhaps even upon this court. It could inflame the passions of those who might look at a harsh sentence as xenophobic, deplorable, perhaps even igniting a call to vengeance, as undesirable and lamentable as that would be.

"Please, Your Honor. We request compassion and leniency if you can find it in your heart."

"Mr. Stonebreaker, before I pronounce sentence, I want to know if you are prepared to serve yours for contempt of court?"

"Your Honor, naturally I'd rather undergo a root canal or a frontal lobotomy than to serve time in your dungeon. That being said, I will surrender myself forthwith at the conclusion of court today, praying fervently that at midnight, my time having been served, I will be released unmolested and allowed to depart, never to set foot in this curious burg again, where Time seems to have stood still for the greater part of this century."

"Mr. Stonebreaker, your eloquence in wordsmithing, combined with your proclivity towards sarcasm, will no doubt lead you to incarceration again someday, if you continue in your trade as a trial lawyer.

"May I suggest a new line of employment, perhaps as a live comedy act on the nightclub circuit of New York City or Las Vegas? The compensation may not be as great as it is in your specific area of expertise, in the defense of high level and well-paying criminal entrepreneurs, but it will keep you out of jail.

"Sheriff Pratt, is the Sheriff's Office fully prepared to protect and defend the citizens and law-abiding visitors of Quayle County, in the event of lawlessness today or henceforth? In other words, should I shirk my duty and render an unjust and anemic sentence in an effort to preserve order?"

"Your Honor, we are prepared today, and we will be prepared in all the days that follow, to protect the law-abiding people in Quayle County."

"Very well. Before I pronounce sentence, I feel compelled to acknowledge the considerable efforts of Mr. Stonebreaker in mounting a vigorous defense of his client, whose behavior was indefensible. You earned every penny of your no doubt, considerable fee, in doing everything you could to keep him out of jail, or at least, minimize his exposure, which was epitomized by earning some jail time yourself, albeit just for a few hours.

"Mr. Schitt, I for one, do not believe you have even one ounce of the milk of human kindness or decency in you. Even so, it is not necessary for me to impose the maximum sentence in order to exact a fair and just punishment on you, in spite of my reputation as 'Maximum Max.'

"First, I must caution any witness to this proceeding who might be contemplating retribution or vengeance on any party to this case, or to Quayle County at large, to take heed. I will live up to my reputation in sentencing anyone who is convicted of 'evening the score,' as it were.

"Mr. Joseph P. Schitt, this court hereby sentences you to six months confinement on count one for disorderly conduct; one year confinement on count two for assault and battery of a citizen; six months confinement on count three for resisting arrest; 15 years confinement on count four for aggravated assault on a police officer; and 25 years confinement on count five for being an habitual offender. Furthermore, I order all sentences to run consecutively. In case you didn't do the math, that's 42 years at hard labor in the custody of the Texas Department of Corrections in Huntsville. You will also pay $75 in court costs.

"Congratulations, Mr. Schitt. You are returning back home where you belong. You will receive credit for time served, dating from Thursday, October 30, 1969.

"I did the math, Mr. Schitt. You are 34 years old. If you live to complete your prison sentence, you will be 76. I suggest that you 'wet your whistle' anywhere but Quayle County when you get out, if in fact, you ever do.

"Court is adjourned."

Judge Sweeney rose and began to return to chambers. Joseph Schitt, his face contorted in anger, yelled, "Fuck you, Judge! You'll be sorry! You'll all be sorry! Just wait and see! This ain't over yet!"

Sheriff Sol and Deputy Atwater yanked him under control by his good arm and his belly chain, and half dragged and half carried him back to his jail cell when his shackled feet could not keep up with their momentum. The rough manhandling didn't seem to matter. Joseph Schitt was in an uncontrollable rage. Pain was inconsequential - at least for the moment. He would pay the price later on once he calmed down.

Deputy Willis lead Mr. Stonebreaker to the jail as well. He suffered another indignity when all of his personal property was taken away and inventoried, and he was processed for fingerprints and photographs, before incarceration in the jail cell across from his client.

CHAPTER 54
AN ALERT IS ISSUED

Barlow escorted Clarice and Sarah through the sheriff's office and out the back door to their car. He watched as they drove away. Then he sought Sheriff Sol for orders. It had been an extremely long and tense day and he was running out of steam. Nevertheless, the entire sheriff's office staff had much to do.

Sheriff Sol instructed Barlow to check out a shotgun and partner up with Deputy Atwater, who had checked out a car. He did and they watched the crowd from the bank parking lot. It seemed unusually subdued, maybe even pensive now that justice had been dispensed. The spectacle was over.

Stonebreaker's chauffeur had taken the secretary and assistant back to the Travelers Rest to await the clock's stroke of midnight.

The outlaw bikers were huddled outside the Dry Gulch, ostensibly being briefed by the club president, who had been present in the courtroom throughout the trial.

The posse was mounted, including those who previously held foot posts. They looked primed for battle.

The citizenry had broken up into little clusters, waiting to see what would transpire.

Without fanfare, the outlaw bikers broke up and mounted their bikes. The president pulled out westbound on America Avenue and slowly crept westward a half block. He stopped and revved his engine.

The eyes of the horses began dart nervously. Most of the horses got fidgety. A few began to rear up. Some of the posse's attention turned from the outlaws to horse soothing.

Slowly, the other bikers fell in behind the president in single file. When all were assembled, they left as one undulating serpent. In two minutes they were out of town.

Atwater and Barlow followed them to the county line. Nary a law had been violated, nor had public tranquility been breached. It was eerie. They radioed the departure from Quayle County and returned to the sheriff's office for a debriefing.

By the time they returned, the crowd had disappeared, including the news trucks. The businesses that had been closed in the morning remained closed. The last remnants of the posse's mounts were being scooped up by the works department, including Jasper Elrod, who could sling manure with the best of them. By all appearances, the impromptu festival was over, and everything was back to normal.

Also, in the interim, Sheriff Sol had been interviewed in front of the courthouse by both of the TV news commentators. They had already interviewed a number of the posse and bystanders. They were looking for Stonebreaker and Barlow, but Stonebreaker was in jail, and Sheriff Sol ensured Barlow wouldn't be available by sending him on patrol with Deputy Atwater. Barlow didn't learn of this until someone mentioned seeing Sheriff Sol on TV the next day. He was thankful Sheriff Sol saw this coming and quietly directed him out of harm's way.

It was 5 o'clock. Everyone looked like they had gone ten rounds with Muhammad Ali. The debriefing was short, but sobering.

Sheriff Sol thanked everyone for his professionalism and dedication to duty. He affirmed, "We 'dodged a bullet' today, but I doubt that we're 'out of the woods' yet.

"Sheriff Fentress from El Paso called. He said there's an even chance the Diablos will retaliate, if they can pull it off without getting busted. Judge Sweeney, Barlow, and Archie are the obvious targets. He thinks Judge Sweeney is numero uno, but if they can't kill him and make a clean getaway, they'll shift to an easier target. That could be anyone in the sheriff's office, to include family members.

"I called in a marker with DOC. They have a transport team in El Paso who dropped off some high-level prisoners earlier today, so there's four corrections officers in two vehicles, more heavily armed than usual. They've been routed to Mosby and will stop by between 2 and 4 o'clock tomorrow morning for a covert pick up. This is not for public dissemination. Neither Schitt nor Stonebreaker are to know. Hopefully, Stonebreaker won't fuck up and will be out of our hair before then.

"We're doubling up on patrol for the next week at least. Everyone will have to work extra. Overtime has been approved by the Board of Supervisors.

"Everyone needs to be extra vigilant, especially off duty when an ambush is least expected. Chief has photos of all known Diablos and straphangers. Spend some time studying them. Learn to recognize them like you would John Wayne or Al Capone."

He excused everyone except Slick and Chief, who would finish the afternoon shift with him. He said for everyone to check the week's updated duty roster on the bulletin board. Finally, he told Arch and Barlow to bug out and not to return until 1 a.m.

Barlow gratefully complied. He checked his truck for a bomb, which as of recent, had become common practice. Finally he hauled his whipped carcass into the truck and crawled home. He was completely empty. Running on fumes. This had been one very long, emotionally charged day. He was hungry but too tired to take time to eat. All he could think about was bed. Sleep first. Food later.

CHAPTER 55

SARAH COMES TO THE RESCUE

Barlow was surprised to see Sarah's car parked out front. Suddenly he was revitalized. He smelled the aroma of bacon as soon as he opened the door. Before he even closed it, Sarah began frying eggs. He saw grits simmering on the stove. The table was set. He heard the dryer tossing clothes.

She said, "You look completely tuckered out, Deputy Adams. Sit down and take your boots off.

"I decided to stop by after court to do some studying, but I saw your clothes were all piled up in the laundry room. What did you think you were going to wear tonight? That wrinkly, old, pitted out uniform?"

"No. Yes. I don't know. I'm just glad to see you."

"Well I hope so. I sincerely hope so. We'll see just how glad you really are after we eat. Put that shotgun away. It isn't the type of big bang I was hoping for. Let me pour you a little taste of Dr. Crow's famous elixir. I'm almost done cooking."

"Don't mind if I do. Looks like you've thought of everything."

He sipped. She cooked. They ate.

She undressed him and then herself. His happiness to see her was more than just intuitively obvious.

She pushed him onto the bed and caressed him tenderly. He became electrified. For a quarter of an hour he was fully energized.

They were lost in the synchronization of their bodies, moving in tandem, becoming one. The intensity kept increasing until it boiled over. They were both spent. She lay in his arms long after he fell asleep.

She covered him and slipped out of bed. She finished the clothes, washed the dishes, ironed him a uniform, set his alarm, and headed home. Gosh, wouldn't it be nice if she didn't have to leave?

CHAPTER 56

SHERIFF SOL COACHES BARLOW

The alarm sounded at 11:30. He dozed off and on until midnight. He was still half asleep after he showered and dressed. He drank half a pot of coffee until he came to. He was touched by all the things Sarah had done for him. She didn't have to and he would never have asked.

He ate two bowls of shredded wheat and a banana for breakfast. He fixed two peanut butter sandwiches for his 4 a.m. meal. He also threw in four Archway oatmeal raisin cookies, and filled his thermos with the other half pot of coffee.

It was 12:45, Saturday, November 15th. His life had been totally consumed for the past eighteen days by his chance encounter with the El Diablos Motorcycle Club. He wanted them out of his life.

Time to go back to work.

Sheriff Sol was seated behind his desk when Barlow arrived. He walked in and said, "Sheriff Sol, there's something I've been meaning to ask."

"Ask away."

"It's what Stonebreaker said about Archie and me being investigated by the FBI for violating Joe Schitt's civil rights."

"Ah, yes. I was planning to talk to you about that. Archie's been through that before. Several of us have to one degree or another.

"About five years ago, the FBI got some new jurisdiction to investigate the real cops for violating a defendant's civil rights. It was generally designed to investigate cops who abused Negroes, but they can use it to go after any cop if he is accused of unlawfully beating or shooting someone.

"The way it works, the FBI is authorized to investigate a police officer if the local jurisdiction decides not to, or if it fails to get a conviction for assault or murder, or even if the cop is convicted but they don't think the sentence is harsh enough. Double jeopardy does not attach.

"This means if a cop is accused of unlawfully shooting someone, and is tried in state court for aggravated assault and found not guilty, the feds get another lick at him in federal court for the same set of circumstances, but since it's labeled as a violation of civil rights and tried in federal court, it's not double jeopardy. How about that?"

"I think it stinks!"

"So do most cops.

"You should know that most FBI agents assigned to investigate civil rights complaints were lawyers before they became agents. Also, the FBI doesn't allow an agent, who was a state or local officer before becoming an agent, to investigate civil rights cases. They think the agent would be biased in favor of the police. How about that?"

"Sounds like the bias against police is already built in."

"Bingo!"

"Anyway, you may rest assured that Stonebreaker did, indeed, file a civil rights complaint against you both. However, I sincerely doubt the FBI gives a damn about some meth-dealing outlaw biker getting his arm busted in a fight with the cops, after he had already violated the civil rights of a helpless citizen, although they probably wouldn't consider that a violation of civil rights. Even so, they are probably required to conduct at least a preliminary investigation.

"My guess is, they think this is bullshit and probably sat on it to see what the state court would do first.

"Also, their modus operandi would be to review the court transcripts before ambushing you or Archie for an interview. If they follow true to form, we're guaranteed to have a 'heads up' since both the clerk of court and the assistant clerk are our friends.

"The FBI thinks they're smarter than local cops because Quantico brainwashes them to think that way. The FBI is convinced that it's 'the best of the best' and the real police are nothing but a bunch of Keystone Kops.

"If the FBI tells a clerk or some bureaucrat, or other witness not to divulge their interest in a suspect, they believe the witness wouldn't dare. They overestimate their shock effect. Also, they don't believe regular cops are capable of making friends or developing snitches.

"They expect to catch their target unawares whenever they swoop in and read him his rights. They usually threaten to arrest him for making a false statement or for obstruction of justice if he doesn't immediately sing like a canary. To say they are overconfident, overbearing, or obnoxious would be an understatement.

"So, if you get ambushed by the FBI, and they read you your rights, tell them you have nothing to say. Once they advise Miranda, that's a declaration that you're a criminal suspect.

"Don't be rude or a smart ass, but do consider them just like you would a rattlesnake or a grizzly bear. They're powerful and dangerous, but definitely not worthy of trust or confidence, no matter how much they buddy up and try to play you like we're all part of some big, happy law enforcement community.

"What a myth! We are not, especially with an organization dedicated to grabbing all the headlines regardless of who they step on.

"Ask for a business card and tell them your lawyer will contact them shortly. Then come get me and we'll sort this out.

"The way I see it, the list of cops who have been investigated by the FBI for civil rights reads like 'Who's Who in Law Enforcement.'

"You and Archie did everything according to law. Don't think for a moment otherwise, in spite of Stonebreaker's assertion to the contrary. He was looking for the smallest crack in your demeanor or confidence to gain an advantage for his client. Unfortunately, that's his job.

"Don't be surprised if the FBI shows up at school and has you called down to the Dean's office, which would be designed to embarrass you and hurt your reputation there. Don't get rattled. Tell them you will speak with them here, in the sheriff's office, after you've spoken with your attorney."

"Sheriff, I don't have an attorney."

"You do if the FBI wants to interview you. We'll get either Able or Sam to represent you. They're our friends and quite capable.

"The FBI is not your friend and never will be under any circumstances, even if we have a joint investigation with them. They always have a hidden agenda.

"And as long as I'm handing out free advice, here's some more. The press is not your friend, ever. Do not believe anything they tell you.

"Also, if someday you move on and join a large police department, never get involved with a police union. Unions have no place in law enforcement.

"Finally, if you do get on a large police department, stay away from Internal Affairs. They're almost as bad as the FBI. Understood?"

"Understood."

"Good. DOC should be here in a little bit. I want you ready to saddle up with me. We're going to escort them out of the county. If the Diablos plan to rescue their man, it won't go well with them in Quayle County.

"And that's another thing. This isn't over with the Diablos. I guarantee they'll try something. I doubt they'd be stupid enough to go after a judge, but you never know. I can see them going after a cop if they caught him alone and unprepared. If you don't already have a set of eyes in the back of your head, you better grow a set.

"Oh, yeah. If they ever find out that you and Sarah are an item, they might try to do something to her. Arthur Baker is a dear friend, and I'll talk to him. In fact, all the folks in Quayle County need to be alert. In my mind, the Diablos are the ones Stonebreaker should have been referring to when he accused the DA of 'making mountains out of molehills.'

"You sorry you took this job now?"

"No, Sir. If anything, I'm even more honored."

"You're a good man, Barlow. The salt of the Earth. We're glad you joined us. Oh, and Barlow, for tonight leave the shotgun behind. Grab us both a Thompson with six mags each."

"Yes, Sir."

Elton Stonebreaker was discharged at 12 o'clock sharp. Within ten minutes of release, he was floating westbound in a protective bubble on his magic carpet, ensconced in the cavernous back seat next to his adoring, stunning, and skimpily clad female companion, who was fawning over him because of this awful ordeal. Suffice it to say, no moss grew under his feet when it came to fleeing Quayle County. However, he probably did grow significantly in his nether regions due to his earthly angel's ministrations, but he was whisked away before anyone from the sheriff's office could see for sure. What a lucky dog!

As a counterpoint in diametric opposition, Sleeping Beauty was enraged when Archie woke him up at 2 o'clock for transport. He could have been real trouble, but his arm was still in the cast and it throbbed whenever he bumped it. Accidents do happen, and it did get bumped once or twice. Or thrice. Nevertheless, he was rousted and dressed in DOC prison wear, and shackled like Harry Houdini getting ready for a magic trick dive in a footlocker in the frigid waters of Lake Michigan in the wintertime, without a hidden handcuff key, that is.

He was placed in an old, DOC Econoline van with heavy wire mesh along the windows and wooden benches along the sides instead of cushioned seats, for convict transport. The only other prisoner was an emaciated hippy doing a 5-year hitch for selling LSD. Ordinarily, this would not have boded well for the hippy, but Joe Shit the Ragman was incapacitated and likely suffering in real pain.

Besides the two pistol-packing correction officers in the front of the van, DOC had a sedan follow-up with two CO's armed with handguns and shotguns.

US Highway 90 might as well have been in Antarctica. Sheriff Sol followed the DOC vehicles all the way through Quayle County and halfway through the next before turning around. They never saw another vehicle in either direction.

The sheriff left for home at 4 o'clock. He had been on duty more than 24 hours. Barlow hero-worshipped him. Sheriff Sol always lead from the front, and he never asked anyone to do something he wouldn't or hadn't done.

Archie and Barlow filed away the rest of the night cleaning weapons that hadn't been fired and talking about the FBI and the Diablos. Mosby was just beginning to stir when he left for home. He didn't see any Diablos or other suspicious characters en route.

He was lying in bed, wondering 'What next?' when he fell into a fitful sleep. He needed Sarah in the worst way. Oh, did he ever!

CHAPTER 57

A BAD FEELING THAT WON'T GO AWAY

Time passed. November 27th. Thanksgiving. Barlow had been a guest at the Bakers'. Now a distant, pleasant memory.

The FBI came and went. They reviewed court transcripts first. Surprisingly, they spoke to Sheriff Sol next. They interviewed both Archie and Barlow at the sheriff's office. It was all very civil. They said, and it appeared, that they were just covering the bases before closing their investigation.

The only sticky wicket concerned Archie, not Barlow. The FBI had Schitt's medical file from the hospital. No surprise there. They pressed Archie hard regarding his rough treatment of Schitt during handcuffing.

Arch said he didn't know how bad Schitt was hurt; he cuffed Schitt as quickly as possible to take him out of commission. The knife was a very lethal weapon and it was somewhere out of sight on the floor.

That seemed to pacify them.

More days passed. Not a peep from the Diablos. Was it over? Barlow wanted to think so but he couldn't make himself. Was this real or was it one big head game? Nobody can maintain full alert forever. Was he becoming paranoid? Maybe it really was over. He prayed that it was.

At least the fall semester at WTJC was over. Barlow had A's in College Math 101, Texas Law 101, Patrol Procedures 101, and Physical Education for Law Enforcement 105. He had B's in English Composition 101 and Spanish 101.

The break couldn't have come at a better time for him. He still wasn't sleeping well.

He enrolled in the spring semester. More of the same. College Math 102, Traffic Enforcement 102, Emergency First Aid 101, Physical Education 106, American Literature 102, and Spanish 102.

Maybe life had already returned to normal and he just didn't know it.

CHAPTER 58

JUDGMENT DAY ARRIVES FOR THE JUDGE

It was Saturday, December 20th. Christmas was five days away. The second semester was three weeks down the road. The weather was crisp and refreshing for Far West Texas. Barlow was invited to spend all day Christmas at the Bakers' and he was looking forward to it.

The sheriff's office was still on alert, but stepped down. They were back on regular shifts. The county couldn't fork out overtime forever, and the Diablos were like a spine-chilling nightmare which had not recurred. Eventually life goes on and returns to normal, except for a nagging fear that Sheriff Sol and Archie and Barlow just couldn't quite shake.

Judge Sweeney took his wife, Monica, Christmas shopping in Alpine. After a pleasant and successful day for her, they decided to dine at the Texas Longhorn Emporium, known for it's tenderloin steaks.

Scrumptious meal consumed, they slowly sauntered back to the parking lot a block away, loaded down with sacks and packages. They turned the corner in the middle of the block, taking a shortcut through an alleyway.

When they came to the end, Judge Sweeney saw Cletus Denton, President of the Diablos, whom he recognized from the courtroom, and another unknown Diablo, both wearing colors. They were standing next to his navy blue, 1969, Lincoln Continental Mark III, about 25 yards away.

Judge Sweeney stiffened visibly, stopped, and gently placed the sacks he was carrying on the asphalt. Initially, Monica did not comprehend the danger. He whispered for her to stay put.

He eased his Colt .45, Bird's Head revolver out of his shoulder holster, cocked it, and held it down by his side.

The outlaws, who had been standing together, split about ten feet apart, and slowly started walking towards him. They were both armed with handguns, Denton with a Government Model, semi-automatic Colt .45 pistol, and the other with an S&W, Model 19, .357 revolver.

Judge Sweeney shifted to his left, expecting Monica to stay where she was, before walking toward the bandits. When they were about seven yards apart, all three raised their firearms simultaneously and commenced firing, as if this had all been choreographed.

The first three shots were so close in succession, it sounded as if only one shot had been fired.

Judge Sweeney shot Denton right between his hate-filled eyes. He was dead before he hit the ground.

Denton shot at the judge and narrowly missed, tearing a hole in the left skirt of his sport coat when the breeze blew it open.

The unknown biker fired two shots at the judge, both of which whizzed by his head like angry hornets, off to the right. Too much recoil or maybe jittery nerves. His second shot came just as the judge pivoted and returned fire.

Judge Sweeney was the better marksman. He scored a hit in the assailant's chest, who began to collapse, but slowly.

Judge Sweeney fired another shot to insure he was completely incapacitated, this time striking him in the head. It turned out to be unnecessary, because his assailant was already shaking hands with the Grim Reaper.

The judge walked over and examined both bandits for signs of life before holstering his weapon. He exhaled a sigh of relief before turning around to check on Monica. He was mortified to see that she was also lying on the ground with a bullet in her chest, blinking tears from her eyes and looking shocked, but nevertheless still breathing. Two passersby ran up to assist. One scooted back around the corner to summon the police and an ambulance, while the other assisted the judge in caring for his wife.

Two hours later at the hospital, Judge Sweeney remembered to call the sheriff's office to warn that the Diablos were on the warpath. It was too late.

CHAPTER 59

THE DAY OF RECKONING

Barlow awoke at 4 o'clock. He showered, dressed, and slipped his revolver into his off-duty holster. He checked the spare loads in his ammo pouch, which he snapped on his belt next to his badge. He picked up his grocery sack filled with wrapped Christmas presents and stepped outside.

He went through his ritual of setting up tells and checking his truck for bombs. He was late leaving for Casa de Baker. They were supposed to put up the Christmas tree before supper. He was invited to help, plus he wanted to put his gifts under it.

He drove slowly eastbound down Zachary Taylor Avenue, planning to turn south on Texas Street. He had just passed Sam Houston Street, when he saw a dark blue, 1962, GMC Greenbriar passenger van pass him slowly westbound. Inside, he saw three Diablos wearing their colors. He recognized the two in the front from Chief's mugshot book. He didn't get a good look at the one in the back seat. It didn't matter. He saw all he needed to see.

Both Barlow and the bikers had a slight delayed reaction before they realized whom they had just passed. The van slowed from twenty miles per hour to five. Barlow slammed on his breaks and dismounted. He knew exactly what this was all about. His heart was racing and his throat felt dry. He slipped the 30-30 from its sheath and chambered a round.

He stepped into the middle of the street about twenty yards from the van, and shot out the left rear tire. The van stopped.

He angled right and shot out the right rear tire. Then he stepped wide left and shot out the left front tire. He backtracked back to his right into a neighbor's front yard, still about twenty yards away. He aimed toward the side passenger doors, where he perceived the greatest threat. His peripheral vision still included the left rear of the van, and he knew he was pretty much screwed if they all came at him at once. All his senses were pinging.

He could see the driver's head, but the front seat and back seat passengers had ducked down and were out of view.

Thirty seconds passed and then a minute. He knew when the shit hit the fan, it would be fast and furious, and over one way or the other in just a matter of seconds. In his right peripheral vision, he could see the neighbor lady in whose yard he was standing, looking his way from a bedroom window.

The passenger doors behind the front seat on the right side of the van were narrow and closed like a pair of French doors. First one, then the other, opened slowly. He saw a head and a pair of empty hands rise over the top of the rearmost side door. He told the man to keep his hands in the air and step out of the van.

Suddenly, the right front door blasted wide open. The Diablo from the right front seat bailed out, made a 180-degree pivot, and aimed an M-16 at him. His face was a mask of visceral, uncontrollable hatred. Barlow recognized the amplified threat of facing the fully automatic rifle, because he was issued one just like it in the Army.

Nevertheless, the astonishing display of acrobatic skill did not pay off for his adversary. Barlow was already primed, and he shot this bandit center mass before he could even get off a shot. He collapsed in a spray of blood, which continued to spurt with each heartbeat.

There was no time for reflection. He jacked a round. The other passenger, who initially showed empty hands, came around the door with a Beretta 9-millimeter pistol. He shot once at Barlow before the gun jammed due to a 'stovepipe.' His shot was hasty and it missed, flying to parts unknown. Barlow punched his ticket with a shot in the ten ring. He collapsed to the ground like an eighty-pound sack of cement dropped from a ten-story building. Lights out.

By then, the driver had exited the van and was stealthily creeping around the driver's side towards Barlow, while jacking a round in a Mossberg 12-gauge shotgun. That particular sound is both unique and riveting. It's like setting off an emergency fire alarm to anyone who's ever heard it.

Barlow didn't let him close any further. Twenty yards away is better than ten when one is facing down a shotgun. The outlaw aimed, but Barlow shot first, hitting him in the upper left chest. He faltered, but didn't surrender. He tried to acquire his target yet again. Barlow shot him a second time a little higher up and to the right, hitting him in the throat. Blood splashed everywhere. This time the bastard dropped to the ground and stayed there.

The 30-30 was empty. Barlow laid it in the neighbor's yard and drew his revolver.

Cautiously, he approached the two bandits on the right. The bandit with the M-16 was still breathing, but just barely. He was bleeding out fast. He only had seconds left to make his peace with God - or not. More likely not. Either way, he was a goner. Barlow picked up the M-16. Sure enough, a cartridge was chambered and the selector switch was on full auto.

The rear seat passenger was lying in a three-foot pool of blood, staring glassy-eyed into nothingness. Barlow picked up his Beretta. This is when he noticed the stovepipe jam, in which the spent shell casing sticks straight up like a chimney, jammed between the breech of the barrel and the back of the receiver. (It's usually caused by not holding the pistol tightly enough, otherwise known as 'limp-wristing.') He picked up both weapons and placed them in the yard next to his rifle.

Finally, he walked over to the driver, and confirmed that he would never again be a threat to anyone. His expiration date had come due. His face had such a look of surprise, like this wasn't supposed to happen to him. "The best laid schemes of mice an' men . . . ."

Barlow recovered all three of the bandit weapons and placed them on the floorboard of his truck. Then he reloaded the 30-30, and was fixing to place it back in its sheath. The neighbor lady, as well as a couple of other neighbors had come out of their houses, wide-eyed, with expressions of horror. They stared at Barlow, but said nothing. It's hard to speak when your mouth is wide open, catching flies.

Screeching tires alerted Barlow to an old, black, Ford F-250, which had just turned the corner on two wheels way too fast, from Texas Street, and was barreling westbound his way. In just a few seconds, the truck was within range. The passenger stuck his arm out the window and commenced firing a revolver at him.

In the interim, Barlow had scrambled to the passenger side of his truck. He leaned over the hood and levered a round. He fired once at the driver. The pickup went out of control but never slowed down. It ran over two of the dead Diablos and smashed into the rear of the van, pushing it ten feet past its original resting place.

Barlow levered another round and walked closer to the truck. He didn't have to walk far. He could see that the passenger was dead. His head was nearly severed, sticking through the shattered windshield. Too bad. Seatbelts save lives.

The driver was also no longer among the living. He had a bullet wound in his chest, but more importantly, the way his head was twisted, it was obvious that he had a broken neck.

Barlow decided to hang onto his rifle while trying to maintain the integrity of the crime scene, just by his presence. How many more bandits were gunning for him? He glanced around, and saw that by now, there were more than a half-dozen curious onlookers clustered together, whispering and pointing fingers at the carnage.

He was relieved to hear a siren. Within moments, Sheriff Sol and Chunk arrived on the scene, both carrying a Thompson. They scanned the carnage and turned their attention to Barlow.

Sheriff Sol asked, "Are you shot?"

He stammered, "I don't think so."

They checked and confirmed that he was unharmed.

Sheriff Sol told Barlow to take a breather in his truck while they sorted things out.

Barlow said he had recovered the weapons from the bikers in the van, but had not had time to search for the guns belonging to the two in the pickup. He said there should be a revolver lying in the road or in one of the north side yards from the dude whose head was sticking through the windshield.

All the sudden, he remembered. He exclaimed, "Oh my gosh! I need to call the Bakers! I'm late! We're supposed to put the Christmas tree up! They're waiting for me!"

Sheriff Sol said, "Barlow, you're not thinking straight. You need to sit down in your truck like I told you. We got this now.

"Chunk get one of the neighbors to let you use the phone. Call Arthur Baker. Tell him Barlow's okay, but he's going to be delayed for a few hours. See if someone can bring Barlow a Coke. Hurry!"

"You got it Sheriff!"

In the next half hour, every deputy except Dewey Carruthers, who was manning the radio, had arrived.

The volunteer fire department arrived and set up floodlights. The crime scene search intensified. Ditto for the database searches relayed to Deputy Carruthers via radio. The outlaws were all positively identified.

As soon as Chief Alex had photographed the scene and made a rough sketch with measurements, the bodies were removed to the mortuary, one by one.

The .357 Magnum, Smith and Wesson Model 27 fired by the passenger, Leland Packer, was recovered from one of the yards. It had four empty shell casings and two live rounds. An Iver Johnson .32 caliber revolver attributed to Edgar Wells, the driver of the F-250, was found on the floorboard. It had not been fired.

Within thirty minutes of the incident, Arthur Baker and Sarah showed up. Chunk tried to talk Arthur out of coming, but Sheriff Sol said it was fine. He wanted Barlow out of there before the newsies or the FBI arrived.

Arthur had to park a block away. The crime scene was roped off and deputies were shooing off gawkers. As soon as Sarah found Barlow in his truck, she jumped into his arms, witnesses or no.

When Sheriff Sol spotted Arthur and Sarah, he broke away from the crime scene. He said, "Arthur, thanks for coming. I need a favor."

"Name it."

"I want Barlow on ice. I don't want him talking to anyone until after I've had time to sort this out. Can he spend the night at your place? I'd prefer it if no one knew where he was, at least until tomorrow at noon, longer if possible, but I doubt that's gonna happen."

"Of course. We'll lock the front gate for a change. I'll get Cordell or Pedro to set up on it to see it's not breached."

"Thanks. I owe you."

"No you don't. We were coming to get him anyway. Does he know about the other?"

Barlow asked, "What other?"

"I haven't had time to go into it. Can you tell him?"

"Tell me what?"

"Barlow, Arthur and Sarah will go back to your house with you so you can pack a bag for a day or two. Take a uniform and your gun belt. Don't dick around. I guarantee the FBI and the El Paso newsies will be here any minute. Once they see you, I may not be able to control the situation. Go now! I'll be in touch later, maybe a lot later. Arthur will fill you in. Get out of here! That's an order!"

"Yes, Sir, Sheriff. Thanks."

Sarah remained in the truck with Barlow. Arthur walked back

to his truck. He said he would meet them at Barlow's house. Slick directed traffic so Barlow could extricate himself from the crime scene.

The escape to the Bar B was anticlimactic. The rest of the night was anything but.

Several hours later, but before Saturday the 20th became Sunday the 21st, DPS, the FBI, a Texas Ranger, and the same two El Paso news trucks had arrived at the scene, along with at least a hundred Mosby onlookers.

CHAPTER 60

THE DEBRIEFING

Once they arrived at the ranch, Arthur told Pedro, his chief vaquero, to wake up Angel or Pancho, and to drive one of them with him ten yards or so from the gate, with rifles, and make sure no one entered the ranch without checking with him first. The only exception would be either Sheriff Sol or Chief Alex.

Once inside the ranch house, Clarice gave Barlow a big hug. She directed him to the kitchen, where she had cooked a huge pot of chili and baked a mountain of biscuits and brownies. A relish tray was on the table.

All but Barlow had eaten. She bade Barlow to eat. In spite of the last couple of hours, he devoured like a ravenous wolf. Two bowls of chili. Three buttered biscuits. Two brownies. Two 7 Ups.

Cordell took Barlow's belongings up to the guest room. One bag was noticeably heavy. It contained several hundred rounds of ammo plus Barlow's reloading kit and supplies. (Barlow wasn't about to be surprised again with Charlie inside the wire.)

Barlow joined Arthur and the rest of the Bakers in the family room where a fire was burning. The Christmas tree was still bare.

Clarice brought an unopened bottle of Makers Mark and a tray full of glasses, where the six of them sat quietly, each absorbed in his own thoughts, while sipping Kentucky's finest.

Arthur told Barlow about the ambush of Judge Sweeney and his wife, Monica. It sounded as if everyone in Mosby, except for Barlow, already knew. The only update was that Monica would be okay. Darnell Sweeney made a call, and a Texas Ranger was detailed to Judge Sweeney until he and Monica returned to their ranch, which was expected to take place on Monday or Tuesday.

A little after 1 o'clock, Sheriff Sol arrived. Clarice opened a second bottle of Makers. The first was a dead soldier.

Barlow slowly recited his encounter with the outlaws, step-by-step, for the first time. Sarah, who was sitting on the couch next to him, squeezed even closer as he recounted the incident. Newton's Third Law of Physics, again.

Sheriff Sol said, and Arthur agreed, that Barlow possibly escaped a concerted three-man attack, but more likely a five-man attack, just by happenstance, leaving his house when he did. Timing is everything, but Barlow didn't determine the timing. God did. He must have big plans for Barlow, because another couple of minutes and he probably would have been completely overwhelmed.

Sheriff Sol also said Barlow turned the tables on the assassins by shooting out the tires of the van, and then by positioning himself where he did before they could exit the vehicle. That was tactically brilliant, but the FBI and the press would probably argue that his actions were completely unwarranted, firing the first shots, even if they were only designed to disable the van, since he knew nothing of the attack on Judge Sweeney. This was bound to come up, so Barlow needed to reinforce his statement that he recognized this scenario as an assassination attempt on his life about to take place.

Of course, the events afterwards confirm this, but someone who has a bias against the police might mock him as alleging to be a visionary or an oracle, as opposed to simply being an astute observer of human behavior.

Sheriff Sol also said the joint gang task force executed a search warrant for the Diablos' strip club as a result of the attack on Judge Sweeney. It was vacant and appeared to have been recently abandoned. They recovered one malfunctioning revolver and some residual meth. They issued a BOLO for the entire gang. In the meantime, they were squeezing all their snitches in an effort to locate them. The incident with Barlow would most likely triple their efforts.

Sheriff Sol promised the FBI, DPS, and the Texas Rangers that Barlow would be available for a full, joint debriefing at 3 o'clock this afternoon in the sheriff's office. In the meantime, Barlow should remain sequestered here, especially since he is on administrative duty, with pay, pending presentation of this incident to the Grand Jury. He should consider this a free vacation.

Sheriff Sol would be back at 2:30 to pick him up. Then, as an afterthought, he said, "Wear your uniform. Make sure you're ready for S.A.M.I. You represent the Quayle County Sheriff's Office. Look the part. I wouldn't be surprised to see you on El Paso TV tonight at 6.

"You can bet the press will be there clamoring for a statement. I plan to be the sole spokesman for the department, unless of course, you want to address them."

"No, Sir. I'd rather not."

"Good decision. One day down the line, if you remain in law enforcement, you will have to deal with them. Right now, you're much better off to leave public affairs to me.

"See you all at 2:30. Outstanding job, Barlow. Very few lawmen would have come out of this unscathed. God must have a guardian angel watching over you. Good night, you all."

Cordell and Darla followed the sheriff out and went home.

CHAPTER 61

BARLOW COMES CLEAN

The four of them remained in front of the fire, lost in thought. Barlow started having random thoughts about Vietnam, particularly about the second time Charlie penetrated the wire. He tried to bottle it up, put a cork in it, afraid the Bakers might discover his . . . uncertainties. What if he woke up in the night screaming? It had happened once before.

Clarice thought Barlow looked peaked, and asked if he wanted to go up to his room.

He said, "No. I can't sleep. I appreciate being here and I enjoy your all's company."

After a while, Barlow broke the silence and said, "I need to get some things off my chest. Maybe you'll send me packing. I'll understand if you do.

"I'm glad all those outlaws are dead. I have no remorse. None. Just like in Vietnam. We almost got overrun twice.

"I'm not sure how many Charlie I killed. Probably a dozen. Maybe more, and that's by rifle. I have no idea how many died as the result of the howitzer I was assigned to. It was them or us. I nearly bought the farm. More than once. Same as with Joe Schitt. Same as today.

"Maybe something's wrong with me. What does it say about my Christianity?

"I love my job. I don't want to quit. I believe I'm needed here, that I'm making a difference. Maybe I delude myself.

"I'll just come out and say it. I love Sarah more than anything in the whole world. I want to marry her. I would marry her today if she agreed. I know we both need to finish school. Maybe after this, you all might not want me in the family. If so, I get it. I hope you all don't think less of me."

Clarice and Sarah were quietly weeping. Sarah squeezed his hand 'til it hurt and she didn't let up.

Arthur cleared his throat and poured everyone another drink. Another dead soldier. He opened a third bottle to top off his own.

He put another log on the fire and sat down. The pause in conversation was pregnant. The only sounds were the crackling and popping of the fire.

Finally he spoke, "Barlow, I think I speak for all of us. Our whole family loves you. We all admire and respect the kind of man you are, as does Sheriff Sol. Few have tread where you have walked. You have the heart of a lion. You have been a blessing to this community.

"Clarice and I have hoped that someday you and Sarah would marry and make your relationship with this family legal and binding. That being said, we do think it would be easier if both of you finished WTJC first. We hope you all will do that.

"As for your Christianity, just know that Jesus loves you. He had something in mind when he made you a warrior. Keep him front and center in your life and He will show you the way.

"Look, you all. It's already 3 o'clock. We probably all should go to church, which is in just six more hours. However, I think it's best, and it would comply with Sheriff Sol's wishes, if Mom and I go and you two stay here. We'll answer everyone's questions without revealing any secrets or getting too deep in the weeds.

"Heck, by next Sunday, everyone in town will know all the nitty gritty details of tonight, anyway, or at least claim they do."

Arthur stood and said, "Good night."

Sarah jumped to her feet and hugged her dad like her life depended on it. She kept saying, "Thank you, Daddy. Thank you, Daddy."

Clarice hugged Barlow. She was still in tears. She whispered,

"They tried to take you from us. You were God's instrument to mete out Justice for what they tried to do to you, and for all the awful things they did to other people less fortunate. Don't lose any sleep over them. Just . . . . take care of yourself, and the rest of us too, and be safe. We love you."

Barlow uttered, "Thanks. I love you all, too."

Clarice started to pick up the empty glasses. Barlow asked, "Would it be okay if I stay up a little while and have another? I can't go to sleep yet."

She said, "Go right ahead. Sarah, you keep Barlow company until he's ready to sleep."

Sarah hugged her mom and said, "Thank you, Momma."

After Arthur and Clarice went to bed, Sarah and Barlow snuggled up on the couch, watching the shadows dance from the burning embers. Two more drinks and an hour later, Barlow took himself to bed. He didn't even undress or get under the covers. Sarah crept in and lay beside him until he drifted off. Then she slipped off quietly into her own room.

CHAPTER 62

SARAH LEARNS A NEW SKILL

Sarah awoke to the aroma of coffee and bacon. She remained in bed until she saw her folks drive off. Then she slipped into the guest room and snuggled next to Barlow. She drifted off into a contented, peaceful slumber.

Around 9:30, Barlow awakened with a start. At first, he didn't know where he was. Then he felt Sarah wedged next to him. Her eyes were open.

"Oh my gosh! Did you sleep here all night?"

"I don't think anyone noticed."

"What?"

"No, Silly. I just came back a little while ago."

"Whew! You gave me a start. I just got here and I don't want to get kicked out after my first night."

"Then you must pay the toll, Mister! I'm the toll collector. Pay me what you owe, Buster, or you're outta here!"

"Can I go to the bathroom first?"

"What! And let the Rock of Gibraltar lose some of its tensile strength? I think not."

"Oh, but it's so hard it hurts! I really need to go bad."

"Well, you better mount up, Cowboy, and work out the kinks. Pay the toll first, and then I'll let you use the bathroom."

Sarah was already naked and she was pulling off his clothes. Once he was stripped like a jaybird, she marveled at the throbbing diamond cutter bobbing up and down of its own volition, like a buoy in the ocean.

She wrapped both hands around it, and then she couldn't believe what she did. She put him in her mouth and sucked him like he had been bitten by a rattler and she needed to draw out all the poison. Only it wasn't poison, and it turned her on, and she went after it like her own climax depended upon it.

Soon Barlow was moaning and thrusting his hips and begging her not to stop. This drove her wild, and she gently stroked him as she sucked until he erupted like a gushing oil well. This enflamed her even more, and she gently lapped his seed with her tongue until it was all gone.

He lay back in ecstasy for a brief moment, then jumped up and ran to the bathroom to empty his bladder. He was gone for a full five minutes.

In the interim she wondered, "What on Earth has come over me? What did I just do? Why did it turn me on so much? Am I a shameless slut?"

When he returned, he was all smiles and full of horny compassion. He cuddled her up, gently rubbed her body, beginning with her shoulders, slowly running down her back, to the backs of her legs with the lightest touch of his fingernails causing a tickle, then onto her feet and her toes, which he massaged with a skill like it was his everyday job. She didn't know a foot massage could feel so divine.

Then he rolled her over and began massaging her legs from the ankles up. He bypassed her pubic area and moved onto her stomach, then her chest, gently massaging her breasts and sucking on her nipples. He ran his tongue down her stomach around her navel, then spread open her thighs and licked all over and around her clitoris.

Now she was writhing in previously undiscovered ecstasy. He gently massaged her womanhood with his tongue, bringing her to a climax she had never imagined could be so intense.

He gave her thirty seconds to recover, before he mounted her with a stiffness not dissimilar from twenty minutes earlier. He brought her up and over, again and again, until she was faint. He peaked, and gave her several extra hard, deep thrusts, culminating in an explosion that left him too weak and winded to move. He rolled onto his back and gasped for air, all done in.

They both drifted off into a light sleep, each silently praising God for the love they shared and the overwhelming sensations they had just experienced.

It was 10:45. Barlow's eyes popped open. He asked, "What time do you think your folks will be back?"

"By 11:00."

"Oh, Gosh! I'm jumping in the shower. Be out in a sec. We got to hurry! If your folks see us now, our gooses are cooked!

"Relax. I'm pretty sure Mom knows and Dad suspects, although they would never imagine that I'm a fellatio aficionado."

"What?"

"A head job artist. I love giving head. It's my new skill set. I'll just add it onto my resume if I ever get around to writing one."

"Oh, Lordy! Don't even think that. Suspicion is one thing. Catching your daughter and her boyfriend in flagrante delicto is a different kettle of fish."

"Shut up and scoot over. I'm getting in with you."

"Thank goodness I'm almost done. I don't want to get shot in my birthday suit."

Barlow cleaned up as quickly as he could. He was going to make his bed, but Sarah had already beaten him to it. His uniform needed ironing, so he put on his jeans and a tee shirt for now.

Sarah stepped out of the shower, parading around in her birthday suit, just to watch him squirm. Back and forth. Back and forth. Licking her lips. Gently massaging her breasts. He got horny all over again. He couldn't stand it anymore, so he skedaddled downstairs for coffee. What if he had a boner that wouldn't go away when her folks got home?

By 11:10 they were both cleaned up, bedrooms and bathroom straight, making a fresh pot of coffee, and scrambling eggs.

Barlow asked about an ironing board, and Sarah said she'd iron his uniform after they ate.

CHAPTER 63

BARLOW AND PUBLIC OPINION

Arthur and Clarice walked in at 11:25.

"My Gosh. You kids sleep all morning?"

"Almost, Mom. What was going on at church?"

Clarice said, "The service was just what everyone needed to hear. Put your faith in God and fear not."

"That's not what I meant."

Arthur chimed in. "The only question we had to answer was if Barlow was okay. Seems like the better part of Mosby witnessed the entire affair and they're 100% in favor of how you handled yourself."

"Well, I know for certain one neighbor witnessed the whole shebang. I also know there were others who saw parts of it. Glad to hear they don't think I'm a monster."

"Heavens sakes alive! Why would you think that?"

"Well, it's hard to say how a person might feel if he saw someone get killed right in front of him, even if he had it coming. It's a dreadful sight. Lots of blood. Stays with you forever."

"Barlow, those Diablos scare the daylights out of everyone. They're like a pack of wolves or coyotes. People around here are peaceable. Heck, a major crime in Quayle County is cattle rustling! Killings almost never happen.

"Consider most folks as sheep. They blend in, go along to get along, try to avoid trouble.

"Then the wolf or the coyotes threaten. The guy who tried to rape Sandra Taft. The two bikers who abused Clifford Biggs. Everyone in the bar felt bad for him, but no one was equipped, mentally, physically, or any other way to step up. All they could do was avert their eyes. Look the other way.

"Finally, when the wolves were preoccupied, Old Man Spellman sneaks in a call to the sheepdogs. The sheepdogs show up and banish the wolves.

"You and Sheriff Sol and Archie and one or two others are sheepdogs. Your purpose in life is to protect the flock. It's who you are.

"It was both your good and bad fortune that the Diablos' planned assassination attempt on you happened when and where it did. Bad fortune in that they wanted to kill you. That sucks! Good fortune in that the odds were three-to-one, but you evened them up by the actions you took. I believe the Army calls that tactics, and you seem to have a sixth sense in that regard.

"Think about it. You forced them to engage in a scenario you set up, not them.

"First, they couldn't drive away. You took out their wheels.

"Second, if they surrendered, they'd be ridiculed by their peers, plus they'd go to prison for eons, most likely, and they knew it.

"Third, they planned it and initiated it, so they had no choice but to fight, except now their plan went up in smoke and they had to ad lib. Their new plan of attack was disjointed and cobbled together in just seconds. Instead of five-to-one, it was one-to-one-to-one-to-one, except you were set and ready and they were reacting, not initiating. These were cowards who planned to blindside you en mass, not take on an opponent who was prepared and willing to engage.

"Fourth, their compadres showed up late. That doofus in the pickup must have been scared out of his wits or too stupid to breathe air through his nose. He began blasting away at you, out of range, from a fast-moving vehicle, with no way to aim the gun. You were in more danger of a lightning strike than getting shot by him. Besides that, how many rounds did that gun hold, forty or fifty? He probably would have run out of ammo if he hadn't gone through the windshield first.

"Fifth, I bet most cops would have shot at him since he was hurling lead, considering him the primary threat. Instead, you took out the driver, an easier target, which took out the truck, which took out the doofus.

"So, do the people of Mosby look at you like a mad dog killer, or as a champion? I think you know the answer in your heart. Cattle and sheep rest easier with a donkey grazing in the same field, because they know donkeys hate coyotes and will kill them on site. The folks of Mosby feel safer having you around. Same, same."

"A donkey, huh?"

"I could have said ass, but you might have taken it the wrong way."

"Touché, Arthur. Thanks. I really do love it here and I want to stay. It's my home."

"We know you do, and we all want you to."

CHAPTER 64

KUDOS FROM ON HIGH

At 1:30, Barlow shined his boots, slicked his hair, and put on his uniform with the razor sharp creases Sarah ironed for him. He pinned on his badge, strapped on his gun belt, and adjusted his Stetson just so. The mustache he began five months earlier was full, and enhanced his appearance as a western lawman not to be taken lightly.

Sheriff Sol arrived at 2:15. He took his old sweet time driving them back to the courthouse.

He said the newsies finally figured out that the cops use the sheriff's office entrance in the rear, so both news trucks set up as close as they were allowed by the back door. Therefore, he was going to park on the street and go in the front, which was locked and vacant, this being a Sunday.

He said it was unlikely Barlow could avoid the newsies once the meeting was over. Therefore, he would prep Barlow and discuss talking points before they left for the evening.

He also said, "Judge Sweeney called. He commended you for sizing up the situation and, in his own words, 'filling them full of lead and erasing them from the gene pool.' He said Quayle County is quote, 'indeed fortunate to have Deputy Adams employed by the sheriff's office' end quote. I concur wholeheartedly."

Barlow blushed. He responded reverently, "Thank you. That means a whole lot to me. I'm still processing the visceral hatred directed at me by the Diablos. They all want me dead, and yet all I want is them out of Quayle County and my life."

"Some wanted you dead. Others went along to stay in favor

with the pack. Now the survivors are in full flight, hoping to evade the pissed off lawmen coming after them, who plan to permanently rectify their wicked ways. Hell! Between you and Judge Sweeney, you wiped out about a fourth of their entire membership! I doubt you'll ever see any of them again, but if you do, treat them like you would any other feral dog.

"Evil is evil, and we'll always have it lurking about. It's our job as lawmen to face it down and protect the citizens. You've more than proved yourself as worthy of their trust.

"This isn't a one-man job, although most of the time we do operate alone. We're a team and whenever possible, we respond as a team. This time, it didn't work out that way. Just a few more minutes and Chunk and I would have been there with you.

"In spite of that, you faced Evil head on, and with God's grace, you prevailed. Five demonic souls perished and descended into the flames of Hell. It was written in The Book of Life.

"Don't overthink it. Something like this can happen at any time. Remember the Boy Scout motto? 'Be prepared.'"

CHAPTER 65

POLICE MEETING AND TV INTERVIEW

Sheriff Sol was right about the news trucks lying in wait out back. Their positioning enabled Barlow and the sheriff to enter unmolested through the front.

The sheriff's office was crowded with lawmen working the case. All the alphabet agencies were represented, to include the U.S. Attorney's Office from El Paso, FBI, BNDD, and ATF, plus DPS, Texas Rangers, EPSO, EPPD, Alpine PD, Brewster County SO, Sheriff Sol, Chief Alex, DA DeWitt, and Sam Davis, who was appointed by Judge Sweeney to represent Barlow, just in case the feds or DPS got confrontational.

They held the meeting in the Grand Jury room to accommodate everyone.

Introductions were made. Sheriff Sol pointed out that Barlow was cleared of any potential wrongdoing by his office and he expected that the Quayle County Grand Jury would concur just as soon as the facts were presented to them. He also said Sam Davis was Barlow's court-appointed counsel, and that he would interrupt any questioning which indicated someone was looking at Barlow as a potential target.

The assistant U.S. Attorney objected, but Sheriff Sol said, "Take it or leave it. I've seen cops railroaded before by zealous prosecutors trying to score points with their constituency, and we're taking no chances here today.

"I do believe we are all here with the common goal of putting the Diablos out of business. We, in Quayle County, are in complete favor of that. We will make full disclosure on everything, and I mean everything, that we've discovered since yesterday afternoon. At the same time, the FBI has already been here questioning Barlow and Deputy Willis regarding a civil rights complaint about an earlier altercation with the El Diablos, so pardon me if we are a little sensitive."

"Special Agent Boyce Jeffries, FBI, Sheriff. I beg your pardon for interrupting. You know we had no choice in that matter. That pompous windbag, Elton Stonebreaker, filed a civil rights complaint against your deputies and we were compelled to follow up. We didn't turn up any improprieties then, nor would we expect to today. Believe me, we want to put the Diablos out of business as much as anyone. Please accept my apologies on behalf of the FBI if we gave you, or Deputies Adams and Willis, or anyone else, the impression that the previous incident or this one were or are witch hunts."

"Very well. Apology accepted.

"Barlow, would you tell everyone here today exactly what happened yesterday, from the point you walked out of your house, until the moment I sent you home on administrative leave?"

Barlow's recitation, tape recorded overtly by Chief Alex and covertly by who knows how many others, was slow, clear, full of details, and complete. As a result, he received very few questions.

At his conclusion, Brewster County Sheriff Leland Waters stood up and commended Barlow, as did everyone else in the room.

Then Chief Alex made a full disclosure of all evidence recovered, some of which had already been turned over to ATF for laboratory analysis. In addition, he read aloud all nine eyewitness statements. He said he would have photographs, as well as a full written report, to include diagrams, available for review by the end of the week if anyone were interested.

Then Sheriff Waters gave a full account of the investigation of the attempted assassination attempt on Judge Sweeney, with additional information provided by Alpine Chief of Police

Roland Godfrey.

Special Agent Gerard Gough, BNDD, discussed information developed by the task force regarding the Diablos organization and personnel. He said they were thrilled with the outcome of these thwarted ambushes, to include the demise of seven full-fledged members of the gang, because they believe this will eliminate the Diablos as a major force in the confederation of southwestern outlaw motorcycle gangs. It might even break up the gang altogether, although if it did, the cockroaches would probably just scurry to another gang for protection. Even so, this was the best possible outcome for law enforcement as well as for Barlow and Judge Sweeney. The gangs will be reeling for awhile after this.

Texas Ranger Avery McCallister said they had leads out statewide in an effort to locate the remaining gang members. Early indications were that a good many of them may have slipped into Juarez. They also believe a few headed north into New Mexico. He expects to know more by Monday.

No one else had any information.

Sheriff Sol concluded by saying, "From everything we now know, Quayle County probably won't have any further input, unless a Diablo returns here. I don't think they will, because staying out of jail is higher on the self-preservation scale, than a second, actually a third attempt on revenge. However, I'm asking you all to call my office if you develop any information affecting Quayle County. In return, I promise to do the same."

After the meeting broke up, Sheriff Sol coached Barlow on what to say, what not to say, and how to comport himself for a brief interview with the TV crews. Everyone else had left the building, except for Kirk, who was duty deputy working one of those rare Sundays in the office.

When they were done, and after Barlow had composed himself with a few deep breaths, they stepped out the front door into a cluster of a half-dozen newsies, including two with cameras. The cameras were rolling. One reporter started the intercourse by asking, "Sheriff Pratt, is this Deputy Adams, who was involved in the Mosby Massacre last night?"

He responded, "My gosh, folks! Are you really calling the foiled assassination attempt of a lawman, in which the lawman killed the assassins in self-defense, a massacre? Shame on you! You think we started this?

"Yes. I am making Deputy Adams available right now, to answer a few questions. Just a few. This will not be a free-for-all. After that, we're leaving and all further inquiries are to be directed to me personally, if you expect any answer other than 'no comment.'"

"Deputy Adams, did you anticipate that the El Diablos Motorcycle Club would target you for revenge after you beat up one of their members and sent him to prison?"

"I did not beat up anyone. I did use the minimum force necessary to subdue two members of the gang because they resisted arrest on the charges of disorderly conduct and assault and battery on a third party. They were tried in a court of law and sentenced by the district court judge, not me. No, I did not anticipate retaliation."

"How does it feel to be responsible for the deaths of five people?"

"Loss of life is always a tragedy. At the same time, they were all felons in possession of firearms, most of them stolen, to include a fully automatic M-16. Some of them fired at me. They initiated the incident. I feel fortunate to be alive."

"Isn't it true you fired first?"

"I did, but only to disable their van by shooting out the tires to prevent their escape. You need to understand. I recognized these gang members as soon as they drove past.

"Look, they live in El Paso. They were driving on my street here in Mosby. It's a dead-end street. My house is the very last one. You can't go any farther. They were almost at my doorstep when we passed each other. I recognized the situation for what it was - an assassination attempt on my life. Why else were they there? My goal was to arrest them all, and to prevent their escape or a high-speed chase.

"I ordered them out of the van with their hands up. Instead, they came out pointing guns and shooting at me. They came to kill me and they nearly did. In fact, the pickup truck came directly towards me at a high rate of speed, while the passenger was shooting at me with a handgun. My answer is simply this. I did not shoot at any individual until my life was in immediate danger."

Sheriff Sol jumped in. "That's all, folks. Your viewers can see for themselves that this situation is just what I reported it to be - an attempted assassination of one of Quayle County's deputy sheriffs. Thank you. Good day."

Sheriff Sol gently nudged Barlow through the crowd and into his car. When they drove away, Barlow saw both talking heads facing the cameras, apparently telling their viewers what Barlow just said, like they couldn't understand plain English.

Sheriff Sol said the Grand Jury would hear the case on Wednesday, December 24th at 10 a.m. He said Barlow would remain on paid administrative leave until Monday, December 29th, to resume his regular midnight shift.

Barlow said he could come back Christmas Eve night so long as he wasn't indicted.

Sheriff Sol said, "Nothing doing. You need time to heal. This isn't enough time, but it will have to do. Go spend time with your new, adopted family. Sarah's brother, Hank, gets in tomorrow from A&M. You'll love him."

CHAPTER 66

PROPOSAL

It was a wonderful Christmas. Barlow proposed to Sarah and she accepted. He gave her a half-carat, solitary emerald engagement ring, set with six prongs, in a band of pink gold.

Sarah burst into tears of joy. "Oh, my gosh, Barlow! I've never seen anything like this! It's so beautiful. No, it's perfect! I love it! Where on Earth did you find it?"

"Linus Farmer made it special just for you. It's an original, same as you."

She ran to his arms and wept for joy. Her mother and Darla wept, too. Arthur got a speck in his eye and had to turn away to flush it out. Cordell grinned like a jackass eating briars and Hank just smiled.

They set the wedding for June 1st, 1971, as soon as Barlow graduated.

Everyone was happy and content.

Classes at WTJC began the second week in January. The pace of life returned to Mosby normal - slow. Life was good. Some might even say boring. Barlow and Sarah settled into a groove. But Life seldom remains boring in law enforcement, even in a backwater burg like Mosby, in Far West Texas. Trouble was lurking around the corner. They just didn't know it yet.

POSTSCRIPT

Associated Press article from the
El Paso Bugle by Dwayne Tuttle

SUNDAY, MARCH 1, 1970

Famous Quayle County Veteran Receives Awards

On Saturday, Lieutenant Colonel Vincent Tapp, Post Adjutant at Fort Bliss, presided over the ceremony in Mosby at the Quayle County Courthouse, in which Corporal Barlow K. Adams, who was honorably discharged from the Army on July 12, 1969, was awarded a Soldier's Medal and a Good Conduct Medal.

On July 10th of last year, Adams, formerly of Benson County, Texas, who was on terminal leave from the Army, was traveling late at night on Highway 90 in Quayle County, when he happened upon a stalled motorist, who was under attack by a would-be rapist.

Adams stopped to render assistance. In an exchange of gunfire, Adams mortally wounded the assailant, identified as Rupert Doyle of Bakersfield, California. He rescued the woman, a resident of Mosby, who was treated at Alpine General Hospital for minor injuries, and released.

It was determined later that Doyle was a convicted felon who had burgled an El Paso residence only the day before. He was driving a stolen vehicle from Los Angeles.

As a result of his heroism not involving actual conflict with an enemy of the United States, Adams was awarded the Soldier's Medal, a decoration for valor ranking below the Distinguished

Flying Cross and above the Bronze Star Medal. He was also awarded the Good Conduct Medal, which according to Lieutenant Colonel Tapp, should have been awarded after Adams completed his tour of duty in Vietnam.

Adams is now employed as a deputy sheriff in Quayle County. He is the same deputy, who, along with Quayle County Circuit Court Judge Maxwell Sweeney, were targeted by the El Diablos Motorcycle Club for assassination. The impetus for the conspiracy to murder both officials was in retaliation to a trial, in which El Diablos member Joseph P. Schitt was sentenced to 42 years at hard labor in the Huntsville State Penitentiary for a multitude of charges, including aggravated assault and the habitual offender act.

Seven members of the El Diablos Motorcycle Club ambushed the officials on December 20th of last year in separate incidents. Judge Sweeney killed two Diablos in a gunfight in Alpine. Deputy Adams killed five Diablos in two separate gunfights in Mosby about an hour later. Both officials were absolved of any wrongdoing.

www.ingramcontent.com/pod-product-compliance
Lightning Source LLC
Chambersburg PA
CBHW061550100726
47898CB00002B/309